ARmaGEDDON oUTTA HeRe

DEREK LANDY

Skulduggery Pleasant

ARMAGEDDON OUTTA HERE

HarperCollins *Children's Books*

First published in the United Kingdom by
HarperCollins *Children's Books* in 2014
Published in this edition in 2022
HarperCollins *Children's Books* is a division of HarperCollins*Publishers* Ltd
1 London Bridge Street
London SE1 9GF

www.harpercollins.co.uk

HarperCollins*Publishers*
1st Floor, Watermarque Building, Ringsend Road
Dublin 4, Ireland

1

HB ISBN 978-0-00-855427-9
Export ISBN 978-0-00-855445-3
ANZ ISBN 978-0-00-855444-6

www.skulduggerypleasant.co.uk

Typeset by Palimpsest Book Production Limited, Falkirk, Stirlingshire
Printed and bound in the UK using 100% renewable electricity at CPI Group (UK) Ltd

* 'The Lost Art of World Domination' first published in *Skulduggery Pleasant*, 2012 Down-under Tour Edition;
'Gold, Babies and the Brothers Muldoon' first published in *Playing with Fire*, 2012 Down-under Tour Edition;
'The Slightly Ignominious End to the Legend of Black Annis' first published in *The Faceless Ones*, 2012 Down-
under Tour Edition; 'Myosotis Terra' and 'The Wonderful Adventures of Geoffrey Scrutinous' first published in
Mortal Coil, 2012 Down-under Tour Edition; 'Just Another Friday Night' first published in *The End of the World*,
2012 Australian Edition; 'The End of the World' first published in 2012; 'Trick or Treat' and 'The Button' first
published on www.dereklandy.blogspot.com; 'Across A Dark Plain', 'The Horror Writers' Halloween Ball', 'Friday
Night Fights' and 'Get Thee Behind Me, Bubba Moon' first published in *Armageddon Outta Here*, 2014; 'Eyes of
the Beholder' and 'Theatre of Shadows' first published in *Armageddon Outta Here*, 2015; 'Going Once, Going
Twice' first published in 2018; 'Outside The Murder-Cottage, By the Sea: A Valkyrie Cain Adventure' first
published in *Seasons of War* eBook, 2020; 'Those Who Watch' first published on twitter.com/DerekLandy, 2020;
Apocalypse Kings first published for World Book Day, 2021; 'A Little Bit Of Weird' first published on thesun.ie,
2022. 'Lesson Learned' and 'Haunted' first published in *Armageddon Outta Here*, 2022.

This book is dedicated to my brand-new nephew, Cameron.

Cameron, I'm sure you'll grow taller as you get older, but right now you're simply way too short. You also can't talk or stand up, and I have yet to see you read a book. None of this is entirely your own fault, however - I blame the parents - so I hope my words don't upset you too much.

The problem is, you're surrounded by a formidable sister and some formidable cousins, so you're going to have to grow up to be an exceptional person. I'll do what I can to help, but the rest is up to you.

UPDATE: OK, Cam, eight years have passed since I wrote this dedication, and all I can say right now is that you remind me so much of myself when I was your age: you're small, weird and you make funny faces whenever someone wants to take a picture of you.

This is a VERY GOOD START to becoming exceptional. Keep it up.

THE TIMELINE

INTRODUCTION

I've always loved Introductions.

They remind me of when I was a kid, wandering through second-hand bookstores, pulling battered old horror paperbacks from the shelves. Those wrinkled covers, those dog-eared pages, that wonderful, slightly stale smell of stories... Those books pulled you into their own history, made you a part of it, and if you were lucky — like, *really* lucky — right before the story started you'd find the Author's Introduction.

This, to a kid who wanted nothing more than to be a writer, was a portal into imagination. I couldn't Google a writer's name and read their blog or watch every interview they'd ever done on YouTube (and I hereby wave to some reader way off in the future who's just read that and is now getting information about "Google" "Blog" and "YouTube" downloaded directly into his brain), so I had to make do with what brief glimpses I was afforded. It was in the Introductions that authors talked about their work and their process, and I scoured these words, searching for the secret to writing, hunting for the Big Clue that would lead me to Where Stories Come From.

I found glimpses of the Big Clue in the words of Stephen King and other masters of the genre, but nothing definite. Still, in many ways it was enough. These glimpses brought with them their own kind of inspiration, and when I was a kid, when I was a teenager, that's all I needed. My early stories dripped with blood. They were soaked in it. Drenched. I had yet to learn concepts such as subtlety or restraint, and there is definitely a place for subtlety and restraint — but it was not a place that held any interest for me. I was all about the blood, the rawness, the viscera. I was reading King and Clive Barker and James Herbert and Michael Slade and Skipp and Spector and Shaun Hutson and dear GOD the list goes on. My life was blood-soaked books, horror movies and heavy metal.

Ah, youth...

And yet, dig a little deeper and you reveal a love of *film noir* and craggy detectives in rumpled suits and cool hats. Dig a little more and you uncover a love of westerns inherited from a father, a love of screwball comedies inherited from a mother (and for a kid who has stammered all of his life, to find these movies where everyone talks really really fast was beyond exhilarating), and a love of science fiction and adventure that blossomed in the eighties because of people like Spielberg and Lucas and shows like *Knight Rider* and *Airwolf* and *The Six Million Dollar Man*...

Taking all this into account, I am the sum of my obsessions. I am every movie I've ever seen and every book I've ever read. I am every song I've ever listened to. I am every comic I've ever bought. I am entire collections by Joseph Wambaugh and Elmore Leonard and Joe R. Lansdale and I am *His Dark Materials* and I am *Harry Potter*.

And in all of these things, I have glimpsed the Big Clue. And these glimpses were enough to open my eyes to the ideas swimming naturally through the soup of my mind. It was from that soup that I plucked Skulduggery Pleasant himself, back in the summer of 2005, and he brought with him every genre I've ever loved.

He is a detective (crime) who is also a skeleton (horror) who takes on a partner (screwball) and they fight monsters (fantasy) and they save the world (adventure). With a little bit of sci-fi thrown in, to stop things from getting boring.

The stories in this collection — arranged here in chronological order for your reading pleasure — are but fragments of the world that Skulduggery has opened up for me. It is because of him that I am able to write a western and sit it comfortably beside a novella about a middle-aged man revisiting the horrors of his childhood. It is because of him that the tones of these stories shift so radically between one and the next. It is because of him that I have the freedom to write the kind of stories I loved, and continue to love, to read.

And if there is a fledgling writer out there who is searching through this Introduction in an effort to find the Big Clue — the secret to writing that I, along with all the other writers, share only amongst ourselves — I am afraid I must disappoint you. This is something you must find out for yourself, fledgling writer, as the Author's Code expressly forbids me from speaking of it in public.

I may already have said too much...

Derek Landy
DUBLIN

Saint Patrick's Day, 2014

ARmaGEDDON OUTTA HeRe

ACROSS A DARK PLAIN

It was the year of Our Lord eighteen hundred and sixty-one, and it was up west of the Missouri River in South Dakota, and the Dead Men were riding again.

This was still years before that damn fool Custer stumbled across all that gold in the Black Hills, years before Wounded Knee and the massacre that took place there. This was back before the territory was admitted into the union, back before Deadwood, back even before that pitiful Treaty of Laramie promised the region to the Lakota people, a treaty that, if ever there was one, was drawn up just to be burned.

It was a time of gunfighters and outlaws and hard living and easy dying and, of course, it was a time of mean-spirited, blood-slicked magic.

The Dead Men had travelled east from Wyoming, tracking their quarry, who'd led them a merry dance. But the longer they tracked, the easier it got. This was on account of the fact that their quarry had taken up with a Necromancer named Noche, who was developing a habit of leaving dead folk in his wake. Not regular dead folk, neither, but the kind that jumped up and ran around and had a madness in their dull eyes and a terrible, terrible hunger that could only be sated by human flesh. The kind only fire or a bullet to the brainpan could put down. Thankfully, fire and bullets were what the Dead Men specialised in.

Seven of them, all Irish, some of their accents a little muddied due to all the travelling and the living they'd done. There was Saracen Rue, all easy charm and easy smiles, like a man trying to convince himself he's nicer than he is. Beside him rode Dexter Vex, one of the more thoughtful of the group, though he wasn't one to show it. The quiet one with the week's worth of stubble was Anton Shudder, and a scarier man was hard to find, even in this forsaken land. There was Erskine Ravel, recently returned from his sojourn to lands even more foreign and forsaken than this one, and Hopeless, a man of one name and many faces.

Riding in the lead was the scarred man, Ghastly Bespoke, and beside him the living skeleton, the one who looked like the Grim Reaper himself, the first of the Four Horsemen written about in the Bible and shouted about from pulpits up and down this wounded and pockmarked country.

And I looked, and behold a pale horse: and his name that sat on him was Death, and Hell followed with him. And power was given unto them over the fourth part of the earth, to kill with sword, and with hunger, and with death, and with the beasts of the earth.

Skulduggery Pleasant's clothes were scuffed and faded, and his coat was long and may have been black once upon a time. Among normal folk, what these men called 'mortals', he'd take that kerchief from around his neck there and tie it over all those teeth that were fixed in that permanent grin, and he'd pull that hat down low over those empty eye sockets. He had two pistol belts, criss-crossing low and held in place with tie-downs, and in those holsters he had guns with pearl handles and long barrels. Colt Walkers, they were. Guns built for stopping men.

They'd been riding for days and their horses were tired and thirsty, and the riders with flesh were chafed and sore. They came upon the town of Forbidden, and didn't think much of it. A town of three streets and dirty people who bathed not often or well. There was a mangy dog lying in the middle of the street, who looked at them with mild indifference as they passed. When they were safely gone, the dog offered up a feeble growl, then lay back down and went to sleep or died. Didn't make much difference to anyone which one it was.

They found the livery down the other end of town and the owner, an ungrateful piece of work called Sully, limped out into the sun, scratching himself in places soap hadn't touched in a long, long time.

"Yeah?" he said with a mouth full of spit. "What the hell d'you want?"

The Dead Men dismounted. Pleasant and Bespoke stayed at the back, them being the most likely to draw attention, and Rue and Vex looked at the proprietor and frowned.

"What the hell do you think we want?" Vex said. "We want our horses fed and watered. You own this place, don't you?"

The piece of work Sully looked at these men, saw the steel in their eyes and the steel on their hips, and he lost some of his scowl and swallowed some of his spit.

"I do," he said. "Proud owner of Sullivan's Livery. If the paint hadn't peeled off years ago, you could see my name on the sign up there, even though it was spelled wrong and the 'y' was missing from Livery. I blame myself, not being able to read, and I blame the fella I hired to make the sign, him not being able to write. But regrets are what regrets are – we all have 'em, and those who don't have 'em don't miss 'em. Fed and watered, you say. You can depend on me, provided you have coin enough to pay for such a service."

Vex tapped Rue's arm. "Show the man some coin, Saracen." He went to join the others, who were walking down the wide patch of dirt called Main Street towards the saloon. The townspeople gave them a decent berth, watched them with wary eyes and waited till they were out of earshot to start whispering. Men with guns were never a good sign. Men who looked like they knew how to use those guns even less so.

Bespoke was first through the doors into the saloon. Inside were a few uneven tables, a solid bar and a cracked mirror. There was a small piano nobody played and the floor was dried mud and sawdust. As far as patrons went, there weren't many here, but all heads turned, and all mouths dropped open. To see a man of Bespoke's scarring was not something you're ever likely to see again, and most people seemed to realise that, so they made sure to stare extra hard when they first met him.

Bespoke tipped his hat to the room and walked up to the bar.

The other Dead Men followed, filing in one at a time. Pleasant came last, found a table in the corner to sit, watching the room from beneath the brim of his hat.

"Good day to you, barkeep," said Bespoke. "What sort of drinks do you serve here?"

The barkeep, a man who'd seen a lot and heard more, had never been one to allow ugliness to get in the way of making money. There was a time he'd even served a leper who had wandered through town, though he served him out back, away from the eyes of his regulars. Money was money, he figured, and it didn't matter a whole lot how many stumps for fingers a hand had if what it was holding could add to the coffers.

Fact is, the barkeep hadn't even washed the mug the leper had used all that much. So the barkeep told the scarred man what was on offer and the scarred man asked for six drinks. Saracen Rue came in as the sixth was poured, and they all drank like thirsty men. Except for Pleasant, of course.

"Now that," said Ravel, "was a long time coming. And it was welcome." He smiled at the barkeep. "We're looking for a friend of ours. Two friends, actually, would've just passed through here. Maybe you saw them. Maybe you served them two of these delicious and refreshing beers."

The barkeep said nothing.

"Our first friend," said Vex, "is like us – he's Irish. Tall and dark-haired and kinda pale, though in this sun he's probably reddened up a little. Wears a glove on his right hand. The other fella wears black and carries a staff with him wherever he goes, the height of a man."

The barkeep looked at the Dead Men and still said nothing.

"It is very important that we catch up to our friends as soon as possible," Rue said. "We have news from home that requires their immediate and direct attention. Tragic news. Time is of the essence."

"Haven't seen anyone," said the barkeep.

"You're sure? Our first friend, he has green eyes. Normally eye colour means very little when talking about a man, but if you'd ever looked into those eyes, you'd remember them. Like a snake's. And the second, as I said, carries a big old staff. That's something to stick in the memory, isn't it?"

The barkeep shook his head. "Can't help you, fellas."

"Well," said Ravel, "that is a shame."

Bespoke turned to the dusty, dirty patrons. "How about the rest of you? Seen anyone like the men we just described?"

A few people kept staring at Bespoke's face. Others looked down at their beers. One or two, and this caught the attention of the Dead Men, flickered their gaze to a man who sat alone with his eyes fixed on his hands. He was so knotted up, he was shaking. The long silence that followed grew heavy and seemed to weigh down on his narrow shoulders. It grew so heavy he evidently couldn't take it any more and he jumped to his feet and went for his gun all at the same time. He made a mess of both, went stumbling and fumbling and panicking, and Hopeless crossed to him so quick no one knew quite what was happening till the man hit the floor with a broken nose and no gun in his hand.

Hopeless walked back to the bar, put down the man's gun and picked up his drink, finished it just as the man realised he was bleeding.

"What did you do that for?" he said. He had a peculiar accent, German or Dutch or some such.

"You were going to shoot us," said Vex.

"I was not," said the man, though there wasn't a person there who believed him.

"People try to shoot me all the time," Rue told him. "Usually because of a wife or a daughter or a sister or a mother. The point is, I'm used to having people shoot at me. We all are. But we generally know why we're being shot at."

The man got to his feet, blood running freely through the fingers that cupped his nose. "I wasn't going to shoot you."

"I'm having a hard time believing you," Ravel said, "seeing as how you were going for your gun at the time."

The man didn't have much to say about that.

"What's your name, friend?" said Rue.

"Joost," said the man.

"Joost? What kind of name is that?"

"Dutch," said Joost.

Rue nodded. It figured. From the accent and all, and anyway, half the world had come west to search for gold.

This was when Anton Shudder stepped forward, and the five other Dead Men at the bar seemed to step back, even though no actual steps were taken. Shudder looked at Joost, and to the poor, panicking Dutchman it seemed like the world was narrowing to a very tight space.

"Tell us what the man with the green eyes said to you," Shudder said in his quiet voice.

"Church," Joost managed. "He said something about going to church."

The church, such as it was, stood on a hill a few miles south. A ramshackle place where not much worshipping went on – and when it did, half of it was half-remembered and most of it was made up. It catered to three different townships, of which Forbidden was one. Its roof sagged and let in water when it rained, its walls groaned and let in wind when it blew, and its doors creaked and let in hypocrites when it suited.

There were two sides of narrow pews and a narrow aisle in between, and there was a table for an altar and the pulpit was a box to stand on. It had once been a barn, and it had never got rid of the comforting smell of cow dung.

In town, there'd lived a man named Wooley, a quick wit who always found amusing, if sometimes crude, names for people and places. He'd come up with a name for this falling-down church-barn that smelled of dung, and it was quite a clever and funny name, but he died of dysentery before he could tell anyone. Mighty unlucky man, that Wooley.

The Dead Men walked up from the bottom of the hill towards this sad-looking church with a single candle burning in its window. It was night, and a warm one at that, and they followed the winding trail between all those graves. They walked single file, with Pleasant in the lead, the moonlight making his skull shine beneath his hat. At the top of the hill the trail widened out, and it was at this point that the Dead Men stood abreast of each other, observing the double doors with the window on one side.

"Nefarian Serpine," Pleasant called, "if you're in there, come out. Come get what's coming to you."

The candle flickered behind the thin, cracked glass. The doors banged gently in the hesitant breeze. Pleasant looked at Rue, who shook his head. No one was in that church.

Pleasant made to step forward, then stopped. The other Dead Men watched him as he turned slowly. They started to turn, too.

Corpses lunged up from the graves all around them, pushing aside packed dirt and overturning markers of wood and stone. They burrowed out from six feet under and less, moaning and groaning and uttering sounds that whistled through dried-up throats. They clambered to their feet and staggered and lurched and shambled, all going straight towards the seven sorcerers who were slowly backing away from them.

More and more crawled to the surface, breaking through to add their sounds to the growing chorus of the dead. Hundreds of graves, going back sixty years. Some of the dead, zombies they were called, were fresh enough, and some were little more than skeletons. Skulduggery Pleasant might've felt right at home at that moment. If he did, he didn't show it.

"Start shooting," he said.

Guns cleared leather and immediately the night was shaking to the thunder of gunfire. The Dead Men stood in a line and fired calmly, making every bullet count. Shots to the legs to slow them down, to the chests to drive them back, and to the heads to give them a death they wouldn't be walking away from. Bullets were easier than magic when it came to zombies. Quicker, too. Even the skeletons, those without a brain, went down when a bullet shattered their skulls.

Bone fragments flew. Rotten flesh burst. Soon enough the Dead Men were standing in a cloud of acrid gunsmoke, and still the zombies came.

"Reloading," Vex said, taking one step back. The other Dead Men closed in, filling the gap. When his guns were ready, Vex said, "Firing," and stepped into the space that was immediately made for him.

That's how they went, the Dead Men, doing this dance, covering for their partners. Guns got hot and fingers got singed, and still they fired and reloaded and fired, and still the zombies came.

Three zombies from the back pushed forward. Fresher corpses, these. They ran at Bespoke and he blasted one of them in the face and one in the throat. The bullet passed right through the spinal cord and the head flopped backwards, tearing decaying skin, then fell off. The third zombie he punched with a column of air that lifted it off its feet. He fired at it as it hurtled backwards, hit it in the back of the head.

The zombies were surrounding them now. The Dead Men moved into a tight circle, constantly turning, a spinning top of death. Empty cartridges fell. New ones slid into chambers. Hammers pulled back and struck down and powder lit and lead flew. Faces, heads and bodies disintegrated. The spinning circle of Dead Men spun its way halfway down the trail. The slower-moving zombies had to adjust their lumbering course a few times just to get within snarling distance.

Pleasant slipped into the middle of the circle and Ravel covered his back while he holstered his empty Colts. He held up his hands, gripping the air. It wasn't easy to do what he was doing. The rifles and shotguns that had stayed behind with the horses lifted from their holsters and packs, and he brought them up the hill, over the heads of the foul-tempered dead.

"I'm out," said Hopeless, returning his pistols to his belt. His rifle, a Sharps, fell into his waiting hands and he brought it to his shoulder and resumed firing.

Rue was next, and he made his Winchester sing, using the butt whenever a corpse got too eager. Shudder had the shotgun, a double-barrelled monstrosity he liked to call Daisy. He fired that from the hip, blowing apart any zombie dumb enough to go up against him. The others all had Henrys, except for Pleasant himself, who favoured the Spencer. They dug in their pockets for shells, reloading as fast as they were able, but it was clear there were more zombies than there were bullets.

A big zombie, a man who'd died scarcely two weeks before, charged into the circle and the circle split apart. Any rational mind watching might think that this'd be the moment to panic, but the Dead Men went about their business, hurried but calm, knowing that one mistake, one fumble or misfire, could lead to being swarmed and torn apart. They dodged among the grasping hands, firing and lashing out, reloading whenever they had a moment.

One by one, rifles were dropped and balls of fire flew. Coloured streams of light burst from Vex's hands, sizzled right through necrotic flesh. Rue went to work with his bowie knife and Hopeless took out that machete of his. Only Shudder was still firing, his pockets providing a seemingly endless supply of shells.

"To the church," Pleasant shouted when it became clear they were about to be overrun, and each of them started making their way back up the hill.

A wave of his hand opened the double doors and they grouped together once more, backing into the shelter of the Lord. But the Lord must've been busy that night, or else He was sleeping on the job, because there was no respite in here. The carnivorous corpses kept coming, clambering over the pews, and the Dead Men kept backing up, shoulder to shoulder. They slowed their retreat some, only stopping when they had to, when the sheer numbers forced them to.

Bespoke gestured behind them and the makeshift altar and the pulpit slid to the side, out of their way. By the time they reached the single door at the other end of the church, every zombie still moving was packed inside.

At Pleasant's signal, Hopeless kicked open the door, held it for his friends, and the Dead Men turned and got the hell out of there. Shudder was last, but instead of running, he turned in the doorway and pulled open his shirt. Pleasant,

Bespoke and Ravel held out their hands, forming a wall of solid air, keeping the zombies from getting at their friend. They dropped the wall when Shudder nodded. The zombies rushed forward.

There are types of magic that are easy, relatively speaking, that take no particular toll on the sorcerer using them. They'll get tired, sure. They'll get worn out, and drained. That's what happens when magic is used. Same as anything a body does.

But then there are types of magic that demand a price. Anton Shudder's magic was one such. The risk he took every time he used it, the pain and anguish it caused him, were immense. Few people ever mastered that discipline of magic. There were those who said it could never *be* mastered. Shudder himself was one such person.

His gist burst from his chest – a screaming, squawking, nightmarish version of Shudder himself. It was made up of every bad thought and feeling the man possessed, and by the look of the fangs and the claws and the madness, those bad thoughts were many, and resourceful. Attached to Shudder by a twisting stream of light and dark, it went at the zombies like they were the things it hated most in the world. Which, at that moment, they were. It went through them and over them and back again, that stream looping over itself like an ever-growing snake. The zombies, with no room to duck even if they'd had a mind to, were reduced to tatters.

Shudder's knees gave out and Rue and Vex each grabbed one of his arms, held him up. With the last of his strength, Shudder called the gist back to him. It hollered and screeched and fought, but the thread between them shortened, and shortened again, and then the gist was sucked back into Shudder's chest, and the night was silent apart from the low moaning of the zombie remains.

Rue and Vex helped Shudder walk away, and Pleasant, Bespoke and Ravel clicked their fingers and filled their hands with flames. They tossed those flames through the door, manipulated them a little, and within seconds the whole church was burning, taking the last of the zombies with it.

The Dead Men headed back down to their tired horses, where Hopeless was waiting for them. He'd collected their fallen rifles and had picked up something extra along the way. A man in black, unconscious, with blood running from his nose and his hands in shackles. Beside him, as he lay in the dirt, was his staff.

They rode back into town, found an empty corner in Sullivan's Livery and dumped the Necromancer in there while the Dead Men took rooms for the night. Only Pleasant stayed to guard him – true dead men never needing sleep. Pleasant stood, arms folded, looking at Noche. Not saying anything. Not moving – not even to breathe.

A few minutes past eight the next morning, the rest of the Dead Men turned up, rested and fed. A bucket of water woke the Necromancer, who sat up with a lunging breath and then rolled over into a series of coughing fits. When he was done with all the spluttering, he looked up at his captors.

"What'll we do with him?" asked Bespoke.

"I think we should kill him," Rue said. "I don't like him. Look at his eyebrows. They're odd. He's got odd eyebrows, and I think they might be magical. He's trying to hypnotise me with his odd, magical eyebrows."

"Nobody is trying to hypnotise you," Shudder said.

"We should shave them from his face and experiment on them."

"I think the stress has finally got to our dear friend Saracen Rue," said Ravel sadly. "He was a good man while he lasted. Annoying at times, perhaps, but a good man nonetheless."

"I will be missed," Rue nodded.

Noche frowned up at them. "You're all insane."

"You should have the measure of insanity," said Vex, "what with all the palling around you've been doing with Nefarian Serpine. Why are you associating with the likes of him anyway? The Necromancers have been staying out of the war. Are you really going to join the losing side right before it ends?"

"My brothers and sisters remain neutral."

"So it's just you, then," said Pleasant. "A rogue Necromancer teaming up with the most notorious of Mevolent's Three Generals. Why? He's been running from us for months, and we're closer to him now than ever. It's only a matter of time before we have him."

Noche smiled, the smile adopting a certain smug quality. "But time isn't on your side, is it? You're absolutely right – Mevolent is rumoured to be injured, his forces are scattered, Vengeous is missing, and the war, they say, is coming to an end. Last I heard, your Sanctuaries were offering a reward to whoever tells them where Mevolent is hiding... But what everyone's talking about is the amnesty. So long as the war is ended soon, and not allowed to drag out, they'll be offering forgiveness to all of Mevolent's followers who aren't yet imprisoned. That's why you're so eager to get to Serpine – because you know that time is ticking away. If you don't get him before the amnesties are granted, you'll lose your chance to have your revenge. Won't you, skeleton?"

Pleasant tilted his head in that way of his. "You're working with him. I really don't care why. Maybe he has something on you. Maybe you owe him. Maybe you're just a glutton for punishment. I don't care about you or your motives. All I want is a question answered."

"You'll not get any information out of me," Noche sneered.

"We just want to know one little bit of information," said Rue. "It's barely worth mentioning, really. Barely worth the breath that would carry the words from my lips."

"Just one tiny bit of information," said Vex, "and then we'll let you go. You can run off and we won't tell anyone you helped us."

"We'll swear to it," said Bespoke.

"Our word is our bond," said Rue.

"Serpine," Ravel said. "Where is he headed?"

Noche glared. "I'll never tell."

"Please?" said Ravel. Another glare, and Ravel straightened up. "Right, well. You are of no use to us whatsoever, are you? I don't even see why you went to the trouble of being captured, I really don't. What's the point of being a prisoner if you're not going to divulge secret plans to your captors?"

"Defeats the purpose," Vex grumbled.

"It does indeed, Dexter," Ravel said. "What do you have to say for yourself? Are you suitably ashamed? You should be. If I were you, I'd have a good long think about what a disappointment you've been to us. We had high hopes."

"The highest."

"That's right, Saracen, the highest. See? You've upset Saracen."

"I just have something in my eye," said Rue.

"I have never seen Saracen Rue weep," Ravel said, "since this morning, but you've made him weep like a little child. I hope you're proud of yourself."

Noche looked at them warily. "You *are* all insane."

Anton Shudder walked forward. "Tell us where Serpine is going. I don't play games like my friends. They're saying all this to confuse you and frighten you. I prefer to simply ask, and I expect a simple answer."

"I would rather die," said Noche, a touch less convincingly.

"Do you know my chosen discipline, little man?"

"You're a... You have a gist."

"That's right. And when I let it out there are times when I just cannot control it. And it's a sight to behold. Terrifying. Ferocious. Merciless. Tell us what we want to know or I shall release it, and believe you me you will garner its full attention."

Noche swallowed like he'd something sharp stuck in his craw. "Serpine... he mentioned Lancaster County, in Nebraska, as somewhere he'd be safe. Sounded like that's where he's headed."

Rue peered at him. "Are you lying?"

"No."

"I don't trust him."

Ravel nodded. "I don't trust him, either."

"I trust him," said Vex happily. "And I've changed my mind about his eyebrows, too. Skulduggery, can we keep him?"

Pleasant tilted his head at the Necromancer. "You're lying."

"No, I—"

Pleasant splayed his hand and Noche flew off the ground, hit the wall, his feet kicking at air.

The Dead Men fell silent, lost their smiles and looks of good humour.

"My friend Anton will kill you," said Pleasant, "but I will kill you worse. Why are you with Serpine?"

"Please, I..."

"You have one chance. If you lie to me, I will start killing you."

Something changed in Noche's eyes, something dripped away. His melting resolve, most likely.

"He's heading for the Temple," he said. "I was to meet him, take him back to it."

"The Necromancers are going to hide him?"

"Y-yes. I don't know why. He has an... an agreement, of sorts. Made long ago."

"He left you here to delay us," said Pleasant, "and went on to the Temple without you. How far is it?"

"Three days' ride," Noche said.

Pleasant curled his fingers, and the Necromancer gasped for breath. "Tell us where it is."

They rode.

On the second day they had grass under their horses' hooves.

The third day they found Serpine's horse. It had snapped its leg in a gulley and Serpine hadn't even had the decency to put it out of its misery. Hopeless laid his hand on its neck and put a bullet in its head, and it was a kindness, and then he remounted and they carried on.

They made good time. Serpine's tracks got fresher. They reached the top of a hill, looked down across the valley and saw a man running and falling, making his way to a rocky outcrop of curiously shaped stones and boulders. Standing outside the opening to what looked like a cave were a dozen figures in black, all in a line, watching Serpine approach.

The Dead Men tore down that hill like the devil's own demon dogs. They got close enough so that when Serpine glanced back they could see the fear and exhaustion painted across his dirty, sweating face.

Then he stumbled through the line of black, and disappeared into the cave behind them.

Pleasant leaped from the saddle, using his magic to propel himself through the air like he'd been shot from a cannon. He landed a couple of strides from the line of Necromancers.

"Move," he said.

The Necromancers, being the contrary lot that they were, showed no intention of budging an inch. The one in the middle, the one who'd stepped aside to allow Serpine to pass, gave Pleasant a smile.

"Welcome to our Temple," he said. "Ours is a place of peace and learning. Do you have business here?"

"Move," Pleasant said again. His voice, usually so smooth, was coarse as the sand they'd travelled across to get here. The Dead Men dismounted behind him, walked slowly up till they formed a wedge at his back. They kept their hands close to their guns.

"Nefarian Serpine is a guest," said the talkative Necromancer. "He has provided us a service in the past, and so he is under our protection. I'm afraid I can't let you through."

"If you side with our enemy," said Pleasant, "you become our enemy."

To his credit, the Necromancer didn't seem all that intimidated by a walking skeleton with guns on his hips. He gave Pleasant another smile. "That's a rather simplistic view of things, isn't it? There's really not much room for manoeuvring around that little philosophy. I prefer, personally, to take each moment as it comes, and to treat every obstacle as an opportunity to do something different. It makes life interesting."

His patience worn to a frayed thread already, conversing with a smiling flannel-mouth such as this one was enough to snap it clean. Pleasant went to push by, and suddenly there was a wall of shadows looming over their heads. The Dead Men went for their guns, but froze before drawing. Once those guns cleared leather, death would come flying and there'd be no turning back.

"You think you scare us?" the Necromancer asked. "They call you the Dead Men, but it is my brothers, my sisters and I who wield the true death magic. You think we're afraid to die? Really?"

"I think you talk big," said Pleasant. "I think you talk about death like it's your friend. But if you really want to get acquainted, we can help you with that."

"Then kill us," the Necromancer said. "But be warned. We stand at the mouth of a Temple. Beneath our feet, there are more of us than you can imagine. They'll tear you to pieces and you still won't be any closer to your quarry."

"Then we'll wait," Bespoke said. "We'll make camp right here and we'll wait."

"As much as I would enjoy seeing you waste your time in such a fashion," the Necromancer replied, "our Temple has hidden entrances and exits leading far and wide. You're just going to have to accept the fact that Serpine is out of your reach, get on your horses, and trot away."

"We don't give up that easily," said Ravel.

"Then you should start," said the Necromancer. "Because you've lost this little game. The skeleton knows it. That's why he's gone so quiet. All this time, all this effort, all this building of hatred and anger... all for nothing. You were a few seconds too late, gentlemen. That can't be easy for you. You have my commiserations. But the game is done. It's over. You can pick it up again in another country, maybe. But when Mevolent does fall – and he will – there will be a treaty, and an amnesty, and then Mr Serpine will be able to walk free without a care in the world, and there won't be a single thing you can do about it."

The Dead Men took their hands from their guns. They'd been alive long enough to know when they were beaten, and they had enough wisdom between them to know there was no shame in it. Sometimes the cards flipped right, and sometimes they didn't.

At Pleasant's nod, they got back on their horses. The Necromancers began to file into the cave, and the wall of shadows became little more than black smoke in the wind. Finally, there were just Pleasant and the Necromancer left standing there.

"What's your name?" Pleasant asked.

That smile again. "Cleric Solomon Wreath, at your service," said the Necromancer. He even gave a little bow.

"Mr Wreath, today you have prevented me from doing my duty."

"On the contrary, I have prevented you from exacting your revenge."

"Which amounts to the same thing. I won't forget this."

"I don't expect you to," said Wreath, but Pleasant had already turned his back on him.

That night they rested their horses by a stream and didn't talk a whole lot.

Pleasant sat by himself, looking out into the darkness. To say he had a peculiar anger would of course be something of an understatement, but a peculiar anger it was, as it wasn't the sort any normal folk could understand. It was a slow-burning heat, capable of firing up at a whim, but never in any danger of puttering out. It kept him. It sustained him. Maybe there was even a part of him that was glad Serpine had wormed his way free.

As long as the man who'd killed him and his family was alive, somewhere out there across the dark plain, Pleasant had a reason to fight, a reason to keep putting one foot in front of the other. But kill the killer, and what was left? Something cold and uncertain. Could be he hung on to what he had – his hate, his anger, his job – because hanging on was all he had. The war was coming to an end. His time as a soldier was coming to an end.

What then? Was there something else out there, something he had yet to discover, that could keep him going when he'd used up everything else? Some thing or some person that would give him a purpose again, that would light a different kind of fire within him?

Most likely, he didn't know. He probably didn't care to think that far ahead.

The Dead Men slept. But not Skulduggery Pleasant.

No, Skulduggery Pleasant just hung on, waiting.

Because it was all he had.

THE
HORROR
WRITERS'
HALLOWEEN BALL

"Hell may well be other people," Gordon Edgley muttered as they entered the ballroom, "but if you're looking for an everlasting purgatory of snide remarks and bitter snipes, look no further than other writers."

The costumed guests mingled and laughed, sipped champagne and wine and plucked tasty but pointless canapés from the trays of passing waiters. A string quartet played from the darkened gallery, as if they'd been shunted to one side to make room in the light for the chosen few. And the chosen few they really were; invitations to Sebastian Fawkes's parties were rarer than an honest coin in a politician's pocket.

That wasn't a bad line, actually, Gordon realised. Needed work, but it had potential.

"Invitations to these parties are rarer than an honest coin in a politician's pocket," Gordon said to his companion, and waited for the response. When none came, he frowned, stored the line away and vowed to play around with it later.

He recognised a few of the faces – the moustachioed face, for instance, of

R. Samuel Keen, an American whose every book had to have either an unnaturally wise child or a psychic dog. His latest one, which Gordon had tried to listen to as a book on tape before the cassette unspooled in his car, had both. It hadn't been very good.

He saw Adrian Sykes, a soft-spoken Geordie whose work was fantastically gory and outrageously imaginative. The theme of the party was, as usual, horror, and Sykes had come dressed as one of Clive Barker's Cenobites, all black leather and hooks. Gordon had met him only once before, and had come away thinking of him as a thoroughly decent person. It was occasionally true to say that the writers of the most disturbing horror stories were among the nicest people you could possibly meet.

There were exceptions, of course. For instance, the gentleman Sykes was chatting to, Edgar Looms, another American, was a man of singular vulgarity. Gordon had first met him ten years earlier, just after Gordon's first book was published, and since then he had developed quite an abhorrence of the man. Tonight Looms was one of many who had come dressed as Frankenstein's monster – from the James Whale movie, not the book.

For his first time here, Gordon himself had come as the Creature from the Black Lagoon – a costume he'd had specially created at no little cost. It was worth it, though, even if the flippers made it difficult to walk and the mask made it difficult to see, hear or breathe. It also made it difficult to be heard, which may have explained why his companion hadn't responded to his politician line.

Gordon leaned in closer, careful not to topple over in his costume, and said, quite loudly and clearly, "Invitations to these parties are rarer than an honest coin in a politician's pocket."

His companion, dressed as he was in a 1930s suit and tie, his head covered in bandages exactly like Claude Rains from *The Invisible Man*, turned slightly, so that Gordon could see his own costume's reflection in those sunglasses.

"Are you having a stroke?" Skulduggery Pleasant asked. "You keep repeating the same phrase. Is it hot in there? It looks hot."

"It is," Gordon admitted. "But I'm not having a stroke. I'm too young. I'm only thirty-five, for God's sake. Though I may start hallucinating, and thirst will likely become an issue before too long."

"How do you take the mask off?"

"I'm not entirely sure. It took two people to get me into this thing. They probably told me how to take it off, but the mask makes it hard to hear properly."

Skulduggery said something.

Gordon leaned in again. "What?"

"I said what about toilet breaks?"

"I hadn't thought of that. Can you see a zip anywhere?"

"It looks rather seamless."

"Damn it. And now I want to pee. I didn't before you brought it up, but now I can feel how full my bladder is. Oh dear God. If I wet myself in front of all these writers, they'll never let me live it down."

Skulduggery nodded. "Writers are small-minded like that."

A waiter came over. Gordon went to wave him away, but his huge flipper hand caught the edge of the serving tray and sent glasses of champagne flying. Even before they'd crashed to the ground, Gordon was spinning on his heels and lurching awkwardly away.

Skulduggery fell easily into pace beside him. "It's hard to look innocent when you're the Creature from the Black Lagoon."

"I suppose that's the one advantage of this mask," Gordon responded. "Nobody knows who I am."

"Gordon Edgley!"

Gordon had to turn his whole body to look round at whoever had called his name. She came out of the crowd like a bespoiled vision in mint green – 1960s skirt and sweater, her blonde hair tied up, scratches all over her face, and attached to her jacket half a dozen plastic birds.

"Tippi Hedren," Gordon said at once, smiling even though she couldn't see it.

"What gave it away?" Susan said, standing on tiptoes to kiss both cheeks of his mask. "It was either this or Grace Jones from *Vamp*, which would have raised a lot more eyebrows, believe me. Who's your friend?"

Susan was a typical upstate New Yorker – talking a mile a minute.

"This is my associate, Mr Pleasant," Gordon said. "Mr Pleasant, may I introduce Susan DeWick, author of the *Chronicles of the Dead* series."

"Mr Pleasant," Susan said, shaking Skulduggery's gloved hand. "How delightfully formal we suddenly are."

"Miss DeWick, it is a genuine pleasure to meet you," Skulduggery responded, his voice beginning to work on her already. "I've been a fan ever since Gordon recommended you. Your latest book is one of your best."

"Oh, you're just saying that because it's true," Susan said, and laughed. She looked back to Gordon. "So, Fishface, is this your first time here? I've been waiting years for an invitation. When it finally came, I have to admit, I squealed a little. Just a little, mind you, for I am a horror writer, and so I comport myself with absolute solemnity at all times."

"Oh, naturally," Gordon said, really wishing he wasn't wearing a stupid mask. "When did you get to London?"

"Wednesday," she said. "I thought travelling all this way for a silly costume party would have appalled my dear late mother, but my dad insists that even she had heard of Sebastian Fawkes and the extravagant bashes he throws. The who's who of the horror elite, all in one place. Kind of gives you an illicit little thrill, doesn't it? Mr Pleasant, are you a writer also? I'm afraid I'm not familiar with the name..."

"I am a mere reader," Skulduggery said. "Gordon allows me to help him with his research and in return I live out my writer fantasies vicariously through him."

"Oh, I like a man with writer fantasies," Susan said, flashing him a smile.

Gordon felt the sudden need to step between them, but doubted he could manage it dressed like a big fish-monster.

A heavily bearded Wolfman swooped upon Susan, nuzzling her neck, and she laughed and allowed herself to be dragged away. She looked back before vanishing into the crowd, but Gordon didn't know if she was looking at him, or Skulduggery.

"She's nice," Skulduggery said.

Gordon made a noise that sounded like agreement.

"She looks a little like Grace Kelly."

"Now listen here," Gordon said, "I didn't invite you to this thing so that you could sweep Susan DeWick off her feet. If anyone is going to be sweeping her off her feet, it'll be me, in a fitting homage to the Gill-man and Julie Adams. Admittedly, it won't be easy. Co-ordination is not what this suit was designed for, and I do have a bad back, and all this heat is making me feel quite weak so I may pass out and drop her, but just the same—"

"No sweeping her off her feet," Skulduggery said, clearly amused. "You have my word. Besides, why would I antagonise a friend who has taken me to the first party I've been to in years?"

"You have the Requiem Ball, don't you?"

"Full of sorcerers talking about Sanctuary business," Skulduggery said, dismissing it with a wave of his hand. "It's an evening of carefully chosen words and awkward silences, where nobody wants to mention the name Nefarian Serpine in case I suddenly get it into my head to kick down his door and kill him. As if that thought isn't constantly swirling through my head as it is. No,

Gordon, you have brought me to a proper party, of mortals. Of mortal *writers*, no less. This is beyond wonderful. This is just what I've been looking for."

"Well, I'm glad," said Gordon. "We weren't supposed to bring guests, but I did suspect that you might appreciate it. And if Fawkes finds out and banishes me to the horror wilderness for the rest of my career, it will have been worth it to pay you back, in some small way, for everything you've done for me."

"Why, Gordon, I never noticed this before, but you are such a sentimental fool."

Gordon laughed. "Indeed I am, my friend, and proud of it."

The lights suddenly dimmed and the string quartet stopped playing as a spotlight fell upon a balcony high above, on which stood their host for the evening. Sebastian Fawkes was tall and thin with high, narrow cheekbones. His black hair was shot through with startling streaks of silver, as was his goatee beard. Even his eyebrows, arched to perfection, each had a slash of silver. Apart from the Dracula costume he wore, he looked, Gordon realised, exactly like his author photo from twenty years ago. The crowd fell into a deep and respectful hush.

"Horror," Fawkes said, casting his gaze down upon the room. He had a deep, musical quality to his voice that made him sound like an English Vincent Price. "Fear. Dread. These are the commodities in which we trade. In return for the devotion of our readers, we conjure for them the stuff of nightmares."

He paused, allowing his words to permeate the air. A tad melodramatic, but Gordon didn't mind melodrama every now and then – just as long as it didn't get too pretentious.

"We are the dark guardians of the soul," Fawkes continued. "The new millennium is a mere twelve years away, and we stand between Scylla and Charybdis to hold back the tide of apathy and indifference that threatens, even now, to engulf us all. We offer glimpses into madness, we bring their hands close to the black fires of terror... and then we guide them, safely, back to the light. Ours is a noble calling.

"Where once we would have sat round the campfire telling our stories, now we sit at our typewriters or our word processors. The world is our campfire now – but while you may think we have banished our demons with our modern technologies, with our VCRs and our CD players and our MTV, they still lurk, out there, in the dark. And we are their hunters."

He bowed his head and the ballroom erupted in applause. Gordon clapped his webbed hands along with everyone else, glad that he was wearing a fish-mask so no one could see him cringe.

Fawkes motioned for silence. "And here we are, gathered together on this most special of nights. A lot of you have been here before. A lot of you already stand within the inner circle. You know the secrets. You have reaped the rewards."

A low murmur rippled through Fawkes's audience. People were nodding and smiling softly.

"But others are here tonight for the very first time," Fawkes continued. "They stand on the cusp of enlightenment. They stand on the edge of wonder. We have seven uninitiated writers among us, writers who have proven their worth, who are ready to be welcomed into our... family."

Fawkes chuckled at the word, and the guests laughed along with him. Gordon didn't know what the hell he was talking about any more.

"But all that is still to be revealed," said Fawkes. "For now, eat, drink, talk, laugh... be merry. And give me a hip hip hooray for horror. Hip hip..."

"Hooray!"

They did that three times in all, and Gordon could only blink at the sudden shift in tone.

Fawkes gave a wave, everyone clapped, and the lights came back on. A few moments later, Fawkes made his entrance into the ballroom and the string quartet started up again.

Skulduggery looked at Gordon. "The man's an idiot."

Gordon nodded. "He does seem to be idiotic."

"I never liked his books. Maybe he's improved with age, but his early work is derivative with definite signs of pretention. And look, he's coming this way. This will be a wonderful opportunity for me to make like the character I've come as, and disappear."

Skulduggery moved backwards into the crowd, and by the time Gordon shifted his position to look around, he was gone.

The mask was ridiculous. He seized it with both hands, squeezed and pulled, and only managed to shift the eyeholes around to his ear. Now he couldn't see anything.

"Help," he said. He reached out and heard a crash. *Another tray of drinks bites the dust.* He stepped back, bumped into someone, heard the unmistakable intake of breath that accompanies a well-dressed lady spilling wine down the front of her dress. "Terribly sorry," Gordon said, spinning quickly, hitting someone else and getting a muffled curse in response.

Suddenly there was a steadying grip on his arms, and he heard Susan DeWick say, "Hold on there, Fishface. You're leaving a trail of destruction in your wake."

"My head's on sideways," he explained.

"I can see that. Want me to take it off?"

"If you wouldn't mind," said Gordon. "Thank you."

He felt her hands take hold of the mask. She twisted and pulled and fiddled, and just when Gordon's claustrophobia was closing in on him, she yanked the Creature's head off. Air rushed in, cooling the sweat on his forehead, and he gasped, laughed and ignored the glares he was getting from the people around him.

"You're a lifesaver," he said, and Susan laughed and handed him back the mask.

"I couldn't watch you flail about any longer," she said. "It was funny, sure, but also kind of sad and pathetic."

"Sad and pathetic are two of my most charming traits."

Susan smiled, a wicked look in her eye, but her response was curtailed by the arrival of Sebastian Fawkes.

"Susan," Fawkes said, kissing her hand, "it is so good to see you again. I'm sure it's been said already tonight by men more charming than I, but you look simply ravishing. Tippi Hedren, yes?"

"Got it in one," Susan replied. "Thank you so much for the invitation, by the way. I was just telling Gordon here how much of an honour it is to be at one of your Halloween parties."

"Ah, yes, Gordon Edgley," said Fawkes, shifting his gaze and holding out his hand. "Very good to meet you."

"Likewise," said Gordon, smiling broadly as he removed one of his gloves. The handshake that followed was unsatisfying and dry. "I've loved your books since I was old enough to read," he said. "I don't wish to embarrass you, but you've been a huge influence on my own work."

"Have I?" Fawkes said. "I haven't read your books so I wouldn't know if I'm supposed to be flattered or insulted." He laughed. Susan laughed, too, but it was hesitant and accompanied by a frown. "And how are your sales, Gordon? Robust, I hope?"

"I can't complain."

"Well, you could," said Fawkes, "but who would listen, eh? Sales can always be better, can't they? It still astonishes me, even to this day, the kind of tripe that sells. Are you one of these exponents of splatterpunk that I've been hearing about lately? Writers who value vulgar gore over genuine chills?"

"I wouldn't count myself as such, no."

"Dreadful stuff. No finesse to their writing. Violence and bloodshed in graphic detail. Where's the character? Where's the theme? Where's the nuance? Cheap shocks, cheap thrills. Blood spills, cheap thrills, eh?" He chuckled at his rhyme. "I'm sure you're successful enough, Gordon. You wouldn't be here otherwise."

"Oh? There's a sales criterion, is there?"

"Oh, absolutely," said Fawkes. "My associates go through the numbers, pick out the writers who are currently in vogue, like you, writers who sell enough books, and their names go on the list."

"I feel so special."

Fawkes's smile faded a little. "I'm sorry, Gordon? I didn't quite catch that."

"I didn't quite throw it."

Now Fawkes's smile was looking decidedly strained. He took a small spiral-bound notebook from his inside pocket, and flipped through it. "Edgley, Edgley... here we are. Gordon Edgley. Writer of, among others, *Caterpillars*. Oh, dear... was that the book about the killer caterpillars?"

Gordon reddened. "That's it."

"The killer caterpillars who eat people?"

"When they swarm, yes."

"I'm interested – are caterpillars known to swarm?"

"I took... liberties with the science."

"I can see that," said Fawkes.

"They're a mutant strain of caterpillar that feasts on human flesh."

"Oh, dear Lord."

"I wrote it when I was nineteen," said Gordon, a touch aggrieved. "It was my first published book."

"You're hugely fortunate it wasn't your last, dear boy. Carnivorous caterpillars, eh? Have you written the sequel yet? *Butterflies?* Or the prequel? *Larvae?*"

Gordon ground his teeth. "They're in the pipeline."

Fawkes roared with laughter. "Oh, that is brilliant! That is wonderful!"

"*Caterpillars* is actually an excellent debut," said Susan, "and it follows in a glorious tradition. You have Herbert's *The Rats*, Hutson's *Slugs*, Guy N. Smith's *Night of the Crabs*, Halkin's *Blood Worm*... *Caterpillars* stacks right up there with the best of them."

"I'm sure it is esteemed company indeed. I apologise, Gordon, I didn't wish to insult or belittle you. I'm sure you have enough critics belittling you without me judging you by my own standards."

Gordon frowned. "That's an apology?"

"It is nevertheless a pleasure to meet you," said Fawkes, smiling again, "and thank you for coming. Stick around – I have a feeling it will be a memorable night for you both. If you'll excuse me...?"

He walked away.

"You're excused," Gordon muttered.

Susan looked at him. "Wow."

"Yes."

"Wow."

"So that was Sebastian Fawkes, eh?"

Susan gave a small shrug. "If it's any consolation, whenever I meet him, he's lovely to me. Always calls me ravishing."

"He didn't call me ravishing."

"I noticed that."

"Maybe he has something against Irish people."

"He probably just hates you," said Susan.

"I think he's racist."

"Are Irish people a race?"

Gordon frowned. "Aren't we?"

"Don't think so."

"Damn. Maybe he just hates me, then. It's probably because I'm better looking than him."

"Oh, I don't know," said Susan.

"What? You seriously think he's better looking than me? He's old!"

"He looks great."

"He's been around forever!"

"Doesn't look a day over fifty."

"Fifty is old," said Gordon sullenly.

"You won't be saying that when you're fifty."

Gordon peered at her, making sure she was telling the truth. "You really think he's good-looking?"

"I really do."

"So why does he hate me?"

"I don't know. Did you sleep with his wife?"

Gordon looked around. "Which one's his wife?"

Susan laughed. "Hey, I think you're a great writer, and I loved the hell out of *Caterpillars*, and every book since just gets better and better, and I'm a ravishing young lady. So who are you going to believe – me or him?"

"Well," Gordon said, "you *do* have better taste."

"See? Now quit your bellyaching and dance with me, you subaquatic fool."

Gordon stopped drinking halfway through the night. He had a longstanding policy – never drink too much in front of rivals and colleagues. Also never drink too much when you don't know where the zip is on your costume. That was an important policy, too, but it was a new one, with limited applicability. Still, what these policies allowed him was the chance to stand back and watch as fellow authors got drunk, and the drunker they got, the funnier it all became. Petty jealousies reared their heads. Comments got snippier. Compliments became barbed. There were many backs behind which many things were said. It was all highly amusing.

He started to notice the crowd being thinned. Very slightly at first, with certain people – all at the low end of the pecking order – being escorted into another room. When it was done, the guests had been split into two groups, with Gordon staying in the main ballroom. Walking with his mask tucked under his arm, he searched for Skulduggery, whom he had glimpsed charming various people throughout the night. Surely Skulduggery would not have allowed himself to be escorted away.

Gordon noticed that the music had stopped and, in fact, the string quartet had left. He was about to ask somebody the time when he saw the waiters and waitresses leaving the ballroom, stepping out as if synchronised, and closing the doors behind them.

The conversation died, and all attention was turned to Sebastian Fawkes, standing where the quartet had been playing. He waited for absolute, solemn silence.

"My fellow writers," Fawkes said, "and here I speak only to the uninitiated... welcome to the darkest of secrets."

Gordon stifled a groan.

"As writers, it is our solemn duty to take our readers by the hand and lead them down a barely lit path, on either side of which lie perils, waiting in the shadows. This we do out of a sense of duty. Someone has to shine a light into the dark, after all."

Gordon examined his mask, wondering if he could put it back on by himself. Then maybe he could look as bored as he felt.

"I was approached, years ago, by a being," Fawkes continued, "an... entity. A man, but... something more than a man. And this being, this magnificent presence, showed me a way to use my talents and be rewarded... not just financially, but also spiritually. Physically. He showed me a way to draw life energy – anguish and pain and emotional suffering – from the hearts and minds of my readers, and to use that energy to keep me successful, young and virile. Behold, Argento."

OK, now Gordon was deciding he should be paying attention. Had Fawkes just talked about how virile he was? How was *that* appropriate ballroom conversation? He became aware of someone moving through the crowd. An excited thrill rippled by, utterly failing to thrill Gordon himself. He stood on his tiptoes, but all he saw were the guests parting before a man in a white toga. He was pale and heavily muscled, and brightness seemed to spill out of him, although that may just have been the spotlight that followed his every step.

Fawkes continued talking as the big man in the toga moved gracefully through the room like a body-building angel. "He showed me the symbols to hide in the words on the page, in the arrangement of the letters, the order of the sentences, of the paragraphs. These mystical symbols not only act upon the readers' subconscious, convincing them to buy multiple copies of my books, but they also draw forth energy, which then flows into me and keeps me young..."

Fawkes smiled beatifically at the people around him. "Fifteen per cent of which goes to Argento, naturally, with twenty per cent for foreign territories."

Gordon had gone cold inside his Creature from the Black Lagoon costume. Fawkes was talking here about magic. Real, actual, supposed-to-be-kept-secret-from-mortals magic.

"I know what you're thinking," Fawkes said. "I thought it, too. I asked the same questions you're asking. We all did. Is this right? Is this fair? But don't we deserve this, after all we sacrifice for them? As writers? We hold a mirror to the face of society, a scalpel to its dark underbelly... Don't we deserve a little extra for the depths to which we must plunge?"

Gordon spotted Susan in the crowd, looking mystified.

"You have been invited here tonight so that you may become one of us. So that you may become family. We will share with you the secrets, the symbols you need to put in your books. You will learn the different types of pain, the particular strain of anguish that is most effective. You will be shown how to get your readers to care about your characters so much that when those characters die the readers are traumatised far past the point of tears. You will be instructed on the best way to bombard your readers with emotions, with feelings."

Susan stepped forward. "So you make your readers suffer, and you draw strength from that?"

"Their pain makes me strong," said Fawkes, smiling. "And your readers' pain can make you strong."

"And you actually believe everything you're saying?"

"You will believe, too, my dear."

"Uh-huh," said Susan. "You said something about draining their life energy. Isn't that, like, bad?"

"No, not necessarily. Is it exploitative? Yes. But fatalities are few."

"Fatalities? Are you saying you've killed your readers?"

"It is regrettable, obviously. We don't want to hurt anyone. We're refining the process even now. Argento is supplying me with new, safer symbols. We want our readers living a long life... so they can keep buying our books!" He chuckled.

Susan looked around. "I don't get what's going on here. Are you all this stupid?"

"There's always one," Fawkes said, his smile growing sad. "Always one who needs convincing."

The crowd parted and a gap opened between Susan and Argento.

"I can feel your doubt," Argento said, his voice soft yet piercing.

"Yeah, no kidding," Susan replied.

"Doubt, uncertainty... these are feelings laced with a bitter aftertaste. Powerful, in their own way, and made all the more so by the fear that always follows."

"Uh-huh," said Susan.

Argento held out his hand. "I will drink from you now."

Susan gasped, her body sagging, and Gordon tried to push through the tightly packed guests.

Argento's hand glowed and he closed his eyes. "Delicious," he said. "Doubt turns to realisation... to the truth... and the truth is a scary thing. Let me taste your fear."

Susan had gone ashen-white, and still Gordon fought to get to her, and then suddenly there was a cry from above and everyone turned, looked up at the balcony from which Skulduggery had just thrown the spotlight operator. He stood there, looking down at them all.

"Terribly sorry," he said, "but I'm going to have to bring an end to tonight's festivities. It's just... I'm disappointed. I wanted tonight to be special. I'm here with my friend, I'm surrounded by writers and I wanted to talk about books and stories and creativity and I wanted to overhear conversations about social responsibilities and the writer as outcast, but... but instead I get this.

"I get an empathy vampire and a group of idiots who are working with him. And he looks ridiculous. I mean we're all here dressed up in costumes, I understand that, but he wants you to think that this is how he dresses normally. It's not. No one dresses like that normally. Why would they? I met a vampire once, an ordinary vampire, who dressed like Lestat. I told him what I'm telling this one – stop reading books about vampires."

Fawkes cleared his throat and looked at Argento, who stepped forward with a dramatic swish of his toga.

"You talk like you know my kind," Argento said. "You, who are nothing to me but an insect, would dare stand upon that balcony and attempt to wound me with insults. I am made of sturdier stuff, my friend. I cannot be hurt by words, nor by blade, nor by bullet. I am eternal. I am the night. I am the day. I am forever. And who are you?"

Skulduggery let his sunglasses fall, then clicked his fingers and set fire to the bandages around his head. They went up in a blaze that died as suddenly as it began, revealing the skull beneath. "I'm Skulduggery Pleasant."

"Oh, hell," said Argento.

"And you're under arrest."

Argento spun on his heels and sprinted away. Skulduggery leaped high into the air, using his magic to boost himself halfway across the ballroom. He landed and gave chase. Argento shrieked.

There was a moment of stunned silence. Then somebody screamed, and the guests surged to the doors, yelling and shouting and tripping over each other. Gordon pushed his way through, catching Susan as she fell. He checked her pulse and her eyes fluttered open.

"That was weird," she said, sounding drunk. "Did that happen?"

"It did," said Gordon, making sure she could stand on her own. "Are you OK? Will you be OK here?"

Susan frowned at him. "Where're you going?"

"I'm going after Fawkes."

Susan grinned. "I'm fine. You go get him, tiger."

He nodded, left his mask with her, and ran as fast as his costume would allow. He got to the door, emerged into a narrow corridor. He followed it to an empty kitchen with three doors leading out from it. He chose one at random, ran the length of it, and found Sebastian Fawkes trying to get out of a window.

"You're going nowhere," Gordon said.

Fawkes turned. "Edgley," he said. "What the hell are you doing here? Go away. There are forces at work you cannot possibly fathom."

"I know all about magic," Gordon said. "I know about the Sanctuaries and the sorcerers. You're not the holder of dark secrets. You're an idiot, and you're not going to get away with what you've done."

Fawkes stopped trying to get away, and regarded Gordon with new eyes. "I don't understand why you're against this. It's power. It's success. It's wealth. And it's a longer life to enjoy all that. Why won't you just go along with it?"

"Because you're hurting your readers," said Gordon.

"Writers hurt their readers all the time! And the readers love it!"

"This is different. This is torture."

"Nonsense! How can it be torture, how can it be cruel, if they don't even know it's happening? We give them stories, they give us longer life. It's a fair trade."

Gordon approached. "So what about the readers who've died reading your books? What do you call them?"

Fawkes shrugged. "The learning curve."

"No. This will not continue."

Colour rose in Fawkes's cheeks. "Who are you to stand up to me? I am Sebastian Fawkes! The *Telegraph* called me the world's greatest living horror novelist. The *New York Times* said my work was artfully sublime. My last novel was heralded as a humane, heartbreaking journey through a nightmare landscape and a triumph in form. What awards have you won? What accolades have you gathered? You're a flavour of the month, easily dismissed, easily forgotten. I am a literary horror novelist. What the hell are you?"

Gordon took a last step towards him. "I'm a storyteller, you pretentious buffoon," he said and he pushed Fawkes.

Fawkes stared at him, his eyes wide. He pushed Gordon back.

Gordon lost his temper, gave Fawkes an extra-hard push to teach him a lesson.

Fawkes let out a roar and charged. Gordon tried to keep him away, but he was too slow. They collided, and stood there, wrestling. Every so often, they'd move their feet slightly. There was a lot of grunting.

Fawkes got a hand against Gordon's face. Gordon squeezed his eyes shut. Fawkes's palm was crushing Gordon's lips painfully. Gordon stuck out his tongue and Fawkes snapped his hand away, yelling in disgust. Gordon tried to press his advantage, but the Creature of the Black Lagoon suit was making it difficult. Fawkes stumbled and flailed, and his elbow whacked against Gordon's chin. Gordon cried out and dropped to his knees, cradling his face. Fawkes stood over him, too out of breath to say anything. Ignoring the pain in his chin, Gordon lunged at Fawkes's leg, wrapping his hands round the left knee.

Gordon held on as Fawkes cursed and staggered back. He weathered the storm of slaps that fell upon his head. One of them clipped his ear – it really hurt – but he didn't let go. Fawkes turned, tried to pull his leg free. Gordon's grip slipped a little, but his fingers tightened again like a vice round Fawkes's ankle. He was dragged a few centimetres across the floor every time Fawkes took a step.

"Let go of me!" Fawkes screeched.

"No," Gordon gasped.

Fawkes overbalanced and fell and, like a ninja, except slower and with less co-ordination, Gordon crawled on top of him. He was sweating badly now. The suit was way too hot to fight in. Fawkes struggled, tried to turn over on to his back to push him off, but Gordon let his body go limp, and he lay on top of him.

Fawkes's breath came in ragged wheezes. "You may..." *wheeze, wheeze,* "think you've..." *wheeze,* "won, but..." *wheeze,* "you'll never," *really long wheeze,* "escape."

Gordon focused all his attention on staying as heavy as possible, and gasped. "Your time is..." *gasp,* "over, you..." *gasp,* "you utter..." *gasp,* "utter nutball."

"Ar..." *wheeze*, "...gento will..." *wheeze*, "tear your soul into..." *wheeze*, "tiny little bits."

"Your friend is..." gasped Gordon, "already in handcuffs..." *gasp*, "and your reign of..." *gasp*, "terror is at an..." *gasp*, "end."

Fawkes shook his head fiercely. Gordon nodded insistently. They lay there like that for some time.

When Skulduggery Pleasant and Susan DeWick found them eight minutes later, Gordon was sitting astride Fawkes like an oddly dressed cowboy riding an exhausted and flattened-out horse.

The Cleavers arrived to take Argento into custody, and a pair of Sensitives talked to the main body of guests, convincing them they'd had a nice, if slightly boring, night, and that nothing unusual had happened.

The writers who knew the intricate details of Fawkes's deal could not be dealt with in the same manner, so they were instead threatened with terrible and gruesome deaths if they spoke a word of this to anyone. According to Skulduggery, threats worked just as well as psychics.

Sebastian Fawkes was released, since an unexplained disappearance would not have gone unnoticed in the mainstream media. His next book, however, failed to reach a receptive audience. The follow-up barely punctured the Top Twenty Bestseller list. After he appeared, uninvited and drunk, on *Wogan*, a light-entertainment talk show broadcast by the BBC, his publishers quietly dropped him, and nobody much cared.

Gordon asked that Susan DeWick's memory of the night be left intact. Skulduggery granted this request. Gordon and Susan were entangled romantically for three months afterwards before she fell for a struggling young actor and he fell for a supermodel. They remained close friends until Gordon's sudden and unexpected death years later. Her book *Stirrings at Norfolk*, the first true horror novel to win the Booker Prize, was dedicated to him. It said, simply, *To Fishface.*

Gordon was to go on to document, in his way, the darker realities of life of which the normal person is not aware. He wrote stories to shock, entertain, thrill and traumatise, and he regretted not one moment of it. His participation in real-life adventures was not quite so prolific (that role would, of course, eventually go to his niece), but he did accompany Skulduggery Pleasant on at least one more case, solving the mystery of the Phantom Killer at Darkenholme House. But that... is another story.

It's also not very interesting. The butler did it.

THE LOST ART
OF WORLD
DOMINATION

With the shadows wrapped around him and the sliver of light falling dramatically over his eyes, the evil sorcerer Scaramouch Van Dreg stood in the dungeon and watched his captive with predatory amusement.

The dungeon was dark and damp and dank, and the chains that bound the Skeleton Detective were big and thick and heavy. They shackled the bones of his wrists to the stone floor, forcing him to kneel.

Scaramouch liked that. The great detective, the living skeleton who had foiled plan after plan, scheme after scheme, was now forced to look *up* at Scaramouch. Like he had always been meant to. Like *everyone* had always been meant to.

The detective, his dark blue suit burnt and torn and muddy, hadn't said anything for almost an hour. In fact, he hadn't *moved* for almost an hour. Scaramouch had been standing in the shadows, gloating, for a little over fifteen minutes, but he wasn't entirely sure that his captive had noticed.

He shifted his weight noisily, but the detective still did not acknowledge his presence.

Scaramouch frowned. There was very little point in going through all this if his efforts weren't rewarded with due and proper attention.

He brought himself up to his full height, which wasn't very high, and sucked in his belly, which was substantial. He gathered his cloak and stepped forward, gazing down at the top of the detective's skull with the pitiless gaze he had practised for hours.

"Skulduggery Pleasant," he sneered. "Finally, you are within my grasp."

The detective shifted slightly, and muttered something.

Good God. Was he *asleep*?

Scaramouch cleared his throat and gave the detective a little kick. The detective jerked awake and looked around for a moment, then looked up with those empty eye sockets.

"Oh," he said, like he had just met a casual acquaintance on the street, "hello."

Unsure how to counter this unexpected approach to being a captive, Scaramouch decided to replay the sneer.

"Skulduggery Pleasant," he repeated. "Finally, you are within my grasp."

"It does appear so," Pleasant agreed, nodding. "And in a dungeon, no less. How brilliantly postmodern of you."

"You have interfered in my plans for the last time," Scaramouch continued. "Unfortunately for you, you will not live to regret your mistake."

Pleasant tilted his head curiously. "Scaramouch? Scaramouch Van Dreg? Is that you?"

Scaramouch smiled nastily. "Oh, yes. You have fallen into the clutches of your deadliest enemy."

"What are *you* doing here?"

Scaramouch's smile faltered. "What?"

"How are you mixed up in all this?"

"How am I...? What do you mean? This is *my* plot."

"*You're* plotting to use the Crystal of the Saints to bring the Faceless Ones back into our reality?"

Scaramouch frowned. "What? No. What do the Faceless Ones have to do with this? I don't want the Faceless Ones back, I don't even worship them. No, this plot is for *me*, to gain absolute power."

"Then... you're not in league with Rancid Fines or Christophe Nocturnal?"

"I've never even *met* Rancid Fines," Scaramouch said, "and I *hate* Christophe Nocturnal."

Pleasant absorbed this information with a nod. "In that case, I'm afraid there's been a bit of a misunderstanding."

Scaramouch felt like he'd been punched in the gut. All the breath left him, and his shoulders slumped. "You mean, you're not here for me?"

"Dreadfully sorry," Pleasant said.

"But... but you arrived at the hotel. You and your partner, the girl. You were asking all those questions."

"We were looking for Fines and Nocturnal. We didn't even know you were in the country. To be honest, and I don't mean to offend you or anything, but I thought you had passed away some time ago."

Scaramouch gaped. "I just took a little break..."

Pleasant shrugged. "Well, at least now I know. So what are you up to these days?"

"I'm... I have plans," Scaramouch said, dejected.

"The absolute-power thing you mentioned?"

Scaramouch nodded.

"And how's that going?"

"It's going OK, I suppose. I mean, you know, everything's on schedule and proceeding apace..."

"Well, that's good. We all need something to get us up in the mornings, am I right? We all need goals."

"Yeah." An unwelcome thought seeped into Scaramouch's mind and lingered there. He tried ignoring it but it flickered and swam, and finally he had to ask, "You don't view me as your deadliest enemy, do you?"

Pleasant hesitated. His skull remained as impassive as ever, but this hesitation spoke volumes. "I view you as *a* deadly enemy," he said helpfully.

"How deadly?"

"I don't know... relatively?"

"Relatively deadly? That's all? I thought we were arch-enemies."

"Oh," Pleasant said. "No, I wouldn't call us *arch*-enemies. Nefarian Serpine was an arch-enemy. Mevolent, obviously. A few others."

"But not us?"

"Not really..."

"Why? Is it because I'm not powerful enough?"

"No, not exactly."

"Then why? What's so different between me and, say, Serpine?"

"Well," said Pleasant, "Serpine had options. He was adaptable. Remember, the deadliest enemies are not necessarily the strongest – they're the smartest."

"So it's because I'm not *smart* enough? But I *am* smart! I am highly intelligent!"

"OK," Pleasant said in an understanding voice.

"Don't patronise me!" Scaramouch snapped. "I have *you* as a prisoner, don't I? You fell into my trap without even a hint of a suspicion!"

"It *was* a clever trap."

"And those chains that bind your powers – you think that's easy to do? You think *that* doesn't require intelligence?"

"No, no," Pleasant said, "I have to admit, you got me fair and square."

"You're damn right I did," Scaramouch sneered. "And you don't even know about my plot yet, do you? You don't even know how intelligent *that* is."

"Well, like I said, I've been busy—"

"Busy with Fines, and with Nocturnal, busy with the threat of the Faceless Ones – but you haven't been busy with the *real* threat, have you?"

"I suppose not," Pleasant said, and then added, "You mean you, don't you?"

"Of course I mean me! I've been smart enough to fool you all into thinking I was dead. I've been smart enough to work under your radar, to set in motion events that will grant me absolute power, which will lead to my total dominion over this world! Now *that*, detective, *that* is smart!"

"Total dominion?"

"Oh, yes, skeleton. How does it feel to know that an opponent such as I, an adversary you would have classified as merely 'relatively deadly', will soon rule this planet with a will of iron, and a fist of..." He faltered. "...iron."

"Um..."

"What?"

"I was just going to say, have you really thought this through?"

"What do you mean?"

"You're talking about ruling the world, right?"

"Yes."

"Not bringing back old gods, not turning the world into some new version of hell, not remaking it as you see fit..."

"Well, no."

"You're just talking about ruling it, then?"

"Yes. With a will of iron and a fist of iron."

"Yes. And again, I'm compelled to ask – have you really thought this through?"

Scaramouch pinched the bridge of his nose with his thumb and forefinger. He was getting a headache. He could feel it coming on. "What do you mean? What is so wrong with planning to rule the world?"

"Well, for a start, think of all the work."

"I'll have minions," Scaramouch said dismissively.

"But they'll still need orders. They'll need you to tell them what to do. You'll be inundated with reports, with documents, with briefings. There won't be enough hours in the day to go over them all, let alone make any decisions."

"Then I'll just order that the days be longer," Scaramouch said. "I will decree that a day stops and starts when *I* decide, not the sun or the moon."

"And how will you cope with warring nations?"

Scaramouch laughed. "When I am ruler, there will be no wars. Everyone will do what I tell them."

"There are billions of people in the world, all with their own viewpoints, all with their own rights. It won't be as simple as telling them to just *stop*. What about famine?"

"What about it?"

"What will you do about it?"

"I'm not sure I understand."

"If famine strikes a country, what will you do?"

Scaramouch smiled evilly. "Maybe I will do nothing. Maybe I will let the country die."

"In which case, you will have an entire country rise against you, because they have nothing left to lose."

"Then I will destroy them."

"And you'll have to deal with the neighbouring countries squabbling over the remains."

"Then I'll destroy them – no, I'll order them to... they'll do what I tell them, all right?"

"And the media?"

Scaramouch sighed. "What about them?"

"How will you cope with the media questioning your policies?"

"There will be no questions. This won't be a democracy, it will be a dictatorship."

"There will always be dissent."

"What did I say? I'll have minions, I told you. *They'll* take care of any rebels."

"You'll have a secret police?"

"Of course!"

"You'll assign minions to levels of power?"

"Naturally!"

"And when these minions get ambitions of their own, and they go to overthrow you?"

"Then I'll kill them!" Scaramouch said, exasperated. "I'll have absolute power, remember?"

"And how do you plan to attain this absolute power?"

"It's all in my plan!" Scaramouch yelled, pacing to the wall of the dungeon.

"What about sorcerers?"

Scaramouch tore the cloak from around his neck. It was heavy, and too warm, and when he paced it was annoying. "What about the bloody sorcerers?"

Pleasant's chains jangled slightly as he shrugged. "You don't really think they'll just stand back and let this happen, do you? I realise I'll be dead, so that's one less you'll have to worry about, but there are plenty more."

"There won't be," Scaramouch said, stepping back into the shadows for dramatic effect. "When my plan is complete, I will be the only one capable of wielding magic."

"So you're going to kill them all?"

"I won't have to. They will be left as ordinary mortals, while I will be filled with their powers."

"Ah," Pleasant said. "OK."

"Now do you appreciate my vast and superior intelligence?"

Pleasant thought for a moment. "Yes," he decided.

"Excellent. I'm sorry we can't talk further, detective, but my Hour of Glory is at hand, and your death will be—"

"One more question."

Scaramouch's chin dropped to his chest. "What?" he asked bleakly.

"On the surface, this plot is fine. Drain the magic from others, and then use this magic to become all-powerful and unstoppable and take over the world. I can't see anything wrong with that plot – in theory. But my question, Scaramouch, is how exactly are you going to achieve all this?"

Scaramouch picked his cloak off the ground, felt through it until he came to the cleverly concealed pocket. From this pocket he withdrew a small wooden box with a metal clasp.

He held the box for Pleasant to see. "Recognise this?"

Pleasant peered closer, examining the etchings in the wood. "Ohhh," he said, impressed.

"Exactly. This container, enchanted with twenty-three spells from twenty-three mages, is one of the fabled Lost Artifacts. I have spent the last fifteen months tracking it down – and tonight, it is finally mine."

"So it's true, then?"

"Of course it's true. Why wouldn't it be?"

Pleasant's head jerked up sharply. "You mean you haven't checked it?"

Scaramouch suddenly felt a little foolish. "I... I don't have to," he said. "Everyone knows—"

"Oh, Scaramouch," Pleasant said, disappointment in his voice.

"I just got it!" Scaramouch said defensively. "Literally, I just got it three hours ago!"

"And you haven't checked it?"

"I didn't have *time*. I had to capture *you*."

Pleasant looked back at the box, and his head tilted thoughtfully. "If that *is* the box from the Lost Artifacts, and it certainly does *look* like it might be authentic, then it contains an insect with the power to drain magic at a bite."

"Exactly."

"Providing that insect is still inside."

Scaramouch looked at the box. "There are no holes in it."

"It's been lost for three hundred years."

"But the insect's meant to live forever, right? It doesn't need food or anything?"

"Well, that's the legend. Can you hear it? You should be able to hear it buzzing around in there."

Scaramouch shook the box, and held it up to his ear. "Nothing," he said.

"Well, it's a thick box," Pleasant said. "You probably wouldn't be able to hear it anyway."

Scaramouch shook it again, then listened for any buzzing. Even a single buzz. Anything.

"Did you pay much for it?" Pleasant asked.

"The guy who found it, he needed to mount expeditions and things. It wasn't cheap."

"How much did he charge?"

"I, uh, I gave him everything I had."

The detective went quiet.

"But I'm going to be ruler of the world!" Scaramouch explained. "What difference does it make to me?"

"He made an awful lot of money by just handing over a box, without even verifying that it contained what you hope it contains."

"How will I know?"

"There's only one way. You have to open it."

"But the insect will fly away!"

"Let it out near me," the skeleton suggested. "You're going to kill me anyway, right? So what do I care if it drains my powers before I die?"

Scaramouch narrowed his eyes. "Why would you make this offer?"

"Because I'm *curious*. Scaramouch, I'm a detective. I solve mysteries. If my final act in this world is to establish whether or not a mythological insect could still be contained in one of the Lost Artifacts, then that, to me, would be a good death."

Scaramouch looked at him, and nodded. "OK."

"Put it on the ground, open it, and stand back. When it's finished draining me, it'll be sluggish. That's when you recapture it."

Scaramouch nodded. He licked his lips nervously, and placed the box on the floor. He undid the metal clasp, felt his heart pound in his chest, and he opened the lid.

He scampered back into the shadows.

The detective gazed down into the box.

"Well?" Scaramouch asked from the corner.

"Can't see anything," Pleasant said. "It's a little dark... wait."

"Yes? What?"

And then, the most beautiful sound Scaramouch had ever heard – a buzzing.

"Amazing," Pleasant said in a whisper.

Something rose from the box, rising into the air after centuries of being trapped. It was unsteady, and weak, but it flew. It *lived*.

"One little insect," Pleasant was saying. "The legends say it rose from the carcass of a slain demon. An insect borne of evil, and wickedness, the demon's last attempt to destroy its enemies." The insect flew up, dancing in a shaft of light. "One little insect, and it could be responsible for bringing this world to its knees."

"Wonderful," Scaramouch breathed.

The insect landed on the ground in front of its box, its prison for all those years. Pleasant looked down at it, then moved slightly and knelt on the insect and squished it.

Scaramouch screamed and the door burst open and Valkyrie Cain stepped into the dungeon.

"What the hell is going on here?" she asked.

Scaramouch charged at her and the girl closed her eyes and flexed her fingers. Her eyes and hand snapped open and the air around her rippled. Scaramouch was hurled back off his feet. He crashed into the far wall, hitting his head and collapsing with a groan. He heard the girl and the detective talking, and he heard the chains being unlocked. Moaning, he turned over and looked up at them.

"It was a trick," he said. "You really *were* here to stop me, weren't you? You really *were* here to foil my plan. This is the last time, you hear me? I will escape whatever prison you send me to, and the next time we meet you will pay for—"

"Who's this?" Valkyrie Cain asked.

Scaramouch paled. "What? What do you mean, who am I?"

"His name's Scaramouch Van Dreg," Pleasant told her.

"She knows who I am!" Scaramouch shrieked. "I am your deadliest enemy!"

Cain raised an eyebrow but ignored him. "Has he got anything to do with Fines and Nocturnal?"

"Nope."

"Then why are we wasting our time? Come on, we've got real bad guys to stop."

Cain walked out. Skulduggery Pleasant looked down at Scaramouch and shrugged.

"I'll just chain you up for the moment, but the Cleavers will be around soon to take you into custody. Is that all right with you?"

Scaramouch started crying.

"Good man. Don't let this get you down, though. We all need goals, and I fully expect to do battle with you again, OK?"

Scaramouch wailed.

"We need more villains like you, you know that? We need more bad guys who want to take over the world. There aren't enough of them. The others think it's just, you know... *silly*."

Scaramouch felt the shackles on his wrists. He had to look up to watch Skulduggery Pleasant leave the dungeon.

GOLD, BABIES AND THE BROTHERS MULDOON

The cemetery was cold and dark, and the dead man was standing on his grave, watching her as she approached.

"Hello," she said.

The clothes he had been buried in were torn and musty, his shoes caked with mud. He stood with a slight stoop and he had, for the most part, skin and hair. The middle of his face had rotted, however, robbing him of lips and nose and eyelids.

"You're late," he grumbled. "Midnight has come and gone."

"Sorry about that."

"Lives hang in the balance. You're lucky I stayed."

"Yes, I am."

"You are Valkyrie Cain."

"That's right."

"Thirteen years old, Elemental by power, partner of the Skeleton Detective, and late."

"I suppose."

"You're lucky I stayed."

"So you said."

"I could have left, you know. One minute past midnight, when you weren't here, I could have walked away. I didn't have to wait here for you. I was under no obligation. But I stayed, because I have no wish to see innocent lives taken."

"You're a corpse," Valkyrie said. "Where were you going to go?"

He glared at her, but didn't answer.

He started walking, shuffling off his grave, up towards the ruined church. She followed.

"I thought the skeleton would be with you," the dead man said as they walked.

"We're quite busy at the moment, so Skulduggery had to stay behind. I said I'd take care of this one on my own."

He looked back, and she was thankful the moon was only a sliver, for his face was mostly hidden. "Maybe you underestimate what awaits."

"No, I think I've got it. Three babies snatched from their cots, being held by a family of goblins who want to exchange them for gold. Fairly straightforward."

"If you fully realised the danger you are walking into, you would not be so calm."

"Ah, I'm sure I would. They're goblins, you know? How bad can they be?"

"They were not always goblins," the dead man said, irritation in his voice. "The Muldoons were sorcerers, descended from a long line of the most powerful mages the world had ever seen. They were rumoured to be descended from the Ancients themselves."

"That was disproved," Valkyrie said.

"What?"

"I asked Skulduggery about that. He said the Muldoons reinvented their own family tree in a sad attempt to appear threatening, and then they actually started to believe their own lies."

"If you know so much," the dead man scowled, "then why are you asking *me*?"

"Oh, right, sorry. Please go on."

The corpse muttered something under his breath, then resumed. "The father died, and the mother went insane, but the children maintained the belief that, because of their heritage, they should be the rulers of the world. They believed in the inherent superiority of those who wield magic, and they despised the mortals, whom they saw as pedestrian and drab."

"Why *are* they called mortals?" asked Valkyrie.

"What?"

"I've been wondering that. Non-magical people, I mean, why are they called mortals? Sorcerers are mortal, too."

"Sorcerers don't claim any different."

"But by calling non-magical people mortal, it's like they're implying that they themselves are *im*mortal. And they're not – magic just makes them live longer."

The dead man stopped suddenly and turned. His brows were furrowed across his unblinking eyes. "Do you want to hear the story of the Muldoons or not?" he asked.

"Sure. Sorry."

He grunted, then turned and carried on towards the church. The breeze caught the mustiness of his clothes and brought it down to her. "The Council of Elders identified the Muldoons as the sorcerers behind a spate of attacks on mortals. In an effort to keep the mortals safe, and to keep the magical communities hidden, the Muldoons were ambushed, and although they escaped, they were not unharmed."

"This is my favourite bit," Valkyrie said. "This is when they get turned into goblins, right?"

"Correct. Over the years they have amassed a collection of gold, for gold is the only thing that could return them to human form, but it has not been enough."

"So they started stealing babies."

"Yes."

They arrived at the ruined church. The dead man looked at her "My role is almost fulfilled. I agreed to make the introductions and witness that both parties keep their side of the bargain. There are innocent lives at stake."

"So you keep saying."

"Earlier, I was with the goblins, and I saw that the three babies were safe and well. Thus far, they have kept their word. And you, Valkyrie Cain, are you here with gold?"

"Yes, I am."

"May I see it?" the dead man asked.

"No, you may not."

"And why not?"

"Because it's not for you to see."

The dead man looked at her, and he gave the slightest of nods. "Very well."

He turned to the open door of the church, and spoke loudly. "It is I, and I stand with the girl, the Elemental and the partner of the Skeleton Detective, and although she is late she is here, which is the important thing, and we are moving on. I ask that the exchange take place, the three innocent lives for the gold she claims to possess, though as of yet I have not seen it. If it makes a difference, she has an honest face, although her eyes are as dark as her hair. Will you bid her enter?"

Torches flared in wall brackets inside the ruin, beating the darkness back. The dead man stepped away.

"You may enter," he said.

"You're not coming?"

"No."

"You wouldn't be letting me walk into a trap, would you?" asked Valkyrie.

"Why would I do that? I'm dead. What do I have to gain? I can't leave this graveyard. There is nothing that brings me joy any more, there is no pleasure to be had, there is nothing I can use so there is nothing that I want. I am empty. My existence is a shallow thing of coldness and—"

"OK," Valkyrie interrupted, "I get it. You're miserable, fine. I'll go in now."

The dead man shrugged. Valkyrie left him there and stepped into the church.

Part of the roof had caved in, and her boots brushed rubble as she walked. Her boots, like the trousers she wore, and the tunic and the coat, were made of impenetrable materials that had saved her life on numerous occasions. Everything she wore was black, and it was a black that melted into the shadows and hid her from unsuspecting eyes. It wasn't hiding her *tonight*, however. Every move she made was being watched. She could feel eyes on her.

There were a few broken pews in the church, but no altar, and no decoration. The flickering torches reflected off wet patches on the stone walls where the rain had fallen.

Valkyrie stopped walking.

"Hello?" she called. "Goblins?"

"Gold," came the voice from behind her.

She turned slowly, making no sudden moves.

The goblin was maybe up to her shoulder, short and squat and distressingly ugly. He had large bulbous eyes and a long bulbous nose, and his nostril hair mingled with a moustache in a way that was far from appealing. His green skin looked unhealthy in the torchlight, afflicted as it was with sores and boils. He wore a filthy grey suit that had lost all the buttons from the jacket. His belly protruded. Hair sprouted from his belly button.

"Give us the gold," he said.

"Give me the babies," she told him. "Then you get your gold."

He shook his head. "Give us the gold, then you get the babies."

"How do I know the babies are here? I can't hear them crying."

"Maybe they're happy."

"Then show me them smiling."

The goblin scratched his belly thoughtfully. "Compromise," he said.

"OK."

"We'll give you half now, you give us the gold, and then we give you the other half."

"There are three babies. How do you give me half?"

He shrugged. "Chop a baby in two."

"You know, even for a goblin, that's disturbed. Bring the kids out, right now, or I walk away with the gold."

The goblin growled in displeasure. "Colm," he said, "Fintan, bring them out."

From behind him, two more goblins emerged. Valkyrie was amazed to realise that the first goblin was the handsome one of the family. His brothers wore rags, torn and dirty, and they carried the babies between them. The babies had dummies jammed in their mouths.

"See?" the first goblin said. "Alive, uneaten, and not chopped or anything. Now, the gold."

Valkyrie reached into her coat and brought out a bag that jangled in her grip.

The goblins stared at the bag, practically drooling.

"Put the kids down," she said. "Just place them on the ground over here, very gently, and step away. Then I'll give you the gold and we'll say goodbye."

One of the goblins, she didn't know which one he was, so she decided that he should be Colm, grunted. "How do we know there's gold in that bag?"

"Because I tell you there is."

"We don't know you. Liam, we can't trust this girl."

The first goblin, Liam, scratched his belly. "We were expecting the skeleton. Where is he?"

"He couldn't make it."

"He sent you instead?"

"Yes, he did," said Valkyrie.

"You're his assistant, then?"

"Partner."

"You're a child."

"You're a goblin."

"Only on the outside."

"And on the inside you steal babies. Looks *and* personality."

"I don't like you."

"You just have to get to know me," she said. "Are we going to stand around talking all night, or are we going to do this ransom thing?"

"The skeleton should be here," the third goblin, Fintan, mumbled.

"Shut up," Liam barked. "We'll settle that later. Right now, give her the brats. I want to see that gold."

Colm and Fintan walked forward, bringing with them an interesting aroma of dried sweat and boiled cabbage. They put the babies on the ground, close to Valkyrie, and the babies gurgled and made baby noises.

The goblins stepped back, rejoined their brother.

"Now," Liam said with a snaggle-toothed smile, "give us our payment."

"And then you'll let us go?"

"Of course."

"Why don't I believe you?"

Liam shrugged. "A deal's a deal – we held up our part, now you have to do the same."

If things turned nasty, Valkyrie would only be able to scoop up one of the kids before the goblins were on her. The goblins didn't look very fast, so she'd probably be able to beat them to the door, but it would mean leaving two babies here. She didn't see any alternative, however, and the goblins' patience was running out.

She tossed the bag, and Liam caught it and yanked open the drawstring. He let the gold coins spill out into his hand.

Fintan licked his lips. "They real? Liam, they real?"

Liam put one of the coins in his mouth and sucked on it a moment, then reached his grimy fingers between his lips to retrieve it. "It's gold," he said happily. His wide eyes glinted.

"Pleasure doing business," Valkyrie said, hunkering down to the kids.

"You're not leaving," said Liam.

Valkyrie sighed. "Is this a double-cross?"

"That's what this is. It'd be better if the skeleton was here instead of you, but when we send him your head, wrapped up in a pretty bow, he'll come looking for us and we'll get him then."

"You have issues with Skulduggery?"

"We hate him," Fintan snarled. "He's the one responsible for turning us into creatures of slime and bad breath."

"I see," said Valkyrie. "Before you kill me, can I ask you a question?"

Liam laughed. "Go ahead."

"Thank you. My question is, what makes you think I came alone?"

Liam's smile faded. "What?"

"You know Skulduggery, right? You've gone up against him before. You know how smart he is."

"Not *that* smart," Colm grumbled.

"And he knows you," Valkyrie continued. "He knows how treacherous you are, and he's told me how you never keep your side of a bargain, and how you always double-cross…"

Liam frowned. "So?"

"So smile, goblin. Skulduggery Pleasant has been here all along, and tonight's the night when he gets to kick your green and wrinkly little—"

There was a crash on the roof above them and the rotten wood splintered and gave, and Skulduggery fell through and hit the ground with his face.

"Oh my God," he muttered as he lay there. "Oh my God, that hurt."

Valkyrie hesitated. No one made a move, and no one made a sound. Even the babies had stopped gurgling. The goblins grinned. Valkyrie chewed her lip.

"This is… slightly unexpected," she said.

Skulduggery Pleasant, the Skeleton Detective, his blue suit ripped and streaked with dirt, rolled on to his back and groaned. If his skull had features, they would surely be twisted in pain. "Don't move," he managed to say. "You're all under arrest."

The goblins laughed.

"You think you're the only one with backup?" Liam grinned at Valkyrie. "You think you're the only one with a surprise?"

Valkyrie glared at him. "So who've you got out there? More of your little buddies? Some assassins? Couple of monsters, maybe? Because I have to tell you, we've faced them all, and we keep winning."

"No assassins," Liam said. "No monsters. Just Peg."

"Who's Peg?"

Liam sneered. "Oh, of course, you haven't met our sister, have you? Peg'll be the one who threw your friend there through the roof. *Peg!*"

A massive shape filled the doorway, and Peg the Ugly Goblin stepped in. She was twice Valkyrie's height, and had legs as wide as tree trunks, and arms as wide as her legs. Her body was a solid slab of meat, clothed in what appeared

ARMAGEDDON OUTTA HERE

to be a half-dozen grimy wedding dresses sewn together, and her hair hung long and lank over her face.

Skulduggery got unsteadily to his feet. "Don't worry," he told Valkyrie. "I have her on the ropes now."

"She threw you over a church," Valkyrie pointed out.

For a moment he was silent. And then he said, "Not *all* the way over."

"Skuluggy," Peg moaned. "Oo uv me."

Valkyrie frowned. "Did she just say what I think she said?"

Skulduggery shook his head quickly. "No."

Peg took another few steps inside. Her brothers cackled and let her pass.

"Skuluggy," Peg moaned again. "I uv oo."

Skulduggery glanced at Valkyrie. "OK. She *may* have a thing for me."

"She *loves* you?"

"Well, yes, but I assure you, it's very unrequited."

Liam grinned. "Weren't expecting *this*, were you, Mr Detective? Probably thought, once a mountain fell on her, you'd seen the last of our sister, eh?"

"To be honest," Skulduggery said, "yes."

"She's tougher than she looks," Fintan said.

"Now *that's* an achievement," Skulduggery murmured.

Peg stood there, a wall in a wedding dress, and held her arms out. A swollen tongue dragged itself over her cracked lips, and she struggled to form her next word.

"Kiss," she said.

Valkyrie arched an eyebrow. Skulduggery nodded, more to himself than anybody else.

"I'm going to have to let her down gently," he said, and ran forward and leaped, slamming both feet into Peg's belly. She roared in anger and swiped at him and he dodged, kicking at the back of her knee. She barely noticed.

78

The three brothers were coming for Valkyrie. She clicked the fingers of her right hand and made a spark, then caught the spark and cultivated it into a flame that burned in her hand.

Fintan was closest. She reached out with her left hand, feeling the air against her skin. He ran at her and she felt the space between them, felt how it connected, and when she found the right spot she splayed her hand and snapped her palm and the air rippled and hit Fintan like a truck. He flew back and smacked into the church wall.

The fire in her other hand was burning fiercely and she threw it. The fireball hit Colm's ragged coat and he shrieked and stumbled back, tearing it off. He raised his head to see her running straight at him, but couldn't do anything to stop the elbow that smashed into his jaw. He spun around, then tipped over backwards and didn't get up.

Liam rushed her and she tried to move but she wasn't fast enough. She was taken off her feet and slammed into the ground, Liam's hands at her throat, trying to throttle her.

Behind him, she saw Peg strike Skulduggery. He hurtled into the shadows.

Valkyrie tried breaking Liam's grip, but his fingers were short and thick and she couldn't pry them loose. She grabbed his wrist and twisted, but he was too strong. His fingers dug into her throat and black spots flashed in her vision, her head swimming. She brought her hands in, felt the air between herself and the goblin, but Liam scuttled up, knelt on her left hand and pinned it to the ground. He took one hand from her throat and held her right wrist away from him.

"Try your little tricks *now*," he snarled, his foul breath hot on her cheek.

Blood pulsed through her temples. Her lungs burned, and although her struggles were getting more frantic, she could feel herself growing weaker.

Spittle dripped from Liam's lips on to her face. Her muscles ached and her body was tired, and darkness seeped into her vision. She couldn't hear anything over the beating of her own heart.

Liam was kneeling on her left hand. His right knee was pressed into her belly, leaving her legs to kick uselessly behind him.

She brought her legs in, bent them, the soles of her boots flat to the ground. With the last ounce of her strength, Valkyrie lifted her backside off the church floor. Liam lurched forward a little and laughed.

"Think that'll do it? I've tamed wild horses, little girl, and they buck a lot harder than you."

Valkyrie took her right foot off the ground. She could feel the air on her face, on her hands, on her exposed skin. Now she struggled to feel the air through her boot. It was possible. She knew it was.

And as her consciousness ebbed, she thought she felt it, a slight resistance, and that's all she needed. She stepped on the air and it shimmered, and Valkyrie's body flipped over backwards, and the goblin screeched as he was catapulted away.

Valkyrie landed on her belly and gasped, sucked in breath hungrily. Tears had sprung to her eyes and she wiped them away, in time to see Skulduggery reach out a hand. A large piece of rubble lifted off the ground. Skulduggery made circular motions and the piece of rubble started to move. Faster and faster it went, in an ever-increasing circle.

The piece of rubble slammed into Peg's jaw and before she could even growl, it had made its way around and slammed into her jaw again. It struck her repeatedly until Skulduggery's hand stiffened, and the piece of rubble hurtled into Peg's face and shattered.

Peg fell back to a sitting position. She held a huge hand to the side of her face and moaned.

Valkyrie stood, and saw Liam. He was on his feet and sneaking towards the babies.

She ran at him and he snarled. She ducked under a punch and he twisted to get at her again. His fist swung and she blocked but her block wasn't strong enough, and his knuckles hit the side of her face and she staggered. He grinned and she smacked him, and goblin blood, the colour of mucus, sprayed from his lip.

In the middle of the church, Peg had Skulduggery wrapped up in a bear hug. He was trying to hit her with a section of a broken pew.

Liam ran at Valkyrie, yelling out a war cry. She clicked her fingers and he stopped and cowered, expecting the fireball. But instead she moved in, stiffened the fingers of her other hand and jabbed into his neck. His head swung around, offering up the perfect target. Her elbow connected with the hinge of his jaw, and Liam the goblin crumpled to the ground.

"You don't really love me," she heard Skulduggery say.

Peg was sitting against a wall, Skulduggery standing over her, the remains of the broken pew in his hands.

"I'm flattered," he continued, "really I am. I'm sure you're a lovely girl."

Peg moaned.

"But the truth is, we don't know each other. Not really. I don't know what your favourite song is, or what flower you like most, or what you like to do on long summer evenings. And what do you really know about me?"

"I uv oo, Skuluggy."

"No, you don't, Peg. This isn't real love. This isn't true love. You deserve someone who can give you true love."

"Oo?"

"No, not me."

"Moh."

"I'm sorry. I didn't want to hurt your feelings."

Peg sniffled.

"He's out there, you know. Your Mister Right. And I'm sure he's looking for you."

She looked up. "Eally?"

"Really. You just have to find him."

Peg nodded, then nodded again, with renewed determination. Skulduggery stepped back as she stood up and brushed some of the dust off her wedding dress.

"Stay away from your brothers, OK? They're not a very good influence on you."

She nodded, and marched for the church door. Before she stepped out, she stopped, and looked back tearfully. "I awah ink awoo, Skuluggy."

"And I'll always think of you, too," Skulduggery replied.

And then Peg was gone.

Valkyrie stood beside Skulduggery. "Anything you want to tell me?"

"No," he said. "Not really. Are all the babies safe?"

"Safe and unharmed. Their folks will be glad to have them back. Are you sure there's nothing you want to tell me? To share?"

"Relatively positive, yes."

"She seems nice. Peg, I mean."

He looked at her. "It's going to take you a while to stop teasing me about this, isn't it?"

She grinned. "Oh, yes."

He sighed. "Then you may as well get started."

THE SLIGHTLY IGNOMINIOUS END TO THE LEGEND OF BLACK ANNIS

Black Annis didn't like living in a ditch, but times were changing, and the England she had known as a child was long gone. She narrowed her eyes – left eye blue, right eye green – and tried to remember what she had been like as a child. It had been so long ago she had quite forgotten.

Had she laughed and played, like other girls? Had she giggled and joked, and run through the meadows and the fields of Leicester, letting the sunshine warm her skin? Highly unlikely. The more she thought about it, the more she remembered. She couldn't recall any friends, nor could she recall any giggling or joking. She seemed to remember a lot of screaming, though. Oh, yes, a whole lot of screaming.

Annis walked to the cave mouth, her feet crunching on bones and human remains. It was almost morning. She hated mornings. She hated the morning, the noon, the early afternoon, the late afternoon, and bright evenings. She hated a lot of things.

What had she been thinking about? Oh, yes, her childhood. Now *that* was a time of her life that had outstayed its welcome. Her parents had been terrified of her. Her father had thought she was the spawn of the devil, but she'd always taken that as a compliment. Whenever she got angry her fingernails would grow long and pointed, and her teeth became jagged and her skin turned blue. She'd never really understood why her skin turned blue, or what purpose it served, but her parents used it as an early-warning system. Annis's temper was not a pretty sight.

All in all, it had probably surprised no one when she started eating people. Her parents' friends had probably nodded when they'd heard, maybe shrugged, saying something like, "Aye, doesn't surprise me one bit, her eatin' people. Always had that look about her, didn't she?" Black Annis didn't mind. By the time she was twenty she'd eaten everyone in her village, parents and all.

That had been... how long ago? Two hundred years, maybe. Now she had streaks of grey in her black matted hair, and her face was lined and she wore her age like an ugly shawl. This was her life – living in a cave that opened into a ditch, kept awake during the day by the tractors that ploughed the field above.

A rat scampered in from the ditch outside and she snatched it up. It was thin and mangy and squirmed in her grip, but she hadn't eaten in a week, so she bit down and the rat squealed and its warm blood ran down her throat.

She munched through it, not bothering with the tail, which was always too chewy, and dropped the remains at her feet. She coughed up a hairball and spat it out, then wandered back to the fire at the centre of the cave.

She heard Scrannel returning, heard the clanging of his armour, and she allowed a spark of hope to permeate her usual dour humour. He was hurrying. Maybe that meant he'd been successful. Maybe he was struggling with someone. She heard him lose his footing and splash and crash into the ditch. She didn't care who he'd brought with him – child, adult, old person, she genuinely didn't care. She was regretting eating the rat now – she should have held off a little longer. She heard Scrannel hiss in pain – either the meal had struck him, or he'd become tangled in the thorns again. Black Annis licked her lips, picturing a plump child, maybe ten years old. She was *starving*.

But when Scrannel appeared at the cave mouth, he was alone. Disappointment became a weight in the pit of Annis's stomach.

"Hullo," Scrannel said, his armour dripping with ditch water. "I'm back." It wasn't real armour, of course. He had made it from an assortment of tin products and segments of corrugated iron. It was held together by nuts and bolts and pieces of frayed string. It clanked when he walked. It clanked when he *didn't* walk. It just *clanked*.

"Where's my dinner?" Black Annis asked, even though the answer didn't interest her. The only thing that mattered was that she wasn't going to eat. Again.

"No one's about," Scrannel said, giving an apologetic shrug that kicked up quite a racket. "Everyone's asleep."

"Of course everyone's asleep," Annis snapped. "It's night. You were supposed to sneak into a house and grab someone."

"I tried," Scrannel claimed, eyes wide with earnestness. "But every time I got close to a door or window, the lights would come on and I'd have to run away. I don't know how they knew I was there. It happened six or seven times."

Annis crossed her arms. Her dress was shapeless and made of sackcloth. "Do you think," she said, her voice quiet and filled with barely restrained rage, "that maybe they hear that stupid armour you insist on wearing?"

Scrannel frowned. "They hear *this*? I don't think that's very likely, Annis. They're probably all psychics. That's what *I* think."

She resisted the urge to tear him limb from bloody limb. Scrannel was, for lack of a better word, a pet. His mother was a troll, to whom his father was nothing more than a drunken blur one dark and stormy night, and so Scrannel himself was a crossbreed, a mongrel, an *oddity*. He had milky-white eyes that were set too far apart, he had no nose to speak of and a mouth wide enough to swallow a decent-sized rock. He had tiny teeth and high cheekbones and only the barest hint of a chin, upon which he was trying to grow a beard. He had been trying to grow this beard for the past three years. His chin looked vaguely fluffy, but that was as far as it had got.

Scrannel was an idiot of a creature, who actually enjoyed living in a ditch, and the only reason Annis had not eaten him was because he tasted dreadful. The first time they had met she'd torn off a chunk of his leg, chewed it for a few moments before spitting it out. She'd spent the rest of the night being sick in a stream, and Scrannel had stuck around, eventually offering to hold her hair back while she vomited.

That had been twelve years ago, and he still hadn't left.

"I have a bit of news," he said, trying to sound casual. "I think I was followed."

She stared at him. "What?"

"I can't be sure now," he said hurriedly. "But there was a woman, and she had blonde hair and a long coat, and I've never seen her before, and she looked, you know, out of place."

"And why do you think she was following you?"

"Because when I ran away, she ran after me."

Annis could feel her skin starting to turn blue.

Scrannel spoke quickly. "I might be mistaken, of course. Could just be coincidence. She might be a jogger, or something."

"A jogger?" Annis growled. "In a long coat? At night?"

"Carrying a sword."

"*What?*"

"I'm fairly certain she was carrying a sword."

Annis felt her fingernails grow long. "That doesn't sound like a jogger, now, does it?"

Scrannel pondered, then shook his head. "To be honest, no, it doesn't. And now that I think about it, I don't think she was even wearing jogging shoes. What kind of jogger doesn't wear jogging shoes?"

"You're an idiot," Annis snarled.

His armour clanked when he nodded.

There was movement at the cave mouth. Scrannel scuttled away, and a young woman with tousled blonde hair, wearing a long coat over brown leather trousers and a brown leather tunic, stepped into the cave holding a sword in her right hand.

"That's her," Scrannel said unhelpfully.

The woman was holding a coil of thick rope in her other hand, which she let drop into the human remains at her feet.

"Nice place," she muttered, almost to herself. She had a London accent. Annis liked Londoners. They tasted great.

Scrannel let out a battle cry, then he ran forward. The young woman didn't use her sword, as Annis expected. Instead, she swayed to one side and slapped Scrannel on the back as he hurtled by. He ran into the cave wall.

Annis could feel her teeth start to lengthen in her mouth. "Who are you?"

"Tanith," the young woman said. "Tanith Low."

Scrannel charged at her again and she kicked out, slamming her boot heel into the piece of tin wrapped around his knee. He hit the ground with his insignificant chin.

Tanith ignored him as he rolled around in pain. "And I'm just guessing here, so don't be offended if I get this wrong, but you must be Black Annis. I've heard an awful lot about you."

"Is that so?"

"Yes indeedy. The blue skin, the nails, the cave littered with the bones of your victims. It's all very impressive."

Annis's jaw dislocated with a loud pop, and her mouth hung open – impossibly wide – to accommodate her growing, jagged teeth.

"Why, granny," Tanith said with a smile, "what big teeth you have."

"You don't know *everything* about me," Annis said. "If you did, you wouldn't have dared set foot in my home."

Tanith shrugged. "I know that you're under arrest, and I know you really shouldn't resist."

Black Annis laughed.

Scrannel forced himself to his feet and threw a punch, but Tanith struck his forearm with the hilt of her sword. The piece of tin that covered that section of arm now had a large dent in it. She kicked him and the corrugated iron that made up his chest-plate rattled as he fell back.

Tanith looked over at Annis. "I know enough. I know that sunlight turns you to stone for all eternity. I know that you've killed and eaten hundreds of people over the years."

"Thousands," Annis corrected.

"Well, in that case, you are doubly under arrest."

"You shouldn't have come here alone."

Scrannel ran to the dark corner of the cave where he kept his stuff, and grabbed the wooden spear he'd been working on for weeks. He ran back towards Tanith and when he was close enough so there was no way he could miss, he hurled the spear and missed. It sailed past her, right out through the cave mouth. She didn't even have to duck.

Tanith jumped and spun, a leg snapping out from nowhere and hitting Scrannel in the jaw. He whirled and clanked and fell and clanked and hit the ground and clanked, and then he lay still and didn't clank any more.

Annis bent her knees, ready to spring. "Any last requests?"

Tanith shrugged. "Fall over and go to sleep?"

Tanith dodged the first swipe of the nails, but only just. Annis pressed the attack, forcing the intruder to retreat. Tanith, panic showing in her eyes, blocked with the sword, but Annis had both hands working, which was the equivalent of ten long knives slashing through the air.

A boot found Annis's knee and she stumbled back and hissed. Tanith came forward, thrusting the sword high then sweeping it low, but Annis had anticipated the feint and the nails of her left hand connected with the blade and forced it down, while her right hand went to carve up Tanith's pretty face.

At the last moment Tanith raised an elbow, striking Annis's arm and making her miss, but the move meant that she had taken one hand off her sword. Annis flicked her left hand and tore the sword from Tanith's grip. It fell between them, then Annis stepped over it, hands flashing.

Tanith stumbled back, desperately trying to dodge another few swipes. Annis's nails struck the cave wall repeatedly, but she was grinning now, looking forward to the meal that was about to come.

Tanith kept moving, however, swaying just far enough so that the nails would miss and hit the wall. Annis was growing impatient, and Tanith moved in, punched her right on the nose, before moving away again.

Annis could see, by the skin of her hands, that she was at her bluest. She felt the anger build, and she let out a roar and her attack became a frenzy of slashing claws that hit nothing but cave wall. She rushed at Tanith, who leaped to the wall and ran sideways along it. Annis howled her rage and tried to reach her. But now Tanith was upside down, above her, and as Annis whirled Tanith jumped and flipped, landed beside her sword, snatching it up.

They went at it, sword against nails, and now Annis could see something new in Tanith's eyes. The panic was gone, the desperation was gone, and Annis suddenly realised it had never been there in the first place. She knew, instinctively, that this had all been planned. But why? What could Tanith possibly have to gain by simply defending, and dodging attacks?

Tanith ducked under another swipe and dropped to the ground. She swung her foot out, hitting Annis in the back of the leg. Annis fell, tried to get up, but Tanith smashed a boot heel into her jaw.

Dazed, Annis swiped at where Tanith had just been, and her nails found nothing but air. She felt something tighten around her ankle, and looked up.

"What're you doing?" she asked dully.

Tanith had tied the thick rope to Annis's leg, and for the first time Annis realised that the other end of the rope trailed out of the cave. Tanith gave the rope a little tug, then stood up and stepped back.

"It's morning," Tanith said. "See outside? That's sunlight, that is."

Annis shook her head to clear it. "So?"

"So," Tanith continued, "there's a farmer out there on a tractor, and the other end of this rope is tied to that tractor, and his instructions are, when he feels a tug on this rope, he is to start driving, very slowly, away."

Annis frowned. The rope was beginning to tighten. After a moment, it was taut, and Annis felt herself begin to move towards the cave mouth.

"You'll turn to stone," Tanith said, "for all eternity. You don't want that, do you?"

Annis, her odd-coloured eyes wide, sat up and slashed at the thick rope with her nails.

"You've gone a bit blunt, I'm afraid," Tanith said. "Striking my sword was bad enough, but that cave wall? That's what did it."

Annis squealed as she was slowly dragged towards the sunlight. She slashed again and again at the rope.

"There's no way you're going to cut through that in time," Tanith said. She took a pair of wrist irons from her coat, and tossed them on the ground. "Put those on."

"Never!" Annis screamed.

"OK."

Annis attacked the rope with renewed vigour. She cut through one strand. By the looks of it, only another two hundred to go. She twisted around.

"Scrannel! Scrannel, wake up!" Scrannel didn't move. He snored gently.

Annis glared at Tanith. "You can't do this! You can't!"

"You eat people," Tanith said. "I pretty much can, unless you put those shackles on and let me take you in."

The sunlight was mere inches away.

"Fine!" Annis screeched. Tanith kicked the shackles over to her and Annis clicked them on around her wrists, the chain dangling. Immediately she felt her powers fade. Her skin began to lose its blue tint, and her teeth and nails shortened and her jaw relocated.

"I hate you," Annis said.

Tanith nodded. "A lot of people in shackles do."

"If I ever get out..."

"You'll come after me? Tear me apart? Cut off my head? I've heard it all before, Annis. It doesn't impress me."

"If I ever get out of prison," Annis said, ignoring her, "I'll find you and eat you."

Tanith smiled. "Well, OK then. Haven't heard that one in a while." She took hold of Annis's arm and pulled her to her feet. "I've got a sack outside," she said. "I'm afraid you'll have to wear it until I get you to the van, just to keep the sunlight off. Hope you understand."

Annis perked up. "Is it a nice sack?"

"It's pretty stylish, as sacks go."

On their way out, they passed Scrannel, who was snoring peacefully in the dirt. Annis gave him an affectionate kick, and he mumbled something and went back to snoring.

"Boyfriend?" Tanith asked.

"Pet," Annis answered.

Tanith nodded. "All the best ones are."

FRIDAY NIGHT FIGHTS

She was food, she was told as they dragged her to the cell. She was lunch. She was little more than a snack, thrown to the beast to reward it for blood spilled. The men were strong, and she kicked at them and they hit her, but still she kicked. She would not go gently to her death. Not her. Not Valkyrie Cain.

Her knees scraped over rough stones and rubble and bled through her jeans. The cold shackles dug into her wrists. Her struggles echoed down through the concrete corridor, as wide as the school running track. The sunlight was too far behind to throw shadows. The darkness was too close in front.

The man holding her arm let go, and keys jangled as he went to the cell door. He slid open a hatch before he unlocked it, to check on the beast. She felt the other man tense, and for a moment his attention was away from her. She twisted from his grip. The light was too far away, so she ran into the darkness. Laughter followed her.

She ran fast. Her tennis shoes splashed in dark pools of stagnant water, and the uneven ground threatened to cut short her escape. She kept her shackled arms up, like a boxer, to protect her head should she run into a wall or a low-hanging pipe. Her eyes were adjusting to the world of shadows, and she couldn't risk a backwards glance.

There was a break in the solid mass to her left, and she veered into a branching corridor. The cold registered on her bare arms, but she didn't feel it. She wouldn't feel anything until the adrenaline faded.

Their voices came, calling for her. Cell doors, iron and old, blurred by on either side. There were people in some of those cells. She could hear them, reacting to the mocking calls of the men. In other cells, there were beasts. They snarled and snapped and hurled themselves against the iron, excited and bloodthirsty, adding to the cacophony.

Concrete steps led upwards to a faint yellow light. Valkyrie left the darkness and took the steps three at a time. The staircase spiralled and the light grew stronger. Another corridor, long and thin, the sunlight streaming through the narrow windows on one side. At the end of the corridor, a wooden door. She ran past the narrow windows and through them saw a small stadium, basic stone seating curving round a lowered arena.

Where the hell had they taken her?

The wooden door opened before she got to it. The man with the keys smiled. Oddly, for someone so dirty and brutal, he had a nice smile. Behind her, the other man was blocking her retreat.

"You'd better be coming along now, girl," the man with the keys said.

Valkyrie went to a window, turned sideways, and squeezed the upper half of her body through. There was an open space of flat concrete twelve metres below, just before the seating started. She managed to get her hips through, but a hand grabbed her leg as she fell. She swung into the wall and did her best to loosen the grip. The man with the keys could barely get his head through the window. His fingers were tight on her ankle.

"Go down and catch her," he said to his friend.

Coins fell from Valkyrie's pocket as she dug into her jeans with her shackled hands, searching for something to break his hold. Something sharp. She unbuckled her belt and pulled it free, held the buckle in her palm with the prong sticking up through her index and middle fingers, and closed her fist. She curled her body upwards, stabbing the prong repeatedly into the back of his hand. It was a crude dagger, and limited. He cursed and yelled and gritted his teeth, but didn't let go.

The muscles in her abdomen were burning. She had to break his hold *now*. She wouldn't get another chance.

Valkyrie released his forearm and grabbed his hand, doing her best to prise a finger loose. She could raise his fingertip off her leg, but that was it. She heard him laugh at her efforts.

Her muscles screaming at her, she dug the buckle prong beneath his fingernail. He cried out for his friend to hurry up. She squirmed the prong deeper and he cursed at her, the pitch of his voice rising with the pain. Finally his nail lifted and she fell with his screeches, turned her body and tucked her chin to her chest. She hit the concrete with her shoulder and tried to absorb the impact through her side. She knew how to fall. She'd been taught how to fall.

But she'd never fallen from this height.

She lay on her back and tried to breathe but couldn't. She tried to move but couldn't. Her arms wouldn't push her up and her legs wouldn't bend.

She made a sound, a long involuntary groan. Her lungs were trying to inflate. Her stomach muscles were bunching up and she had to fight the urge to curl into a ball. When the first bit of control returned to her, she arched her back and groaned again.

A sliver of breath, in through her lips.

Valkyrie turned over, got up, saw the other man running for her. She stumbled away from him, still trying to breathe. He was fast and he was gaining. Her legs struggled to find a rhythm, but at least she was running again. Valkyrie jumped on to the stone seating, leaping from seat to seat, moving diagonally down to the arched tunnel that led out of the stadium. He was behind her all the way.

Her breathing was ragged, but back under her control as she dropped from the last seat. The tunnel lay ahead, opening out on the other side to a view of magnificent green countryside. She ran for it. She could lose him in the fields, or the trees, or even swim a river to get away. She could flag down a car on the road. She could pick up a rock and smash his brains in. Once she got through that tunnel, she could do a lot of things.

She was halfway through when there was a rattle and a rumble, and a gate began to lower. It was one of those old latticed gates, the kind that protected medieval castles. It was waist-height as Valkyrie neared, and she had to throw herself down and roll beneath it, springing up immediately on the other side.

Her pursuer shot his arm through the gate, but she was well out of reach.

She looked round, hands behind her head, sucking in air and gearing up for the next run. She was standing in a large makeshift car park that pushed back the countryside as far as it would go. Hills of green rolled like frozen waves towards the horizon. To her left was a forest that spread unchecked, enveloping everything within reach, and to her right were houses in the distance. She counted seven, isolated from each other on the sides of the hills. But for all Valkyrie knew there was a town beyond that clump of trees, or a village hidden by that hedgerow.

"Don't go too far," the man behind her said. "We'll get you soon enough."

She took off at a quick jog, following the trail that led away from the car park. She could hear Skulduggery's voice in her head, telling her to stay off the path, telling her that was making herself an easy target. But the trail would lead to a road, Valkyrie knew, and a road would mean cars, and other people.

She took the trail downhill, where it evened out and became a small road. She turned the jog into a run. The road joined another, and as she approached a tractor passed. She waved but the driver didn't see her, and it was round the next bend before she reached the junction. She took off after it, wishing she had something with which to tie her hair back. She didn't like running with it loose.

The tractor was ahead of her, trundling on its way. It was old and, by the look of it, ran primarily on rust. It didn't have any wing mirrors, so Valkyrie's frantic waves were going unnoticed. She had to slow, she had to, and she glared at the tractor as it trundled on.

She heard another engine, a car or a van, coming from behind, and had visions of the van the men had been driving when they'd grabbed her. She was about to jump into the ditch when a blue sedan came round the corner and stopped sharply. The woman behind the wheel stared at her, then opened the door and stepped out.

"Are you OK?" the woman asked. She was about sixty, with short grey hair.

"Two men are chasing me. I need to get away."

The woman waved her hand at the passenger side. "Get in."

Valkyrie did as she was told, and buckled up as the woman put the car in gear.

"What happened?" the woman asked as they overtook the tractor and sped on. "Who's chasing you?"

What was Valkyrie going to say? Was she going to tell the truth? Of course not. "Bad men," she said. "They kidnapped me, brought me here. I got away, but they're chasing me. I have to get back to my friends. They'll be able to help."

"What's your name?"

"Valkyrie," she said without thinking.

"Valkyrie... what an unusual name. I'm Grace. I'm not from around here, so you're going to have to tell me where to go."

"I don't even know where we are."

"I think we're in Kildare. I'm so sorry, I'm kind of lost."

"Do you have a phone? They took mine."

Grace winced apologetically. "I have, but the battery's run out, and I left the car charger at home. I think the best thing we can do is just head for the nearest town." She took a right turn. "I passed one about five minutes ago."

Valkyrie frowned. "We're going back?"

"Not the same way. I think this road loops around."

"I really think we should be getting as far away from here as possible."

"You don't have to be afraid. There's no one about."

"I don't think you're getting how serious this is. They're not going to just let me *escape*." Valkyrie frowned. "Are you sure we're not headed back on the exact same road we were on? This looks familiar."

"Oh, no," said Grace, "I'm quite sure. Why are you looking at me like that? You seem almost... Oh, my. You think I know those men, don't you? You think I'm bringing you back to them?"

"Let me out," said Valkyrie. "Let me out right—"

The van reared up at Grace's window and swerved into them, and there was a crunch of metal and the world spun and Grace was screaming. The car dipped sickeningly and hit something and the air bags rushed out, knocking Valkyrie's head back.

Suddenly it was still. The engine was running, but they weren't moving.

Valkyrie opened her eyes. She heard Grace moan, and started to push the air bag down. They were in a ditch. Her thumb clicked the seat-belt release catch, and she reached for the door, but it wouldn't open. She moved her head, looking back at Grace. There was movement outside. Someone was opening the driver-side door.

"Help," Grace said softly.

The man reached in and took hold of Grace's head, and he twisted until her neck broke. Then he looked over at Valkyrie.

"Told you we'd get you," he said.

They dragged her to the cell and this time they didn't take their attention off her. The man with the keys opened the iron door and his companion threw her inside.

Valkyrie stumbled in. Her foot hit something and she fell. The door shut and darkness swarmed. She stayed very still, on her hands and knees, and listened for the beast, but she could only hear her own breathing.

Moving slowly, she tracked her hand back to whatever she'd tripped over. There was a cold metal ring bolted to the middle of the floor, and a thick chain led from it and snaked towards the far right corner of the cell.

Valkyrie moved backwards, wincing every time she made a sound. She got to the door, her foot loud against the iron. After waiting a moment to make sure this hadn't roused the beast to attack, she crawled sideways to her left, sat back into the corner, and pulled her knees into her chest.

She held her hand in front of her face and couldn't even see movement. The ground was smooth, with no rocks to use as weapons.

She still couldn't hear the beast. Had they been lying? Toying with her? She thought of Grace and the sound her neck had made, and she folded her arms across her chest and brought her knees in closer. She was starting to shake. It was freezing in here and the adrenaline had worn off. She felt the panic rise, from her belly to her throat, and bit her lip. She wasn't going to cry. They could have a camera on her right now, and she wasn't going to cry. She did her best to close down her mind, but one thought slipped through, and that was all it took.

I wish Skulduggery were here.

Her face crumpled and tears came, and she lowered her head and cried.

When there were no more tears to fall, Valkyrie wiped her eyes. She was fairly certain she was alone in the cell. Anything that hadn't been woken when she'd been thrown in would surely have stirred since then. So they'd been playing little games with her. She wasn't food for anything. So what, then? Was she to be used as leverage against the Sanctuary? She doubted Grand Mage Thurid Guild would negotiate too much over her fate.

"Hello," said a voice.

Valkyrie cursed in fright and pressed herself back into the corner, widening her eyes to try and distinguish shapes in the dark.

"I'm not going to hurt you," the voice assured her. It sounded like the voice of a young man. "Probably."

"Who are you?" Valkyrie asked, her voice loud and harsh.

The voice was smooth and quiet. "I'm Caelan. This is my cell. You're sitting in my favourite corner, you know. Switching corners every few days is the only thing that makes life bearable in this place. Keeps things fresh."

She frowned. "Sorry."

"It's OK. You can have it."

"What's happening?"

"They haven't told you? Usually, they tell people."

"They just said I was going to be food."

She could almost sense him nodding.

"So they *have* told you. But technically you wouldn't be food. You'd be drink."

Valkyrie went cold. "You're a vampire."

"Aha," he said slowly. "You must be a sorcerer, then? Don't suppose you could use your magic to get us out of here?"

She held her hands up in the dark. "These shackles are bound. I can't use magic."

"Ah. It was a nice idea while it lasted. What's your name?"

"Valkyrie. Valkyrie Cain."

"You say it like that name is supposed to mean something to me."

"I work with Skulduggery Pleasant."

"The Skeleton Detective," Caelan said. "Now, him I *have* heard about. I heard he was gone, though. Sucked into another dimension or something equally stupid."

"He is. I'm going to get him back."

There was a moment's silence. "And you're doing a wonderful job of that."

She glared at the darkness. "So what about you? What are you doing here?"

"Right now? Right now I'm on hunger strike."

"Since when?"

"Since this morning. It's going pretty well so far, but I always falter around dinnertime..."

"What are you striking about?" asked Valkyrie.

"I don't want to play their game any more. Have you seen the arena? The pit?"

"Yes."

"Every Friday night," said Caelan, "we're taken to the pit and we're made to fight each other."

"*We?*"

"The others like me, in the other cells."

"Vampire pit fights?"

"Not just vampires. All sorts of creatures. It draws a crowd. Of course, I'm not allowed to change fully. The beast I'd become would rip apart anything it faced, and where's the fun in that? So they give me a half-dose of serum to trap me halfway through the change. For the sport. If I win, I'm taken back here and before my next fight I'm thrown a morsel to keep my strength up. You are said morsel. If I lose, I'm dead. Real dead, not just vampire dead."

"So you're not drinking my blood because...?"

"They want me strong when they put me into the pit. That's the only way the crowd will be satisfied. Who wants to pay to see a starving vampire flail at a zombie or a bridge troll? If I don't eat, they won't put me in the pit. I've been here three months, and I'm not going to do it any more."

"That doesn't make any sense," said Valkyrie.

"You really don't want to be talking me out of this, you know. I've been draining every person they throw in here. You're lucky today's the day I've changed my mind."

"Who are they? The men who do this?"

"You mean are they sorcerers?" asked Caelan. "They are not. They're mortals who know more than they should. Those shackles binding your power are just one of the things they've picked up over the years. Everything they have is scavenged. The big one's Bruno. I don't know the name of the smaller one.

"As far as I can tell, the whole thing is run by a man who calls himself the Promoter. And the audience that gathers every week? Mortals, also. They keep all this a secret from the press to prevent the Sanctuary from noticing them and sorting them out. I've come to the conclusion that mortals are far worse than any vampire or sorcerer."

"What'll happen when they realise I'm still alive?"

"If I don't feed on you, they're going to give you to someone who will. What day is it today?"

"Thursday."

"Then you'll be dead by tomorrow night."

Valkyrie didn't say anything to that.

*　　*　　*

She didn't have anything to say for the next four hours, either. She was cold, and getting colder, and she was hungry, and she had other needs.

"I have to pee," she called out.

For a moment there was just darkness and silence.

"Well," Caelan said slowly, "that's a little awkward."

Embarrassment made her angry. "So what do I do? Knock on the door, or what?"

"I'm really not sure. No other meal has survived long enough to want to go to the bathroom. You're going to have to just go in here."

Valkyrie got up, felt her way to the door, and banged her fist against it. "Hey!" she shouted.

She heard the voices from the other cells shouting "Hey!" back.

She kicked the door. "I have to use the toilet!"

The responses she got to *that* one were predictably disgusting.

And then a new voice, clearer than the others. "Shut up in there!" It wasn't a voice she recognised.

Most of the other prisoners quietened down, and those that didn't got a sharp rap on their iron door as a warning. Valkyrie waited until she could be heard.

"Hello?" she called. "I need to go to the bathroom. Hello?"

She heard striding footsteps getting louder, and then the door rattled and the viewing hatch slid open. The beam of a torch blinded her and she immediately looked away.

"What's going on?" the man demanded. "Why isn't she dead?"

"I need to use the toilet," she told him, blinking her vision back.

The man ignored her and repeated his question. "Why isn't she dead?"

"I'm on hunger strike," Caelan said.

The man shoved the torch through the hatch in an attempt to see into

Caelan's corner, and Valkyrie reached out and grabbed it, wrenching it from his grip.

"Give that back!" the man roared.

"You let me go to the bathroom and I'll give it back."

"You're supposed to be dead!"

"Well, I'm alive and I need to pee."

"Keep the bloody thing!" he snarled, and slammed the hatch shut. She heard him striding away.

"I won't look," Caelan said, "I promise." Angrily, Valkyrie swung the torch to the sound of his voice.

The beam fell upon a boy around her age, maybe a bit older. He languished with his back to the corner, one long leg stretched out straight along the floor, the other pulled in. His boots were scuffed and his jeans dirty and torn. His torso was bare, the light flowing over the lean muscles of his arms. But it was his face that caught her attention – black hair falling to his brow, and a smile so wicked and cheekbones so sharp. He had one hand up, shading his eyes.

"I won't even tell anyone about it," he continued. "Your dignity is safe with me, I swear."

She let the torch beam drift down to his torso again, and allowed herself a moment to marvel at the way the light caught his abdomen.

"Excuse me?" he said. "I'm starting to feel just a little bit objectified here."

"Don't flatter yourself," she retorted, but still the beam lingered. "You're kind of good-looking, in your own way, but you're really not my type."

She was, of course, lying.

She swept the beam to his outstretched leg, to the shackle that was attached to the heavy chain. She scanned the walls, looking for cameras or windows, but there were none.

She pointed the torch at one of the free corners. "I'm going to go here."

"I'm not looking."

Valkyrie went to the corner and kept the torch on him, to blind him if he did look. But it appeared that he was going to keep his word. His face was turned away and his eyes were closed.

She hesitated, then undid her jeans and hunkered down.

"Talk," she ordered.

"What?"

"Talk to me, but do it loudly. I don't want you to hear me."

That smile again, playing with the corners of his mouth. "What would you like to talk about?"

"I don't care."

"Very well. Your friend, the skeleton. How do you plan on rescuing him from this other dimension?"

"It's a long story," said Valkyrie. "It's complicated. I'm almost there, though. I just have one more thing I need to get and that's it."

"And what is this one more thing?"

"The Murder Skull."

"I'm afraid I'm not familiar with it."

"You don't have to be. I've been trying to find it for ages now, trying to find out who has it. That's what got me in trouble, actually. The guy who has it is a man called Chabon. In my efforts to get in touch with him, I've been mixing with a bad crowd."

"What a nice way of putting it."

"Thank you. The bad crowd led me to the big guy... What did you say his name was?"

"Bruno."

"Bruno, who figured out I was a sorcerer and thought I was coming to arrest him or set him on fire or something... I turn away for one second and *bam*. I wake up in a van with my wrists shackled."

"Just when you'd got within arm's reach of your goal."

"I'm a little more than arm's reach away. I don't know anything about this Chabon guy."

"He's a criminal," said Caelan. "Thames Chabon, an information broker-slash-lowlife from London."

"You know him?"

"I know some people who can get in touch with him."

"Can you help me?"

Caelan laughed softly. "Sure. We'll just explain to the Promoter that we've got stuff to do and he'll let us walk out of here."

"If I can get you out, will you set up a meeting?"

"You're chained up in a cell, about to be fed to whichever monster isn't picky about its food. You're not getting anyone out."

"But if I do?"

He sighed. "If you get me out, I'll owe you a favour, I suppose."

Valkyrie stood, doing up her jeans. "Good." She walked to her corner, but didn't sit. Instead, she leaned back against the wall and turned off the torch. "How long have you been a vampire?"

"Longer than some," he said. "Not as long as others."

"How did it happen?"

In the dark, there was silence, and then he spoke. "I was in love. Her name was Anna. Our parents wouldn't allow us to be together, they said we were too young, so we planned to run away and get married."

His voice changed as he spoke. The rhythm became slower, like he was suddenly living in a different time.

"We quietly sold our possessions and saved our money, and every night I'd climb through her bedroom window and we'd lie in each other's arms, and we'd talk about the things we were going to do. We planned to go to England, and then France, and Africa. I could see my whole life in her eyes, and she could see hers in mine."

Valkyrie sat while Caelan continued.

"Her family owned a tavern. She was used to leering men and wandering hands, and she had no patience for either. And then the tavern door became darkened by the presence of a stranger. She'd tell me about him as we lay together. He'd sit at his table and he wouldn't touch the drink he'd ordered, and his eyes would never leave her face.

"Night after night he'd sit there, looking at her, always with a smile beneath his beard. One of the regular patrons was sweet on Anna, as many of them were, for she was a beautiful girl, and he took offence at this stranger. This patron, and two of his biggest friends, attempted to eject the man from the premises. Anna was fetching wine from the cellar at that moment so she didn't witness the fight, but according to the bartender it was over as quick as it had begun.

"He said the stranger had lifted one of the men over his head and thrown him the length of the room. He said he then gripped the shoulder of the second man and pulverised the bone. And the patron who was seeking to defend Anna's honour, he was dragged outside and no one saw him again.

"After that night, the stranger started talking to Anna while she served him. She said he was rough but educated, and he was charming, in his way. She found herself telling him a great many things. She told him about me. She even told him of our plans to run away. He seemed... interested.

"One night, he was waiting for me in the garden below her window. He dragged me to the willow tree and bared his fangs. But he didn't drain all of my blood, and he didn't kill me. He just threw me away."

"And that's all it took?" Valkyrie asked softly. "Just one bite?"

"That's all. I crawled through a narrow window, dropped down into the tavern cellar. I lay hidden by barrels for three days while the fevers took me.

"When my senses returned, I smelled blood, and I was starving. It was a hunger I had never experienced. I left the cellar. The tavern was dark and empty and I went up, to the living quarters. The stranger had visited only hours before, and he had torn Anna's family limb from limb. Blood painted the walls, still wet. I can't recall if there was a part of me that was horrified by the scene. All I remember was the blood, and that it was the only thing that could satisfy me."

"You... drank it?"

"I lapped it off the floor. I licked it off the walls."

Valkyrie didn't say anything.

"It was orchestrated, of course. The stranger did like his little games. In the three days I had been gone, he had convinced Anna that I had left without her. She was distraught, and he was her comfort. And he manipulated events so that when I was at my weakest, on my knees and smeared with blood, Anna would return home and see me.

"She fled to him, and he took her to his bed, and when he was finished he cut out her heart and left it for me, as a gift."

"Did you ever find him again?"

"No. I tried but he was gone. I never even knew his name."

Valkyrie looked into the darkness where Caelan sat. "I didn't know vampires could be like you," she said.

There was quiet amusement in his voice. "Known many vampires, have you?"

"Only one," she admitted. "And I gave him a scar that'll never fade, so he doesn't like me very much."

There was a moment of silence. "Dusk," said Caelan.

Valkyrie's eyes widened. "Yes. He's not a friend of yours, is he?"

"No," said Caelan softly. "No. Not a friend."

She slept badly.

She was cold and there was no padding on the ground. She was hungry and thirsty, and every time her defences lowered she thought about Skulduggery and how she was his only hope, and here she was, chained up and about to be killed. The thought that she was going to fail him brought tears to her eyes.

Sleep came in fits and starts. In the cell, time wasn't something that could be judged. Time was something that went on outside. The door would open whenever it would open, and then time would be allowed to flood in. But until that happened, there was only the cold and the dark and the vampire across the floor.

She thought of her parents, living the rest of their lives with the reflection standing in for their daughter. She thought of her friends – of Tanith and Ghastly, and Fletcher. They'd have noticed her absence by now. They'd be worried. They'd talk to the reflection, and the reflection would tell them that Valkyrie hadn't even taken her armoured clothing when she'd gone off to do her investigating.

That's what she got. That's what she got for letting this take over her life. She made stupid mistakes. She talked to the wrong people without taking the proper precautions.

That's what she got.

Morning came. Valkyrie heard the men making their rounds. The hatch in the door opened and the light fell on her. She heard a grunt, and the hatch closed.

"They're not happy with me," said Caelan.

His voice was weak.

*   *   *

He didn't talk much that day. When he did, his voice was dry and thin, and there was something else behind it. A hint of anger. No, not anger. Fury. Violence. He was trying to hide it, but it was too sharp to disguise.

More hours passed, until he said, "I'm sorry."

"For what?"

"They're coming, Valkyrie. The stadium is filling up. I can hear them talking and laughing. I can hear the cars outside."

"What will they do with me?"

He didn't answer for a moment. "They'll feed you to someone else."

Outside the cell, a light switched on. The edge of the door lit up.

Valkyrie stood. The torch was in her right hand, and she gripped it tight. "I'll make a run for it," she said. "The moment that door opens..."

"You won't make it," he told her wearily. "There'll be too many of them."

"I'm not going to just wait here," she spat. "If I'm going to die, I'm going to make them *hurt*."

He managed a last laugh before the hatch rattled, and slid open. Yellow light burst through.

She pressed her back to the wall, her eyes on the light, blinking quickly to help the adjustment. The door opened and when the big man, the man Caelan had called Bruno, stepped in, she launched herself at him. The torch cracked against his head and he cursed and flung her back. She tripped over the chain and sprawled on to the ground.

"What the hell is this?" he snapped.

"I told you," said the man behind him, the one whose torch she had stolen. "I told you he wasn't drinking."

"Vampire," Bruno said, "why isn't she dead yet?"

"We talked about this last week," Caelan said calmly. "I'm on strike."

"And what makes you think that changes anything?"

"You have a crowd out there baying for blood," Caelan said, "and as much as they hate me, I'm still the biggest draw you've got. They'll be expecting a certain standard. It's not going to be a very thrilling fight when I'm as weak as I am."

Bruno laughed. "So you think we're going to let you forfeit, simply because we don't want to upset your fans?"

"That would seem to be the reasonable thing to do."

"I hate to burst your bubble, vampire, but you're really not that entertaining, and there are quite a few people out there who think you've been given too easy a time in the pit."

"That's ridiculous and you know it."

"Hey, if you don't want to take part in the scheduled fight, then so be it. We'll shake things up a little, what do you say? We're going to give them a spectacle tonight. Yes, indeedy, we are. Caelan, the weakened champion, going up against Victor, the eager young contender."

Caelan's voice changed immediately. "You... can't put me up against Victor."

"And yet we are."

"He won't do it. Vampires are forbidden to harm other vampires."

"That didn't stop you, now, did it? And it's not going to stop Victor, either."

Bruno stepped to the side, and two burly men came in and unlocked Caelan's shackles. They started to pull him to the door.

"You can't put me in the pit with him," Caelan protested. "He's at full strength."

"Then you should have fed when you had the chance."

Caelan looked at Valkyrie and there was something in his eyes that made her step back. "Just give me a second," he said.

Bruno shook his head. "To the pit, boys."

Caelan reached for her. "I'll just take a little sip..."

There was an electric flash and Caelan jerked and then slumped, and the men dragged him out.

Bruno smiled at Valkyrie. "I don't know how you managed to keep him away from you, girl, but you're back on the menu tonight."

He grabbed her shackles and shook the torch from her hand, then pushed her out of the cell. The men dragged Caelan on ahead, but Bruno took Valkyrie another way. Already she could hear the chanting of the crowd.

He took her through a narrow passageway that linked to a larger tunnel. She glimpsed the night sky, but she was forced in the opposite direction. The chanting got louder.

Eventually, they came to a set of large wooden doors that sealed off the tunnel. Valkyrie could hear the crowd on the other side, working itself into a frenzy. Like the cells, these doors had hatches, and Bruno opened them and pushed Valkyrie forward.

They emerged into a fenced-off area in the stands, the pit opening out below them. There were two doors opening on to the arena, both shut. Valkyrie looked at the crowd. They were wrapped up in coats and hats and a lot of them had colourful umbrellas, anticipating rain from the clouds that were blocking out the stars. They sang and chanted and laughed like they were at a football game.

This was *insane*.

The crowd grew quiet, and Valkyrie shifted her position to watch a tall man walk into the centre of the pit.

"Ladies and gentlemen," he called, his voice carrying, "welcome to the fights!"

That drew an appreciative roar from the stands. Valkyrie figured they were an easy crowd to please.

"And what a night we have in store for you," the Promoter continued. "Vicious animal against vicious animal. Inhuman killer against inhuman killer. Monster against monster. And we have a surprise or two. Oh, yes, ladies and gentlemen, we can see that you're growing complacent up there. We can see that you have your favourites, and you're betting accordingly.

"There's a lesson we have to teach you, my friends and neighbours. When it comes to monsters, you can take nothing for granted. Am I right?"

The crowd roared, and the Promoter nodded.

"They'll sneak up on you, won't they? They'll steal through the night to your open window, girls and boys, and what will they do then? They'll bite your neck and drain your blood!"

Some of the audience squealed in horrified delight.

"When it comes to vampires, especially, expect the unexpected. That's the only way we'll ever rid our lands of these parasites. And so our first fight of the evening is the rarest of the rare. There's a code that vampires live by, to never harm another one of their kind. And yet, here tonight, we have two vampires who have forsaken this code. Ladies and gentlemen – place your bets!"

The doors to Valkyrie's left opened, and a man was led through, shackled hand and foot. He wore blood-splattered tracksuit bottoms, cut off just below the knee. His body was a map of pain, criss-crossed with scars both old and new. His head was badly shaved, like he'd done it himself, in the dark, with a blunt razor. His eyes were black, his sharp teeth splitting his gums.

"Victor," the Promoter said, drawing down a chorus of booing. "Eight fights in, he's proving himself to be a capable little monster, aren't you, Victor?"

Victor didn't respond. He was trapped halfway through his transformation into full vampire. Valkyrie could see it by the pain on his face, by the way his body twitched. She'd seen it before with Dusk, when he'd been jabbed with vampire serum in the middle of a change. That time, Valkyrie herself had been responsible.

The doors to her right opened, and the Promoter swung round, pointing to the newcomer as he was led out into the light.

"And tonight, for your sporting pleasure, for your entertainment and your education, Victor will be facing... Caelan!"

The crowd roared their cheers. Caelan stumbled, and the man behind him poked him in the side with the barrel of a shotgun. Valkyrie glimpsed the claws that tipped his fingers. He, too, was caught halfway between his two natures.

The fighters were brought to opposite sides of the pit, where their shackles were taken off as the Promoter left the pit. The men, half a dozen for each fighter, backed off warily to the doors, sealing Caelan and Victor in.

The Promoter appeared in the stands, sitting down in a chair that could only be described as a throne.

"Vampires," he shouted, "begin the slaughter!"

Caelan and Victor started circling each other, knees slightly bent, shoulders hunched. Victor bared his fangs and attacked and Caelan spun him away, keeping the space between them.

Victor moved in again, forcing Caelan to retreat and cutting off his avenues of escape. Victor was bristling with energy – every movement was sharp. Caelan's movements were tempered with a controlled wariness, and he looked positively sedate compared to the other vampire.

Valkyrie hoped this was a deception. She hoped he wasn't really as weak as he'd said. If he was, she had a feeling that this would be a very short fight.

Victor came in and this time Caelan had no room to manoeuvre, and the blow caught him across the jaw. He stepped back and Victor's claws slashed open his chest.

The crowd roared its approval.

Caelan managed to hook an arm round Victor's body, then heaved and twisted, slamming Victor to the ground. He kicked him while he was down there and Victor spun on his back and swept Caelan's feet out from under him.

Both fighters scrambled up, but Victor was noticeably faster – they collided and Caelan was thrown hard against the curved wall of the pit.

Above them, bets were being shouted, and there were people wearing bright sashes across their jackets, furiously scribbling into notebooks. Bruno was shouting, too, struggling to have his voice heard. Valkyrie tried to wriggle from his grip, but he was far too strong.

Victor pummelled Caelan, knocking him round the arena, only letting him get up just so he could have the pleasure of knocking him down again.

When they broke away from each other again, the Promoter's voice came blasting through the speakers. "How're you enjoying the spectacle, folks?"

The crowd roared.

"This is indeed a special night, isn't it? This night could not get any more special, now, could it? What's that? It could?"

The crowd went almost quiet in anticipation.

Valkyrie could hear the grin in the Promoter's voice. "Ladies and gentlemen, tonight, for our main event, we are not only giving you, for your viewing pleasure, a rare and thrilling vampire versus vampire match-up, but we're also throwing a third party into the mix! Friends, family, colleagues, you've heard about them, you've heard the stories, you've heard what they can do, but you've never seen one in action... until now! Patrons of the arena, she's young, she's beautiful, she's magical... I give to you our third and final fighter – the Sorceress!"

"What?" said Valkyrie, and then Bruno kicked her right in the ass, sending her stumbling over the lip and falling into the arena.

She landed on her knees, the sheer volume of noise from the crowd threatening to overwhelm her. She looked back at Bruno, who gave her a smile and tossed her a key. It glinted in the bright lights as it fell, and she caught it, spun immediately, making sure Victor and Caelan weren't making any moves. The two vampires stood on the opposite side of the pit, both staring straight at her.

Her hands were trembling so much the key scraped against the lock of the shackles for an eternity before it slid in. One twist to the right and both wrists were freed, and she felt the magic flood her body. But the sound of the shackles hitting the dirt-packed ground was all the signal the vampires needed.

They sprinted for her and Valkyrie pushed at the air, sending Caelan tumbling backwards. Victor dodged around, came at her, and she whipped the shadows at him, taking him off his feet. He hit the arena wall, landed in a crouch, shaking his head to clear it. His snarls were drowned out by the roar of the crowd.

Caelan burst at her. She went down, rolled, staying away from his claws and fangs. She tried to kick him off her, but it was like kicking a wall. Sharp nails dug into her leg, drawing blood, and he dragged her close. She turned over, clicking her fingers and shoving a fistful of fire into his face. Caelan lurched away, yelping like a wounded dog. Valkyrie scrambled up.

Victor thudded into her from behind. His claws raked her shoulder blade. She cried out, twisted, stumbled and fell, Victor getting tangled in her legs. He fell on top, snapping at her. She held him back. Barely. He pushed her head to one side, exposing her throat, but as his head darted in she filled his mouth with shadows. He recoiled, gagging, and she sat up, but in his blind panic he kicked out and found her jaw and the world sparked and tilted and Valkyrie was lying on her back, blinking slowly in sudden silence.

Gradually, the sounds from the arena soaked back into her hearing.

Without moving, she looked over at Caelan and Victor as they thrashed around in the dirt, snarling and biting and punching. Groaning, she rolled over, looked up.

The Promoter was leaning forward in his throne, watching the contest with an eager, greedy delight on his face. The wall of the arena was lower where he was, allowing him a better view. It wasn't low enough for a vampire to jump, but maybe if there was a sorcerer nearby willing to give a little boost...

Valkyrie got up, clutching her left arm. Blood ran freely down her back, and her leg was pretty bad. She ignored the pain, ignored the snarling, snapping vampires beside her, and limped towards the throne. When she was close enough, she turned back to the vampires, put two fingers in her mouth, and blew a short, shrill whistle.

The vampires stopped fighting and looked over. The audience stopped roaring and peered closer.

The vampires bolted for her. Valkyrie waited until they were close enough and then swept her arms in and up, lifting them off their feet so that they hurtled over her head. All she heard was the Promoter's panicked cry before all hell broke loose.

The audience stampeded. People screamed and shouted and scrambled over each other. Extra lights snapped on over the stands. Doors that should have been closed were opened, and doors that should have been opened were closed. Behind the screams of panic were screams of pain, of people getting torn apart. Valkyrie wasn't the least bit sorry.

She found a door in the arena wall, used shadows to smash the lock. She hurried through, gritting her teeth against the pain. Men with guns passed and she shrank back till they'd gone. She could hear gunshots now. A lot of them.

Ahead was the tunnel out of here, the tunnel to the outside. Two men were guarding it, arguing among themselves about what they should be doing. They had guns, too.

Valkyrie hurled a fireball at the ground between them. They cried out and jumped back, and the shadows slammed them into the walls. They collapsed. Dead or just broken, she didn't know and she didn't care. She ran out, between the rows of parked cars. Headlights swooped all around. Panicking people crashed into other panicking people. Horns blared. There were gunshots closer now – outside the arena.

Someone grabbed her, tugged her, and she was on her knees before she even realised Caelan was beside her. Up close, his fangs were ragged things that split his gums. He wasn't looking at her. He was trembling. Resisting.

They stayed low, moving quickly. Around them, excited voices and angry shouts. Accusations and orders. Valkyrie heard Bruno organising the search, telling people to get in their cars and spread out. They stayed in the dark while people ran through the rows on either side. Bruno's voice got closer.

Valkyrie shrank back as Bruno hurried to a jeep just ahead of them. Someone called to him and he called back, and as he did so he looked her way and frowned. He took a single step in their direction, and then his eyes widened. He opened his mouth to alert the others.

Caelan's hand wasn't closed round Valkyrie's wrist any more, and he wasn't by her side. Instead, he was a dark blur, rushing Bruno, dragging him down into the space between the jeep and another car. He went for the throat, and Valkyrie saw Bruno's arms spread wide in shock, and then scrabble madly against Caelan's shoulders and back. But Caelan was locked on, and there was nothing that could shift him now.

She watched in horrified fascination as he fed.

Headlights swarmed her and she rolled from her position, then the car reversed and the headlights swept away again. She was going to be seen. Any moment now, they were going to find her.

She looked back at Caelan. Bruno's arms were limp. His legs were twisted beneath him, like he'd been trying to push himself up, right until the moment his life left him. Caelan dug inside Bruno's pockets, found what he was looking for. The serum. Without hesitating, Caelan jabbed the syringe into his skin and a moment later he straightened, his back arched, his muscles rolling beneath his moonlit skin. She saw his hands go to Bruno's head and he wrenched it to one side. She heard the pop of bone.

"We have to go," she said softly.

Caelan pulled on Bruno's coat and used the sleeve to wipe his mouth. Valkyrie was glad it was too dark to see much. He found the keys for the jeep in the jacket pocket. They got in and kept their heads low, waiting for the van in front to pull away. They followed the trail of cars to the road, and the first chance they got they broke away and sped on.

There was a phone charging on the dash, so Valkyrie called Ghastly, told him what had happened. A truckload of Cleavers and a truckload of sorcerers were on their way before she'd even hung up. Valkyrie and Caelan waited down a side road for the cavalry to arrive.

When it did, they returned to the arena. A dozen dead. Another dozen injured. The Promoter was found ripped to pieces. He had a ledger in his jacket with the names of the people who'd paid in it. Sorcerers visited each one of those people. Some were convinced to never speak of any of it. Others were taken away to places mortal lawyers couldn't help them.

The creatures, vampires and various fighters in the cells were released. There was no sign of Victor.

Caelan was human again. His scars were already beginning to heal. Valkyrie talked to him, but got the barest of responses back. He was different, she realised. His rediscovered freedom was unnerving him. Back in that cell, with death so close it could happen at any moment, he had nothing to lose. Despite the chains, he was free. But now that the chains were off and his world had expanded, he himself was shrinking away from it. By morning, she had forgotten what his smile looked like.

"The Murder Skull," he said, breaking the silence between them. "You want it."

"Yes," she said. "I know you don't owe me anything – I got you free, but you saved my life, so we're even – but if you can help out at all, I'd be—"

"We're not even," he said. "I still owe you."

"For what?"

He didn't answer. Instead, he looked at the Cleavers and the sorcerers and then he looked back at her. "I'll be in touch," he said, and walked away.

Valkyrie watched him go. He was a dangerous one, of that she was sure. Attractive, though. There was no denying that. But she wasn't a girl to fall for the cliché. She wasn't going to be won over by brooding good looks and a tortured soul, not when the risk was so obvious.

She was a teenage girl and she made stupid decisions sometimes – but she wasn't a *complete* idiot.

LESSON LEARNED

It was a little after ten, still warm but just getting dark, when the Bentley pulled up at the pier and Valkyrie got in. As they drove out of Haggard, they chatted and exchanged gentle yet barbed insults, and then Skulduggery asked, "How was the class?"

Valkyrie looked at him. He kept his face turned towards the road ahead, but she knew he knew. Of course he knew. She briefly considered lying, just to see how long he'd indulge her, but finally she just rolled her eyes. "You know I didn't go."

"I know you didn't go where?"

"You know I didn't go training," she said. "You know I didn't turn up. Do you know why I didn't turn up? I was going to. I was all set to turn up. But do you know why I didn't?"

"You didn't turn up because you didn't think you needed to," Skulduggery said.

"Exactly," Valkyrie responded. "Why do I need someone else teaching me how to fight when I have you and Tanith?"

"Tanith and I have vastly different combat styles."

"Which is why it's all I need. Tanith focuses on kicks and punches, and you teach me what to do when I'm in too close to kick or punch. I'm getting a wide range of instruction. That's a good thing, isn't it?"

"Tanith has astonishing agility, and I don't have tendons," Skulduggery said. "You need instruction from someone who understands your body's limitations."

"My body doesn't have limitations," Valkyrie announced. "It's awesome, and so am I. Besides, why do I need to fight when I've got magic?"

"There'll always be someone with more magic."

"I'll get by. It's what I do."

"Can I tell you a story?"

"Does it have sharks in it?"

"It does, actually. There was this little shark, and it was a very special little shark, and everyone knew how special it was, including the shark. The little shark was very good at a lot of things, but it was especially good at two things in particular – swimming and magic. But, because it was so good at these two things, it didn't really practise either of them, and didn't develop its skills. There came a day when it needed to swim like it had never swum before, but it couldn't because for years it had taken its talents for granted. And then it died for some reason."

"Wow," said Valkyrie.

"I managed to sneak an important lesson into the middle of the story. Did you spot it?"

"It was subtle, but I think I did. Was the swimming, like, a metaphor for fighting? And was the magic a metaphor for magic?"

Skulduggery nodded. "You did spot it."

"That is so clever. It was a very good story, Skulduggery. What was the shark's name?"

"Sharky."

"Did it have any brothers or sisters?"

"Forty-eight brothers and thirty-three sisters."

"That's nice and cosy."

"I feel you may have missed the point of the story, though."

"Pretty sure I got it."

"So, if I reschedule your lesson for tomorrow afternoon, you'll actually turn up?"

Valkyrie made a face. "Don't I know enough people? Like, I know loads of people already, and I forget half their names, and I'm just worried that if I meet this instructor guy then he'll be added to the list of people I know, and someone else on that list will be kicked off, and it'll just be really unfair. Also —" she made a noise like she was being strangled — "I really like training with you and Tanith, and I don't want to start training with anyone else."

"Because you're shy?"

"Because I'm rude, but you and Tanith don't seem to mind."

"This instructor is used to rude. He teaches soldiers how to kill."

"Is he going to shout at me? I can't handle people shouting at me. If he shouts at me, then I'm just going to shout at him, and we'll never get anything done."

"He probably won't shout."

"Probably?"

"You are very annoying."

Valkyrie grinned. "I am."

"He's very good at what he does, though, and you'll learn fast. Once he's done with you, I'll take over and guide you through the more advanced levels, but you really should kick this off with someone made of flesh and blood. If I take you through what he's going to take you through, I'll end up snapping every muscle and tendon you have. Shall I reschedule the lesson?"

"Fine," she grumbled.

Skulduggery's phone beeped in his pocket, and a moment later her own phone buzzed. Valkyrie read the message, and her mood brightened.

"Better not reschedule it just yet," she said. "There's been another murder."

* * *

They drove through the city, and the night-time traffic eased off. Passing a roadworks crew who'd cordoned off the street, they parked behind the vans and got out. Valkyrie recognised one of the crew, a sorcerer she'd spoken no more than five words to, and he nodded to her and she nodded back.

It was a nice night, quiet, as they approached the dead body lying just beyond the corner of an old abandoned building. The Necromancer ring on Valkyrie's finger turned cold.

She hunkered down, squinting into the mess. "Well," she said, "this is disgusting."

"Disgusting," Skulduggery echoed, and gave a nod. "Excellent work, Detective Cain. Incisive analysis. Do you have something for me that's a little more professional?"

Valkyrie sighed. "I don't know. What more do you want? It's *really* disgusting? Like... ew?"

"That's much better."

"I mean, with the way the head's been chewed off – that's pretty gross. It's probably the grossest thing I've seen since last night, when I saw the previous victim. Missing head and open chest cavity. Bite marks and claw marks. The internal organs that remain have been chewed, which probably means the internal organs that are missing have been eaten. Also, we've got these footprints in the blood, which we haven't had before. They look like they were made by an animal, although it's no animal footprint I've ever seen. My technical, professional opinion?" She stood up. "A monster did it."

"I concur," said Skulduggery. "So how do we find it?"

Making sure not to step in any of the evidence, Valkyrie backed away from the body, giving her the space to look around.

"The previous victims were all killed in the early morning, between midnight and five a.m., and there was a lot less of them left at the scene. Tonight, it's barely gone half ten, and we already have a body. This isn't like the other attacks. We're not in someone's home or a secluded area – we're outdoors, on a city street, where it's quiet and empty, but anyone could stumble across what was happening. I think the monster was interrupted, or was about to be interrupted, and had to abandon its meal."

"So?"

"So it might still be hungry, and it might still be in the area. I reckon we get the Cleavers in to scoop up the remains before some poor mortal wanders by, and then we go hunting."

"Lead the way," said Skulduggery, and followed her back towards the roadworks crew. Halfway there, he put a hand on her arm and a finger to his lipless mouth.

They turned quietly and retraced their steps to the corner of the abandoned building. Valkyrie became aware of a new sound – a chomping, a chewing, a guzzling. She raised an eyebrow at Skulduggery as he drew his revolver. She'd been right: the monster was still in the area.

Skulduggery took a few quick steps round the corner, and Valkyrie jumped out beside him, shadows curling round her right fist as the creature that had been crouched over the dead body jerked backwards and held up its clawed hands defensively.

"Don't shoot!" it cried.

Valkyrie blinked. Skulduggery lowered his gun a fraction.

"I don't mean you any harm," the creature continued.

It was large, about twice the size of a gorilla. Powerful. Its skin was rough and its eyes were yellow and its mouth had fleshy mandibles that clicked.

"I understand that this must look bad – it must look very bad indeed – but I assure you, I'm not a threat."

Its voice was deep and garbled, but understandable behind the clicking of those mandibles, like a bear who'd learned to talk. It spoke with a refined British accent.

"What are you?" Skulduggery asked.

"My name is Amios Adroit. I'm a Sensitive."

"No. What are you?"

"Oh," said Amios, looking down at himself, "you mean this? I suppose, technically, I'm one of the Shalgoth Reth."

Valkyrie frowned. "You're from the caverns below my uncle's house."

"Am I?" Amios looked confused. "Maybe I am, but the underground caverns that the Shalgoth Reth inhabit stretch for incredible distances in all directions. Some of them link up to other systems; some are entirely self-contained. It is possible that this form I'm inhabiting might have originated from the system you're referring to. I myself hail from Hampstead, in London."

"So what's a British psychic doing in the body of a Shalgoth Reth, in Dublin?" Skulduggery asked.

"Experimenting," said Amios. "Over the years, I have trained myself to inhabit the bodies of various birds and animals, casting my consciousness into their minds, experiencing life from a drastically different perspective. I've long since been fascinated by tales of the Shalgoth Reth, monsters created by the Faceless Ones to hunt down the Ancients and feed off their magic. I thought this would be the ultimate journey for one such as myself and so, four months ago, I commandeered the creature you see before you."

Skulduggery had lowered his gun to his side, but hadn't put it away. "And then what happened?"

"I'm not entirely sure," said Amios, "but, in order to send my consciousness to inhabit another form, I enter into a trance state. Unfortunately, I do have a history of sleepwalking, and I entered into this particular trance state while sitting cross-legged on the top of a very tall cliff."

"So you think you got up and sleepwalked off the edge?"

"Seeing as how I have been unable to return to my own body, that is exactly what I think happened. I'm dead, and my consciousness now has nowhere to go."

"You're not very bright, are you?" Valkyrie said.

"Not as bright as I thought I was, no. I taught myself to speak, though, which hasn't been easy, and although I mangle a few words every now and then I take small victories where I can."

"Speaking of mangling," Skulduggery said, "this trail of half-eaten bodies you've been leaving behind..."

"Ah," Amios said, his features contorting in what Valkyrie assumed was a wince, "yes. That. It seems the longer I inhabit this creature, the more it seeks to re-establish itself as the dominant personality in this pseudo-relationship. It has its urges, and I seem to be faltering in my resistance to them."

Valkyrie nodded. "So you're killing people."

"Sadly, yes."

"Butchering and then eating them."

"And feeling really guilty about it, I must say."

"And yet you haven't turned yourself in to the Sanctuary."

"I was going to," Amios said quickly. "I fully intended to. Once I realised that murder was on the cards, I decided that I could no longer hide away in the shadows. Killing the first person was the absolute final straw for me. Killing the second person was irrefutable proof that this wasn't a one-off event. The third person I killed and ate opened my eyes to the fact that I now had a serious problem that must be dealt with. From there, my determination to find a workable, liveable solution only grew stronger."

"I admire your resolve," Skulduggery responded, "although I can't help but notice that you're still killing people."

"I am, yes," said Amios.

"And eating them."

"Eating parts of them, yes."

"And though you might intend to stop—"

"I definitely intend to stop."

"—the fact remains that you have not stopped, and, even as I'm talking, you've taken another bite."

"Sorry," mumbled Amios, his mouth full. "Corpses go off surprisingly quickly."

"Mister Adroit," said Valkyrie, "we're obviously here to take you in. Hopefully, the experts at the Sanctuary will be able to find a way to help you, but this, this whole killing-and-eating-people thing, it has to stop."

Amios finished chewing. He swallowed, and nodded. "Yes. You're absolutely right. When would be a good time for me to turn myself in?"

"You don't have to. We can arrest you right now and get you the help you need."

Amios hesitated. "Now?"

"It's for the best."

"Now, though?"

"We may as well. We're here; you're here. We have special chains in the car that should be able to hold you. If we arrest you now, you won't have to be in a position to hurt anyone else."

"That does, in theory, make sense," said Amios, then shook his head. "I'm dreadfully sorry, but I don't think that arrangement is going to work. Even now, at this moment, I can feel the creature's impulses strengthening. It understands, you see, that incarceration is imminent. I seem to be getting quite angry about it."

"There's no need for anger," Skulduggery said.

"Oh, I think the creature might disagree with you there," Amios responded, shaking his head again, and growling.

Valkyrie hesitated. "Mister Adroit?"

Skulduggery took a step forward, and Amios lashed out, catching him full in the chest and flinging him off his feet.

Valkyrie backed away, her hands up. "Now, just hold on a second," she said. "You don't want to hurt me, Mister Adroit. I know you don't. You don't want to hurt anyone, do you?"

Amios snarled.

He swiped at her, and she dodged, stumbled, ran. She sprinted down a side street and Amios came after her, claws clicking right beside her ear. Valkyrie grabbed a fistful of shadows and hurled them. They broke against his skin, and the back of his hand found the side of her head and she went flying, a rag doll tossed from a baby's pram.

She fell backwards through an empty doorway, tumbling into the darkness of a burnt-out warehouse. She picked herself up, her skull ringing, her knees shaking. He came through the doorway after her and she threw a fireball into his face. He recoiled, and Valkyrie snapped her palms against the space between them. The air rippled, and he staggered.

Fire, though conjured with magic, was still fire, and a wall of air, though propelled by magic, was still a wall of air. Necromancy, though, her strongest weapon, was pure magic, and that was the kind of stuff the Shalgoth Reth drank in. So her strongest weapon was pretty much useless.

Amios thundered behind her as she ran. She didn't look back, couldn't, had to keep her eyes on the path ahead. She dropped and slid beneath a collapsed beam and was up and running again as Amios smashed into it, getting tangled in the fallen architecture.

There was a ramp of debris, and Valkyrie took it, climbing to the floor above by grabbing bits of wood and girders and metal pipes and cables. If any one of the things she grabbed had come loose, she would have fallen into the monster's arms as it followed her, snapping and snarling.

The ramp cracked behind her as she reached the top, the whole thing collapsing under Amios's weight, but he dug his claws into the blackened floorboards and sprang up after her.

Valkyrie tripped in the dark and stumbled, and those claws of his swung into her and took her off her feet. She hit something and flipped, and her shoulder crunched when she landed. She rolled to her feet on pure instinct, wheezing for breath, and Amios took hold of her coat and tossed her through the darkness. A pillar smacked into her and Valkyrie fell, unable to even wheeze any more. Blinking, she watched the Shalgoth Reth close in.

"If I had a throat to clear," Skulduggery said from the shadows, "I'd clear it now."

Amios stopped and growled and looked round, and now Valkyrie could see Skulduggery standing there, holding the biggest rifle she'd ever seen across one shoulder. She blinked as she tried to breathe, not quite believing what she was looking at. He was being all cool with a rifle that he had obviously gone back to the car to get. He had left her to possibly die while he went and fetched a bigger gun.

The monster roared at Skulduggery with untold rage, and Valkyrie knew how it felt.

Skulduggery, for his part, merely took the gun off his shoulder, raised the sight to his eye socket and said, "Amios, if you can hear me, I really would advise you to calm down."

Amios went to run at him, and Skulduggery fired. Amios spun and staggered, but didn't fall.

Skulduggery chambered another round as casually as brushing lint from his lapel. "Seriously," he said, "I've got plenty of bullets and plenty of time. If you don't behave, I'll be forced to do something I'll regret."

Crossing his massive arms in front of his head, Amios charged, and

Skulduggery fired twice before Amios crashed into him. The rifle went flying, and the monster slammed Skulduggery into the wall, then grabbed his leg and swung him into the closest pillar. Amios swung again and again, and Skulduggery bounced off walls and broke wooden beams, and then he was flung towards Valkyrie, sailing over her head. She kept her eyes on Amios as Skulduggery landed and went rolling away behind her.

Blood leaking from his arms and chest, Amios filled the building with his roar. Taking as deep a breath as she was able, Valkyrie grabbed Skulduggery, and they ran on, squeezing through gaps too small for the creature to follow. Staying low and staying quiet, they manoeuvred to the opposite side of the warehouse and ducked down. A minute passed.

"You're mad at me for some reason," Skulduggery whispered.

Valkyrie ignored him, kept watching for Amios.

"If you're mad at me because we've walked into a dangerous situation without adequate backup," he continued, "then may I point out that we've walked into far worse? I'm not sure what marks this occasion out as special, other than the fact that I've lost my hat. Are you mad because I've lost my hat? Is that it? Do you feel somehow responsible? Valkyrie, I assure you, while you may be at least *partially* responsible for the loss of my headwear, I do not actually blame you. Any blame is reserved solely for Amios Adroit. Do you hear me, Valkyrie? I forgive you."

She turned to him and glared. "You went back to the car to get that rifle."

He cocked his head. "That's why you're mad at me? It's got nothing to do with my hat?"

"You left me alone with a Shalgoth Reth while you went and got a gun that didn't even work!"

"The gun did work. Firing bullets is exactly what a gun is designed to do."

"But it didn't stop him, did it? He's still hunting us, isn't he?"

Skulduggery glanced at his pocket watch, and then put it away. "Probably not, actually."

She narrowed her eyes. "What do you mean?"

"That was a hunting rifle, Valkyrie. Do you think I drive everywhere with a hunting rifle in the back of my car?"

"Yes."

"Oh. Well, I don't. We've been on the trail of a monster, so I brought along a gun that would stop one."

"But it didn't stop one. That's my point."

"Ah," Skulduggery said, "you think I meant to kill the creature. Not so. Those bullets were coated with a special tranquilliser of my own design. A dart wouldn't have pierced its skin, so I needed something bigger."

"So Amios is unconscious?"

"He's probably unconscious, yes."

"How probably?"

"He's very probably unconscious," Skulduggery said, and straightened up. "Come on. Let's go and see if I'm right."

Amios Adroit opened his bleary monster eyes and blinked. "What's happening?" he asked.

Skulduggery clicked shut the last of the padlocks, securing the chains in place, and hunkered down in front of him.

"You attacked us," he said. "You tried to kill us. You destroyed my hat. I shot you, tranquillised you, and now we have secured you with chains, but that is of little comfort to my hat, which remains destroyed."

"Oh, dear," said Amios. "I'm dreadfully sorry."

"It was a very nice hat."

"Will you stop talking about your bloody hat?" Valkyrie said, stepping into

Amios's view. "Amios, we're waiting on a Teleporter to take you to the Sanctuary where, hopefully, someone will be able to help you."

"Thank you," said Amios. "Thank you very much. I am so incredibly sorry for attacking you. It is as I feared: I am increasingly losing control over this body." He sniffled. "You may have to put me down like a rabid dog."

Skulduggery tilted his head. "A rabbit-dog?"

"Rabid."

"You're saying rabbit."

"I'm saying rabid."

"Rabbit, yes."

"Rabid with a d."

"That's drabbit," Skulduggery said. "That's not even a word."

Amios frowned. "You're joking with me, aren't you?"

"I am," said Skulduggery. "We're not going to put you down, Amios, whether it be like a rabid dog or a rabbit-dog. We're going to help you because helping people is what we do."

"Thank you," said Amios.

"Sometimes."

"Thank you very much."

"If we haven't already killed them."

The Teleporter arrived a little before dawn and took Amios to the Sanctuary, and Skulduggery drove Valkyrie back to Haggard. They didn't speak until the Bentley pulled up beside the pier. The tide was in.

"You're still mad at me," Skulduggery said.

"I could have been killed," she responded, winding down the window to smell the sea air. "And I know why you did it. You left me alone with that monster to teach me a lesson, didn't you? You let me face an enemy that couldn't be defeated with magic because you wanted to demonstrate that I shouldn't be so confident that magic will get me out of whatever mess I find myself in."

"Interesting theory," Skulduggery conceded. "Of course, you wouldn't have been able to defeat the monster with your fighting skills, either."

"But doesn't that just reinforce your point about not becoming complacent about the skills I already have?"

Skulduggery tapped his chin. "It might at that. Do you really think that's what I was doing?"

"I think it might have been."

"And if that was, indeed, what I was actually doing, did it work?"

"No. Not really." She glowered. "Although I suppose I could start training with the new guy."

"This afternoon? After you've slept?"

Through gritted teeth: "I *suppose*."

"Then today is a good day," he said, and Valkyrie got out of the car.

She closed the door and leaned down to look in at Skulduggery through the window. "So? Did you plan this whole thing just to teach me a lesson or not?"

"I did not," he said.

"So you left me alone with a monster for no other reason than you wanted to go and fetch your rifle?"

"That's right."

"And you just... you just had *faith* that I wouldn't get myself killed?"

"I know you well enough by now to know that you wouldn't allow that to happen."

"Skulduggery, that's... That's *incredibly* irresponsible."

"Isn't it?" he said happily, and drove off.

In 2011 Derek ran a competition for German fans to come up with a new character who would feature in a one-off Skulduggery short story. The response was staggering, making it especially difficult to pick a winner – however, there was something special about Myosotis Terra that made her stand out from the rest.

Here is how Alena Metz described her character's abilities:

"… Her magical quality is more of a curse than a gift. The ability to make everyone forget her immediately after meeting her makes her feel very lonely. However, it is a very useful gift for spies and thieves, and at least it helps her to earn her bread and butter. People will only be able to remember Myosotis if they have got an item which belongs to her or if they get the chance to touch her. However, dementia sufferers are able to remember her perfectly."

MYOSOTIS TERRA

"Caves," Valkyrie Cain muttered. "I hate caves."

She reached the bottom of the stone steps, stepping into the light cast by the flame in Skulduggery Pleasant's hand.

"This isn't a cave," he told her. "At least, not a natural one. This has been carved out of the rock. Man-made. From what I can gather, we're about to enter a series of interlocking caverns that could stretch on for as much as twelve miles. Quite impressive when you think about it."

"And do I have to think about it?"

"Well, no, not really..."

"Good," she said. "It's freezing down here. Far too cold to be thinking about things."

She clicked her fingers, summoning her own flame, and started walking through the darkness. "So we're here on a rescue mission?"

He sighed as he walked after her. "Yes."

"What was that? What was that sigh? Why are you sighing?"

They walked side by side. "Do you remember who we're here to rescue?" Skulduggery asked.

"Yes," she said. "Wait. No. I mean, I do, it's on the tip of my tongue, but I can't... I just can't..."

"We're here to rescue Myosotis Terra."

She shook her head. "No, we're not. That's not the name. I'll know the name when I hear it, but that's not it. I've never heard that name before."

"That's not strictly true. She's actually a friend of yours."

"Nope. I think I'd know if I had a friend called Myo-Something Whatsit."

"Myosotis Terra. And you wouldn't know, actually. Or to be more precise, you wouldn't remember."

"You've lost me."

"I'm used to it."

Rock walls appeared in the gloom around them, signalling the narrowing of the cavern. They headed for a gap and Skulduggery went first, squeezing through.

"There is a sorcerer named Myosotis," he said, "from Germany. You first met her a few months ago, and got along very well, I have to say. You both get quite annoying when you talk, but again, I'm used to *that*, too. Myosotis is, amongst other things, a spy. What makes her so very good at her job is the fact that once she moves out of sight, you forget all about her. The human mind can't retain any information concerning Myosotis at all. We've actually had this conversation eleven times over the past few hours. You always have the same reaction."

"Bull."

"That's the one."

"You're serious?"

"Quite serious."

They emerged on the other side. Torches hung in rusted brackets on the walls, and they followed the flickering trail of light through the darkness.

"Her power doesn't work on me because of my fabulous mind – and the fact that I have no physical brain," Skulduggery continued. "And if she could turn her power off, I'm sure she would."

"You're sure who would?"

"Myosotis."

Valkyrie frowned. "Who?"

"Ah," Skulduggery said. "You're forgetting about her already."

"That's amazing," Valkyrie said. "Forgetting about who?"

"The spy, the girl who's been taken captive."

"Right," Valkyrie said, "the rescue mission. Gotcha. Who has taken her?"

"The inhabitants of this place. It was once a prison of sorts, hundreds of years ago. Now it's a refuge for sorcerers who can't bear to live on the surface. The people down here are... damaged. Some are quite dangerous."

"And what was..."

"Myosotis."

"And what was Myosotis doing down here?"

"The Sanctuary in Berlin sent her over to investigate the disappearance of one of their own. He was last seen around these parts, so the natural assumption would be that he found his way down here. And disappeared."

Valkyrie nodded. "And we're here to rescue him."

"No, we're here to rescue Myosotis, the operative sent to rescue him. If we happen to rescue him along the way, it's a bonus. But she is our main priority."

"Who is?"

"Oh dear God," Skulduggery muttered. "This is astonishingly aggravating."

He froze and she stopped, splayed her hand, felt the air move against her skin, and then she heard something, a whisper from behind.

They spun, but there was a rush of dark figures and Skulduggery went down in a tangle of arms and legs. Someone hit Valkyrie and she stumbled, couldn't do anything to stop the boot that smashed into her. She went back, rolling on the hard ground. Rough hands grabbed her, hauled her up. There was a crowd around Skulduggery, lashing in kicks, throwing down punches. Valkyrie's arms twisted and she cried out, feeling them twist almost to the point of breaking.

The crowd stopped kicking Skulduggery. They stepped away, and through the gaps she saw him, on the ground and not moving. All eyes turned to her.

They were dirty. Filthy. Unshaven. They wore ragged clothes, worn thin. They were skinny, all of them. Sunken cheekbones, sunken eyes, eyes that glittered in reflected firelight.

"We're not here to fight you," Valkyrie said.

One of the men observed her for a moment before opening his mouth. "Doesn't matter," he said. "You come down, invade our home, and you expect us to just stand by and let you? You think we're not ready to do battle? You think we're weak?"

"No," she said, "I don't think that at all, but we're not your enemy—"

"We're not weak!" the man roared, and the others joined in. "We eat moss and mushrooms. We drink from stagnant pools. We survive."

All around her, mutterings. "We survive," over and over.

"We like new people," the man said, and everyone laughed. "Yes, we do. Too bad for you."

"Too bad," said one of the men holding her.

"You're tall," said the leader. "We like tall. Your clothes might fit us. Some of us. Enchanted, are they? Protected? They'll last. They'll last forever. But you. Tall. Strong. Pretty. You won't last as long."

Skulduggery moaned, and someone kicked him.

"The Skeleton Detective," said the leader, looking down at him. "We'll take him apart. Use his bones as weapons. He won't last, either. But we can't eat him." The leader looked back at her. "We *can* eat you."

There was a woman holding Valkyrie's left arm. Valkyrie pulled her in, smashed her forehead into the woman's face. She yanked her right arm free, reached for the shadows, but the air rippled and she flew back. More hands grabbed her. Someone started to hit her and she turned her head, eyes closed, mouth tightly shut. They dropped her and she latched on to a leg as others kicked. She held that leg and didn't let go, letting her clothes soak up most of the impacts. A bare foot came in, caught her on the side of the jaw and the strength left her arms. She collapsed, sounds growing dim, her vision darkening.

"She'll do," she heard the leader say. "We'll divide her up. We get half. The Beast gets half."

She heard someone laughing and she slipped downwards, away from it all, plummeting into unconsciousness.

They had managed to get a set of shackles to close tightly enough to secure Skulduggery's hands to the frame of old wood and hardened root. He hung there, arms above his head, feet tied below, in the centre of what could be considered the village. Small huts of stone and rock emanated outwards from a large campfire. The frame on which Skulduggery hung was on one side of the fire. The frame on which Valkyrie hung was on the other.

The villagers milled around, talking amongst themselves. She watched them through one half-open eye, feigning unconsciousness. Her jaw ached and her head throbbed. Some of the villagers were talking about who should get which item of clothing. Others were talking about how best to cook her.

Even if her own power hadn't been dimmed by the chain that bound her to the frame, she doubted she'd be able to do much. Everyone down here was a sorcerer of some description, be they Necromancer or some other Adept discipline. They couldn't have snuck up on someone like Skulduggery if they weren't using the air to hide their approach, so there had to be more than a few Elementals around, too.

A scuffle broke out amongst the villagers. There were curses and raised voices, and then a man stumbled through.

"Mine!" he roared. The crowd came after him and he spun, snarling, "She's mine!"

The crowd parted and the leader came forward. "We share our food, Josef."

Josef shook his head. "You're not in charge any more, Owain. I am. I'm leader. I say she's mine!"

"And what about the Beast?" Owain asked. "Do you cheat the Beast out of its meal, too?"

Josef hesitated. "Beast can eat," he said at last. "After I have fed!"

Owain narrowed his eyes. "You would anger the Beast?"

Josef faltered. "I... I need to feed... and I will! I am leader!"

Owain signalled, and a man walked up and handed him a heavy wooden club. "Then we battle. Battle for leadership. Like the old ways."

"Yes," Josef said, "like the old ways. Where is my weapon?"

"Bring Josef his weapon," Owain commanded. Another man moved through the crowd, and handed Josef a twig.

"Um..." Josef said.

Owain whacked the club into Josef's head, and Josef sprawled on to the ground.

"Cook him first," Owain said. "Save her for later."

There were protests from the crowd.

"But Josef's scrawny!" cried a woman. "Not enough to go around!"

Owain sighed. "Fine. Cook Josef," he said, then nodded to Valkyrie, "and we give the Beast one of her legs. Tonight, the Beast eats well."

The crowd cheered.

In the next few hours, they'd chopped up Josef and slow-roasted him over the fire. Valkyrie did her best not to look.

A shadow moved between the stone huts, steadily sneaking towards her. She closed both eyes, slowed down her breathing...

"Hello." Someone nudged her leg. "I know you're awake. You can stop pretending."

She thought about it for a moment, then opened her eyes and looked down at him. He was thin and filthy, with long matted hair and a wispy beard. He looked to be in his early twenties.

"What's your name?" he asked.

He looked wild, dishevelled, but otherwise harmless. "Valkyrie," she said. "Who are you?"

"I'm Baffle. How are you?"

"Not doing too well, to be honest."

He nodded, grabbed the frame and clambered up until they were at eye level. He stank of bad breath and body odour.

"I don't like eating people," he said.

"Maybe you shouldn't do it."

"Can't say no. It'd be a waste, wouldn't it? We kill you and cook and serve you – you'd want us to eat you, wouldn't you? Otherwise, what's the point?"

"Baffle, I really don't want to die. It's not fair. I never did anything to hurt any of you."

"Life isn't fair."

"You could help me."

"I could?"

"Sure. You just said you don't want to eat me, right? So you could help me, couldn't you?"

"I... I suppose."

"You'd have to be really sneaky about it."

He nodded. "That's true. If the others found out, they'd be very cross."

"So you'll do it?"

"If I do, will you be my friend?"

"Of course."

"Then, yes," he said, and smiled, "I'll help you." Then he threw his head back and started singing.

"Stop!" she hissed. "Shush!"

His eyes were closed, and he sang louder. It was 'Be My Baby', by The Ronettes. Her mum used to sing that to her all the time when she was a kid. She strained against the ropes.

"Hey! Shut up!"

Baffle stopped singing.

She glared at him. "What the hell do you think you're doing?"

"I'm... I'm helping."

"How is that helping?"

"It'll make you feel better. It might make you forget we're going to eat you."

"But you don't *want* to eat me! You want to let me go!"

He looked horrified. "No, I don't! Why would I do that?"

"Because we're *friends*, Baffle."

He shook his head. "I know friends. Friends don't shout at each other. Friends sing to each other to take their minds off bad things that are going to happen."

"Baffle!" someone shouted from inside a hut. "Are you singing to our dinner again?"

"No!" he called back.

"You better not be!"

"I'm not!"

He waited, but got no further response. Stifling a giggle, he turned back to Valkyrie. "Did I help?"

"Sure," she said, totally deflated. "You did great. You know another way you could help me? We're looking for someone. A girl. A woman. Her name is..." Valkyrie frowned. "OK, I'm not sure what her name is, but she's got... she's got...

she's got hair, I think, I imagine, though I don't know what colour, but... I imagine she has hair. Or she might be bald. Or she might be a he. Do you remember anyone like that arriving down here in the last few days?"

Baffle shook his head. "No one's been down for ages. Not since the man."

"What man? Did he have an accent? Did he have a German accent?"

"Don't know what that is. He talked funny, though."

"What happened to him?"

"The Beast ate him."

"Oh. Where is the Beast now?"

"Out there," Baffle said, waving at the darkness. "Waiting. Watching. We feed it what we can. Sometimes, Owain says we must feed it our friends and families." His voice turned sad. "The Beast ate my sister."

"I'm sorry to hear that."

"I was given a bit of her leg to cheer me up."

"Right..."

There was a sound, like a growl, low and threatening, that echoed up to them.

Valkyrie raised an eyebrow at Baffle. "That's the Beast?" she asked.

"Yes," he breathed. "It doesn't come this close to the village, not usually. Not unless it's very hungry." He looked worried. "We might not get to share you after all."

There was another shout from one of the huts. "Baffle!"

"What?" he yelled back.

"Stop talking to the food!"

"I wasn't!"

"Baffle!"

"Sorry," Baffle whispered to her. Sighing grumpily, he jumped down from the frame and trudged away.

"About time," said someone from the darkness. "I thought he'd never leave."

A girl stepped into the light. She looked to be around twenty and her blonde hair hung long and wavy. She was pretty, with green eyes behind her glasses. Smaller than Valkyrie, in good shape, wearing grey jeans and a silver-grey coat.

"Myosotis," Valkyrie said, the memory of the girl flooding back into her mind, bringing with it their friendship. "Love the coat."

"Isn't it gorgeous?" Myosotis responded. "I got it a few weeks ago from a little shop in Langenfeld. It's a bit dirty now, of course, but I suppose that's what happens when you're running around somewhere like this, searching for an idiot of a man."

"Ah," Valkyrie said. "That man. I'm pretty sure he's dead."

Myosotis frowned. "So I've been searching mile after mile of dark caverns for him, and he doesn't even have the common courtesy to stay alive until I find him? That *is* irritating."

"So what are you guys doing here?"

Valkyrie hesitated. "We're here to rescue you."

"Really?"

"Really."

Myosotis nodded. "And how's that going for you?"

"I have to admit, it could be going better."

"I would agree with you. It's the thought that counts, though, isn't that what they say?"

"It is."

"In which case, thank you for coming to rescue me."

"You're welcome," said Valkyrie. "Can you get me out of these shackles now?"

"What are friends for?" Myosotis asked, then clambered up the frame, took a lock pick from her sleeve and set to work on the shackles. After a moment, she paused.

Valkyrie raised an eyebrow. "What?"

"Nothing," Myosotis said. "It's just... I'm not used to having a friend. It's a little odd, you know?"

"Yeah. You could probably work a little faster on the shackles."

"Shut up, I'm being sincere and vulnerable."

"Can't you be those things *and* work a little faster?"

"The problem with people forgetting you when you're gone is that nobody actually cares if you don't come back."

Valkyrie regarded her as the lock picks scratched and scraped. "Sounds lonely."

"It can be," Myosotis said. "But this is the life I chose. Mystery and intrigue and anonymity. There are things one must sacrifice in order to be a good spy."

"You could give it up, you know. Become a regular operative."

Myosotis smiled, her thin lips rising. "My Sanctuary values my expertise too much to allow that. But do not feel sorry for me. I never do." The shackles clicked open. "There. My rescuer is freed."

Valkyrie's magic washed over her as they jumped down from the frame. Myosotis handed her a bracelet. "Wear this, it's one of mine. So long as you keep it close to your skin, you won't forget me."

"I'm honoured."

"You should be."

"Though it's a pretty cheap bracelet."

"I buy in bulk."

"I'm still honoured."

"You still should be."

Valkyrie's grin caught on her lips as a low growl reached them. It was close. It was far too close. "The Beast," she whispered. "It's behind me."

Myosotis nodded.

Valkyrie turned slowly, ready to click her fingers and summon a fireball, ready to grab the darkness and hurl spears of shadow. Instead, she frowned.

The Beast was two feet tall, with small arms and tiny hands. It was covered in fur, everywhere except its face, where two large eyes blinked above a small snout. It had little ears that twitched, and big feet.

"Uh," Valkyrie said. "That's it?"

"That's it," said Myosotis.

"Does it grow? Is it suddenly going to expand into a giant and devour us in one bite?"

"Nope," Myosotis said. "That's the size it stays."

"Does it have razor claws that are going to pop out, or huge teeth, or...?"

"Nope."

"Is it... I mean, is it really bad-tempered?"

"It's quite good-natured, actually."

"Then I don't understand. Why is it so terrible?"

"Who said it was terrible?"

"What do you mean? Everyone's terrified of it. From the moment we got here they've been talking about feeding the Beast, how the Beast must be fed, all that kind of stuff."

"And the Beast *must* be fed," Myosotis nodded. "Otherwise it'd go hungry. But they're not scared of it. They love it. Look at it – it's adorable."

Valkyrie had to admit, it was pretty cute. It kind of wobbled when it walked.

"I think they named it the Beast because they thought it was kind of funny," Myosotis continued. "It's their pet."

"And how exactly would that little thing eat us?"

"From what I can gather, it's going to just stand there, and then the people who are sneaking up behind us are going to cut our throats, chop us into bits, and feed us to it over the next week or so in very small chunks."

Valkyrie turned, and a dozen villagers froze mid-step. Baffle was the closest.

He looked embarrassed to have been caught out. "Ah," she said. "So this is where we fight."

She snapped both hands against the air and Baffle flew backwards, yelling as he crashed into his fellow villagers. She grabbed the shadows, brought them in low, knocking a big man off his feet before he could get to her. Fire flared in her hands and she lobbed it into the middle of the crowd, scattering them. She slammed her elbow into a woman's face and stomped on the knee of another man. They were everywhere, all around her, but unable to use their magic in case they hit one of their own. Valkyrie didn't have that problem.

She caught sight of Myosotis, taking on three at a time, but then more villagers were running in, joining the fight, and Myosotis was blocked from view.

Valkyrie knew there were too many of them. She knew this wasn't going to end well.

A beam of blue light flashed by her face and she jerked back. It hit the man behind her and he dropped instantly. Villagers were stumbling out of the way as one of them, a man in rags with crazy hair, swung his arms wildly, like he couldn't control the energy that was pouring from his fingertips. Valkyrie dived to the ground, and the blue beam swept over her, taking down half a dozen villagers in one go. Everyone was screaming at Crazy Hair to stop, but he looked terrified, like he'd forgotten how to turn off his power.

And then Myosotis was behind him, grabbing his arms, redirecting the beams into the crowd above Valkyrie's head. Villagers fell around her, unconscious before they hit the ground.

But then the beams sputtered and died, and Crazy Hair sagged, exhausted.

"Thanks for that," Myosotis said, and punched him. He did a little twirl and fell down.

Valkyrie scrambled up before the remaining villagers could grab her. She ran through the stone huts, Myosotis behind her, towards Skulduggery. A man crashed into her and she went down, rolled over, dropped an elbow into his face and hauled herself to her feet.

Skulduggery raised his head. "Oh, hello," he said. "I see you've found Myosotis."

"Thank you for saving me," Myosotis called as she ducked the swipe of a crude blade.

"Not a problem," Skulduggery answered happily. "So this is the exciting battle part, is it? I do so love these parts."

"You might have to stay up there just a little while longer," Valkyrie called, using the air to hurl three villagers off their feet.

A fist came in, crunched against her cheek and she stumbled against Skulduggery's legs.

"How long?" he asked.

She kicked out, brought her elbow to the hinge of the villager's jaw. "Just another few moments."

"I feel I have to ask," Skulduggery said as a woman with earrings made from other people's ears brought Valkyrie down, "do you have anything resembling an actual plan here, or are you making it up as you go along?"

"We have a plan," Myosotis said after a headbutt. "But we're also making most of it up."

"Best of both worlds," Valkyrie grunted, shoving the woman off her. She got up, turned, something swung into her face and the world exploded with light. She was aware of her body falling backwards, but couldn't feel the impact as she hit the ground. She was barely able to crack open one eye, but when she did she saw Owain standing above her, holding that club.

"You think you can invade our home?" he snarled. "Attack my people?"

"Owain," Skulduggery said, "we're not here to invade. We came looking for a friend—"

"Quiet!" Owain roared. He looked around. He was the only villager left standing. "This is what you've done. We are a peaceful village, but you come and ruin it all."

Valkyrie heard the scepticism in Skulduggery's voice. "No offence, Owain, but you're a village of cannibals. That's not, strictly speaking, peaceful."

"We will pull you apart, skeleton," Owain sneered. He looked down at Valkyrie. "And you," he said, "are dinner."

Owain raised the club in both hands, ready to bring it down on Valkyrie's head, and then a voice said from behind, "Hey! Forget about me?"

He turned and Myosotis hit him, slugged him right across the jaw and his knees wobbled. He swung wildly and she caught his arm and cracked his elbow. He howled in pain and dropped the club, but Myosotis grabbed it before it touched the ground and smashed it into the side of his head. Owain staggered and gurgled and fell down and didn't get up.

Myosotis helped Valkyrie to her feet, and then searched through Owain's clothes. She found the key to the shackles and freed Skulduggery. He jumped from the frame and looked around.

"You didn't leave any for me," he said.

"Sorry," Valkyrie said, before groaning in pain.

"You can kick him if you want," Myosotis said, nodding down at Owain.

"He's already unconscious," Skulduggery sulked. "It's not fun if they're already unconscious. Wait – what about the Beast? We've still got to fight that, don't we?"

"Uh," Valkyrie said, "no. And we're not calling it the Beast any more."

"We're naming it Fluffy," said Myosotis.

Skulduggery tilted his head. "You named the terrifying monster Fluffy?"

"It actually isn't a monster after all," said Valkyrie. "It's a cute little furry thing with big eyes. No fighting necessary."

Skulduggery looked at her. "So who do I get to punch?"

Valkyrie looked at Myosotis, who shrugged. "No one," Valkyrie said.

Skulduggery sighed. He picked up his hat and put it on, then walked over to Owain, whom he kicked. "Well," he said, straightening his tie, "it's better than nothing."

GOING ONCE, GOING TWICE

Valkyrie Cain – fifteen years old, dark-haired, dressed all in black – was sitting in the office with her feet up on the desk, reading a battered paperback, a good old-fashioned private-detective story, when the door opened and a nervous man with nervous eyes poked his head in the room.

"Um," he said.

Valkyrie looked up, and waited for him to continue.

"I'm looking for Skulduggery Pleasant," the nervous man said. "Is this his office?"

"He doesn't have an office," Valkyrie replied, and went back to reading her book. It was a good one. It was about two tough guys in Texas who were on the trail of a serial killer. The writer had a way with one-liners. Valkyrie appreciated that.

The nervous man cleared his throat. "This office isn't his?"

"Nope," said Valkyrie.

"Do you... do you know him?"

"The question isn't do I know Skulduggery Pleasant," Valkyrie said. "The question is, does Skulduggery Pleasant know me? And yes, he does. He thinks I'm awesome." She made a note of the page she was on, and put the book down as she took her feet off the desk. "It doesn't seem like you're going to go away, so I may as well ask what you want. Are you here to kill him?"

A look of horror washed over the nervous man's face. "Dear Lord, no. No! I would never!"

Valkyrie shrugged. "I didn't mean to offend you. Plenty of people want to kill Skulduggery. He's that type of person. I've known him for three years and I've wanted to kill him for at least half that time."

The nervous man stepped into the room. "Are you Valkyrie Cain?"

She smiled. "You've heard of me."

"I thought you'd be older."

"Well, I'm not. I'm the age I am. Who might you be?"

"My name is Whist Simple. Ghastly Bespoke said I'd be able to find the Skeleton Detective here."

"You're a friend of Ghastly's?"

"Kind of," said Whist. "Well, not really, but I spoke to him, and he directed me to this office. I assumed this is where Mr Pleasant conducted his business – but, if this isn't his office, then who owns it?"

"It belongs to a man," Valkyrie said, "whose life is in danger. We're helping him out. Why were you looking for Skulduggery?"

"I... I need someone to find my wife. She's been kidnapped."

"Oh. Wow. That's awful."

"I can pay, of course. Whatever it takes."

"Payment isn't the issue," Valkyrie responded. "We don't really, you know, take on outside cases. We work for the Sanctuary, mainly, or we just stumble into trouble and then, along the way, end up saving the world or something. That's generally how it works."

"But I've got nowhere else to turn."

"You should call the Sanctuary, and they'll assign your case to someone who takes care of this kind of thing."

"My wife isn't in Ireland, though. I believe she's been taken to America."

"Well, talk to the American Sanctuary."

"I can't go to them," said Whist. "I think they're in on it. Or one of their operatives is. A detective called Gumshoe Grady."

"That's a silly name."

"I know."

"So why did Gumshoe kidnap your wife?"

"A few hundred years ago, they courted. She ended the relationship, and he's never been able to forget her. I think he finally snapped."

"They *courted*?"

"That's... that's what they called it back then. Please, I'm sure he's dangerous. Once he realises she doesn't love him any more, I don't know what he'll do. Her life may be in danger. I think she's in Florida."

Valkyrie narrowed her eyes. "Where in Florida?"

"South of Orlando."

"Where exactly?"

"A place called Kissimmee."

"Is that near the theme parks? Is that near the Magic Kingdom and Universal Studios and, to a far lesser extent, the Epcot Centre?"

"I... I suppose so."

Valkyrie nodded. "We'll take the case."

"No, we won't," Skulduggery said from the corner.

Whist swung round, startled. "Detective Pleasant? Are you... are you invisible?"

Valkyrie smirked. "He's not invisible. He's hiding behind that chair."

The armchair was old and frayed, and sagged in the corner beside the door. A gloved hand emerged, and waved. "Hello," said Skulduggery.

Whist hesitated. "Why are you hiding?"

"I told you," Valkyrie said. "Someone wants to kill the guy who owns this office, and we're helping out. I'm the bait, so I've been sitting here for two days. Skulduggery's the trap, so he's been hiding behind that chair."

"For two days?"

"Yes."

"Mr Simple," Skulduggery said, "my colleague was right when she suggested you take your case to the American Sanctuary."

"Nonsense," said Valkyrie. "We'll do it, Whist. Can I call you Whist? What do you do, Whist?"

"You mean for a living?" Whist asked. "As a job? I'm an archaeologist, actually. I travel the world and get into, um, well, adventures. You might not think it to look at me, but they, heh, they call me the magical Indiana Jones..."

"Do they?" Valkyrie asked. "Really?"

Whist's smile faltered. "No."

"Why do you think your wife is in Kissimmee, Mr Simple?" Skulduggery asked.

"Oh, um, well, that was a bit of detective work I did all on my own," said Whist. "Her last credit-card transaction was at a motel there."

"So you think her kidnapper is using her own credit card to rent the room he's keeping her in?"

Whist frowned. "Um... yes?"

"What's her name?"

"Liana. Liana Lacuna."

"And why do you think she was kidnapped?"

"Because... because why else would she go?"

The door burst open and a crazy man with a sword burst in and Skulduggery stood up from behind the armchair and kicked the door and it slammed into the crazy man's face and he dropped to the floor, unconscious.

Whist stared.

Valkyrie was used to being around Skulduggery, so she often had to remind herself what it must be like for people seeing the tall skeleton in the exquisite suit for the very first time. But right now she didn't care. Right now only one thing mattered.

"The job's done," she said. "We can go to Florida now, can't we?"

Skulduggery adjusted the brim of his fedora so that it slanted over his left eye socket. "What is it with you and Disney World?"

"I've never been," said Valkyrie. "When I was a kid, my parents didn't really take holidays, but I used to go online and look at pictures of the Magic Kingdom and the castle, and I'd imagine myself going on all the rides..."

"Your boyfriend's a Teleporter. Get him to take you."

Valkyrie scowled. "Fletcher has a thing about queues. He won't line up for anything. And I don't want to go around on my own – that's just sad. Skulduggery, this is literally a childhood dream of mine. Please don't crush my childhood dream. It's the only one I have left."

He sighed, and looked down at Whist. "Mr Simple," he said, "apparently, we're going to Florida, so please tell us more about your missing wife."

An hour later, Skulduggery and Valkyrie were hiring a car in Orlando. They would have been there sooner, but Fletcher didn't pick up his phone for ages. When he finally transported them over, he started grumbling about how no one appreciated him for who he was, and everyone just called when they needed to get to places quickly. Valkyrie nodded along and waited for him to disappear.

She had ditched her black clothes and was wearing yellow shorts and a white T-shirt. The heat pressed in from all directions. Her sunglasses could barely take the glare from the sun. It was magnificent.

The car they hired wasn't as classy as the Bentley, but it was air-conditioned and roomy, and Valkyrie stretched out her legs as they drove along the wide highways of Orlando.

"Where do you want to go first?" she asked. "The Magic Kingdom or Universal? I say we go to the Magic Kingdom."

"We're going to the motel where Liana Lacuna last used her credit card," Skulduggery said.

"Absolutely," Valkyrie said. "We've got a job to do, and we're professionals. But, after that, we can go to the Magic Kingdom, right?"

"Who knows what the future may bring?"

"I do," she said. "I know what the future may bring. It brings Mickey Mouse ears and It's a Small World."

Skulduggery didn't say anything to that.

They got to the motel. Skulduggery's disguise was only good for half an hour at a time, so he stayed in the car while Valkyrie left the cool confines of the rental and braved the fourteen steps to the air-conditioned office.

A guy in his twenties came to the desk. He had a little beard and scrawny arms, and his name tag identified him as Greg. He didn't look like a Greg. He looked like a Spencer, or a Finn, or some indie-sounding name. "Hi there," he said. "How can I help?"

"I'm looking for this woman," Valkyrie told him, holding up a picture of Liana that Whist had given them. "I think she's staying here?"

Greg looked at the picture, then back at Valkyrie. "Is she your mom?"

"No," said Valkyrie, "I'm just looking for her. Do you recognise her?"

Greg smiled. "Where's that accent from? Scotland?"

"Ireland."

"I've always wanted to go to Ireland. My great-grandmother was from there. I heard it's really green."

"It has green parts, yes."

"Do you have electricity in Ireland?"

Valkyrie made sure to smile. "I'm sorry?"

"Do you have electricity?"

"We do."

"That's cool. Well done."

"Thank you. This woman, Greg. Have you seen her?"

He laughed. "Why?"

"Because I'm looking for her."

"You playing detective, are you?"

"I'm not playing."

This made him laugh even louder. "Aw, that is so cute!"

Valkyrie bristled. She wasn't used to this. She wasn't used to disrespect. Usually, when she asked a question, people answered.

"Is it the outfit?" she asked.

"Say what?" Greg responded, still grinning.

"The outfit," she said. "Is it the fact that I'm wearing yellow shorts and a T-shirt? Is that why you're failing to take me seriously? Usually, I'm dressed all in black. Usually, I look a lot more intimidating."

"I'm sure you do," said Greg.

Her phone rang. It was Skulduggery. "You're taking a long time," he said. "Do you need help?"

"No," Valkyrie answered. "I'm fine."

"I can see you through the window. You look agitated."

Greg was still grinning at her. She forced a smile. "I'm not agitated. I'm just building a rapport with the motel clerk. These things take time."

Greg sniggered.

"Don't hit him," Skulduggery said.

Valkyrie took a step away from the desk, to make sure Greg couldn't hear what Skulduggery was saying. "I'm not going to."

"Stay calm."

"I'm very calm."

"He's a civilian. And a mortal. He doesn't know that you've saved the world and that he owes you his life. Just stay calm, be polite, and find out which room Liana is staying in. But hurry up. There's nothing to do out here."

Valkyrie frowned. "You've been sitting in the car for three minutes."

"It's a very boring car."

"You once told me that ninety-five per cent of detective work is waiting around."

"Which is why we tend to operate in the five per cent where things actually happen. I like kicking down doors, and occasionally people if they really, really deserve it. Hello."

"What?"

"I'm not talking to you. There's a bee outside the car. It's tapping at the window."

"Uh..."

"I think I'll let it in."

"What? No, don't do that. I don't want a bee in the car when I come back."

"Too late. It's flying around. Hello, bee. It's sitting on the steering wheel. Now it's bouncing lightly against the windscreen."

"This is fascinating stuff."

"Oh."

"Oh what?"

"It flew through my eye socket. It's in my skull. It's flying around inside my head."

Valkyrie sagged. "Why are you like this?"

"What was that? I didn't hear. The buzzing is *very* loud right now."

"I'm going to hang up. Please make sure the bee is out of the car when I return." She put her phone away, stepped back to the desk, and showed Greg the picture again. "Have you seen this woman?"

Greg put both hands flat on the desk – somehow managing to make that a patronising gesture – and said, "Listen, what's all this about, huh? Just level with me."

"I'm looking for this woman," said Valkyrie. "I think she's staying here. Her life may be in danger."

"That's a very dramatic thing to say."

"It's a very dramatic world, Greg."

"I used to say dramatic things when I was a teenager. It got me the attention I was so desperately craving."

"I'm not craving attention, Greg. I'm searching for this lady."

"Where are your parents? Was that your dad you were just talking to?"

"Most definitely not."

"Where are they, huh? Who's taking care of you?"

"Greg, I swear to God, answer my question or I will smack you."

Greg recoiled. "There's no need for that."

"Do you recognise the woman in this picture? Have you seen her? Have any of your staff seen her, maybe when they were bringing fresh towels or something?"

"Yes," he said, clearly getting irritated. "She checked in a few days ago."

Valkyrie frowned. "She checked in? Was there anyone with her?"

"She was by herself, from what I could see."

"Did she seem to be here against her will?"

Greg bristled. "This motel isn't that bad."

"How did she seem when she checked in, Greg?"

"She seemed fine," he answered. "It was all normal. Nothing stood out, OK?"

"Is she still here? What room is she in?"

"I can't give you that information."

"Can't you? You won't know until you try. Is that where it's written down? In that ledger there?"

Greg picked up a thick black ledger and placed it on a shelf behind him. "No," he said.

"You're a bad liar, Greg."

"You should leave."

"Fine."

Valkyrie went to the door, glancing back at Greg who was eyeing her suspiciously. She stepped outside. It was like stepping into soup – really, really hot soup. She glanced back again as the door began to close, watching Greg head into the room behind the reception desk.

She reached her hand out, connected with the stifling air, found the links between the spaces, and the black ledger flew off the shelf towards her. She caught it and started walking, the door finally shutting behind her.

She found Liana's mortal name, the name all her credit cards were under, and walked over to the assigned room. She waved to Skulduggery and he got out of the car. He tapped his collarbones and his façade flowed over his skull. The face he wore was a pale one with a beard.

Valkyrie knocked, and, when no one answered, Skulduggery started picking the lock. He was buzzing.

"Is that bee still in your head?" Valkyrie asked.

"Not any more," he said. "It's flying around my ribs."

"Isn't that weird?"

"A little," he admitted.

The door opened, and they stepped in. Skulduggery deactivated his façade.

The motel room was small, with a double bed, neatly made up. They searched through Liana Lacuna's things, but didn't find anything of interest.

When they had finished, they stood in the centre of the room. Valkyrie's hands were on her hips. Skulduggery's arms were folded. The bee flew out of his right eye socket, and then flew back in through his left.

The door swung open slowly, and they turned to see a shabby man in a shabby suit standing there. He raised an eyebrow at Skulduggery, but didn't freak out. Sorcerer.

"You're Skulduggery Pleasant," the shabby man said. "Which makes you Valkyrie Cain. It's very good to meet you both. My name's Gumshoe, Gumshoe Grady. I'm a detective for the Sanctuary here. Thanks for saving the world, by the way."

"Finally," Valkyrie said. "Someone says what we're all thinking."

Gumshoe walked in and closed the door behind him. "You're a little far from your regular stomping ground, aren't you?"

"We're looking for Liana Lacuna," Skulduggery said.

Gumshoe put his hands in his pockets. "Uh-huh. Yeah, I should've figured. Why are you after Liana?"

"Because you kidnapped her."

Gumshoe frowned, and scratched the stubble on his cheek. "I did?"

"Apparently."

"Huh. That's news to me. I mean, I guess it could have happened. I'm always forgetting stuff, like where I put my keys, whether I paid this bill or that bill, that kinda thing... But I don't know if I've ever forgotten kidnapping someone. You'd think that'd be something that'd stick in your head, you know?"

"So you're saying you didn't kidnap her?"

"That's what I'm saying."

"But you do know her?"

"Yeah, I know her. She came to me a few weeks ago, looking for help. Then she disappeared. I tracked her here. Same as you, I expect."

"What did she need help with?"

"A rare and powerful artefact was stolen from her, she said, and she was looking to get it back. She had a feeling it might be going up for auction right here."

"What's the item?" Valkyrie asked.

"Doesn't matter," Gumshoe said. "It was a lie. All of it. My black market contacts had no idea what I was talking about, so I did a little digging, and found out that the artefact is safely tucked away in a private collection somewhere in Europe – where it's been for the last fifty years."

"So what did Liana get out of all this?"

"I really don't know. As you can see by her choice of accommodation, she barely had two nickels to rub together, so why she wasted her money coming to Florida and hiring me, I can't begin to guess."

"She paid you?" Skulduggery asked.

"Half upfront," said Gumshoe. "I'm not overly optimistic that I'll ever see the rest."

Skulduggery tilted his head. "Did you keep Miss Lacuna updated on your progress?"

"She insisted on it."

"Did you tell her the names of your contacts?"

"Clients don't need to know those things."

"Could she have found out? Maybe glanced at your notes?"

Gumshoe frowned. "I guess she could have, at that."

Skulduggery turned to Valkyrie. "Have you figured it out yet?"

"What?"

"Have you figured out what Liana was up to?"

"Oh," said Valkyrie. "No, sorry. I stopped listening. I was thinking about Big Thunder Mountain. You carry on, though. You two look like you're having fun."

"She used me," Gumshoe said slowly.

Valkyrie smiled. "Who used you?"

"Liana," he growled. "She used me to get the names of people who'd be in a position to hold an auction for a rare and powerful artefact."

"I think it's time we called Whist," Skulduggery said to Valkyrie.

She took out her phone, dialled and put it on loudspeaker. "Whist," she said when he answered, "we found Gumshoe Grady."

"You got him!" Whist exclaimed. "Well done! Did he put up a fight? Oh, I hope he did! I hope you taught him a lesson! I hope he's bruised and battered and crying like a little baby!"

"Actually," Valkyrie said, "he's standing beside us right now."

"Hi there," said Gumshoe.

There was silence on the other end. Then, "Hello."

"Gumshoe claims that he didn't kidnap Liana," Skulduggery said. "He says she went to him, looking for help."

"I see," said Whist. "But, and I don't mean to sound rude here – I'm sure Mr Grady is a very nice man – isn't that just what a kidnapper would say?"

"We have good reason to believe him," Skulduggery responded. "Mr Simple, you're an archaeologist, yes? You travel the world in search of historical objects?"

"Yes. My main area of expertise is finding magical artefacts."

"And have any of these magical artefacts gone missing recently? Mr Simple? Hello?"

"Why, um, why do you ask?"

"Shall I take that as a yes?"

Whist sighed. "A few months ago, I found a stone tablet on a dig in West Asia. Inscribed on it was a language of magic I'd never seen before, and, below it, a language I recognised, but only barely. I think both texts are the exact same passage."

"You found a Rosetta stone," Skulduggery murmured.

Valkyrie held up her hand. "I don't know what that is."

"In this case, it's a means to translate a language of magic that's so ancient we haven't, as yet, been able to understand it," Skulduggery told her. "This artefact is the starting point. This is where we can start to decipher the code."

"OK," Valkyrie said. "Cool. So what?"

"Those old languages are dangerous," said Gumshoe. "If the wrong person cracks the code, the world could be put at risk."

"I'm sorry," Whist said, "but what does my missing tablet have to do with my missing wife?"

"She must have taken it," said Gumshoe. "Then she left Ireland, thinking she could come here and sell it without any alarms being raised. She used me to find the people who could set up such an auction."

"She's going to sell it?" Whist said, startled.

"Unless we stop her."

"I'm coming over," said Whist. "I'm catching the next flight!"

"It might be best if you stay in Ireland," Skulduggery said. "We'll find out where and when the auction is being held and we'll keep you in the loop, but things might get dangerous."

"I'm an archaeologist," Whist said. "Danger is what I do."

He hung up.

Gumshoe took out his own phone. "I'll see if I can find out if there are any auctions coming up. Shouldn't be too difficult."

He dialled a number and stepped out of the room.

"OK," Valkyrie said, "I'm not entirely sure what's going on because I wasn't paying attention, but let me know if I've got this part straight. We're waiting for information on something. Which means we're not doing anything right now. Which means that if we hurry, we can still make the Illuminations in the Magic Kingdom."

"Let's just wait and see if Gumshoe comes up with anything," Skulduggery said.

"But that'll take ages," she said. "Does he strike you as someone who works fast?"

"Not particularly."

"We might be waiting all night."

Gumshoe came back in. "Found it," he said.

Valkyrie grumbled.

"Everyone's talking about it," he continued. "A major auction tomorrow night. The tablet's going up for sale. People are flying in from all over the country – all over the world."

"Well, OK then," Valkyrie said, clapping her hands together. "You call your buddies at the Sanctuary, get a squad of Cleavers ready to arrest everyone, and our work here is done."

Gumshoe made a face. "I don't think that's a good idea."

Valkyrie sagged. "Why not?"

"The more people know about it, the higher the chance there'll be a leak. The only way to be sure that the auction goes ahead is if it stays between the three of us."

"I agree," said Skulduggery.

"Do I get a vote?" Valkyrie asked, narrowing her eyes. "Do I?"

"Of course."

"Then I vote we tell the Sanctuary."

"Noted. But that's still two against one."

Valkyrie glowered. "Stupid maths. So what do we do until then, eh? I suppose we've got to stick around in case Liana Lacuna comes back to her motel room, do we? So we've got to stay in this horrible motel overnight?"

"Actually, yes," Skulduggery said. "That's a very good idea."

"Of course it's a good idea," she responded, a little harshly. "It's mine, isn't it?"

So they stayed at the motel for the rest of the night and most of the next day, and Valkyrie sulked the whole time.

Once night had fallen again, her mood lifted. Now they were doing something. She much preferred doing something to doing nothing. Doing nothing was boring. Doing nothing meant sitting in a motel room, looking out of the window and listening to a bee buzzing somewhere within Skulduggery.

But, once the sun went down, they got in the rental and followed Gumshoe's car to a well-kept estate with strangely unwelcoming lawns. When they left the cars and proceeded on foot, Valkyrie bent down to touch the grass. It was spiky and horrible.

"The grass is weird," she said.

Gumshoe and Skulduggery ignored her.

They continued on, breaking through a row of dark trees and emerging behind a brightly lit stage. Rows of seats were set up, and every single one of those seats was occupied.

"There," Gumshoe whispered, pointing. "Liana."

Liana Lacuna stood to one side. A pretty woman with short blonde hair, wearing a nice dress that wasn't exactly in fashion. She had nervous hands.

The low-key murmuring died down as a man in a suit came up to the podium.

"Ladies and gentlemen," he announced, "human and not-quite human, welcome to today's auction. You will be bidding on a singular item of singular purpose — a tablet that can unlock the most ancient of the ancient languages of magic. Undreamed-of power could be yours — if you're willing to pay."

Valkyrie couldn't see the auctioneer's face, but she could tell by his voice that he was smiling.

"Shall we begin at, say, one hundred million dollars?"

Liana's face brightened as hands went up.

"One fifty."

"Two."

"Three hundred."

Valkyrie watched the bidders bid, and started to get freaked out by how calm they all were. The dollar count rose, and kept rising, and, when it reached impossible levels of ridiculousness, people started holding up different things.

A guy at the back, a large man with a face like the side of a mountain, held up a glass sphere filled with swirling lights. "Three souls," he said.

Another sphere was raised, this time by a woman with chalk-white skin. "Five," she said.

A burly man held up a leather-bound book, and the elderly gentleman beside him said, "The only surviving copy of *The Fatalist's Grimoire*."

There were some gasps at that, and many envious, greedy glances.

"I have an idea," Skulduggery said quietly.

Valkyrie frowned. "A plan? You have a plan?"

"I have a plan, yes."

"Your plans are not good."

"What are you talking about? My plans are great."

"What's this one?"

"We're going to bluff."

She shook her head. "No."

"Bluffing might work."

"It will not work," she said. "It really won't and then we'll be killed."

"I've been killed before," he told her. "It's not that bad."

"That totally contradicts everything you've ever said on the subject. I vote no."

"If we allow the tablet to fall into the wrong hands," Gumshoe said, "terrible things could happen."

"*Could* happen?" Valkyrie pressed.

"Yes."

"Not *will* happen? *Could* happen? I can live with *could* happen. *Could* happen isn't all bad – it means *might not* happen. Skulduggery, let's leave. For all we know, the person who buys the tablet might not be evil or bad in any way. They might just really like tablets."

"My plan will work," Skulduggery said.

"Your plan isn't a plan."

"So no one will be expecting it."

Skulduggery crept forward before she could grab him, and Valkyrie groaned as he bounded onstage. Guns were drawn and hands lit up with fire and energy.

"Wait, wait," Skulduggery said, waving his arms, "let's not rush to judgement here. Let's all calm down. I realise what a shock this must be to you. You arrive here for a respectable night of bidding for a tablet that could make you into the most powerful sorcerer in the world – and here I come, the Skeleton Detective, to spoil all the fun."

No guns went off. No streams of energy were let loose.

Skulduggery gently pushed the auctioneer to one side and stood at the podium. He leaned on his elbows, surveying the crowd. "I'm not going to lie to you," he said, "but that's exactly why I'm here. However, I'm going to do you a big favour. I'm going to give you the chance to walk away. I understand why you're here. I understand why you want to bid and I don't blame you for it. You want power. Of course you do. Who doesn't? You want to crush your enemies, maybe take over the world or something hilariously old-fashioned like that.

Again, I get it. I'm not taking this personally. So pack up your things and grab your coat – the valet is waiting with your car."

Nobody moved.

Then someone at the back shouted. "Kill him!"

Skulduggery took off his hat, laid it on the podium. "I give you the chance to walk away and your first response is to shout *kill him*? Who said that? Who was it?"

Nobody stirred.

Skulduggery sighed. "You've all heard of me. You've all heard of the things I've done. Chances are, you know someone who I've defeated, or arrested, or at the very least punched. And here I am, standing before you, giving you the opportunity to run away. I don't give that chance to too many people."

A man with a stupid beard stood up. "We outnumber him," he announced loudly. "We can take him!"

"And who's going to lead this charge?" Skulduggery asked. "You? Really?"

The man with the beard hesitated, and faltered, and sat back down.

"Violence is not the answer," Skulduggery told the audience. "Not for you. For me, it usually *is* the answer, and I'm OK with that. But you, all of you, should leave before something nasty happens. Go on. Yes, that's it. Pick up your things. Walk away."

Valkyrie heard a low murmur spread through the crowd. She saw them glance at each other anxiously, waiting to see who'd be the first to move. The old man, the one with the large bodyguard and the book, grunted, and stood, and suddenly they were all doing it.

"It worked," she whispered. "It actually worked."

With Gumshoe following along behind, she joined Skulduggery onstage as he took a heavy chunk of stone, covered in strange markings, from the hands of the auctioneer.

"Thank you," Skulduggery said, "you can go now."

"But..." the auctioneer said. "But..." He looked like he might cry.

"Get outta here or I'll arrest you," said Gumshoe. "Go on. Scram."

He waved him away, and the auctioneer blinked, and then hurried off.

"See?" Skulduggery said to Valkyrie. "My plans are amazing. Everyone's gone and no one got hurt."

"Um," Valkyrie said, as Liana Lacuna stormed on to the stage, a gun in her hand.

"I can't believe you did that," she said. "This was my chance. This was my ticket to a better life!"

"The tablet isn't yours to sell," Skulduggery said.

"I was going to be rich!" Liana screamed. "Rich beyond imagining! I don't care about magic! I don't care about being a sorcerer! I was never really that good at it anyway! But I always dreamed about being rich... and now you've taken that away from me."

She extended her arm, her finger tightening on the trigger.

"Liana!"

Whist stepped out behind her. She whirled and Valkyrie made to run at her, but Skulduggery held her back.

"Liana," said Whist, walking forward slowly with his hands out, "please... please come home. I love you."

Tears ran down Liana's face. "Oh, Whist," she said. "After everything I've done?"

"After everything," he said. "I just want us to be happy again. I know you didn't mean those things you said. Those incredibly hurtful, detailed things... I love you and I know that you love me, and we can still be happy together."

Liana sobbed. "But... but they're going to throw me in prison!"

"No, they won't," said Whist, and looked at Skulduggery. "You're not going to imprison her, are you?"

"We are, actually," Skulduggery said.

"Really?"

"Technically, the tablet doesn't belong to either of you, and she was trying to sell it, so that's a crime."

"Oh."

"She probably won't get too long, though. A few years, then she'll be out."

"Do you hear that?" Whist said. "A few years, sweetheart. That's nothing. And I'll be waiting for you. I'll be counting down the days."

"Oh, Whist," said Liana, and the gun fell from her fingers as she collapsed in her husband's arms.

"It's OK, my darling," he said, stroking her hair. "I have you. I love you. And I know you love me."

"I do love you," she sobbed into his jacket. "It... it might not be an all-consuming love, but it's love nonetheless."

He nodded. "You probably didn't have to say that, my sweet. Our love is real and that's all that matters."

"It is real!" Liana cried. "Small, but real."

"Hush now. Stop talking."

She wept. He cradled. Valkyrie felt awkward.

Gumshoe took Liana away, and Whist went with them. Valkyrie stood with Skulduggery.

"What are we going to do with the tablet?" she asked. "I know of one collector in particular who'd be delighted to have it."

"I'm sure she would," Skulduggery said, "but, in the wrong hands, this tablet could spell disaster on a planet-wide scale. There are some languages best left untranslated, Valkyrie, and some secrets best kept hidden."

"So what do we do?"

"Florida is known for its alligator-infested swamps. I say we find the deepest swamp we can, and throw the tablet in."

"And then we go to Disney World?"

He sighed. "And then we go to Disney World."

He buzzed, and the bee flew out from behind his cheekbone, and flew away.

"Goodbye, George," Skulduggery said.

This story was written for Charlie Smith, who won a competition to create a new character to appear in *Mortal Coil*.

The character Charlie came up with was Geoffrey Scrutinous, and this is how Charlie described him in his competition entry:

"Wears khaki shirts (Indiana Jones style), short trousers and maroon socks with leather sandals. Lots of beads and chains, lots of rings on one hand. Has a small goatee and wild frizzy hair with piercing blue eyes. A frantic, disbelieving nature and is very erratic in both appearance and personality. He sorts out disturbances in the non-magical population. He has the ability to get you to agree with anything he says, without you realising it."

You'll have seen Geoffrey in *Mortal Coil*, of course. But as an added bonus, here's a little story all about him...

Thanks, Charlie!

THE WONDERFUL ADVENTURES OF GEOFFREY SCRUTINOUS

The cop frowned. "But there's a dead body in there. I have to... I can't let anyone into the house. It's my job to preserve the scene for the forensics people, to investigate and... and solve the crime..."

Geoffrey Scrutinous nodded. "And you will do a wonderful job of preserving and investigating, I know you will. But for the moment, you want to delay all this hustle and bustle."

"I do?"

Scrutinous nodded. "Oh, yes, very much so. I have some friends coming, they're special investigators, and they have to look around a bit first."

"Who are they?" asked the cop.

"Just some friends. A tall man and a teenage girl. They're very good at this kind of thing."

"I'm not sure I should be allowing this."

Scrutinous smiled, maintained eye contact and poured more magic into his words. "It's perfectly fine. You know it is. You can feel it, that reassuring feeling that everything is going to be fine. You can feel it, can't you?"

"I... I suppose... They're good, then?"

"Very good."

"You think they'll be able to crack the case?"

"If anyone can, they can."

The cop nodded. "Good. I was hoping I wouldn't have to. I have no idea how someone could be run over by a train in their own living room."

Scrutinous patted the cop's shoulder. "Don't you worry," he said. "They handle this kind of thing all the time."

"I have to confess," Skulduggery Pleasant said as he took his hat off in the dead man's living room, "I have no idea what's going on here at all."

Valkyrie Cain nodded up to the corner of the room. "What's that bit?"

"It's his head," said Skulduggery. "You can see the rest of it there, hidden behind the curtain."

"Oh, yeah. That's disgusting."

"Nobody ever said being hit by a train was a neat way to die."

Valkyrie turned to Scrutinous. "And you're sure that's what they said?"

"Oh, yes," Scrutinous answered. "Neighbours reported hearing an old-fashioned train. Like a steam engine, they said, with the 'choo choo' and everything. The walls of every house on the street rattled as it passed."

Skulduggery murmured something to himself. The living room was small and tidy, the furniture in place, the TV still on with the sound muted. It was three o'clock in the morning and the lamps gave the place a gentle, warm light. It would have been a perfectly good room in which to spend an evening were it not for the man who had been splattered across every imaginable surface.

"Well," Skulduggery said, "purely to get this out of the way, I'll just go ahead and say it. There does not seem to be any sign of a railway track on the carpet or, indeed, a train hiding behind the sofa. And I don't think one could have fitted through the door."

"Maybe it was a ghost train," Valkyrie said. "Do ghost trains exist?"

"I've seen two," Scrutinous said. "But I've never heard of a ghost train that could run over anything living. A ghost train would be able to run over a ghost, not a man."

"And yet something big killed him," Skulduggery said. "And it was powerful and fast-moving. Just like a locomotive."

Valkyrie examined a couple of framed photographs on the mantelpiece. "Who was he? He wasn't a sorcerer, was he?"

"His name was Brendan Cassidy," Scrutinous said. "From what I can gather, he was a perfectly normal mortal. He worked as an assistant manager of a local store. Nothing whatsoever to do with us or anyone in our community."

Skulduggery took a bag of powder from his jacket and threw some into the air. It fell as a light cloud, shimmering with faint colour. "Definite traces of Adept magic," he said, "but I'm not getting a read on an exact discipline. Which only proves that he didn't explode of his own volition."

Scrutinous watched the two of them work, and tried not to get in the way. He wasn't a detective, after all. He worked in Public Relations – he convinced mortals that they didn't see what they actually saw. All this looking-for-clues lark was a tad beyond him. He liked to think of himself as a simple man.

He wandered over to a lamp. It was a very nice lamp. He'd seen better, of course he had, but this was a very fine example of a perfectly nice lamp. It suited the room. He approved. Beside the lamp was a fountain pen. He picked it up. It was an old pen, a classic. He wasn't an expert on pens, but he knew an old, classic pen when he saw one. He remembered when pens like this had first gone on sale, over a hundred and fifty years ago, when they were brand new and cutting edge. He'd probably owned a few. There was a pad of paper on which the pen had been lying, and he looked at it now, at what was written across the top page.

I'm going to be hit by a train, it read.

Scrutinous frowned. "Um," he said.

"Yes?" Skulduggery asked, from somewhere behind him.

"Um, I'm not sure, but I think I may have found a clue."

Skulduggery and Valkyrie joined him, and peered down at the pad.

"Ah," said Skulduggery. "I think you're right. That is indeed a clue. I don't know what it tells us, apart from the obvious, but it definitely tells us something. Valkyrie?"

"It tells us Cassidy knew what was going to happen," Valkyrie said.

Skulduggery nodded. "Anything else?"

"Uh..."

Skulduggery hunkered down and poked the pad with his finger. "The handwriting is very clear. Very legible. When he wrote this, he was calm. That tells us one of two things. Either he had already accepted his fate, or he didn't believe it would happen. Or he wasn't aware that he was writing it."

"That's three things," Valkyrie said. "How do we know it's even his handwriting?"

"There's a half-finished crossword by the armchair. Most of it is impressively wrong, but the handwriting is a match." Skulduggery straightened up. "Out of those three possibilities, Valkyrie, which one would you dismiss first?"

Scrutinous stepped away to let them converse. It was always fascinating watching detectives work.

"I don't think he'd accepted his fate," Valkyrie said at last. "There's nothing else here to suggest that he was preparing to die. There's no note to family or friends, the dinner plate in the kitchen hasn't been put away... He wasn't expecting this."

Skulduggery nodded. "Which leaves us with options two and three – he didn't believe what he'd written, or he wasn't aware he was writing it."

Scrutinous picked up the newspaper by the armchair and glanced at the crossword. He wasn't a fan of them, to be honest. There were enough confusing things in the world without crosswords.

"If Cassidy didn't believe what he'd written," Valkyrie said, "then why not tear out the page? This should be crumpled up in a bin somewhere, as just another bit of nonsense. But he didn't tear it out."

"So he wrote it, but didn't know he was writing it," Skulduggery said. "Which means something or someone was guiding his hand."

"Someone wanted him dead?" Valkyrie asked. "A sorcerer? Why?"

"There's something we're not seeing," Skulduggery said. "Geoffrey?"

Scrutinous looked up. "Yes?"

"What are you doing? I thought you hated crosswords."

"I do, yes."

"Where did you get that pen?"

"It was on the pad."

"What are you writing?"

Scrutinous laughed. "Writing? I'm not writing anything." And even as he said it, he heard the scratching of pen on paper, and looked down. "Oh," he said. "Oh, dear." He dropped the pen to the carpet.

Skulduggery held out his hand. "Let me see."

Scrutinous handed over the newspaper.

Skulduggery read what Scrutinous had written. *"I'm going to be eaten by a shark."*

"Oh, dear," Scrutinous said again. "This does not bode well for me."

Valkyrie waved her hand, and the pen drifted up off the ground and hovered at eye level. "Haunted pen?" she asked.

"Cursed, more likely," Skulduggery said. "Physical contact seems to be enough for the curse to pass on. Geoffrey, you had no idea what you were writing?"

"I had no idea I was writing *anything*," Scrutinous replied. "I hate to be a pain, but do you think there's anything you can do to help me? I really don't want to be eaten by a shark tonight. The next round of my bowling tournament is on Wednesday and we're not doing too badly, all things considered. I'd hate to miss it."

"If a shark does come for you, it won't be tonight," Skulduggery told him. "The ink on the pad is at the very most a day old, Cassidy died four hours ago, and these kinds of curses really like the twelve-hour rule. Any more than that and the power starts to wane."

"So I have twelve hours before a shark eats me?"

"Or you have twelve hours for us to save you, if you want to be glass-half-full about it. Cheer up, Geoffrey, you have our full attention focused on your dilemma. Wait, where's my hat?"

Valkyrie picked it up off the armchair and handed it to him.

"Perfect," he said. "*Now* you have our full attention."

Scrutinous smiled gratefully, suddenly reassured that everything was going to be all right. The Skeleton Detective and Valkyrie Cain were on the case, and they would stop at nothing to solve it.

"I'm hungry," Valkyrie said.

Skulduggery nodded decisively, said, "Then let's find you something to eat," and Scrutinous sagged.

They sat in the diner, Valkyrie doing her best to eat a burger that kept slipping from its bun. Skulduggery had activated one of his false faces, one which gave him a slightly bewildered look. He had placed the pen in a wooden box and was peering at it. Scrutinous sat in the booth and did his best not to worry. He had a glass of water in front of him that he didn't touch.

"This store," Skulduggery said, "where Mister Cassidy worked – where is it?"

"Donnybrook," said Scrutinous.

"Donnybrook," Skulduggery repeated. "Interesting. Do you know of any sorcerers living in Donnybrook? I don't. Thoroughly nice area, but no sorcerers."

"This burger is hard to eat," Valkyrie muttered.

"You're doing a fantastic job," Skulduggery said happily. He closed the box and put it in his pocket. "Now then, Donnybrook. No sorcerers in Donnybrook. No sorcerers around where Cassidy lived. So how did he meet the sorcerer who killed him?"

Scrutinous found it hard to know when Skulduggery was addressing him or merely thinking out loud. The eyes on his false face were slowly swivelling in every direction.

"Unless," Skulduggery said, "he never did."

Valkyrie asked a question with her mouth full.

Skulduggery's head tilted. "What I mean is, this is a curse that passes from one person to the next, yes? The pen keeps moving around. Brendan Cassidy may not have been the first victim, which means it's possible he had no contact *at all* with the sorcerer who started it. Which means that there should be more unexplained deaths that we haven't heard about. Excuse me for a moment."

Skulduggery took his phone from his pocket, then slipped out of the booth. He went away to make a phone call. Scrutinous looked back at Valkyrie. She had managed to shove half of the burger into her mouth but now froze, her eyes on his.

She mumbled something that sounded like, "Sorry."

He looked away, and she munched on.

A few minutes later Skulduggery slid back into the booth. "Excellent news," he said. "There have been four unexplained deaths in the past two weeks. The first three were all sorcerers, and the fourth was a mortal woman who *knew* the last sorcerer killed and who lived in Donnybrook. Before she died, she could have left that pen in the store in which Brendan Cassidy worked. He picked it up, took it home, and got hit by a train."

"Who was the first sorcerer killed?" Valkyrie asked.

"His name was Elwood Satchel. Low-level Elemental. If the curse did start with him, then the killer must have some connection. We find that connection, we find the killer, we save Geoffrey."

"Then let's do it," Scrutinous said. He paused. "How do we do it?"

"We talk to someone who knew Satchel well. He has a brother who's out of the country right now, and a friend who lives close by."

"So we talk to the friend," Valkyrie said. "Let's go."

They got in the Bentley, drove to the friend's house and knocked on the door. There was nobody home, so they went back to the Bentley and waited. Skulduggery didn't move for hours, and Valkyrie fell asleep. Scrutinous sat in the back seat and thought about sharks all night.

Satchel's friend returned home at ten the next morning. He was a sorcerer but, like Satchel, he wasn't a very powerful one. He worked nights as a security guard to pay the bills.

"It was a clear day," he said when Skulduggery asked him how Satchel had died. "The sun was shining. There were no clouds. But Elwood was... panicking. He kept running around, looking up at the sky. He ran into a café, ran right back out again, screaming something about how it didn't have a ceiling. And then... And then he jerked backwards, flew right off his feet. He was all twisted up, and you could smell burnt hair."

"He was electrocuted?" Skulduggery asked.

"Yeah. Apparently. The doctors said it was a massive electrical current. But I didn't see anything, and he was running across the park when it happened. There was nothing electrical around."

"Did you find a note?" asked Valkyrie.

The man frowned. "What? How did you know about that?"

"Then you *did* find a note."

"Yes. Well, we think. A few days after he died, Elwood's brother found something written on the back of a receipt. It said 'I'm going to be struck by lightning'."

Skulduggery nodded. "Did Elwood have any enemies?"

"I... suppose. I mean, doesn't everyone?"

"Any enemies he had recently made?"

"Oh. Oh, yeah. One. Davit Maybury. They were friends once."

"What happened?"

"Ah, I don't know. The usual."

"I don't quite believe you," said Skulduggery.

"Look, Maybury's a weirdo, OK? He comes out with these weird things, and he looks... odd. He's got crazy eyes, you know? But Elwood grew up with him, they were childhood friends, and then... Elwood kind of stole Maybury's girlfriend."

"Ah."

"I suppose it was kind of a sucky thing to do. Maybury found it hard to talk to girls, because of his whole weirdness thing, and he finally found one who liked him and Elwood comes in and sweeps her off her feet... You think Maybury had something to do with his death?"

"Perhaps," Skulduggery said. "Do you know where we could find him? We just want a little chat."

Davit Maybury's house was quite nondescript from the outside. Skulduggery knocked a few times, then kicked the door in. It was quite a nondescript house from the inside, too. Skulduggery went first, hand open and fingers splayed.

"The air hasn't been disturbed for weeks," he said. "It doesn't look like anybody's home."

"So what are we going to do now?" Scrutinous asked. "It's almost eleven o'clock. I have one hour before a shark eats me."

"You'll be fine," Skulduggery said, poking around. "Everyone spread out. Look for clues."

Skulduggery and Valkyrie went wandering, examining things and muttering to themselves and each other. Scrutinous bit his lip and checked his watch.

Almost three quarters of an hour later, Skulduggery found something in the main bedroom.

"It's a door," he said, rapping his knuckles against the wall. "Very well hidden. Whoever installed it knew what they were doing."

"Where does it lead?" Scrutinous asked, and shifted his weight. The carpet in here was soggy, and water spilled through his sandals to wet his socks.

"It could be a stairway leading to a tunnel, or it could be a single room." Skulduggery stood back. "Maybury isn't the strongest sorcerer out there, and by all accounts he doesn't have many friends. It is therefore entirely conceivable that the moment he released the cursed pen upon Elwood Satchel he secluded himself away until it was all over. If something went wrong with the curse, if it didn't work, then Satchel might come after him."

Valkyrie peered at the wall. "So you think he's still in there?"

"Mister Maybury," Skulduggery said loudly, "we need to talk to you. If you can hear me, please open the door. I am a detective with the Sanctuary – we're not going to hurt you."

They looked at the wall and waited, and nothing happened.

"Um," said Scrutinous. "Where's that water coming from?"

Valkyrie looked around. "What water?"

Scrutinous splashed his foot a few times.

"That's the carpet," Valkyrie told him.

"And why is it covered in water?"

She frowned at him. "What are you talking about? It's not. It's just a regular carpet."

"It's a regular carpet covered in water, Valkyrie. You're standing in it, too."

"No, Geoffrey, I'm not. My feet are perfectly dry, as are yours. Are you feeling OK?"

He stared at her. The water was rising. It was up to her ankles. It had completely covered his own sandals. It was cold and wet. "You can't see this?" he asked. "You can't hear the splashing? You can't feel it?"

She hunkered down, put her hand in the water, flat on the floor. Her eyes were on him the whole time. "Am I touching the water now?"

He nodded. She brought her hand up. It was perfectly dry. No drops fell.

"Oh, dear," Scrutinous said.

"Interesting," Skulduggery murmured. "The curse must deliver a reality that only the victim can experience."

"Which explains how a train fitted into Cassidy's living room," Valkyrie said.

Scrutinous peered into the water, and his eyes widened. "I see a fish," he said. "A small one, a tiny one, but... it's a fish." He looked up. "When there's enough water, the shark will appear, won't it?"

"I'm afraid so," Skulduggery said. "Which means we have to get through this door."

Skulduggery and Valkyrie walked through the water without disturbing it, Scrutinous splashing noisily after them. They ran their hands all over the wall, feeling for imperfections.

"There has to be a lever here somewhere," Skulduggery said. "The time and the effort was put into making this door virtually undetectable, not into making it impenetrable. At Maybury's price range, it's one or the other. So there has to be a lever somewhere nearby."

Even as he spoke, something clicked beneath his fingers. The wall shifted, the door swung open, and Skulduggery led the way in.

It was a small room, windowless, with an armchair and a side table. On the side table there was a thick book and a scalpel. There was water in here, too. Now it was up past Scrutinous's knees. His legs were freezing, and every now and then a school of tiny fish would brush past and he'd jerk away.

"We may have a problem," Skulduggery said.

Scrutinous stopped scanning the water and glanced up, saw a corpse in the armchair. Valkyrie had her hand covering her mouth and nose, but all Scrutinous could smell was the briny sea.

"That's Maybury?" he asked. "But... he's dead. He *is* dead, isn't he?"

"He must have trapped himself inside," Skulduggery said.

"He starved to death?" Valkyrie asked.

"I'm afraid he ran out of air long before that could happen. He obviously didn't think this through too well."

"But if he's dead," said Scrutinous, "how can he lift the curse? Who's going to lift the curse?"

"The important thing to remember is not to panic," Skulduggery said.

"How can I not panic? A shark is going to eat me!"

"It's really not as bad as it sounds. I was attacked by a shark once, back when I was alive. Well, not so much a shark as a rather large fish. And not so much attacked as looked at menacingly. But it had murder in its eyes, that fish. I knew, in that instant, if our roles had been reversed and the fish had been holding the fishing pole and I had been the one to be caught, it wouldn't hesitate a moment before eating me. So I cooked and ate it before it had a chance to turn the tables."

"That," Valkyrie said, "is one of the most useless stories you've ever told me."

"I'm just trying to make Geoffrey feel better."

"You went fishing, Skulduggery. That's not the same as being eaten by a shark."

"It shares similarities."

"Like what?"

"It was wet. Also, one eats the other. When looked upon like that, the main points are practically identical."

"Um," Scrutinous said, "could we start talking about how we're going to lift the curse if the man who started it all is dead?"

"Yes," Skulduggery said, "of course. All is not lost. While it would have been easier to have Maybury simply cancel the whole thing, that is only one way to solve the problem. Davit Maybury was not an evil man. He was a weird one, by all accounts, but not evil. As such, it does not make sense that he would want many people to die, when all he was after was revenge on the one man who had stolen the woman he loved."

He took the wooden box from his jacket and opened it. Hesitating only a moment, he took the pen from the box. "Well," he said, "now we're in this together, Geoffrey." He held the pen in both hands, and twisted. The outer shell cracked and he pulled it away. He murmured something, then held up the pen for Valkyrie and Scrutinous to see. Four symbols had been cut into the inside. "The curse," he said. "I think Maybury made a mistake. Instead of the curse afflicting the first person to touch the pen, it has instead afflicted *every* person to touch the pen. Maybe he used the wrong symbol or misjudged the depth or the width... Every aspect of these sigils has to be perfectly judged."

"How does that help us?" Valkyrie asked.

"It means we don't have to lift the curse – we just have to correct his spelling."

"He carved the wrong symbol, so now we have to carve the right one?"

"In theory, once we do, it will mean the curse will have fulfilled its purpose the first time it was used, and all this will just... stop."

"In theory?" Scrutinous pressed. His teeth were chattering.

"Yes."

"That doesn't s-sound very certain."

"It's a very strong theory, Geoffrey. In much the same way that gravity is a very strong theory. It's almost certainly true. If I were you, I wouldn't worry about it."

"I have ten m-minutes left. The water has reached the ends of my shorts. There are f-f-fish swimming all around me and the floor has changed to a s-seabed. How do you expect me to not w-worry about this?"

"By taking deep, calming breaths."

"Do you know how to correct it?" Valkyrie asked.

Skulduggery picked up the scalpel from the side table, before opening the book. "This is obviously what Maybury used to start it all, but because he got it wrong I would be disinclined to trust the same instructions he followed. We'll have to ask China."

Valkyrie raised an eyebrow. "But China isn't here."

"Your b-boyfriend," Scrutinous said. "He's a tele... porter... He can bring her."

"Fletcher's never been here," Valkyrie said. "He can't teleport anywhere he's never been."

"Well," Skulduggery said, taking out his phone, "where magic fails, technology prevails." He took a picture of the pen, then made a call.

Scrutinous glanced behind him, just in time to see a pale fin sink beneath the water's surface.

"It's here!" he screeched. "It's over there!"

Valkyrie jumped in front of him protectively.

"That won't do any good," Skulduggery said.

"I know!" she snapped. "But we can't just stand around while he gets eaten!"

Scrutinous took a deep breath and ducked his head into the water. The confines of the room did not exist down here. Down here, he was in the middle of the ocean. He saw a dark shape move out of the corner of his eye, and then it was gone. He came up for air.

"It's huge," he said. "Oh, God, it's h-huge."

"China," Skulduggery said suddenly. "We have a bit of an emergency here. I just sent you a picture, did you get it? Excellent." He waited a moment, listening to her talk. "But that's just the thing. It *is* a mistake. The gent who set the curse didn't mean it to apply to *everyone* – he meant it to apply simply to the *first* one."

Scrutinous took another breath, and ducked down for another look.

The shark, and it must have been a Great White judging by its size, was visible in the distance, turning towards him. Scrutinous broke the surface, gasping for air. "It's coming!"

"But my question," Skulduggery was saying, "is how to correct the curse so that the original intent overrides the mistake? Really? Oh, that's interesting."

"It's coming!" Scrutinous screamed.

"Geoffrey, please," Skulduggery said, "I can't hear what she's saying." He put the phone back to his head. "Carry on."

"Splash about," Valkyrie said. "Make a lot of noise. Scare it away."

Scrutinous splashed at the water and kicked his legs and screamed and yelled and hollered.

"A shark's coming for him," Skulduggery said into the phone. "Oh, have you? OK, I'll tell him." Skulduggery looked over. "China was attacked by a shark once, just like I was, except it was an actual shark and she was actually attacked. She says you're not to splash about, she says that makes you look like a seal, and sharks really like eating seals."

Scrutinous froze, and Valkyrie winced. "Oh, yeah," she said. "I saw that once on TV. Sorry."

"So it's just the upwards slash, then?" Skulduggery was saying, peering at the pen. "Is it too long or too short? How long should it be? No, shouldn't be a problem." He put the phone on loudspeaker and placed it in his top pocket, then readied Maybury's scalpel. "OK, making the cut now..."

China's voice came from the phone. "Has the shark eaten him yet?"

"Not yet," Skulduggery muttered, focusing on his task. "What happens if I do it wrong?"

"Geoffrey gets eaten," China said. "Am I on loudspeaker?"

"Yes, sorry, should have told you. Valkyrie and Geoffrey are here."

"Can they hear me?"

"Yes, they can."

"Hello, Valkyrie," China said.

"Uh, hi," Valkyrie said back. "Is this going to take long? The shark's coming for him."

China said something in response but Scrutinous didn't hear it. The shark came at him like a torpedo, its mouth open impossibly wide and all those teeth biting in at him. Scrutinous shrieked, dimly aware of Skulduggery gesturing, and then he was sent deeper into the water, tumbling head over heels, the shark missing him by inches.

Scrutinous turned, twisted, saw the shark flick its great tail and shoot back towards him, coming in for another go. In desperation, knowing it was useless but doing it anyway, he started to swim away from it. But there was nowhere to swim to, nowhere to hide, and then something snagged his right wrist.

An invisible force yanked him to the surface, the shark passing so close that its rough skin scraped like sandpaper across his leg. He broke the surface, gasping, realising that Valkyrie had grabbed his arm and pulled, and for a moment he saw the both of them, the alarm in Valkyrie's eyes, Skulduggery still working on the pen, the room around them, and then he dropped again, below the surface, and Valkyrie and Skulduggery disappeared and there was only the shark down there in the middle of the ocean.

Oxygen bubbles filled his vision and he jerked his head from side to side, trying to get his bearings, trying to work out what direction the shark would attack from. Then he saw it, that huge mouth, those huge teeth, coming in on top of him and there was no way out, not this time, and the massive jaws closed over him just as the water went away and Scrutinous fell to the floor.

"There," Skulduggery said. "I think that did it."

Scrutinous sat up, gasping, looking around in astonishment.

"Is he dead?" China asked from the phone.

"Not even remotely," Skulduggery said. "He's back on dry land. Many thanks, China."

He hung up as Valkyrie helped Scrutinous to his feet. The water was gone, the shark was gone. Scrutinous wasn't even wet any more.

"It had me," he said. "The shark had me. I was, literally, about to be torn in two. You saved me. In the nick of time, you saved me."

"You're welcome," Skulduggery said.

"I was talking to Valkyrie."

Skulduggery's head tilted. "But I'm the one who worked the whole thing out."

Valkyrie grinned. "You're very welcome, Geoffrey, although I can't take all the credit. China helped, you know."

"But I carved the right symbol," Skulduggery said.

Scrutinous clasped Valkyrie's hand in his. "If there is anything I can do for you in the future, anything at all, do not hesitate to ask."

Skulduggery looked at him. "Can I ask, too?"

"No."

"Why not?"

"Valkyrie cared that I was being attacked. You told me to shut up."

"That's because your screaming was very annoying. How is that my fault?"

"If you'll excuse me," Scrutinous said, "I'm going to go for a walk. A nice, long walk, on solid ground."

He left them, heard them bickering behind him, and then Valkyrie was laughing and Skulduggery was acting offended. Scrutinous emerged into the midday sun, took a deep, calming breath, and headed off in search of some lunch.

Possibly seafood.

There are no animals featured in this novella, and yet this novella is dedicated to a whole lot of them.

This is to Groomer and Sansa and Bowie and Lorelai and Rory and Salem and Tilly, for all the love and all the laughs.

And this is also dedicated to the pets that have been lost over the years — so this is to Ziggy, to Sylvester, to Mammy Cat, to Pooper, to Sherlock, to Mabel and to Ali — the inspiration for Xena and the greatest dog who ever lived.

To all the good girls and all the good boys. If you have a pet, you are their whole world, so love them accordingly. If you don't have a pet but you have a younger sibling, pretend they're a kitten and love them too. Also, dress them up in stupid outfits and laugh at them.

For isn't that what Christmas is REALLY all about?

APOCALYPSE KINGS

I

A dedayo was fourteen when he discovered that he was magic.

Up until then, he'd lived what he reckoned to be a normal life. He was on the school football team, which he enjoyed. He was on the school debating team, which he didn't. He had his family, he had his friends, he liked dogs but was wary of cats, he didn't like spiders, he hated rats and he ran away from wasps. All pretty normal. All pretty standard.

The magic thing happened over the course of a few weeks, when things started to come to him. Not answers, or knowledge, or insight, or anything like that – but actual *things*. Lamps, and bottles of water and big, heavy books. They'd fly at him as soon as he looked at them and he'd have to duck or jump back or run screaming from the room.

At first, Adedayo thought he was being haunted. Then he thought that he must have annoyed an invisible man at some point. One afternoon, after a teapot had collided with his face, he covered the kitchen floor in flour and waited for a footprint to appear. His mother appeared first, of course, and yelled at him, told him to clean it up. Adedayo was more scared of his mum than he was of an invisible man, so he did what he was told and wondered why he was being singled out for torment by this invisible gentleman when his two younger sisters were way more annoying than he ever managed to be.

Then his grandmother came to stay. She was a small Nigerian woman who didn't speak much English, but her health wasn't the best and she couldn't stay on her own any more. Adedayo's sisters were told they had to share a room and their grandmother – their beloved *iyá agba* – moved in. It took some time to adjust to a new person in the house, but she was lovely, so nobody minded, and a few weeks later she knocked on Adedayo's door.

Adedayo didn't speak much Yoruba, his grandmother's language. His parents were both English speakers and, once they'd moved to Ireland to start a family, that's how they'd raised him and his sisters. They'd tried to teach him a few words over the years, but he didn't have much interest in learning, so, when his grandmother sat beside him on the bed, he prepared himself for a few long, long minutes of hesitations and the slow searching for words in English that always accompanied the rather pointless stories of her childhood. But she was his *iyá agba*, and he loved her, so Adedayo smiled and pretended with all his heart to be interested in whatever she had to say.

She surprised him, then, by telling him something so brain-punchingly interesting that it changed his life forever.

She told him, in that hesitant way of hers, that magic was real, and that she was magic, and so was he.

At first, he thought she was just telling him a story to entertain him, but when she clicked her fingers and conjured a fireball into her hand it all started to make sense. The odd occurrences, the weird coincidences, the objects that moved on their own – that was magic. His grandmother explained that there were rules for people like them; there were styles of magic he could specialise in, other magical people – sorcerers, or mages – he could meet. She told him about the Sanctuaries around the world, and the wars that had been fought between the sorcerers who wanted to enslave ordinary people and the sorcerers who wanted to protect them.

He had such a life ahead of him, she said. Such wonders to uncover.

She taught him some things – how to move objects by manipulating the air around them; how to make strands of energy dance in the palms of his hands; how to click his fingers and generate sparks. She told him about the three names that sorcerers have – the name they're given, the name they take, and their true name, the source of all their power.

But she was an old, old woman, and, a few weeks after his fifteenth birthday, her health deteriorated so much she had to be taken to hospital. Her energy dipped so that she lost all of her English and could only speak the language of her childhood. When Adedayo went in to sit with her, she woke, took his hand and said weakly, "*Má ṣi àpótí.*" Then she smiled, and closed her eyes.

Má ṣi àpótí, he repeated in his head. *Má ṣi àpótí*. He made a note to ask his folks what that meant, but it slipped his mind, and his grandmother passed away later that night, and Adedayo was left with a lifetime of questions, a heart full of grief and a polished wooden box.

His grandmother had insisted that it had to go to him, apparently. That only he would know what to do with it.

The box was the size of a biscuit tin. It had carvings across the lid and along the sides – carvings that looked like letters, that looked like words, but weren't. There was no lock, no latch, no way to open it. There was nothing inside, though. Or there didn't seem to be when Adedayo's mum shook it. His dad tried prising the lid off with a screwdriver. Didn't work.

*   *   *

The wooden box had been sitting on Adedayo's desk, under a pile of pristine textbooks and dog-eared graphic novels, for weeks when Adedayo woke in the middle of the night, suddenly *knowing* how to open it.

He got out of bed, crossed the dark room and cleared the junk off the lid. He tapped the carvings on the box's left and right sides, then pressed, then tapped again and moved his fingers in a swirling motion.

A dim blue light shone from between the carvings, travelling across the box in strange, swirling patterns. There were sounds from inside, like wooden cogs turning.

And then there was a click.

2

Suddenly apprehensive, and not a little nervous, Adedayo ever so slowly lifted the lid. Inside was dark. Inside was empty.

But something in that emptiness reached out and Adedayo went rigid, his fingers splayed, his legs locked straight, his head back and the muscles in his neck standing out. He felt a consciousness, more than one, poking through his mind, picking out his language, sorting through what he knew of the world, and then his knees wobbled and he went floppy and staggered back a few steps before collapsing.

A hand emerged from the box.

The hand became a forearm and then there was an elbow, and the elbow pressed down on the table for leverage and a shoulder appeared and then a head, a head with a black veil and horns poking out, a head far too big to be squeezing through a box the size of a biscuit tin.

This thing, this being, was called the Sathariel. Adedayo didn't know how he knew that – he just did. It was like there was a swimming pool full of weird knowledge and he'd just cannonballed into it. He watched the Sathariel climb out of the box and stand by the table, his black robes long and ragged, his breathing heavy, his horns sharp.

He had mottled green hands tipped with black nails, and from his robes he drew a gnarled staff as tall as he was. The smell he brought with him was pungent and made Adedayo think of people screaming.

Something else came out of the box: a tentacle, wet and dripping. It probed the air, then found the table, and a second one came out to join it, then another. Then there were a dozen tentacles, some as thin as a cat's tongue, some as thick as an elephant's trunk, and once they'd gained purchase they lifted the Cythraul straight up out of the box.

The Cythraul, the Many-Tentacled One, hid most of his body beneath a robe of soiled crimson, but Adedayo caught a flash of pale, squirming flesh that made his stomach roil. The Cythraul had a wide, gaping mouth lined with small, sharp teeth, like a lamprey eel, and a single black, blinking eye. He looked down at Adedayo and then, thankfully, away.

There was another creature in the box. The last of the Apocalypse Kings unfurled himself from his confinement and stepped into the bedroom. Tall and thin, black-haired and pale, long-faced and red-eyed, the Deathless wore a robe of rags and filth that fitted him like kingly vestments.

He looked round Adedayo's bedroom and breathed in, then smiled.

"Smells like feet," he said, and all three of them vanished.

3

For reasons both completely outrageous and totally understandable, Adedayo found it hard to concentrate in school the next day.

He had said nothing to his parents or his sisters about the creatures that had emerged from the box. He had said nothing to them about anything, in fact. His *iyá agba* had told him that his sisters might develop magical abilities as they got older and, if they did, it would be his job to guide them. But, until that happened, it was safer to keep the truth from ordinary people. Safer for them, and safer for Adedayo.

He'd walked to school, met up with his friends, wearing a smile and laughing when the others laughed, but not paying one bit of attention to what anyone was saying. As he sat in class, he ignored the teachers and stared at the pages of his books and worried – for there was a lot to worry about.

The first lesson of the day was given over to debating practice, in which Adedayo performed even worse than usual. He'd joined the team because he needed at least *one* extracurricular activity for when he eventually applied to university, but he wasn't very good at debating. He found it difficult to come up with a coherent argument at the best of times, and this was certainly not the best of times.

The hours passed in a confusing, hazy blur, and suddenly Adedayo was in maths, the last lesson of the day, his eyes on a long line of equations the class had to solve. There was a knock on the door.

"Hello," a girl said, coming in without waiting for an invitation.

She was around Adedayo's age, fifteen or so. Taller than him, with long dark hair. She was wearing the school uniform, but he didn't recognise her.

"Yes?" said Mr Hopkins, frowning with irritation. He didn't like his lessons being interrupted.

"Hi there," said the girl. She had a nice confident smile. "I was wondering if I could speak to Adedayo Akinde."

Everyone looked at Adedayo, except for Mr Hopkins, whose frown deepened. "Who?"

"*Adedayo Akinde*," the girl repeated.

"No, no, who wants to speak to him? The principal? Another teacher?"

"Oh," the girl said, and laughed. "No, only me."

Mr Hopkins blinked at her. "Are you a student here?"

"Yes, exactly. I'm new, though. I just need Adedayo for a moment. Maybe two moments. Three at the very most."

"I don't know how they did things in your last school, young lady, but here we don't have pupils calling on other pupils in the middle of classes."

She didn't respond right away. She just looked at him as if she couldn't understand why he wasn't simply doing what she wanted. "I'm sorry," she said, "I think we got off on the wrong foot. I need to speak to Adedayo. Thank you." She turned to the class. "Adedayo, are you here?"

Once more, everyone looked at Adedayo, but he put up his hand anyway, and the girl smiled.

"A word?" she said, indicating the doorway.

Adedayo stood, but Mr Hopkins was quicker. "Adedayo, you are not to leave this room. Young lady, unless I get a full explanation—"

"What is this class?" the girl asked. "Maths? I'm a maths prodigy. I'm so far beyond genius that they don't even have a word for what I am. People like me have a club, and we think Adedayo might belong in it."

Mr Hopkins looked insultingly sceptical. "You think Adedayo is a maths prodigy? Adedayo, what do you think of this idea?"

"Um," said Adedayo.

"That's what I thought."

"The problem with prodigies such as ourselves," said the girl, "is that mainstream schools fail to challenge us, and, in doing so, fail to recognise our vast, vast intellects."

Mr Hopkins folded his arms. "And do you have anything to back up these claims of yours?"

The girl walked over to the whiteboard, picked up a red marker and started writing a sequence of bracketed numbers. She wore a thick black ring on one of the fingers of her right hand. "This equation, for super-geniuses, is as easy as falling into a ditch, and, if you've ever fallen into a ditch, you'll know how easy that is. If you, or anyone in this class, come even close to solving it by the time I've finished talking to Adedayo, that'll be all the proof you'll need." She popped the lid back on the marker and tossed it to Mr Hopkins. "Adedayo, out here, please."

Adedayo didn't know what to do, so he hurried into the corridor.

"I'm a maths genius?" he asked once the girl had shut the door behind them.

"What?" she said, glancing at her watch. "Oh, God, no. I mean, maybe you are. Are you? I haven't a clue. I hate maths. Always have. Too many numbers."

"Then what was that equation you wrote on the board?"

"Complete gibberish," she said. "In fact, your teacher will figure that out in a few seconds, so do you mind if we walk as we talk? Thanks awfully."

She began to stride away, and Adedayo, unable to think of what else to do, followed her.

4

As they neared the end of the corridor, the new girl turned to him and smiled. "Adedayo, my name is Valkyrie Cain. I heard you had some interesting visitors last night."

He stopped. "How did you know about that?"

Valkyrie took his arm, started him moving again. "I'll explain everything later, I swear. Or maybe I won't. It kinda depends on the threat level we're facing, to be honest. But I'll tell you what we know, OK? It won't take long, because we don't know a huge amount. Three creatures appeared in your house last night and then promptly left."

She paused. "And that's it. That's as much as we know. Well, apart from the fact that these creatures – they're pretty bad news. But I probably don't have to tell you that. Do I? I probably don't."

"Who are you?"

"Like I said, my name's Valkyrie Cain. I'm the good guy."

They heard the door open behind them.

"We can run, if you like," she said, smiling, and broke into a jog. Adedayo jogged alongside her round the next corner.

"Did they say anything, the creatures?" she asked. "Did they mention who they were, what they wanted, anything like that?"

"All they said was that my bedroom smelled of feet."

"Huh," Valkyrie said. "That's a little mean, isn't it? Even if your bedroom *does* smell of feet, they didn't have to say it. Didn't have to point it out. You know the problem with supernatural creatures? They're rude. Yes, a lot of them also want to kill humans and/or destroy the world, but I'd say their main problem is the rudeness."

"Where are we going?" Adedayo asked as they jogged past the balcony overlooking the sports hall.

"That way," said Valkyrie, nodding to the exit at the bottom of the stairs.

He slowed. "What? I can't leave school."

"Of course you can. You do it every day."

"But classes haven't ended. I'll get in trouble."

Valkyrie put a hand on his shoulder and led him down the stairs. "I used to worry about things like that," she said. "I used to worry about teachers and homework and detentions, and what other people thought of me, and what my friends said, and what to wear, and what music to listen to, and none of this is true. I didn't worry about any of that because I'm way too cool and always have been, but at least I've managed to distract you long enough for us to get outside."

She pushed open the doors and they emerged into the fresh air. Adedayo looked around, expecting a horde of teachers to come sprinting up. Instead, an empty crisp packet skipped lightly over the ground.

"Come along," said Valkyrie, and strode across the courtyard. He didn't know why, exactly, but he followed her. They passed the Old House, a tall, imposing building that used to be the main school a hundred years ago, but was now for staff only. They walked right by the window of the principal's office. No one saw them.

There was a big black car parked in the staff car park – an old-fashioned car that gleamed in the sunlight. No one else was around.

"You're a sorcerer, aren't you?" Adedayo asked.

Valkyrie looked at him, surprised. "You know about us?"

"My *iyá agba* – I mean, my gran – told me. She said I'm one of you."

"Oh, thank God," Valkyrie said, laughing. "I hate having to explain to mortals that magic and monsters exist and yes, there are bad guys, but *we're* the good guys and please, please stop screaming. I hate when they scream, y'know? It's just so unnecessary."

"Totally," said Adedayo.

A man got out of the car – a tall man in a dark blue suit, with a crisp white shirt and a dark blue tie. His hands were gloved and he wore a hat, like a detective in an old black-and-white movie.

"Adedayo," said Valkyrie, "this is my partner, Skulduggery Pleasant."

Adedayo was about to remark on such an unusual name when Skulduggery Pleasant tapped his shirt, just over the collarbones, and his face melted, actually *melted*, flowing off his bare bones and disappearing beneath his collar, so that what Adedayo saw looking at him now was just a skull wearing a hat.

"Hello, Adedayo," the skeleton said, "very pleased to meet you."

And Adedayo screamed.

5

Skulduggery and Valkyrie waited for Adedayo to finish screaming. It took a few seconds.

"Excellent," Skulduggery said, opening the door and moving his seat forward. "In you get. We need to talk, and privacy is required."

Adedayo should probably have run away. Instead, he climbed in.

Skulduggery got back behind the wheel and Valkyrie slid into the passenger seat. The car started with a gentle purr, and they left the school grounds and turned on to the road.

"Um," said Adedayo, "are you kidnapping me?"

"No," Skulduggery said immediately.

"No," said Valkyrie.

"Absolutely not," Skulduggery said.

"Are we, though?" Valkyrie asked.

Skulduggery shook his head. "If he agrees to come with us of his own free will, then it's not kidnapping, it's a day out."

Valkyrie looked back at Adedayo and shrugged. "There you go."

"Cool," Adedayo said, trying to smile. "I just wanted to check. Could I ask what's going on? And also how are you a skeleton?"

"The story of how I became a skeleton is a long one," Skulduggery said. "Thankfully, it is also a really interesting one because it's about me. The year was 1690, and the war with Mevolent had reached—"

"We're just going to skip this," Valkyrie interrupted, "because, like we said, we don't have an awful lot of time. Skulduggery, Adedayo already knows about magic. He's one of us."

"Oh, good," said Skulduggery, turning right. "That cuts down on the tedious explanations and the screaming."

"I was just saying that."

"I don't know an awful lot, though," Adedayo pointed out. "*Ìyá Agba*, my grandmother, she was magic and she taught me a few things in secret. The rest of my family don't know. Things like . . ." He clicked his fingers a few times, but nothing happened, and he frowned. "Usually sparks fly out."

"It can be difficult to make magic work when you're nervous or scared," Valkyrie said. "Or when people are trying to kill you."

Adedayo blinked. "Will people be trying to kill me?"

Valkyrie and Skulduggery glanced at each other.

"No," Valkyrie said unconvincingly.

"Adedayo," Skulduggery said, "we know a few psychics and they had some rather disturbing dreams last night. The details are rather vague, but they all saw three beings at your address, they saw you, and they saw these beings abruptly depart. Then they saw these three beings destroy everything and kill everyone on the planet. Pretty standard apocalyptic stuff, to be fair – but it's our job to make sure that doesn't happen. So that's why we're here. We visited your home first, of course. Don't worry, no one was there, but we did find a wooden box in your bedroom. This is where the creatures emerged from, I assume?"

Adedayo nodded. "My grandmother left the box to me."

"It will, with your permission, be examined by experts at a later date, but from what we've seen the box appears to be an ancient but incredibly sophisticated prison. It's quite astounding, really."

"You get excited about the weirdest things," Valkyrie muttered, before turning back to Adedayo. "What can you tell us about the creatures that climbed out of it?"

"Everything," said Adedayo.

Valkyrie frowned. "Everything?"

"I . . . I don't know exactly how to describe it, but I think they kinda looked into my head? To learn about the world and the language and stuff? But, when they looked in, I don't know, it's like they left the door open to their minds. So I went in. Only it was more like I was jumping into a swimming pool full of knowledge. It was amazing."

"Oh, Adedayo," said Skulduggery, taking another right, "you just might be my favourite person I've met since you got in the car. So who are they?"

"Gods," said Adedayo. "All these gods, countless gods, lived, like, billions of years ago. Then the people came and started worshipping them and sacrificing each other, and things were good – if you were a god. The worshipping was nice, but all those sacrificed souls were . . . nourishment, I suppose. They made the gods stronger. So then one race of gods would attack another, and wars broke out, and . . . Anyway, there was this one race, called the Faceless Ones—"

"We're acquainted," Valkyrie said.

"Oh," said Adedayo, "cool. So they hunted down and, like, eradicated all the other gods. Three races – the Cythraul, the Sathariel and the Deathless – were on the verge of being wiped out and they wanted to make sure that the Faceless Ones starved to death once they were gone. Just to, like, teach them a lesson or something. So each race sent one of their last survivors to kill all worshippers. The humans, basically. To cut off the source of souls, you know? But the Faceless Ones managed to trap them in a magical box, the box my grandmother had. They put it aside and forgot about it for all that time and . . . and then last night I opened it and let the Apocalypse Kings out. That's, I think, roughly what their, like, collective name is." He sagged. "I'm such an idiot."

"Hey," said Skulduggery. "Hey."

Adedayo looked up. "Yes?"

"Hey," Skulduggery said again.

Valkyrie glared at the skeleton, then smiled at Adedayo. "You're not an idiot. There's no way you could have known what was in that box or what would happen once you opened it. I mean, it's a box. Boxes are meant to be opened."

"I know another lady who said that," Skulduggery muttered, turning right again. "Her name was Pandora and things did not go well for her."

"Oh, really?" Valkyrie said. "You knew Pandora, did you?"

"Yes," he responded. "Pandora Willoughby-Smythe, a very nice English lady who owned a rather nasty Pomeranian that got itself locked in a trunk one sunny afternoon. When she finally let it out, it had peed all over her cashmere blankets." He shook his head. "It was a massacre."

Valkyrie closed her eyes. "You will never not be weird."

"So how are these Apocalypse Kings going to destroy the world?" Skulduggery asked, taking the next right.

They'd done a loop, and were arriving back at the school.

Adedayo winced. "I didn't get a chance to find out before I had to leave the, uh, the swimming pool of knowledge that I mentioned. Sorry."

"And how much time do we have?"

"Not long. All they have to do is get their strength back. They're going to be feeding on souls. They're going to, like, attach themselves, I suppose, to people and they'll feed until they're strong again. They don't need to be as strong as they once were, just strong enough to do whatever it is they're gonna do. But I think I know how to beat them."

The car pulled up outside the school, and Skulduggery tilted his head. "Something you saw in their minds, while you were paddling around in the swimming pool of knowledge? A weakness?"

"Not exactly," said Adedayo, and cleared his throat. "*Má ṣi àpótí.*"

"What's that?" Valkyrie asked.

"It's the last thing *Ìyá Agba* said to me. I think it's a spell. I think, maybe, it'll stop them, or maybe trap them in the box again. *Àpótí* means *box*, I think."

"A spell, eh?" Valkyrie said, looking doubtful.

"What?" said Adedayo. "Don't you do spells?"

"Not really," Skulduggery said. "Spells can be useful in focusing your intent, distilling it down to its basic and most potent essence . . . but, in general, spells aren't really a thing."

"Oh," said Adedayo. "OK." He nodded, like he was accepting what they were saying, but he still thought his grandmother's words were a spell. He still thought they could be useful. "Can you stop them?"

"That's why we're here," Skulduggery said with utmost confidence.

Relief flushed the anxiety from his bones, and Adedayo smiled. "Thank you. Thank you." Valkyrie and Skulduggery nodded. Didn't say anything. "So, uh . . . will I just get out?"

"Yes," Skulduggery said. "That would be a splendid idea."

Valkyrie let Adedayo out on her side, then got back in. Before Adedayo could say anything else, they drove off.

He hesitated. Then waved.

6

The next morning he felt better. Valkyrie Cain and Skulduggery Pleasant were going to take care of things. They were going to stop the Apocalypse Kings and life would return to normal, and nothing bad that happened would be his fault. Adedayo could go back to focusing on the debates.

"Argue with me," said his dad at breakfast. He held up a slice of toast. "Convince me to give this piece of toast to you."

Adedayo frowned. "But that's your toast."

"This is practice. Training. Come on now. Convince me."

Adedayo nodded, frowned at the piece of toast, his mind working to come up with persuasive arguments. "Please can I have that toast?" he asked.

"No," his dad said, sighing.

"Aw," said Adedayo, "please?"

"Ade, this is not an argument. When you debate, you have to *convince*. That's the whole point of debating. Convince me to give you my toast."

"Dad?"

"Yes?"

"Give me your toast."

"Dear God," said his dad, "you are dreadful at this."

"I told you," Adedayo said, slurping his orange juice. "I told you I was really bad at debating. But everyone said I should do it."

"He's too nice," Adedayo's mum said to her husband. "That's his problem."

"Thank you, Mum," said Adedayo, "even though it sounded like an insult, the way you said it."

His mum grinned. "You're going to be late for school."

"But I haven't finished breakfast."

She took the slice of toast from her husband's hand and gave it to him. "There you go."

"Hey," his dad said.

Adedayo took a big bite. "Victory."

He was halfway to school when the big black car pulled up beside him, and Valkyrie hopped out, still wearing the school uniform, and held the door open. Adedayo didn't know what else to do, so he got in.

"What's going on?" he asked, once they started driving.

"Our psychic friends," Skulduggery said, "they tracked these Apocalypse Kings to your school."

"What?" Adedayo said, his eyes widening. "Why? Why would they go there?"

"They scanned your mind," said Valkyrie, "and your school is somewhere you know well, with plenty of people walking around, each one fitted with a juicy little soul, ready for plucking. It makes sense that they'd choose it for a hunting ground."

Adedayo stared. "They're going after the people in my school?"

"Don't worry," Skulduggery said as they approached the school gates, "we'll be here to search for them, stop them, and keep everyone else safe." He pressed his collarbones and a new face flowed up, one with a hooked nose and a moustache. "How's this? Is this one OK?"

"It's fine," said Valkyrie.

"Fine, but not great?"

"It'll do."

"I need it to be great. I'll be wearing it for hours."

"Then it's great."

"OK. I believe you."

They drove slowly into the school, the crowds of students parting, staring at the car as it passed.

"What, um, what's happening?" Adedayo asked. "What's going on?"

"We're going undercover," said Valkyrie. "I'll be a student, obviously, and he'll be a teacher."

"No," said Adedayo. "What? No. That's not a good idea."

"Nonsense. It's a wonderful idea," Skulduggery said, stopping in the far corner of the staff car park. Safely away from prying eyes, they got out and Skulduggery opened the boot. He placed his hat on the carved wooden box that had started this whole mess, and took out a teacher's black robe. He put it on, completing the look with a six-sided hat sporting a golden tassel. He stood there with his hands on his hips and said, "Am I not magnificent?"

Valkyrie frowned at the hat. "What's *that*?"

"It's called a tam, Valkyrie."

"You're not wearing that."

"I am, as it turns out."

"No, you're not."

"May I remind you that I'm a teacher and you're a student? Therefore, you will do as I command."

Valkyrie flicked her hand and the six-sided hat flew into her grip. She clicked the fingers of her other hand and suddenly she was holding a ball of flame. She set fire to the tam, then dropped it.

"I see," Skulduggery said slowly.

"But I don't think any of this is a good idea," said Adedayo. "I think you might, like, raise suspicions or something."

"Why would we do that?" Skulduggery asked, taking another six-sided hat from the boot and putting it on.

"Because you don't seem to be very good at keeping a low profile."

Shadows leaped from Valkyrie's ring and slashed the tam from Skulduggery's head.

"We are excellent at keeping a low profile," she muttered. "Skulduggery, don't you dare put on another—"

He put on another, the tassel dangling in front of his face.

Valkyrie glared. "How many of those do you have?"

"Eight," he said.

"And you're aware that they're ridiculous and they make you look stupid?"

"I am aware that they are amazing and they make me look like a teacher."

"No teacher wears any of that stuff any more."

"Then I will usher in a revival of the trend."

She glowered. "Fine. You want to look stupid, you go ahead and look stupid."

"Thank you, I will."

"Will you even be allowed into the school building?" Adedayo asked.

Skulduggery shut the boot and locked the car. "Don't you worry, Adedayo. As far as the faculty is aware, I am a substitute teacher filling in for an absent member of staff, and Valkyrie has just transferred here. Most of the necessary paperwork has already been forged."

"Most?"

Skulduggery adjusted his tassel, and grinned. "Quite. Most is all you need, most of the time. And, for those times when most isn't enough, unswerving confidence is bound to see you through. Come now. We have a world to save."

7

Adedayo took his seat in Irish class and waited for the room to fill up. Valkyrie was the last one in, and Miss Coll tapped her ruler on the desk to call for silence.

"We have a new student joining us today," she announced. "Valerie, is it? Valerie, welcome. Most teachers would embarrass you by making you stand up and tell us a bit about yourself, but I've always found that to be needlessly cruel, so stand up and tell us a bit about yourself, there's a good girl."

It seemed to Adedayo that there wasn't a whole lot that could embarrass a girl like Valkyrie, and she stood there like she was standing in her own living room.

"Right," she said, "yes. Hi, everyone. I'm Valerie. A few of you might know me from my appearance in maths class yesterday. Like I said, I'm something of a prodigy, something of a genius, but I'm modest, and I hate showing off, so don't ask me to prove it in any way. I don't know anyone here apart from Adedayo, so I'd appreciate it if I could sit next to him just until I get settled. Because of how shy I am." She fixed Massoud with a look. "I'll take your desk, if you don't mind."

Massoud blinked at her for a moment, then looked round the room for support. When he received none, he sighed, gathered his stuff and moved to the empty desk at the front of the class.

"Cheers," Valkyrie said. "Also I don't have my books yet, so I'll have to share." She moved the desk closer to Adedayo's, and sat.

Miss Coll looked at her. "You're quite an assertive young lady, aren't you?"

Valkyrie raised an eyebrow. "Am I?"

The lesson began, the class splitting up into pairs to hold conversations in the Irish language.

"What are we meant to be looking for?" Adedayo whispered. "The Kings won't be just walking around out in the open, will they?"

"Wouldn't that be nice?" Valkyrie responded. "Oh, that would make our job so much easier. But no, they'll probably disguise themselves, so we'll have to stay alert for something out of place. We don't know how these guys are gonna do what they need to do, so just keep your eyes open, you know?"

"Eyes open," Adedayo repeated, looking round the room. "Right."

"And we can't discount the possibility of possession."

He looked back at her. "I'm sorry, what?"

"Possession," Valkyrie said again. "When these Apocalypse Kings choose a target, there's the possibility that, in order to feed on the soul, they might have to possess that person."

"Like, *possess* possess? Like control their actions?"

"I might be wrong, but it's something to look out for."

"Have . . . have you ever been possessed?"

"Not me personally, but I know people who have. It's not nice. Even after it's over, you feel rotten, apparently. People like us, we'd recover a lot faster than mortals, but even so . . . Does not sound like a good time to me."

"So anyone in this school could be possessed right now?"

"It's a possibility." She sighed. "This whole thing is totally unfair, to be honest."

"What do you mean?"

Valkyrie gave a quiet grunt. "The Faceless Ones may have been a threat way back when, but the last time they tried to break through into this reality we pushed them out again. So the Apocalypse Kings want to destroy the world to starve the Faceless Ones . . . but there *aren't* any Faceless Ones to *starve*. They came, they saw, we conquered."

"Do you think the Apocalypse Kings will realise that?"

"I doubt it. They've been in that box since long before recorded history, and the only thing they've had to focus on has been the destruction of every living being on the planet. I don't think they'll be changing their minds any time soon."

"Good point."

"Make sure," Miss Coll announced loudly, "that whatever it is you're talking about it is *as Gaeilge*, yes? *In Irish*. That's the whole point of the class, after all."

She raised an eyebrow at Adedayo and Valkyrie, and Adedayo frowned back suspiciously.

After Irish, it was history. Once again, Valkyrie sat beside Adedayo as his classmates chatted and laughed among themselves. The teacher was late. A feeling of cold dread overtook Adedayo.

And then Skulduggery swept into the room, his robe billowing behind him like a cape caught in a crosswind. The class went quiet.

"Oh dear," Valkyrie muttered.

8

Skulduggery got to his chair, frowned at it, and looked up. His moustache twitched, like it was about to bolt from his face.

Niall put up his hand.

"Aha!" said Skulduggery. "A question already! Yes, young sir? What do you have burning inside you, curiosity-wise?"

"Why are you wearing gloves?"

"I have cold hands," Skulduggery answered.

Clodagh leaned forward in her seat. "Why are you wearing that hat?"

"It keeps my head warm."

"Why are you wearing a cloak?" asked Bolanle.

"It billows impressively when I walk."

Seimi folded his arms. "What's with the moustache?"

Skulduggery tilted his head. "I have a moustache?"

The students stared.

"Welcome," Skulduggery said loudly, "to this class of –" he looked at the books on his desk – "history. Ah, excellent. That's one of my specialist subjects, you know, as I was there for most of it. My name is Mister Me. You may call me 'sir' or 'Your Lordship'."

"Your name is Me?" Cian asked.

"Yes."

"The *word* Me?"

"The *name* Me, actually, but yes."

"That's not a name."

"Yes, it is. It's mine. I happen to come from a long line of reluctant narcissists. We don't like to talk about it."

"So . . . so *you* are *Me*."

There were a few laughs, and Skulduggery took a moment, then broke into an unnervingly huge grin. "Ah! I get it! Yes! Wonderful! You, boy, have a keen wit! I shall call you Barnaby!"

"That's not my name."

Skulduggery waved away the objection. "I have neither the time nor the inclination to learn names – and that goes for all of you – so I will call you by whatever pops into my head. Try not to be offended by my casual indifference to your feelings – we'll get on so much better if you can manage that. Now then, as a class, what topic are you studying right now?"

"Uh," Rafaela said, "we're revising the Great Famine."

"Ah, the Great Famine!" Skulduggery repeated. "Thank you, Winifred! Also called the Great Hunger or the Great Starvation – *great* as in widespread, not *great* as in wonderful. Caused by what? Can anybody tell me?"

Caitlyn raised a hand. "Potato blight."

"Potato blight," Skulduggery said, "yes! The dreaded *Phytophthora infestans* that swept across Europe in 1845 had a particularly devastating effect on Ireland because . . . why . . .?"

"Because people loved potatoes," said Raunak, and everybody laughed.

"Did they, though?" Skulduggery asked. He perched on the edge of his desk, adjusted his tassel, and observed the class grimly. "Let me tell you a story, then, of a nation forced to export huge quantities of livestock, fish, beans, peas – even honey – to Britain while being left with nothing but fields of rotting potatoes for themselves. Let me tell you a story of pain, of prejudice, of cruelty and of sacrifice. Let me tell you a story of people. A story of . . . yes?"

Haley lowered her hand. "Mister Me—"

"Please," Skulduggery said, "call me Your Lordship."

She sighed. "Your Lordship, we have our notes, and a test at the end of the week. We really don't need stories of people."

"But that's what history is!" Skulduggery exclaimed. "History isn't a list of dates or a collection of events – history is people. It's the decisions they make, and the consequences of those decisions. History is a jigsaw puzzle, and when you have all the pieces in place you can step back and finally see the whole picture laid out before you. History is a mystery waiting to be solved."

Rania held up her textbook. "Mystery solved, sir."

"Ha!" Skulduggery barked so loudly that Adedayo actually jumped. "You can't get history from a textbook! You can't find truth in a Contents page! History is a living, breathing thing!"

"Hold on," said Conor. "So history is people, a jigsaw puzzle, a mystery, *and* it's a living, breathing thing?"

"It's all of these things and more," Skulduggery said, "and it's a mistake to think that it can be captured and placed into a safe little cage on a safe little page to be memorised. History defies your tests and it denies your exams. But they don't want you to know that."

"Who?" asked Lucy. "Who doesn't want us to know?"

"Governments," Skulduggery said, almost whispering. "Corporations. Text-book manufacturers. They're all in on it. That's why I could never be a teacher – the idea that I'd be regurgitating falsehood upon falsehood for generation after generation would be, frankly, more than I could handle."

"What do you mean, you could never be a teacher?" Cian said. "You *are* a teacher."

"Once again, Barnaby, your quick wits impress me. Have a gold star." Skulduggery dug into a pocket in his robe and flung a fistful of tiny gold stars across the room.

"Uh, thank you," said Cian, brushing them from his hair.

9

Ian Tynan had been a teacher at the school for eighteen years, and he was proud of the fact that he made time to chat to each and every substitute teacher who passed through those hallowed doors, no matter how short a time they were here for. The new guy, the one called Me, was a tall one, with an interesting moustache, and he wore a robe and one of those six-sided hats. He stood in the middle of the staffroom, peering at every teacher who passed.

Ian walked up to him. "Welcome to the madhouse," he chuckled. "Name's Ian."

They shook hands. "Hello, Ian. The name's Me. Honolulu Me."

Ian frowned slightly. "That's quite an unusual name you got there."

"And yet believable," said Honolulu. "My parents met in Hawaii, you see. It's where they fell in love. After a whirlwind romance, they got married, and I was born nine months later, which you'll find is the customary length of time for a pregnancy to come to full term. They named me Honolulu, after the city that changed their lives. This is not an unusual decision, as many people are named after geographical locations."

"That's actually very sweet."

"Is it?" said Honolulu. "Good. They died soon after in a terrible parasailing accident."

"Oh. Oh, no. They were sharing the same parasail when it . . .?"

"No, actually, they were on separate parasail wings, as they're called, but the boats that were towing them passed too close to each other and, well, I'm sure you can imagine what happened next. Still, at least they died in each other's arms."

"That's . . . awful."

"After their sad demise, I was raised in a series of orphanages, in which I had many adventures, and eventually I grew up and became a teacher. That's the story of my life. Do you have a story of your life, Ian?"

"Not . . . not one as eventful as yours."

"Then I thank you for not sharing it with me. Can I ask you a question, though? Have you noticed anything unusual lately?"

"What kind of unusual?"

Honolulu chuckled. "Oh, nothing sinister, I assure you! Just regular levels of unusual. Have you noticed, for instance, somebody acting strangely, or someone seeming drained of energy, or maybe you've seen some ghostly apparitions, anything like that?"

"Apparitions?"

"Ghostly apparitions, yes. What about voices? Have you been hearing any voices?"

"You mean apart from yours? No, no voices."

"Oh, good," said Honolulu, failing to hide the look of disappointment on his face.

"You're a strange man, Honolulu."

"It's a strange world, Ian."

10

Alesha Walsh had been a student at the school for three years, but she remembered quite clearly the feeling of walking in and not knowing anyone, so, when she saw the new girl sitting alone in the cafeteria, she walked over and sat next to her.

"Hi," she said. "I'm Alesha. You're Valerie, right?"

"Yes," the new girl said, smiling. "Hey there."

"Just to let you know, everyone's having a big discussion about why you're switching schools in the middle of term. Some of my friends reckon you got kicked out of your last school for fighting, while others reckon you just burned it to the ground. Are either of those close to the truth?"

"Not especially," Valerie said. "My folks got new jobs and we had to move – that's the entire story. Sorry to disappoint."

"I'm sure they'll get over it," Alesha said, and smiled again. "This place isn't so bad. You've got your different groups that you need to be aware of, though." She nodded to a table in front of them. "Those are the sporty types, the jocks, as the Americans would say, although they're not really that sporty, all things considered, and they do have plenty of other interests."

She indicated a table next to one of the windows. "Over there, you have the geeks, and all they ever talk about are comics and movies and books, but they're quite well liked because everyone loves that stuff."

She pointed again. "There you have your popular girls, the pretty ones. Some of them are really nice, and, while there are a few who aren't classically beautiful, everyone's welcome, you know?" She scanned the room. "After that, there are the weirdos, the burnouts and the losers, but they tend to mingle with all the other groups because everyone has redeeming qualities and no one is left out. And I think that's it, really."

"And where does Adedayo fit into all this?"

"Oh. To be honest, I'm not too sure. He's not the *best* at sports, and he's not *amazingly* geeky, and he doesn't get the *best* grades, but, um . . . oh! He's a member of the debating club, did you know that?"

"I didn't."

"I mean, yeah, I'd say he's quite a reluctant member, if you know what I mean? He doesn't really like arguing all that much, which is a drawback. But he's cute and he's nice and he's just the right kind of weird, so if you fancy him, I say go for it."

"I'll keep that in mind," Valerie said, smiling. "It sounds like a nice school."

Alesha shrugged. "Ah, it has its problems, the same as everywhere. You get bullies, and you get people being mean to each other, and you get those who just can't seem to fit in . . . but, on the whole, it's not bad."

"And you're the welcoming committee, are you?"

"Ha! Hardly. I just thought you could use some company."

"Well, that's very nice of you."

"I'll introduce you around and you'll make friends in no time, just you see."

A girl went past their table, her head down. "Hey, Lorna, come say hello! Lorna? Lorna!" But Lorna just kept walking, and Alesha rolled her eyes. "OK, that wasn't the best example, but everyone else is lovely, I swear!"

Valerie grinned. "I'll take your word for it."

II

Debating practice went disastrously, as it usually did. Adedayo was given the task of arguing against the idea that society should eat the rich, but ended up persuading everyone – himself included – that eating the rich would probably be a good idea, all things considered.

The bell sounded, the corridors filled with students heading to their next class, and Adedayo rushed for the toilet. He got halfway there when Valkyrie appeared at his elbow.

"Who are you following?" she asked, peering ahead of them.

"What?"

"Who's your suspect?"

"I don't have one."

"Then why are you sneaking around?"

"I'm not sneaking," said Adedayo. "That's just how I walk when I'm bursting to go to the loo."

"Oh." He squeezed through the throng. She barged through after him. "What's your next class?"

"Chemistry," he said.

She made a face. "I hate chemistry."

"But, like I said, I have to go to the toilet now."

"Cool," she said, still at his elbow.

"You can't follow me in there."

"Sorry? Oh! Yeah, of course. Duh."

He went to walk off, then turned. "What happens if we don't find the Apocalypse Kings before the final bell?"

"Then we start again tomorrow."

"And do you think, um, Mister Me will come back? It's just, I don't feel he's blending in as well as he thinks he is."

They watched Skulduggery march down the corridor, smiling at nothing.

"Yeah," Valkyrie said, "he's pretty awful at it. It's been so long since he was, y'know, alive, that he's completely forgotten how to act around normal people. I'm much better at it."

"Yeah," Adedayo muttered.

She looked at him sharply. "What?"

"Sorry?"

"You said *yeah* like you didn't mean it. You don't think I'm blending in?"

"I don't know. I suppose it kinda depends on your definition of blending in."

"I'm a sixteen-year-old blending in with a bunch of other sixteen-year-olds. I can't *not* blend in. That's like saying a blade of grass isn't blending in with the rest of the lawn. Why do you think I'm not blending in?"

Adedayo chose his words carefully. "You're very confident."

"So?"

"Most people aren't that confident – especially when you're the new kid."

"But this is how I've always been."

"Oh. OK. Is this what you're like in your own school? Do you even still go to school?"

"Of course I do," Valkyrie said. Then shrugged one shoulder. "Well, technically, it's not me."

"I'm not sure I understand."

The corridor was emptying fast so she lowered her voice. "Technically, it's my reflection. It steps out of the mirror and goes to school in my place and does my homework and spends time with my family, stuff like that. It means I'm not missing out on anything."

"You have a magical reflection? And it takes over your life?"

"Only the boring bits."

"I'm not really sure how to, like, process that."

"*You* can have a magical reflection too, you know."

"Seriously? So I could, like, send it in to do my exams and stuff?"

"Magic, dude. It's awesome."

Her phone beeped, and Adedayo swallowed the urge to tell her that they weren't allowed to have their phones on during school hours.

"Elliot," she said, looking at the screen. "Skulduggery suspects a teacher called Elliot."

"This way," said Adedayo, and Valkyrie followed him. They got to Mr Elliot's classroom. The door was still open and they watched him sitting at his desk, his shoulders hunched, staring into space and completely ignoring the students.

"Is this normal behaviour from him?" Valkyrie asked, keeping her voice low.

"Not really," Adedayo answered. "He doesn't look well."

"Having a hungry god leech off your soul will do that to you, I suppose." She took Adedayo's arm and moved them on. "OK, so we have our first suspect. Now we need two more."

"Cool," said Adedayo. "But you head on to chemistry, OK? I'll meet you there."

Valkyrie frowned. "Where are you going?"

He went to answer and she clicked her fingers.

"Toilet! Yes! Go! Pee! Pee and be free!"

She walked off and Adedayo shook his head. She was so weird.

He hurried on. A couple of boys were at the urinals so he stepped into one of the cubicles. He heard the boys leave and then he finished up, flushed the toilet, and stepped out.

Lorna stood at a washbasin, staring at her reflection in the mirror. She was pale. Her spine curved.

"Lorna?" Adedayo said. "Everything OK?"

She turned suddenly, smiling. "Yes," she said brightly. "Everything's great. How are you, Adedayo?"

"I'm, uh, I'm good. Lorna, these are the boys' toilets."

She blinked. "Oh," she said. "Oh dear."

There was a flash, like a light bulb flaring, and in that instant Adedayo saw the hazy figure of the Cythraul looming behind Lorna, his tentacles stuck in her head. Then he was gone again, almost immediately.

"I should get to class," Adedayo said.

"Oh dear," Lorna said again. "You saw, didn't you? Oh dear, oh dear. What *are* we going to do about that?"

Her smile widened.

12

A dedayo bolted, but she was on him before he reached the door, and she tossed him behind her like he was nothing but an old coat. He somehow managed to keep upright as he bounced off the wall, stumbling into the cubicle.

"You saw me," Lorna said.

He slammed the cubicle door. Locked it. The latch rattled loosely. "No, I didn't!" he called.

"You saw me," Lorna sang. "That's a pity. We were going to leave you alone. We thought it polite. You're the one who set us free, after all. The least we can do is refrain from eating your soul."

Adedayo pressed his hands against the door. "I won't tell anyone, I promise."

Through the gap between the hinges, he watched her shape get closer. "I know," she said.

She shoved the door and it was like a truck hit it, flinging Adedayo back. He scrambled on to the toilet seat as she reached for him and vaulted clumsily over the cubicle wall. He hit the ground and bolted as she lunged, grabbing the back of his jumper. He turned, twisted, pulling his head and arms free, and then he was sprinting into the corridor.

She came after him.

Adedayo ran, adrenaline pumping through his system, painfully aware of how close she was, of how her fingertips grasped at the shirt on his back. Up the stairs, turning right, running alongside the balcony that overlooked the sports hall. She was going to get him. He was going to slow down or trip or make a mistake and then she was going to have him and this time there'd be no escape. He knew it. It was inevitable. He was dead unless he did something unexpected.

He launched himself over the balcony and Lorna screeched and grabbed his wrist and he swung back and hit the wall, but her grip wasn't good and she had to let him go and he fell, slamming down on to the soles of his feet, jarring his knees, teeth crunching together, and then he was spinning, running on shaking legs, bursting through the double doors into the sunlight.

"Adedayo!" Valkyrie yelled from the Old House, and Adedayo sprinted across the courtyard. She grabbed him. "Let's go," she said, bolting for the stairs. "Skulduggery's waiting. We have a plan."

"What kind of plan?" Adedayo gasped, trying to keep up.

"A good one," she said. "Well, kinda."

He glanced back as the door burst open. Lorna stormed in, looked up, right at him, and smiled.

Adedayo tripped over the top step, would have fallen if Valkyrie hadn't kept him upright, turning him to the second set of stairs. She stopped suddenly and he crashed into her. Mr Elliot stood halfway up, the hazy image of the Sathariel looming over him.

"Hold on," Valkyrie whispered, wrapping an arm round Adedayo's waist. She brought her other arm in and it was like the air seized them and flung them high over Elliot's head.

A small part of Adedayo's fear-spiked mind recognised how exhilarating it all was.

They crashed on to the landing and Valkyrie led the way onwards, to a part of the Old House Adedayo had never been. Down a narrow corridor they went, up some steps, turning a corner, up more steps, before arriving in an attic space the size of a swimming pool. The room was clean and empty, the ceiling high, the windows flooding it with light.

"So what's the plan?" Adedayo asked, trying to get his breath back. "Where's Skulduggery?"

"He's supposed to be here," Valkyrie said, frowning.

Adedayo kept his eyes on the door. "Maybe you should call him? Maybe you should call him now, like? It's a bit of an emergency, don't you think? Lorna said – or, no, the Cythraul controlling her said – they were going to eat my soul."

"They're *not* going to eat your soul," Valkyrie said firmly.

"He said they weren't planning on it, out of politeness, but he's changed his mind and he's gonna eat it."

"He said that, did he?"

"He did."

"Well, I can assure you, Adedayo, we are *not* going to eat your soul."

Adedayo stopped moving for a few seconds, and then he turned, ever so slowly. Valkyrie stood there, smiling calmly, while the Deathless stood behind her, his fingers inside her head.

13

"Oh dear," said Lorna, joining them in the attic, Elliot at her heels.

Adedayo backed up against one wall, keeping all three of the Apocalypse Kings in sight. "How long?" he asked.

Valkyrie's smile widened. "How long have I been controlling her? Only a few minutes. I had attached myself to one of your school friends but, once I sensed Valkyrie's sheer power, I couldn't resist the – what's the word? – *upgrade*."

"We should eat their souls," Lorna said.

"We agreed that we would keep the damage we inflict to a minimum," Valkyrie responded. Her face, her voice, his words. "When they are dead, they will need their souls to move through to what comes next."

Elliot nodded. "We will feed but not devour. It is what we agreed."

"But that was before," said Lorna. "You can feel it as I can. It will be better for us if we consume their souls completely. It will make us stronger."

"This isn't about strength," Valkyrie said. "This is about punishing the Faceless Ones. And we are strong enough already – it is time to stand on our own."

"I agree," said Elliot.

Valkyrie stiffened, and the Deathless stepped away from her, letting her collapse. He stood there, clenching and unclenching his fists, rolling his shoulders, working his jaw – getting used to having his own flesh-and-blood body once more.

Mr Elliot grunted and then sank to the floor, as unconscious as he was ungraceful, and the Sathariel stood over him, his hand going to his brow as if the light was hurting his eyes behind his veil.

"I object to this," Lorna said.

"I know," the Deathless replied.

She arched her back and gritted her teeth, and her knees gave out and she fell – but the Cythraul caught her, and lowered her gently to the ground.

"This isn't right," Adedayo said softly.

"You will be treated fairly," the Deathless said. "You have my word."

"Well, you're planning on killing everyone, so right now your word doesn't mean much to me, no offence."

"The Deathless sit in judgement," said the Cythraul.

"The Deathless do not lie," said the Sathariel.

"I would not mislead you, Adedayo," the Deathless said. "The other races, the Faceless Ones among them, relied on my kind to be impartial, to be just. We even had the confidence of Those Who Slumber, Whose Name We Dare Not Speak Lest They Rouse to Waking. But that was before the Scourge, before the Great Betrayal."

Adedayo frowned. "I recognise some of what you're saying. Those Who Slumber, Whose Name We Dare Not Speak Lest They Rouse to Waking. They were in your mind when I looked into it, in the swimming pool of knowledge, but . . ."

"But I hid the details from you," said the Deathless, "as I hid so much else. There are truths you are not ready for – truths that would harm you and tear you in two."

"How very considerate of you," said Skulduggery, walking in. His teacher's robe and six-sided hat were gone – as was his face. He was just a skeleton now, and he wore his other hat, the one that went with his suit, dipped low over one eye socket. "So what is it going to be?"

The Deathless turned to him. "I beg your pardon?"

"How are you going to do it? How are you going to kill everyone? Plague? Pestilence? Are you going to snap your fingers and we'll all crumble to dust?"

"No," the Deathless said. "We're going to die."

"I see," Skulduggery said slowly.

Valkyrie sat up, blinking. Mr Elliot and Lorna – mere mortals, without the benefit of magic in their blood – stayed unconscious.

"Our passing will cause our souls to reverberate," said the Cythraul, "and those reverberations will shake this world to pieces."

The Sathariel continued. "The ground will quake and the mountains will tumble. Fire will rain from the skies and the seas shall boil and reclaim the land."

Skulduggery nodded. "So, bring your umbrella is what you're saying."

"*Can* you even die?" Valkyrie asked the Deathless as she stood.

"Do not allow our name to mislead you, Valkyrie. In our arrogance, my kind named ourselves, for we thought there existed no power that could rob us of life. We were, as in a great many things, wrong. By the time the Faceless Ones betrayed us all, we had already been thoroughly humbled." He smiled. "But the name stuck."

"They're not here," said Adedayo. "The Faceless Ones. You're doing this because of them, because of what they did to your race, but they're not even around any more. They've been banished."

"Yet this world reeks of them," said the Sathariel. "The air has grown stale with the stench of them. They have made their mark here and they wish to return."

"They see this place as their rightful home," the Cythraul said. "While they still live, they will seek to cross realities until they are worshipped here once again. But, when they arrive, we want them to set foot on the remnants of a barren land – a land devoid of humanity."

"Then how about you help us?" Valkyrie said. "How about, instead of spoiling their home, you stand by our side if they ever come back?"

"There are but three of us," said the Cythraul, "and the Faceless Ones' numbers are immeasurable."

The Deathless shook his head. "If we fight them, we may lose, and forgo our chance at retribution. Destroying their food source, however, destroying their homeland . . . that is guaranteed to inflict damage."

"Fair enough," said Valkyrie. "I mean, if you're happy with merely *damaging* the Faceless Ones, instead of actually fighting and possibly destroying them, then hey, you do you."

"You will not change our minds."

"Nope. Looks like you decided what you're gonna do a long time ago, and you've got no intention of changing."

"Your attempt at reverse psychology will not work."

"I don't even want it to."

"You are amusing," said the Deathless, as he took a glass ball from his robe. Energy flowed from his hand into the ball, and Adedayo watched the Deathless sag. When he was done, he handed it to the Sathariel, who took his turn.

"Let me guess," said Skulduggery. "That orb is your equivalent of loading a gun with three bullets, yes?"

The Sathariel slumped, and handed the orb to the Cythraul.

"Then what do you do?" Skulduggery continued. "It looks fragile, so I imagine you destroy it, releasing the bullets that will then seek you out?"

The Deathless smiled. "You've seen this before?"

"I've seen something like it, yes. A way to ensure you all die at the same instant."

The Cythraul handed the orb back to the Deathless. The different-coloured energies flickered around inside like fish in a bowl.

"Something to hang on the Christmas tree," said Valkyrie. "Cute."

"You won't have to wait long," said the Sathariel. "Once the orb settles, we will end your suffering."

Valkyrie rolled her shoulders. "Putting all that energy into the orb really took it out of you, didn't it? Even the way you're standing right now – you look dead on your feet. Don't you think so, Skulduggery?"

"Yes, I do," Skulduggery said.

"We are still more than strong enough to restrain you," said the Sathariel.

Skulduggery tilted his head. "You think so?"

The Sathariel raised an arm, but Skulduggery flew across the room, smashing into him.

The Cythraul moved to help, but shadows leaped from Valkyrie's ring and wrapped round him, binding his many tentacles.

The Deathless backed away from it all, then turned and ran out of the room.

"Adedayo!" Skulduggery called as he wrestled. "Stop him!"

Adedayo nodded. Then shouted, "*What?*"

The Sathariel slammed Skulduggery back against the wall.

"We can't do it!" Skulduggery yelled. He punched the Sathariel, drove a knee into his leg, followed it with an elbow shot to the face. "We're a bit busy! You'll have to!"

"But I can't use magic when I'm panicking!"

"It's not about magic!" Valkyrie cried as the Cythraul broke free of her shadows. "It's about trying your best, you muppet!"

The tentacles grabbed her, picked her up, hurled her across the room.

Adedayo hesitated – then ran after the Deathless.

14

He caught a glimpse of the Deathless turning a corner, and sprinted after him. This was stupid. This was amazingly dumb. What did he know about fighting a god? But he had no choice. There was no one else around to do it. There was no one he could turn to for help. This had to be him. He had to try. The fate of the world depended on him. His parents, his sisters, everyone he loved depended on him.

A small set of stairs led to a door that was just swinging closed. Adedayo charged up, clicking his fingers until he had a small ball of flame in his hand. He burst out on to the roof of the Old House. The Deathless stood on the roof's edge, his back to him.

Adedayo hurled the fireball. It barely made it halfway before going out.

He tried pushing at the air, but all he could manage was a slight breeze.

The Deathless turned to him slowly. Adedayo had one chance left. One slim chance.

"*Má şi àpótí!*" he shouted.

The Deathless raised an eyebrow. "Pardon?"

Adedayo frowned, wondering if he'd got the pronunciation wrong. "*Má şi àpótí,*" he repeated, a lot quieter this time.

The Deathless didn't react. The spell didn't work.

Adedayo realised his fists were clenched. He unclenched them. "Please don't do it," he said.

The Deathless gazed at the orb in his hand. "I promise you, what awaits your soul in death is far greater than what this life has had to offer you."

"Maybe it is, but I don't want that yet. Barely anyone does. You're robbing us, all of us, all of humanity, of who we are."

"Who you are is wonderful," said the Deathless, looking at him, "but ultimately unimportant. Your soul is eternal, Adedayo, or as close to eternal as can be. By contrast, you, your memories, your personality – these things exist for so brief a time that it could be argued they don't exist at all."

Adedayo took a step forward. "But they exist *now*. I exist now. I'm right here. I'm talking to you. I'm asking you not to destroy us."

The orb started to pulse with a soft glow. "It is ready," said the Deathless. "It is time."

"Wait! Please wait! I get that you think I'm unimportant, that humanity is unimportant, but who are you to decide this?"

"I'm a god," said the Deathless.

That was, admittedly, a good point. "OK, right, you're a god, so I'm asking you to be a merciful god. You want to destroy the Faceless Ones because they wiped out your race. But what are you about to do? You're going to kill my race the same way the Faceless Ones killed yours."

"I am fully aware of the hypocrisy of my stance."

"Then be better than them. Isn't that the least you can do, after what happened? Isn't that how you defeat them?"

"We are under no illusion, Adedayo. We have long since lost this battle." He raised his hand, preparing to hurl the orb to the ground.

"Not yet you haven't," Adedayo said quickly. "Not while you're still alive. Yeah, they murdered your race, they murdered the Cythraul's race and the Sathariel's race – but they couldn't kill you, could they? They could only trap you. You know what that says to me? It says they're scared. It says they feared you getting out. And now what? Now that you're out, instead of fighting them, you're going to end yourselves to spoil their food source? I don't know anything about what's out there on other planets or in other dimensions – but what's to stop the Faceless Ones from finding another world full of worshippers with souls they can eat?"

The Deathless hesitated. "This is still their home."

"So you're going to ruin it just to spite them?"

"I don't expect you to understand."

"But if you can't make me understand, maybe that's not a fault with me. Maybe that's a fault with your argument."

The Deathless said nothing.

"I don't know what the best thing to do is, but Skulduggery and Valkyrie, and other sorcerers like them, I'm sure they'll have plans. You don't have to be the bad guys here. You could be the heroes. You could do your races proud."

"You are a good boy, Adedayo. A good human. It is a pity it has come to this."

"But I'm not alone," Adedayo responded. "I'm not the only one. The human race, we have our problems, we do, but there are plenty more good people in this world than there are bad. Give us a chance, please."

"A chance to do what? To poison your planet further? To kill yourselves your own way?"

"At least give us the chance to decide our own fate – a chance the Deathless were never given."

"You are trying to convince me that humanity is worth sparing – even though I have already looked inside your mind. I know about their petty cruelties."

"You can't judge us by the idiots, though. Judge us by the nice people. That's what you do, isn't it? Sit in judgement? All those other gods, they trusted your kind to be fair. That's all I'm asking now. Just be fair."

"This accord between my kind, the Cythrauls, and the Sathariels has long been in motion."

"That doesn't mean you have to see it through. You can change your mind. You can focus on helping us instead of hurting us. The Faceless Ones are still out there somewhere. Don't you want to fight back? I know you do. You can deny it, if that makes you feel better, but I saw it when you let me look inside your mind. You want to fight. Not like we fight, not like humans fight, but you want to . . ." He searched for the right words. "You want to be better than them. You want to prove that you're better than them. And for you that doesn't mean beating them physically. It doesn't even mean ruining their home. It simply means that you beat them by being better than they are. You could do what you're planning to do. I can't stop you. But it's just . . . it's revenge. That's all it is."

"Revenge," said the Deathless, "is all we have left."

"That's not true, though. You've got so much more because you *are* so much more. You're talking to me. You're hearing my side of the argument. The Faceless Ones wouldn't listen to a word I said – but you're not them. You're listening. You *are* better than they are. Or, at least . . . you can be. But taking revenge on someone, on anyone, that just brings you even with them, doesn't it? It means you're operating on the same level."

The Deathless raised an eyebrow slightly. "And you want us to operate on a higher level?"

"I do. And so do you, I think. You could have the revenge that you planned, right now, by smashing that orb thing. Or you could choose not to. You could pass over it. You could let it go. And be better than them."

The Deathless smiled sadly. "You are wise, Adedayo Akinde."

"I am?"

"I will consider your words. If I decide that you are right, then we will return to our confinement. It was, if nothing else, peaceful in there. If, however, I decide that I am more right than you, that our plan is truly the way to proceed, then I hope your death is swift and painless."

Adedayo hesitated. "Cool."

The Deathless inclined his head ever so slightly, and Adedayo fainted.

15

Adedayo opened his eyes.

It was dark. Oh, God, he'd failed. He'd failed and the Apocalypse Kings had destroyed everything and everyone was dead and the world was in darkness all because of him and his stupidity and his . . . no, wait – it was night.

He was lying on the roof of the Old House, and it was night-time. Yes. That made sense.

"There you are."

He sat up as Skulduggery walked out on to the roof. "What happened?"

"You did it," Skulduggery said. "The Deathless came back down and the fighting stopped. He explained to the other two what you talked about up here and made them understand. They're quite a reasonable bunch – for gods, I mean. They abandoned their plan, retrieved their energies from the orb, and agreed to return to the box until they decide what to do with themselves. We can't lock it like the Faceless Ones did, but when you're dealing with beings like the Apocalypse Kings, you take what you can get." He stood beside him. "Well done."

"Thank you," Adedayo said, getting up. "How long have I been out here?"

"About five hours."

"Oh." His eyes widened. "My parents are going to kill me!"

"Probably."

"What about Lorna? And Mr Elliot?"

"Both fine," said Skulduggery. "They're mortals, so they won't remember anything about what happened. That's always best, I find. Things like this tend to traumatise mortal minds."

"You found him," Valkyrie said, walking on to the roof. She was wearing all black. "Wow, it's chilly up here."

Adedayo suddenly realised how cold he was, and crossed his arms. Valkyrie slipped off her jacket and handed it over.

"Go on," she said. "Until you warm up."

He accepted it gratefully.

"This is a moment, Adedayo," Skulduggery said. "In life we are offered so very few moments to truly savour – so, when they occur, you must take the opportunity to sear them into your memory. This would be, I imagine, your first time saving the world?"

"I saved the world?"

"We all did, which means the three of us can say both *We saved the world* and *I saved the world*. Go ahead. Say it."

"Uh . . ."

"Don't be shy."

Adedayo cleared his throat. "I saved the world."

"Yes, you did," said Skulduggery. "I want you to stand here on this rooftop, Adedayo, and reflect on those words. Do you know what makes a hero?"

"Bravery," said Adedayo. "Or . . . maybe fear. You can't be brave unless you're feeling scared, right? So bravery in spite of fear? Is that what makes a hero?"

Skulduggery shrugged. "I was going to say *punching*, but sure, yours is OK, too."

"What do I do now? Like, do I go back to my normal life and forget about all this, or do I abandon my normal life and focus on learning magic?"

Skulduggery took a moment before answering. "I don't care," he said.

"Oh," said Adedayo.

"It's up to you," Valkyrie said. "Skulduggery can't tell you what to do. It wouldn't be right."

"And also I genuinely don't care," Skulduggery said.

Valkyrie ignored him. "When I found out about magic, that was it for me, I couldn't let it go. I wasn't about to return to my old life, not after what I'd seen – but everyone's different. Do you like your life?"

"I mean . . . I suppose."

"Do you ever feel as if something's missing?"

He was quiet for a bit. "Not before now."

"It's up to you, dude. You get involved in magic, and it can be really, really dangerous. You could get killed doing this."

"Or you could get killed in your bedroom playing video games," Skulduggery said. "A meteor could come through your window and take your head clean off. I've seen it happen."

"You have not," Valkyrie said crossly.

"Yes, I have."

She folded her arms. "You've seen a meteor take someone's head off in their bedroom, have you?"

"Maybe not *exactly* that," he responded, somewhat grudgingly. "OK, fine, it wasn't a bedroom, it was a kitchen, and it wasn't a meteor, it was a rock, and it didn't take their head off, but it left a bruise."

"Skulduggery, did you throw a stone at someone while they were standing in their kitchen?"

"I did, yes."

She sighed, and turned her attention back to Adedayo. "It's your choice. I'm gonna leave a number with you for a place called the Sanctuary. If you decide you want to explore magic, they'll be able to help. Oh, and take a name, all right? If you become a sorcerer, you'll need a new name."

"OK," said Adedayo. "Sure. What name should I take?"

Valkyrie smiled. "I can't tell you that. If you decide to learn magic, if you're capable of putting in the work and the practice, you'll be a new person. You've just got to decide what this new person will be called."

Skulduggery checked his pocket watch. "And now we must be off. I have a tailor friend who has a new suit waiting for me to pick up, and he gets unreasonably grumpy when I'm late." He stepped right to the edge of the roof and turned. "Adedayo, it's been a pleasure working with you. Maybe we'll do it again sometime. Maybe not."

He let himself fall backwards off the edge, and disappeared.

"What a show-off," Valkyrie muttered.

Adedayo passed her back her jacket and shadows flowed from her ring, enveloping her. "See you around," she said, and, when the shadows dispersed she was gone, and Adedayo was alone on the rooftop.

16

Adedayo got home and apologised for being so late. He told his parents he'd been out walking, thinking about his *iyá agba*. They seemed to accept that, and let the matter drop.

His sisters arrived in the kitchen and announced that, even though *Ìyá Agba* was gone, and so a bedroom was suddenly available, they wanted to keep sharing. They announced this like they expected their request to be denied – his youngest sister's eyes were already brimming with tears. When they were told that was fine, they shrieked and hugged and hugged their parents and even hugged Adedayo, and ran back to their room.

Adedayo's dad chuckled and went into the living room.

"Mum," said Adedayo.

She was making herself a cup of tea. "Yes, sweetie?"

"What was *Ìyá Agba*'s life like? Back in Nigeria?"

His mum paused. "I'm not too sure, actually. She never talked about it all that much. She was happy, though. I know that." She smiled. "She used to tell me stories, when I was your youngest sister's age. All kinds of stories she'd make up about people with amazing names all over Africa. People with magical powers. And in the stories she was always in the middle of the adventure. Always having fun. I miss her."

"I miss her too."

His mother's smile turned sad, and she took a packet of biscuits down from the cupboard and held it out. "Take two," she said, "and don't tell your sisters."

He took two, and she winked and carried her tea to the doorway.

"Mum," said Adedayo, "what does *má ṣi àpótí* mean?"

She frowned. "What?"

"It's just something *Ìyá Agbà* said to me in hospital. What does it mean?"

"Are you sure that's what she said?"

"I mean . . . I might not be remembering it exactly right, but I think so."

His mum shrugged one shoulder. "It's just it's an odd thing to say, that's all. It means *don't open the box.*"

Adedayo looked at her, then nodded. "Yep," he said. "Makes sense."

In December 2011 Derek launched a competition on his
blog (dereklandy.blogspot.com) to find two characters for
a new short story, to be published exclusively in this book.
One of them had to be Australian, and one of them had
to be New Zealandish... New Zealandan... um,
from New Zealand.

After much deliberation over all the fantastic entries,
Derek chose:

Tane Aiavao, of New Zealand, created by Josie. Tane is a
laid-back Maori Elemental with zero planning skills.

Hayley Skirmish, of Australia, created by Sparky
Braginski. Hayley is a strong-willed, plain-speaking Adept
with the ability to jump, flip, and run along walls and
ceilings.

Congratulations to Josie and Sparky! And now read on
for the brand-new story featuring their amazing
characters...

JUST ANOTHER FRIDAY NIGHT

"Zombies," Tane Aiavao muttered as they crept closer to the mausoleum. "I hate zombies."

The night air was filled with the stench of the dead. It wafted through the headstones and played with the long grasses of this remote Brisbane cemetery, and it was all Tane and Hayley could do to stop from gagging whenever one of the shambling, rotting things got too close. They stayed low, moving through the shadows, ready to run or fight in an instant should their luck change.

Hayley Skirmish, her brown hair tied back in a ponytail, held the axe in a two-handed grip. Tane, his own hair sticking up in a clump, followed behind her and did most of the complaining. Unlike his Australian companion, Tane didn't cherish these calm moments before the storm, and he cherished the storm even less. Tane was a New Zealander, a Kiwi, and even more than that he was a Maori, and he reckoned Hayley could learn a thing or two from him on how to relax. Not that he'd ever suggest it. Tane was a big guy, but not all of it was muscle, and there was something about Hayley that was just flat-out *intimidating* to a bloke like him. She was athletic and pretty and impressive, looked to be around seventeen, so she was a bit younger than he was – but even so, she was in charge, and that was the end of it.

Hayley moved her hand in a quick motion and they stopped where they were, within sight of the rusted iron gates of the Doherty family crypt. They could hear movement all around them. Tane peered about and caught glimpses of things that had once been people, lurching with each step. He disguised his whimper behind a terrified moan, and realised that Hayley was looking at him, like she was waiting for something.

"What?" he whispered.

"The amulet," she whispered back impatiently in that broad Aussie accent. "Hurry."

He frowned at her. "I don't have the amulet."

"What? You were meant to bring it!"

"I thought you were meant to bring it."

"I brought the axe!"

"No one told me I had to bring the amulet."

"I told you! Before we left!"

He let a moment pass. "I thought you were joking."

"Right," she whispered decisively, turning so she was facing him. "I'm going to kill you."

He flinched away from the axe. "I thought we didn't need the amulet – didn't Skulduggery say they'd be able to do this without it?"

Her grip on the axe was turning her knuckles white, and she had that look in her eye, the look that meant she was barely controlling her anger. "He did say that. And then Valkyrie said no, they *hoped* they'd be able to do this without the amulet, but that if they couldn't, they'd use the amulet as a last resort."

"A last resort?"

"To save the world."

Tane gave a feeble smile. "See? We've got nothing to worry about. I mean, when was the last time we used a last-resort-type weapon?"

"Monday."

He chewed his lip. "I'm sure we won't need to do it again so soon, though. It'll be fine."

She leaned in close, real close, close enough to bite his nose clean off. "You," she said in a whisper so coarse it was sliding off sandpaper, "are an idiot."

He shrugged and muttered something and went to retie his bootlace before he remembered gumboots don't have laces, and eventually Hayley looked back at the mausoleum. When they were sure they wouldn't be seen, they hurried to the gate. The lock had been snapped, but the hinges still creaked as they slipped through. Tane's feet crunched on pebbles, but Hayley's bare feet moved over them with barely a sound, and within moments they were passing through the heavy door into the dank confines of the final resting place (in theory, anyway) of the once great Doherty clan. Two flaming torches, held in wall brackets on either side, illuminated the ancient coffins that lay empty and broken all around them. Moving slowly, they approached the crumbling hole in the ground, a pit so impossibly dark it could have led into the infinitely fathomless depths of Hell itself.

"Looks pretty deep," Tane said.

Hayley didn't bother answering him. She did a quick check around to make sure all the coffins were indeed empty, and then moved back to the door. Hayley was good at standing guard. She was alert, and she didn't get bored as easily as Tane did, and she didn't start fidgeting or go for a wander, the way Tane tended to.

His eyes scanned the crypt, not finding a whole lot of interest. The plan was that they wait here for the sign, and then they help Skulduggery and Valkyrie close over this gaping pit, which was the reason the dead were walking. Skulduggery had explained it to them that very afternoon, how they had figured it all out, about the centuries-old family curse and the last of the Doherty bloodline and something else about how the wicked shall not rest and something about a dog. Or a bog, or something like that. Maybe a log.

"What does a log have to do with all this?" he asked Hayley.

"Nothing whatsoever."

He nodded to himself. It was definitely either dog or bog. He looked down into the pit. Could it really be called a pit? What made a hole a pit? It was about two metres in diameter and very dark, but apart from that, it was just a hole. He picked up a small piece of rubble and dropped it into the darkness. He listened for the sound of it hitting the bottom. Nothing. Either the hole was very, very deep or the piece of rubble was way too small. He picked up another piece, a heavier, chunkier piece.

"What are you doing?" Hayley asked suddenly.

He hid the chunk of rubble behind his back. "Nothing."

"You're doing something. What are you doing?"

"I'm not doing anything," he said. "I'm standing here, that's all."

Her eyes narrowed. "Stay away from the pit."

"It's more of a hole, really."

"Shut up, and stay away from it."

He didn't respond. She glared at him once more, then went back to peering out of the door. In Tane's experience, Australians were fine most of the time, but whenever they were in dangerous situations they tended to lose their sense of humour. Making sure he wouldn't be caught, Tane tossed the chunk of rubble into the hole and listened for a sound. It came almost immediately, a soft thud and a moan. Tane frowned. A moan?

The zombie pulled itself up and grabbed his ankle and Tane shrieked. He kicked out and fell back and the zombie was clambering from the hole/pit/ whatever it was, its flesh rotten and disgusting. Tane was aware of Hayley dragging him away as the zombie reached for him again.

"What did you do?" she hissed.

"I just wanted to see how deep it was!"

"I told you not to go near it!"

"Who are you to be giving me orders?"

She dropped him and strode forward. "I'm the one with the axe."

Zombies are scary and all, and there's the whole loss of identity and mindless savagery side to them, but one on one, they're not very effective. Now in an enclosed space, if you're outnumbered and there's nowhere to run, you can offer up a prayer to whichever god you believe in and prepare to have your brains eaten. In that kind of situation, you're pretty much doomed. But when there's only one of them, and they're as slow and clumsy as they usually are, and they're facing an Australian girl who's had experience wielding an axe, they don't really stand much of a chance.

The zombie had only just got to its feet when Hayley swung, and Tane had to admire her proficiency. The only way to kill a zombie is the tried and true – destroy the brain or sever the head – and where Tane would have chopped and hacked and made an unholy mess of it, one swipe was all it took for Hayley to get the job done. The head hit the ground and the body crumpled, and she glanced back at him and her eyes widened.

"Look out!"

Tane twisted just as the mausoleum door burst open and the zombies staggered in. He scrambled up as they poured through the doorway, a seemingly endless parade of decomposing corpses, moaning and snarling in that guttural way of theirs.

He pushed at the air and a few zombies went stumbling back, but he'd be the first one to admit that he wasn't the best Elemental the world had ever seen. Hayley was doing better, jumping and flipping and taking off heads, but there were just too many of them. Enclosed space. Outnumbered. Nowhere to run.

"This is bad," he said to Hayley as they backed up to the edge of the pit.

"Yes, it is..."

"OK, listen," he said. "I've got a plan. You run at them, do that jumping-around thing you like to do so much, let them eat you, and I'll try to escape."

"Good plan."

"Thank you."

"Or how about *you* run at them," said Hayley, "do that standing-around thing *you* like to do so much, let them eat *you*, and I just stay and watch?"

"I think I prefer my idea."

They were doomed. There was no way out. The zombies were closing in. Tane looked at Hayley. So much he wanted to tell her. So much he wanted to say. And then they heard a voice behind them.

"Thought I told you to stay *away* from the flesh-eating zombies from beyond the grave?"

They whirled as a skeleton in a mud-stained suit and a seventeen-year-old Irish girl with blood-matted hair climbed from the pit. Skulduggery held a wooden staff and Valkyrie threw him a headpiece carved from stone. He fixed it to the staff, then held it up for the zombies to see.

The shuffling stopped. The moaning stopped. They stared, transfixed.

"Hear me," Skulduggery said loudly. "You are the Doherty clan, the last of the great families. You have been cursed to an un-death, cursed to never know peace because of the sins of one man, centuries ago. That man, your ancestor, has now been punished. I have seen to it myself. The curse is lifted. This staff belonged to the one who cursed you. It is yours to destroy."

Skulduggery stepped back, held the staff over the pit they had just emerged from, and let it go. A moment passed where nothing happened and then, as one, the zombies lurched forward. Skulduggery and Hayley went one way and Valkyrie and Tane went the other, parting so that they wouldn't be caught in the surging mass of bodies that started to topple into the hole. Like lemmings they went, albeit uglier and smellier, without even a murmur as the darkness swallowed them. When the last of them disappeared into the pit, the pit itself closed over, and so was neither a hole nor a pit any longer.

"Told you we wouldn't need the amulet," Tane said, wiping the dust from his combats.

"How did you do it?" Hayley asked Skulduggery as he checked his pocket watch. "What's down there? What happened?"

"Assorted things," Skulduggery said as he led the way to the door.

"We've got to kind of hurry a little bit," Valkyrie said, walking after him.

"But how did you lift the curse?" Hayley asked. "How did you punish their ancestor?"

Skulduggery was already out the door, but Valkyrie hesitated just as she was about to leave, and turned. "He lied. We didn't lift the curse. We didn't punish anyone. We stole the staff to get the zombies to go away. And if we're not out of this graveyard by the stroke of midnight, in exactly seventy seconds, we will inherit the curse. Providing the Hound doesn't kill us first."

The Hound. So it was *dog*, not bog, and certainly not log. Tane remembered it now. The Hound was the spectral guardian of the curse on the Doherty family, and it was meant to be very, very mean. Feeling pretty chuffed with himself that he had managed to remember that much, Tane spoke up.

"So how big is it, this Hound? Big as a German Shepherd?"

Skulduggery stepped back inside the mausoleum, and nodded to just over Tane's shoulder, said, "Oh, it's about as big as that one," and Tane looked back.

The Hound stood where the pit had been. It was huge and scarred and ravaged and it was sniffing at the ground and pawing at the earth. And then it looked up at them with fiery red eyes and its hackles rose and it growled, and Tane felt very strongly that they should be running away now.

They bolted from the crypt. As they sprinted over people's graves, Tane could hear Hayley hissing apologies. He felt no such remorse. He'd run across a thousand graves if it meant delaying his entry into one of them.

The Hound burst through the mausoleum door, taking it from its hinges, but it hit the gate and for a moment it stalled, unable to find a way past. It solved its dilemma by leaping clean over the rust-tipped spikes, and landed on the far side in a crouch, its muscles rippling beneath the welts and the fur.

The road outside the cemetery was ahead. They were halfway there when the Hound caught sight of them and gave chase. Tane started laughing, one of his nervous reactions when being pursued. Skulduggery and Valkyrie and Hayley were ahead – if the Hound was going to pounce on anyone, Tane knew it was going to pounce on him. He was unlucky that way, always had been.

He didn't dare look back. He didn't need to. He could hear the Hound gaining on him. It was all over. He thought it had been all over before, in the crypt, but he had been premature. Now, *now* it was all over. His life, snatched away, extinguished like a candle in the wind, like in that song, 'Candle in the Wind'. And then Tane tripped and fell on his face and the Hound passed right over him, snapping at the space where his head had been.

Strewth, bro, that was lucky, a chirpy little voice in the back of his mind piped up.

The Hound landed and skidded on the gravel but snapped its body around, eyes fixed on Tane, saliva dripping from its bared fangs. Its body tensed, coiled, prepared to spring. One lunge would be all it took to close the distance between them, and Tane, lying belly-down on the ground, was in no position to even try to escape.

The chirpy little voice wasn't saying much of anything now.

There was shouting. Valkyrie and Hayley were at the very edge of the cemetery, calling out to the Hound and hurling stones. One of the stones, probably hurled by Hayley, hit Tane, but he didn't utter a sound. The beast snarled and reluctantly shifted its stare, snapping its jaws in the direction of the other two.

And then Skulduggery came darting out, waving his arms, and the Hound took a single step towards him and Tane kept his head down, didn't move an inch, and proved to be such an uninteresting target that the Hound quickly switched focus. It leaped for Skulduggery and Tane scrambled up and ran straight at Hayley. As he ran he saw Skulduggery sprint for a large Celtic cross, made from stone and standing as a proud testament to some dead guy's life. Right before he ran straight into it, Skulduggery turned his body sideways and let his momentum carry him forward. His shoulder collided with the cross and he spun and hit the ground, but the Hound hit it head-on.

Tane noticed something approaching from in front of him and realised it was Valkyrie, but she was standing still, and in fact it was he that was moving. He crashed into her and they tumbled back over the low wall and sprawled on to the road in a mass of flailing limbs and cursing. It was mostly Valkyrie cursing. Out of the corner of his eye he saw Skulduggery running for them, the Hound, having recovered, right behind him. Skulduggery dived out of the cemetery and the Hound leaped after him and then kind of faded into nothing, like the air had come and whipped it away. Skulduggery landed and rolled and was on his feet again, checked that the Hound was gone, and then looked down at Tane and Valkyrie.

"Having fun?"

Valkyrie hit Tane and got up.

"Is it over?" Hayley asked, looking around warily.

"It's over," said Skulduggery, straightening his tie. "Stroke of midnight, so it was in the nick of time, but when isn't it for us?"

"Always in the nick of time," Valkyrie mumbled. "Why can't we ever solve a problem *early*?"

Skulduggery tilted his head at her. "Where's the fun in that?"

Hayley peered at Tane. "You OK down there?"

"A dog tried to eat me," Tane said, not getting up.

"If it's any consolation," Skulduggery told him, "it tried to eat me, too."

"Yeah, that's no consolation at all."

"I need a shower," Valkyrie said. "I'm covered in gore and zombie guck, and I don't want to get on the plane reeking. It's a long flight back to Ireland."

"Was this your first trip to Australia?" Hayley asked her, suddenly all friendly now that the threat was averted. Bloody typical, that.

"No, but it was definitely my goriest. Are you sure your friend is OK?"

Hayley scowled down at Tane. "He's not really my friend. He's just an idiot that I know."

"She loves me," Tane whispered. The others talked a bit more, discussed this and that, but Tane stayed on the ground and didn't join in. He was alive. He was alive and he was going to stay alive, and he was going to enjoy living again. He suddenly had a mad urge for fishnchups. He poked his head up. "Anyone hungry?"

"I don't eat, I'm afraid," Skulduggery said, "and we really have to get going."

Valkyrie smiled. "Thanks for the offer, though."

Hayley looked at him and sighed. "Fine," she said, "I'll go get some grub with you. But you better not talk to me."

He grinned, and Hayley helped him up.

A LITTLE BIT
OF WEIRD

The door burst open, and Eddie shrieked and whirled and fell backwards over the stupidly low coffee table his wife had insisted on buying, despite Eddie's tendency to shriek and fall backwards over things.

As he lay on the thick carpet (that went with the walls and the curtains, but gave him a static shock whenever he walked across it, wearing socks), he watched a tall man stride into the house. A tall and thin man – a tall and *very* thin man – dressed in a suit and a hat, a fedora, like one of those old-fashioned private eyes in the black-and-white movies. Except all of those old-fashioned private eyes at least had the decency to wear a face with their fancy suits and fancy hats. This guy just had a skull.

"Hello, Eddie," said the skeleton, and, for the second time in thirty seconds, Eddie shrieked.

A girl walked in behind the skeleton. She couldn't have been more than sixteen years old, and her hair was as black as her clothes, so Eddie (who found teenagers vaguely scary, especially when wearing black) took an immediate dislike to her – but at least she had a face. So that was something.

"Help!" Eddie cried. "It's a skeleton!"

The girl ignored him, went into the other room as the skeleton looked around.

His shoes were shiny. His hands were gloved. The brim of his hat was pulled low over his left eye socket.

"House is clear," the girl said, walking back in. She frowned. "He still on the ground, then?"

"He appears to be," said the skeleton. "Eddie, how are you? I'm sure you're very startled right now, but I'm going to have to insist that you snap out of it as soon as possible. Bad things are happening, and we need your help."

Eddie's brain wasn't co-operating. This happened sometimes, usually when his boss, Mr McKenzie, invited him into his office for chats, which had been happening a lot lately. Eddie didn't do well under pressure.

"He doesn't say much, does he?" the girl said.

"Some people don't have to," the skeleton responded. "Eddie here strikes me as the strong, silent type. Would I be correct in that assumption, Eddie?"

Eddie gargled.

The skeleton nodded. "See? What did I tell you? Eddie, my name is Skulduggery Pleasant. This is my associate, Valkyrie Cain. We are sorcerers. We use magic. We use that magic, in large part, to protect people like you from various threats – though sometimes we use it to show off."

"It's about fifty-fifty," said the girl, Valkyrie Cain. That was a weird name. So was Skulduggery Pleasant, for that matter. Eddie didn't like weird stuff. It unsettled him.

"We're here," Skulduggery Pleasant continued, "because one such threat is on the loose, and we think it's coming for you."

Skulduggery waved his hand, and the air around Eddie shimmered, seemed to grab him and lifted him off the carpet. It deposited him back on his feet and dispersed. Eddie didn't know how to react to that, so he laughed, and then started crying.

"Oh," said Skulduggery.

Valkyrie stepped forward. "Eddie. Eddie, look at me. Stop crying and look at me. I understand that dealing with a living skeleton is a lot to take in, so maybe focus on me. I'm not scary, am I? I'm totally and completely normal, right? You're not scared of me, are you?"

"I... I am a little bit," Eddie confessed, sniffing back his tears.

Valkyrie narrowed her eyes. "But I'm not scary," she said scarily, and Eddie started crying again. She scowled and went to stand by the window, and Skulduggery took over.

"Eddie, there is a man, a sorcerer, like us, except he's bad, a bad man, and a psychic. Do you know what a psychic is?"

Eddie nodded. "People who can read minds. But they don't exist."

"Some of them don't exist, absolutely, but some of them very much do. This one's name is Hornswoggle Ra."

"That's a funny name."

"It is," said Skulduggery, chuckling. "It is a funny name. Hornswoggle Ra wants to devour your brain, Eddie."

Eddie was appalled. "But he can't. It's the only one I have."

"Hornswoggle doesn't care about that, I'm afraid," Skulduggery said, leading Eddie to the sofa. "You see, he's what we'd term a psychic vampire. Do you know what a vampire is?"

Eddie sat. "Creatures who drink your blood, who don't exist either."

"Correct on the first part, sadly mistaken on the second. Hornswoggle Ra makes you feel strong emotions – usually anger, or sadness, or outrage, or fear – and, instead of drinking your blood, he drinks all that energy back up. If he drinks too much, he'll leave you as little more than a husk, and you'll go through your life as an empty shell of a man."

Eddie swallowed. "Why is he after me?"

"Who knows how psychic vampires choose their victims?" Skulduggery asked, then paused. "Well, actually, I do, because I'm a detective, and knowing things is part of my job. But we don't have time to get into it, Eddie, because Hornswoggle Ra is on his way here as we speak."

"You've got to help me!"

"That's why we're here," Skulduggery said happily. "Helping people is what we do, Eddie. Helping them, rescuing them, saving them from the very jaws of danger itself. You'll be perfectly safe with us. Have no fear."

"But you will have to act as bait to draw him in," Valkyrie said.

"Oh, yes," said Skulduggery, like he'd just remembered. "That's right. He'll have to see you and come in and actually begin the attack in order for us to sneak up undetected, so, if you could disregard everything I just said about being perfectly safe with us, that would be great, because actually the amount of danger you're going to be in will be quite extraordinary."

Valkyrie stepped away from the window. "He's here," she said.

Eddie got up, and Skulduggery placed his hands on his shoulders.

"I'm going to need you to be brave now, Eddie. Can you be brave?"

"You're... you're going to leave me alone?"

"No, Eddie. Never."

"Yes, we are," said Valkyrie.

"Yes, we're going to leave you alone," Skulduggery said, nodding, "but only because he'll sense Valkyrie's presence if we stay. He won't sense me because my thoughts can't be detected by psychics."

"Then why can't you stay?" Eddie asked, desperation creeping into his wavering voice.

Skulduggery hesitated. "Because that's boring," he said at last. "It'll be much more fun to burst in when he least expects it. Probably through the window."

They left quickly, before Eddie had time to properly beg, and so he was left alone, standing in his quiet house.

He heard footsteps. The front door opened. A well-fed man walked in.

"Mr McKenzie?" said Eddie.

"Hello, Eddie," said his boss. "You weren't at work today. We missed you. We were worried about you. While you may not technically be a funny person or a fondly regarded colleague, you are an essential part of our business – much like the photocopier or the coffee machine."

"Neither of those things work any more," Eddie said, thoroughly puzzled and understandably wary.

"That's something else you're going to have in common," said Mr McKenzie. "Eddie, I have some bad news."

"Are you sick?"

"No, Eddie, the bad news is not regarding me. The bad news is regarding you. I'm afraid I am not Mr McKenzie, affable boss and all-round good egg. My real name is Hornswoggle Ra."

Eddie swallowed. "That's a funny name."

"It is, isn't it?" said Hornswoggle Ra with a small smile. "I've been feeding off your emotions for some time now, Eddie, and today was supposed to be our final meal together, after which you would shuffle away to live out the rest of your life as a sad grey little man. But you didn't come into work, so now I've had to come to you. To eat out, as it were."

"You're a psychic vampire," Eddie whispered.

Hornswoggle frowned. "Now where did someone like you hear a term like that?"

The window exploded as Skulduggery Pleasant jumped through and Hornswoggle Ra spun, but Valkyrie Cain was already charging in, and Eddie shrieked and fell backwards over the coffee table, and he lay on the carpet with his eyes closed until things went quiet again.

He raised his head and blinked. Hornswoggle Ra was unconscious and handcuffed. Skulduggery did that thing with the air that raised Eddie to his feet.

"Is it over?" Eddie asked.

"It is," said Skulduggery. "Normally, we would have someone come in to alter your memories, but that tends to work best with, and I don't say this to be mean, but it works best with imaginative people, and you're not overly imaginative, are you, Eddie?"

"No. I'm about as imaginative as a... foot."

"So we're going to trust you not to tell anyone what happened here," said Valkyrie.

"And that's it? You expect me to go back to my normal life after this? After living skeletons and psychic vampires and scary teenagers? How can I return to the ordinary now that I know real magic exists in the world?" His eyes widened. "Unless I join you. Unless I leave my old life behind and go on adventures with you. Can you teach me magic?"

"No," Skulduggery and Valkyrie both said at the same time.

Eddie sagged.

"But you don't need us to," Skulduggery continued. "Because it's not about knowing magic, Eddie. It's not about using magic as a weapon or a shield or a tool. You know why? It's because the magic – the *real* magic – has been inside you all along." And Skulduggery tapped Eddie's chest, just over his heart.

Eddie smiled. "Really?"

"No," Skulduggery and Valkyrie said at the same time, and they carried Hornswoggle Ra out of the house.

Eddie's wife got home a little later and asked why the window was broken. Eddie couldn't think up a convincing lie, so he just blinked and waited till she got bored. It seemed to do the trick.

After he'd cleaned up the glass, and she'd gone to bed, Eddie sat on the sofa and thought about his life. He tried to imagine himself as a magical detective, saving people from psychic vampires and psychic werewolves and psychic ghosts, but in his wildest imaginings the furthest he got was putting on his shoes and standing in the doorway to adventure. In his wildest imaginings, he couldn't picture what was even one step beyond.

So, in his imagination, Eddie closed the door to adventure, and in the real world he got off the sofa and went upstairs.

This story is dedicated to cover artist extraordinaire,
Tom Percival.

For most people, the cover is the reason they pick up a book in the first place. The amount of correspondence I get proves this, as people go on and on about how the cover caught their eye, made them want to read about a Skeleton Detective, how the covers are the best things ever, how the covers blah blah blah...

I think it's a generally agreed-upon fact that I could draw the covers if I really wanted to. I have the raw talent, I have the eye, and I have that one year of art college under my belt.

And I think Tom knows this, which is why he pushes himself to excel each and every time, why he pushes himself to make these books stand out from the others on the shelf. The threat I pose is important. The threat I pose is a good motivator.

Keep pushing yourself, Tom. My time is coming.

PS You're welcome.

THE END OF
THE WORLD

I

The man with the unfortunate face stood in the aisle between the Science Fiction section and Crime, and he seemed to be trying to blend in with the bookshelves. He wasn't doing a particularly good job of it. When an old woman shuffled too close, he snarled at her – actually *snarled* – and the old woman yelped like an injured puppy and hurried away as fast as her little old legs would carry her. People weren't used to snarling, not in a public library. For as long as he'd been coming here, Ryan certainly hadn't witnessed any snarling. Until today, of course.

He watched the man out of the corner of his eye, watched him whispering with his companions. They were an odd bunch. The snarling man was the biggest – arms like tree trunks, black matted hair completely failing to hide a face that was in no way attractive.

The smallest one of the group was a middle-aged man who stood very still and didn't join in with the whispering. He looked like an accountant who'd wandered out of the office one day and had accidentally joined a biker gang.

The woman beside him wore battered leather and had short spiky hair. She was pretty, in a sinister sort of way, but she didn't have a very nice laugh. It carried through the quiet building, unnerving all who heard it. The librarians, usually so strict about things like that, pretended not to notice.

The final member of the gang seemed to be the leader. He was lean and his arms looked strong. He had tattoos curling down from beneath his T-shirt. His jeans were black and his boots were scuffed. He had dark hair that hung over his brow. The big man and the woman would whisper to him and he'd nod. He never stopped looking around, though. Once or twice he almost caught Ryan's eye.

Ryan sat back in his chair, exited his email account on the computer. No emails. As usual. No one ever sent him emails. Not even spam. Maybe if he made more friends, like his mother was always saying, maybe then he'd at least be sent some junk every once in a while. Fifteen years old and no friends. It was kind of sad, when he thought about it. He didn't think about it much.

He got up, walked through the Children's section, running his fingers along the spines of the books he passed. He found himself in History and picked a book at random. Something about the Second World War. He didn't care. He was just here to waste time, after all – waste time and build up the courage to run away.

It wasn't his mother's fault. It wasn't even his new stepdad's fault. Ryan didn't have a problem with either of them. He just missed his father so much, and every moment spent living in that house reminded him that his father was dead and gone and never coming back, and Ryan didn't want to live like that any more. So he was going to run away to... somewhere. Somewhere else. Just for a little while. Just to get away.

He put the book back and went to take another one, but something fell from the shelf. He saw a flash of silver – what looked like a clasp, or a brooch – and without thinking he reached out and caught it, closed his fingers round it tight. It was cold to the touch, but immediately turned hot. Pain lanced up his arm and he cried out. He opened his hand to drop it, but the only thing he was holding was silver dust. The clasp, whatever it was, had crumbled away in his grip.

The pain was gone, too. Not wanting to make a mess, Ryan emptied the silver dust on to a gap in the bookshelf, then brushed at his hand. There was something smudged on his palm. He tried to wipe it away, but it wouldn't come off. Then he realised his skin wasn't smudged – it was burnt. The clasp had burned itself into his flesh.

"What you got there?"

Ryan turned at the sound of the voice. It was the leader of the gang. The other three stood behind him. They were all looking at him like he was prey.

"Nothing," Ryan mumbled, closing his hand.

"We heard you cry out," said the man. "We heard you cry out and Mercy said – that's Mercy over there – Mercy said let's see if he needs any help."

"I said that," the woman with the spiky hair confirmed, nodding her spiky head. "I was worried. Because I care."

"She does care," said the leader. "She wanted to know if you'd hurt yourself. Have you hurt yourself? She wanted to know if you'd hurt yourself and Obloquy said – Obloquy's the big lad – Obloquy said how is he going to hurt himself in a library? Is he going to paper-cut himself to death?"

The leader laughed, and Mercy laughed, and the big one grinned.

"I'm funny," he said.

"How did you hurt yourself?" the leader asked, coming down off the laugh with a friendly chuckle.

"I didn't hurt myself," said Ryan. "I'm fine."

"But we heard you cry out," said the man, suddenly frowning. "We heard you. Didn't we hear him?"

"I heard him," said Mercy.

"I heard him too, Foe," said Obloquy.

The middle-aged man, the accountant, didn't say anything.

The leader, Foe, examined Ryan curiously. "You don't have to be scared of us. Is that what's wrong? You're scared of us? You don't have to be. We're not bad people."

Obloquy laughed, and Mercy jammed an elbow into his ribs to shut him up.

"I know you're not supposed to talk to strangers," Foe continued, "but aren't you a bit old for that? Isn't that rule more for kids? You're not a kid any more, are you? What are you, fifteen or so?" He reached out, dipping a finger into the silver dust on the bookshelf, then bringing it to the tip of his tongue. He tasted it, and smiled at Ryan. "And if you don't talk to strangers, how are you going to make friends? Friends are important. We want to be friends."

"We really do," said Mercy.

"And we were standing over there," said Foe, "talking about books, because that's what we like to do, we like to talk about books, and we heard you cry out and we came over because we were worried, and we care, and now we're here, having a conversation. Having a friendly conversation with our new friend."

"I didn't hurt myself," Ryan said, really wishing he were somewhere else right now.

"Friends don't lie to each other," Foe said.

"I'm... I'm not lying."

"You're lying a little bit," Foe said, smiling. "What's your name?"

"Ryan."

"Good to meet you, Ryan."

Foe stuck out his hand. Ryan hesitated, then went to shake it. Instead, Foe grabbed his wrist and turned his palm to face upwards. The gang looked at the symbol imprinted on to his skin, and Foe released Ryan's wrist and put his hand on Ryan's shoulder. "Ryan, my friend. You're going to have to come with us now."

Ryan shook his head. "I should be going home. My dad will be here in a minute to pick me up."

"Ryan," said Foe. "If you don't come with us right this second, we're going to kill everyone in this building and then we're going to drag you out through the blood and the gore and what remains of their dead bodies." Another smile, this time with narrowed eyes. "So really, buddy, it's up to you."

Ryan wanted to scream for help and run away, but his legs wouldn't work and his chest was too tight. He looked at them. Foe, with his smile and his eyes. Mercy, an eager look on her face, like she was really hoping she'd get to kill someone today. Obloquy, standing there looking dumb and dangerous. And the accountant, whose gaze had never faltered, who was as still as a statue, completely detached from what was going on. The accountant was the scariest of them all.

And then, whistling.

2

Through the gaps in the books, Ryan could see someone in the next aisle over, moving slowly. Someone in black. Someone whistling. Ryan recognised the tune. It was the theme music to *Harry Potter*.

A pretty girl appeared at the corner of the bookcase. Tall, with long dark hair. Maybe a year or two older than Ryan. Wearing a jacket that was zipped up, tight trousers and boots, and a ring on her finger. All in black. All made from materials Ryan couldn't identify.

And still, whistling. As she whistled, her dark eyes wandered from Ryan to Foe, to Mercy and Obloquy, and then to the accountant. When she got to the accountant, she stopped whistling, and looked back at Ryan.

"Hi," she said. "My name's Valkyrie. Are these people bothering you?"

Ryan wanted to tell her to run, but he knew the gang would be on her in an instant.

The girl looked at Foe. "I'm part of Library Security," she said. "We've had some reports of overdue books in this area, and I'm going to need to ask you all some questions. We can do this here or downtown – where we'd actually have more space and access to a coffee machine."

Something was wrong. Foe didn't threaten her and Mercy didn't say anything at all. In fact, Mercy and Obloquy were glancing around, like they expected someone else to show up. Even the accountant looked wary.

"You really want this to happen?" Foe asked, his voice low. "Here? In a public place? Where all these innocent people might get caught in the crossfire?"

The pretty girl, Valkyrie, gave him a shrug. "I'm just looking for a way to spoil your day, Vincent. The choice is yours. Stick around and get beaten up and thrown in a cell, or leave, now. Immediately."

"Sure," said Foe. "We'll just take Ryan here with us."

Valkyrie shook her head. "Ryan stays, I'm afraid."

"Ah. Well, see, now we have a problem."

"That's too bad."

"That's just what I was thinking."

Valkyrie moved, snapping her palm against the air and the air shimmered and Foe shot back off his feet, colliding with Mercy. Before Ryan could even wonder what had just happened, she grabbed him and then they were running through the aisles. A stream of red energy sizzled by his ear and Ryan shrieked, tried to throw himself to the ground but Valkyrie wouldn't let him.

"Keep moving," she snapped.

He stumbled after her.

There was a roar, and the crash of a bookcase being toppled. Ryan glanced back, saw Obloquy go hurtling through the air, and a man stepped into view – a tall man, thin, wearing a dark blue suit and hat, like one of those old-fashioned private eyes.

Another stream of red energy burst through the bookshelf to his left and Ryan forgot all about the thin man and focused all his attention on not dying. Mercy smashed into him and he went sprawling across the floor, the wind knocked out of him. Then Valkyrie was there, running straight for Mercy who turned to her, opened her mouth wide, and let loose another stream of energy. From her mouth. *From her mouth.*

Ryan blinked.

Valkyrie dived, rolled, came up and threw herself into Mercy. Mercy grunted, the stream cut off, and they went down. They grappled, throwing elbows and pulling hair. Mercy grabbed a handful of Valkyrie's hair and yanked, and Valkyrie slammed her forehead into Mercy's face. Mercy screamed with pain and rage and Valkyrie was on top now, Mercy trying to push her off. Valkyrie trapped one of Mercy's arms and moved up, too fast for Ryan to work out what was happening, but somehow she swung her leg over Mercy and was now leaning back sharply. She snapped Mercy's elbow and Mercy howled, and then Valkyrie was scrambling towards Ryan, pulling him to his feet.

Ryan wished he could have said something intelligent to her at that moment, but all he could manage was "Muh". It was not very impressive.

Around them, the good people of the library cowered behind cover or ran for the exits. Ryan would have given anything to be allowed to cower. His entire body ached to find a dark corner and collapse into it like some kind of jelly. But the pretty girl who was gripping his hand kept pulling him on through the stacks, and Ryan was suddenly determined not to embarrass himself in front of her. So he forced his legs to stay strong and when Valkyrie hesitated, he overtook her.

"This way," he said, and now he was pulling her through the stacks, and she was probably thinking what a great guy he was, and look how take-charge he is, and even though he's a year or two younger than I am he'd probably make a great boyfriend and when all this is over, I'll probably want to kiss him or something. Ryan nodded to himself. Yeah, she was probably thinking all that as he led her through the aisles and the stacks, and then they came to a wall with a nice picture on it.

"Moron," Valkyrie snapped, turning and yanking him after her.

"Sorry," he said.

"I thought you knew where you were going!"

"I thought there was a door here."

She stopped suddenly and he ran into the back of her. He was halfway through apologising when he saw the accountant standing ahead of them.

Elsewhere in the library, the thin man was still battling the others. There were a lot of crashes and yells and screams and grunts. But here, with Ryan and Valkyrie and the accountant, it somehow seemed really, really quiet.

The accountant took a step forward. Valkyrie took a step back. She stepped on Ryan's foot and he said "Ow" and then apologised. She didn't hear him.

She snapped her hand against the air. The space rippled and a bookcase was blasted back, but the accountant was already moving. Then Valkyrie clicked her fingers and Ryan yelped when fire suddenly flared in her palm. He tore off his jacket and flung it over her forearm, batting out the flames.

"What the hell are you doing?" she raged, trying to push him back.

"You're on fire!" he squealed manfully.

She pulled away from him, her hand still ablaze, and then she flung the fire, but the accountant twisted, impossibly fast, and the fireball missed him, exploded against the side of another bookcase. The accountant darted out of sight.

"Oh," Ryan said.

Valkyrie backed up against him. "If you see an exit," she whispered, "you run to it. Understand?"

He nodded.

Something moved above them and the accountant dropped down on to Valkyrie. She cried out and Ryan stumbled back, watched as the accountant grabbed her and threw her like she was nothing. Valkyrie disappeared among the stacks.

Ryan spun, and ran. He didn't know where he was going, but anywhere was better than where he'd just been. The accountant was following, but he had leaped back up so he was off the ground, gliding from bookcase to bookcase, like a hawk chasing a terrified field mouse.

Then Ryan saw it – a green EXIT sign over a fire door. He changed direction, almost tripped over a cowering man who was hiding in the Reference section, and ran on. He was almost at the door when he glanced back over his shoulder, saw the accountant leaping for him. Valkyrie emerged from the stacks and something was happening to her right hand – it was covered in writhing, moving shadows. She whipped her hand and a trail of darkness reached for the accountant, wrapped around his leg. Valkyrie pulled back, hard, and the accountant crunched to the ground.

He snarled, sprang up and turned, and Valkyrie sent a wave of shadows crashing into him. He hit the far wall and that's all Ryan saw, because Valkyrie was pushing him out through the fire door. The alarm wailed as they emerged into the narrow alley behind the library. With Valkyrie's hand pressing into his back, Ryan sprinted towards the road. A gleaming black car was parked illegally, like it was waiting for them. It looked old, but a brand-new kind of old.

Valkyrie opened the door, bundled him in the back. She got behind the wheel, leaving the door open. She started the car and the engine roared, and she slipped into the passenger seat and buckled her belt.

"Seatbelt," she ordered.

Ryan buckled his seatbelt. He looked at the empty driver's seat. "Does it drive itself?" he asked.

"Don't be thick," she replied, looking back at the library. "He just hates it when I drive the Bentley, that's all."

The thin man came sprinting out of the library, clutching his hat in one gloved hand. Ryan blinked. The way the sun caught his bald head made it seem almost white, almost like...

Ryan swallowed. It wasn't the sun. The thin man wasn't bald.

The thin man was a skeleton.

Ryan screamed as the skeleton jumped in behind the wheel.

"Shut him up, please," the skeleton said as the car shot forward.

"Shut up, Ryan," said Valkyrie.

Foe came charging out of the library but the car, the Bentley, was already slicing through traffic. And still Ryan screamed.

"Ryan," Valkyrie said, "stop that."

"He's a skeleton!" Ryan yelled. "Look at him! They killed your friend!"

"No, they didn't," said the skeleton. "But they punched me. A lot. And one of them hit me with a desk. Have you ever been hit with a desk, Ryan? It's sore."

"I was hit with a desk once," Valkyrie said.

"Oh, that's right," said the skeleton. "It really hurts, doesn't it?"

"It does."

Ryan sat in the back seat, petrified. Valkyrie turned to him, sighed, and then gave him the kind of smile usually reserved for idiots, or toddlers, or idiot toddlers.

"Hi," she said. "I'm Valkyrie Cain. My partner here is Skulduggery Pleasant. We just saved your life. The least you can do is not throw up in our car."

3

The skeleton's jaw moved when he talked, but he had no tongue. He had no lungs, or vocal cords. There was nothing at all to give him a voice, and yet Skulduggery still talked. Good God, did he talk.

"The short version," he said as they drove, "is that magic exists. Monsters exist. Sorcerers, like myself and Valkyrie, fight to stop other sorcerers, like Foe and his friends, from doing bad things. We're the heroes, if you really must give us a title. They're the villains. We try to stay out of the public eye as much as possible. It's really quite straightforward if you don't think about it too hard."

"But I don't understand," Ryan whispered.

"That's the spirit," Skulduggery said. "We don't have an awful lot of time, so there are some things you're just going to have to accept."

"You're a skeleton."

"Like that."

"But how can you move?"

Valkyrie undid her seatbelt and climbed into the back. "Ryan," she said when she was settled, "the world is an amazing place. It's full of wonderful things and fascinating people and deep mysteries just waiting to be uncovered. In order to not annoy me, though, you've really got to put all of that to one side and concentrate on what we tell you. He's a walking skeleton. I wear tight trousers. Do you have any questions so far?"

"Uh, no."

"Excellent."

"You can feel safe with us," Skulduggery said. "We've saved the world a few times and we've become quite good at it. Really, if I were you, there's no one else I'd rather be with at a time like this."

"Skulduggery," Valkyrie said, "your façade."

"Oh, yes," he said, and his gloved fingers tapped his collarbones. A face flowed up, covering his skull with skin and hair and features. He smiled at a lady in a car they passed and she frowned at him.

"He can only wear a face for half an hour every day," Valkyrie whispered to Ryan. "So he tends to overdo it on the sociable front."

"But all that went on in a library," Ryan said, finally confident enough to form a complete sentence without gibbering. "It's going to be all over the news."

"Actually," Valkyrie responded, "it's not. We have people for that sort of thing. Sometime within the next hour a very nice man called Geoffrey is going to convince everyone who witnessed that fight that they didn't see what they thought they saw. He's kind of a Public Relations officer, in a way – making sure the civilian world doesn't notice the rest of us as we go about our business."

Skulduggery glanced at Ryan over his shoulder. The face he wore was dark-haired and sallow-skinned. "Some people, like Geoffrey, find they are suited to non-combative roles. He's what we call a Sensitive – someone with psychic abilities. Some Sensitives read minds, some see the future – Geoffrey just makes you believe whatever he tells you. Another Sensitive was a man called Deacon Maybury. Which is where you come in."

"I've never heard of him," Ryan said.

"Of course not," said Valkyrie. "I hadn't, either, up until a few days ago. I'd heard of his brother, Davit, who died. There were sextuplets, apparently. Six identical Mayburys. Only four now, though."

"This Deacon Maybury, he's dead, too?"

Skulduggery turned the Bentley off the busy road, down a quieter street. "Deacon was a Sensitive who worked for the Sanctuary – where we work. Sometimes we arrest criminals for whom there is no redemption. If they're susceptible, it's possible to enter their mind and insert a new personality. It's always been a controversial procedure, and it only works if the criminal's will is weak, but the old personality would be subdued, the new one would have a life and a history and memories, and the criminal would get a chance at a normal life. Inserting new personalities was Deacon's job."

"But he got bored," Valkyrie said. "We spoke to people who knew him. He wanted adventure and excitement. He wanted money and power. So he fell in with the wrong crowd – Foe and his gang."

Skulduggery nodded. "A very bad lot. Vincent Foe was a mercenary during the war. I won't tell you what war, I don't want to complicate things. Mercy Charient is, to all intents and purposes, a serial killer. Obloquy, I doubt you'll disagree, is something of a moron – but a savage moron. And then there's Samuel."

Valkyrie made a face. "Bloody vampires."

Ryan sat forward. "That was a vampire? That guy who looked like an accountant?"

"We don't talk about vampires," Skulduggery warned.

"But it was daytime. How could he have been out during the—"

"We don't talk about vampires!" Valkyrie said sharply.

Ryan shrank back. "Sorry," he said.

"Don't worry about it," Skulduggery told him. "Valkyrie used to date a vampire, that's all."

"We didn't *date*," Valkyrie said immediately.

Skulduggery held up a hand. "I'm not judging."

Valkyrie scowled, and looked back at Ryan. "Anyway, Deacon Maybury fell in with Foe's gang, and Foe's gang are nuts. Some people want to take over the world. Some people want to change the world. Foe and his mates want to destroy the world." She shook her head. "They're idiots."

"Nihilists," Skulduggery corrected.

"Idiots," Valkyrie repeated. "There's something called a Doomsday Machine, Ryan. Yes, I know how that sounds. And, yes, it is as stupid as it appears. Some genius went ahead and built a bomb that could blow up the planet. He said he built it so that if the Faceless Ones ever returned, we could kill ourselves and kill them at the same time so that they could never travel to and infect other realities."

Ryan frowned. "Faceless Ones?"

"Don't complicate things," Skulduggery said.

"Yeah, sorry, Ryan," said Valkyrie. "Anyway, that's why it exists. So it was sitting there, existing, not harming anyone, and then a few years ago it was stolen. Foe and his gang stole it and hid it – which wouldn't be an easy thing to do because the Machine is bigger than a house."

"Why did they hide it?" Ryan asked. "Why not just set it off?"

"Because they didn't have the key," Skulduggery said. "They spent the next few years searching for it. That's when Deacon joined them. They finally found it, nine days ago. But Deacon had no intention of activating the Machine. He hid the key, shaped like a clasp, to sell to the highest bidder."

"But Foe's gang caught up with him before the auction could take place," Valkyrie said. "They chased him and he accidentally fell into a wood chipper."

Ryan winced.

"Yeah," said Valkyrie.

"So now Foe is hunting for the key," Skulduggery said. "Their hunt led them to the library, and our hunt led us to them. And both hunts have led to you, Ryan."

Ryan looked at his hand. "But the key's gone. It crumbled when I held it. It's just dust now."

"The key wasn't what you held," Skulduggery said. "It's the imprint it left on your skin. I've got good news and bad news for you, Ryan. The bad news is that you're the only one in the world who can activate the Doomsday Machine, and Foe and his gang are never going to stop coming after you. The good news is that with myself and Valkyrie protecting you, you stand a very good chance of emerging from this relatively unscathed."

Valkyrie looked at the back of Skulduggery's head. "You said they'd probably try to cut his hand off."

"I said relatively," Skulduggery reminded her.

4

Deacon Maybury's apartment was trashed.

Skulduggery and Valkyrie went first, to check if it was safe, and Ryan crept in after them. Papers littered the bad carpet. The ugly couch had been slashed open and its stuffing had been pulled out like fluffy intestines. Chairs were overturned, picture frames smashed and every drawer taken from its slot, the contents dumped and scattered.

"What exactly are we looking for in this mess?" Valkyrie asked.

"Foe secured the Doomsday Machine somewhere," Skulduggery said, picking through the debris. "We need to find out where. Maybe we'll get lucky and discover that Deacon was an avid journal keeper. But if we can't find a solid lead to take us to the Machine, there might be something else here, a clue or a name, something that will take us a step further."

Valkyrie sighed. "I hate looking for clues."

Ryan smiled at the cuteness of Valkyrie's sulk.

"Looking for clues is an integral part of detective work," Skulduggery told her.

"I prefer the part where we hit people."

"That's just because you have a violent nature. You should endeavour to be more peace-loving, like Ryan."

Ryan stopped admiring Valkyrie and frowned. "Why am I peace-loving?"

"Hmm?" Skulduggery said, looking up. "Oh, I meant nothing by it. I just assumed you were peace-loving because you seem to be terrible at violence. Plus, you scream a lot."

"Just because I don't go around getting into fights every day doesn't mean I can't fight," Ryan said, his face growing warm.

"Not being good at violence is nothing to be ashamed of," Skulduggery said, standing a filing cabinet upright and sifting through it. "If there were more people like you in the world, there'd be less need for people like us."

"I don't have a violent nature," Valkyrie growled.

"And I'm not peace-loving," Ryan insisted.

"But you do scream a lot," Skulduggery said.

"How can you know that?" Ryan asked. "You've known me for, like, two hours."

"And in those two hours, you have spent most of your time screaming." Skulduggery shrugged. "I really can't see how my logic can be faulted."

"I don't have a violent nature," Valkyrie repeated.

"Of course you don't," Skulduggery said as he continued to sift the files in the cabinet. "Entirely my mistake."

Valkyrie scowled and started sorting through the papers on the floor. She hadn't been too interested in Ryan's defence of his manliness. He couldn't say he blamed her. She was a sorcerer who battled evil villains every other day. He was a chubby loser who needed girls to fight his battles for him. The only way he was going to change how she thought of him was to do something so brave and noble that she couldn't fail to be impressed. He turned and screamed at a middle-aged woman who stood in the doorway.

The middle-aged woman was startled by the scream, but not half as startled as Ryan himself. It had been a surprisingly high-pitched scream this time, and to make matters worse, it resulted in Valkyrie leaping in front of him protectively.

"Oh," said the middle-aged woman. She wore a floral dress and a cardigan. As middle-aged women went, she wasn't particularly frightening.

Skulduggery walked forward, a new false face smiling broadly. "Hello there," he said. "How are you on this fine day? Come in, come in. And you are...?"

"Francine," the woman said, a little flustered. "I live down the hall... What are you doing in Deacon Maybury's apartment?"

"You know Deacon?" Skulduggery asked. Valkyrie walked behind her, checked the corridor for anyone else, then stepped back in and closed the door.

"Well, yes," said Francine, frowning at Valkyrie and then looking at Skulduggery. "He's my neighbour and he's a good man. If you're robbing him, I must warn you – we don't take kindly to that sort of thing here."

"We're not robbing him," Skulduggery said. "But I'm afraid I have some bad news."

"Is it Deacon?" Francine asked, her eyes wide.

"It is."

"Is he sick?"

"It's a little worse than that."

She gasped. "He's dying?"

"He was briefly dying," said Skulduggery. "Now he's dead."

Francine's mouth dropped open. "What? Deacon... Deacon is *dead*?"

"I'm afraid so."

"Oh, no. Oh, no, no, no." She sagged, and Valkyrie caught her before she collapsed. "My Deacon... My poor Deacon..."

Valkyrie staggered over to the only upright chair, and dumped Francine into it.

"He was so strong," Francine sobbed. "So proud. So much dignity. How did he die?"

"Wood chipper," said Valkyrie.

Francine wailed again, pounding the table with her little fists. "Why?" she cried. "Why did you take him, Lord?"

Valkyrie looked at Skulduggery, and Skulduggery shrugged.

"Uh," Valkyrie said. "I'm sorry for your, you know, your loss. I'm sure he was a great... I'm sure..." She faltered, and gave a shrug of her own. Ryan looked at Skulduggery, but he showed no signs of offering any real comfort to the poor woman.

"You obviously loved him very much," Ryan said, surprising himself by stepping forward.

"I did," Francine sobbed.

"I'm sure he loved you back."

Francine looked up, her eyes red and puffy and pleading. "Did he ever mention me?"

Ryan hesitated, and Valkyrie smirked at him from behind Francine. "All the time," he said. "Yes. God, every time I spoke to him he was all, Francine this and Francine that and... ohh, how I love Francine."

"He said that?"

"Uh, something along those lines, definitely..."

Francine clasped her hands to her chest. "I knew it," she said. "I knew he loved me. All those long silences. All those awkward moments. I should have told him I felt the same way. Then we could have... Then we could have..."

She broke off into a fit of sobbing. Behind her, Valkyrie gave Ryan the thumbs up. He had a feeling she meant it sarcastically.

"Did you talk to Deacon much?" Skulduggery asked, leaning down to gently pat her hand. "Did you tell each other about your days? Did you confide in each other...?"

"With a love like ours," Francine warbled, "we didn't need words."

"How inconvenient," Skulduggery muttered, straightening up immediately and walking away.

"Francine," Ryan said, "we're looking for something that Deacon was keeping for us. Do you know where it is? It'd be big, now, as big as a house."

Francine blinked away tears. "What could he have had that was as big as a house?"

Ryan frowned. He really had no answer to that.

"A house," Valkyrie said quickly. "He had a house. He was keeping it for us. One of those mobile houses, you know the kind."

"A mobile home?" Francine asked.

"Something like that. A little bigger. Do you remember if he ever mentioned a warehouse, or some kind of big storage facility that he visited?"

Francine frowned. "Well, I... I heard him on the phone once. I remember him saying something about having the paperwork for a warehouse that was cluttering up his files."

"It has to be here somewhere," Skulduggery said, going back to the filing cabinet. Valkyrie went into the bedroom, and started pulling the place apart.

"Did I say something wrong?" Francine asked.

"No," Ryan said. "Actually, you've been a big help. Would you like something? A cup of tea or...?"

"I should get back to my apartment," Francine said, standing slowly. "I need a lie-down. This is all... this is all a big shock to me."

"I'm really sorry," Ryan said.

She smiled weakly, took a step and swayed. Ryan jumped for her, wrapping one of her arms round his neck.

"I'll help you," he said.

"Thank you," she replied. A tear rolled down her cheek. "You're very nice."

While Skulduggery and Valkyrie searched, Ryan hobbled along with

Francine out of the apartment and down the corridor. She was light but awkward.

"Your friends are a little odd," Francine said.

"I know."

"The girl's pretty, though. Is she your girlfriend?"

Ryan gave a laugh, realised he was blushing. "No, she's not. We've just met, actually."

"My apartment's around the corner," Francine said, gesturing ahead of them and sniffling. "Do you want my advice? Don't make the same mistake I made with Deacon. Tell her how you feel."

"I really just met her."

"But you like her, don't you?"

"I, yeah, I suppose."

He helped her round the corner.

"Seize the moment," Francine said. "You never know when you might get another chance at happiness."

"I'll think about it," he promised, hoping that she'd change the subject before anyone overheard them.

"My apartment's just up ahead," Francine said, standing a little straighter. "You really are very nice. Such good manners, helping me all the way to my door."

"It's no trouble at all."

"Unfortunately," Francine said, "it will be."

"Sorry? It will be what?"

"Trouble," Francine said. "It will be a lot of trouble."

Vincent Foe walked out of the apartment ahead of them.

5

Ryan spun, grabbed Francine, tried to drag her with him, but she laughed. She got an arm round his throat before he could call for help and hauled him backwards. He kicked and struggled, but she was much too strong, and then he was in the apartment and Foe was closing the door behind them.

Francine released him, and Ryan jumped away, almost colliding with Obloquy. Samuel watched him from the corner of the room.

"If you shout or scream," Foe said, "we'll kill you."

"And then we'll kill Valkyrie," said Francine. She looked at Foe, and grinned. "He's got a little crush on her."

Foe raised an eyebrow. "Is that right? Well, can't say I blame you, Ryan – she is a fine-looking girl. If I were a few hundred years younger, I'd be in there like a shot, believe you me. I'm not altogether sure what she'd ever see in *you*, though. You don't seem quite up to her standard. No offence, but you're kind of... unexceptional."

"Maybe he's hoping she'll like him for his sense of humour," Obloquy chuckled.

"Young love," Foe said, almost wistfully. "If you're lucky, you might have a chance to confess to her your eternal devotion, so long as you do exactly what I tell you."

Ryan's mouth was so dry his voice was a croak. "I'm not going to help you destroy the world."

"Yes, you are."

"It doesn't make any sense. If you want to die, why don't you just kill yourselves and leave everyone else out of it?"

"Where's the drama in that?" asked Francine.

Foe glanced at her. "That's getting really disconcerting, you know."

"Ain't that something?" she murmured, and Ryan watched as Francine flickered, and he glimpsed someone underneath, someone slimmer, wearing black, with a bandaged arm... And then Francine was gone, and Mercy stood there. "That better?"

"Much," Foe said, turning his attention back to Ryan. "We're going to destroy the world because there is absolutely no point to its continued existence."

There were a hundred things Ryan wanted to say. *That's it? That's the reason? You want to kill everyone because you can't see the point? What kind of stupid, pathetic, selfish reason is that?* But he didn't say any of it, because he was too scared. Because he wasn't the hero. Because he was the one who was waiting for someone to rescue him.

There was a knock on the door.

"Francine?"

It was Valkyrie's voice. Mercy stepped up to Ryan, pressing a blade against his belly.

"Francine," Valkyrie called, "is Ryan in there with you?"

Foe looked at Ryan, and held his finger to his lips as Obloquy went to the door. The knife dug into Ryan's skin painfully. He had to warn her. He had to. He couldn't just stand here and keep quiet.

"I know what you're thinking," Mercy whispered. "I can see it all over your face. Just know that if you make a sound, I'll kill you and cut off your hand."

Valkyrie knocked again, and Mercy looked towards the door, and a sudden pressure built up inside Ryan until he shoved her away from him. And then

Samuel was there, a hand closing round his throat and Ryan was moving with his feet off the ground, slamming back into the wall. Samuel's fingers were like steel and Ryan's vision clouded, dimmed, and a distant part of him knew he was about to pass out.

The window exploded. Ryan dropped. He sucked in air and his head pounded. There was movement all around him. Foe flew backwards over the couch. Skulduggery was there, flipping Mercy over his hip. The door came down, on top of Obloquy. Valkyrie, clambering over it, shouting at Ryan to run. Ryan's legs, like concrete. Around him shouts and curses and the sound of breaking things. Samuel, hitting Valkyrie so hard she folded in mid-air. Foe diving at Skulduggery.

The floor moved and Ryan realised he was stumbling. He didn't even remember ordering his legs to do it. He climbed over the door, slid down it, rolled out into the corridor. Got to his hands and knees, trying to get his brain back in gear.

"Oh, God, oh, God," he muttered, and stood, walked and ran, ran down to the corner, through the corridor, running for the stairs, leaving Skulduggery and Valkyrie to fight behind him. He got to the stairs and stopped. He couldn't. He couldn't leave them. They'd saved his life. He had this stupid key imprinted on to his hand and they were fighting to protect him. He couldn't abandon them. He had to help. There was nothing he could do, but he had to help. He had to try. He had to do something. They would want him to run, he knew that. They would want him to run to safety, to leave the fighting to the professionals. They didn't expect him to turn back and help. But he had no choice.

Ryan turned, ran back the way he had come. An old man was in the corridor, blinking.

"I've phoned the police," he said.

"Get back inside," Ryan told him. "Lock the door."

The old man nodded, shuffled out of the corridor, and then Valkyrie came crashing through the wall of his apartment in a shower of broken plaster and chipboard. The old man howled in shock, ran past Ryan, sprinting round the corner with surprising agility. Valkyrie was on the floor in a cloud of dust, groaning and trying to get up. Obloquy climbed through the broken wall after her and saw Ryan.

"Run!" Valkyrie shouted.

Ryan ran.

He got to the corner before he heard Obloquy's voice in his head – *pain, feel pain, too much pain to move* – and Ryan staggered, doubled up, sweat breaking out on his forehead. He looked back, saw Obloquy, and now he dropped to his knees, trying not to cry out. The pain was building, intensifying, the closer Obloquy got to him, and then Valkyrie was there, covered in dust and swinging both arms, and the pain went away as Obloquy hurtled into the wall.

Mercy stepped out behind her and Ryan shouted a warning, but even as Valkyrie spun, Mercy was opening her mouth, and that red stream of energy slammed straight into Valkyrie's chest, throwing her back. Skulduggery leaped from nowhere, barging into Mercy, and Ryan scrambled over to Valkyrie, his eyes wide, expecting to see a gaping, bloody hole. But when she came to a groaning stop, there was no injury – just trails of steam that rose from her jacket. He grabbed her, pulled her up.

There were gunshots, and with every deafening bang, Ryan yelped and flinched, but he managed to drag Valkyrie round the corner before either of them was horribly killed. She straightened up, taking a deep breath and rubbing her chest.

He had to ask. "Why aren't you dead?"

"Protective clothing," she said, eyes scanning the corridor. "You don't think I wear this outfit just because it's tight, do you?"

She ran to the window at the end of the corridor, flattened both hands against the air. The glass exploded outwards and the frame splintered. "Come on," she said, climbing on to the narrow sill.

"Uh," Ryan said.

She looked back in. "Move!"

He swallowed, and did what she ordered. As he searched for the securest position possible, fingers curling round the edge of the wall, he tried not to look at the concrete courtyard below them. "We're... we're not going to jump, are we?"

She took hold of his arm, and said gently, "Not if you don't want to."

He relaxed, his grip on the edge of the wall loosening slightly, and that's when she stepped off the sill and yanked him after her.

Ryan screamed as they plummeted to the ground, the wind rushing into his mouth and up his nose and through his hair and suddenly it was buffeting them both, slowing their descent. He saw Valkyrie's hand move, like she was orchestrating the air. They landed heavily, but at least they didn't go splat.

Ryan staggered away from her. "Oh my God. Oh my God."

Skulduggery dropped down in front of him and Ryan screamed again.

"Well said," Skulduggery muttered, reloading his revolver. "We'd better hurry, now. Come along."

They ran through the tunnel connecting the courtyard to the street on the other side of the apartment buildings. Skulduggery put his gun away and let his façade flow over his skull. They got in the Bentley and the car roared and shot forward.

"Everyone OK?" Skulduggery asked.

"I'm in pain," Valkyrie groaned. "Ryan?"

Ryan nodded quickly. "I'm fine. I'm OK. I'm not hurt."

"Are you shaking yet?"

Ryan looked at his hand. "No."

"It'll start any minute now."

Ryan's hand began to tremble violently. "Oh, wow, yeah. I'm definitely shaking now." He laughed. It was a weird sound.

"Geoffrey's going to have his hands full explaining this one," Valkyrie said as she brushed the dust off her jacket. It rose from her in small clouds.

"Please don't do that in the car," Skulduggery said.

"You didn't say Mercy could do that," Ryan said. "She changed shape. She's a shape-changer."

"Actually," Skulduggery said, "she's not. Francine was a psychic image. Basically, an illusion. Physically, there *was* no disguise. That was Mercy sitting at the table, talking to us, in her normal form. But our minds reinterpreted Mercy as Francine. We heard Francine's voice."

"I smelled her perfume," Ryan said.

"All an illusion. The only person in Dublin, in all of Ireland really, capable of disguising her like that is a man called Robert Crasis. In wartime, his skills were invaluable. We might have twenty people ready to storm an enemy position, but thanks to Crasis it would look like we had a thousand."

"So he's a good guy?" Valkyrie asked. "Then why did he help Foe?"

"I don't know," Skulduggery said. "I suppose we'll have to ask him."

6

On the way to see Crasis, they stopped off so Ryan and Valkyrie could get something to eat. They each bought a Coke and a sandwich, but Skulduggery made them eat with their heads sticking out of the window to avoid crumbs being dropped. Ryan didn't dare open his Coke in case it fizzed out over the seats, and by the time the Bentley pulled over, his throat was parched.

Skulduggery led the way to an old workshop in a quiet part of town. He knocked on the door and waited. When Robert Crasis opened the door, he looked at Skulduggery and Valkyrie, but barely glanced at Ryan. He was a man in his sixties. He was tall, broad-shouldered. His hair was grey, his jaw coated in stubble.

"Can I help you?"

"Hello, Robert," said Skulduggery. "Mind if we come in?"

"Skulduggery?" Crasis frowned, peering at him. "Since when do you have a face?"

"It's a relatively new addition. We'd like a word, if that's OK."

Crasis hesitated, then stepped back to allow them through the door.

They walked into a carpenter's workshop, to the smell of wood shavings and varnish. It was a big space, no windows, lit in spots that allowed the darkness to soak in around the edges.

Skulduggery let his face melt away, and he took off his hat. "This reminds me of your place in Venice."

"Before it was burned down," Crasis responded. "Skulduggery, I don't mean to be rude, but I was really hoping never to see you again."

"You know why we're here."

Crasis shook his head. The muscles in his jaw tightened. "All I want is to be left alone. I'm out of that game, but people... people keep pulling me back in. After years of not being involved in any craziness, suddenly there's one after another, when all I want to do is be a carpenter and grow old."

"You *want* to get old?" Valkyrie asked, sounding surprised.

"Staying young isn't all it's cracked up to be," Crasis said. "I've been young and strong and healthy for two hundred years. I've had to leave my home countless times to stop my mortal friends from wondering why I never seem to age. Then I met Sarah, and she became my wife, and suddenly I had someone I wanted to grow old with. So I stopped doing magic. Up until two weeks ago, I hadn't done magic in nearly fifteen years. I went grey. Last month I noticed a bald spot. It was working. I was ageing again. But now? Now it'll take years for me to age a *day*."

"This last job you did," Skulduggery said, "it was for Mercy Charient, wasn't it?"

Crasis nodded. "They came in the back, the whole lot of them. Deacon Maybury, the idiot, had mentioned what I used to do for the Sanctuary, and they remembered. Of course they remembered. So they came in, threatened me, threatened my wife, my kids... What could I do?"

"We're not blaming you," Skulduggery said.

"So I did it. I made her into a frumpy little woman. It wasn't my best work, but it would do for a few hours, which is all they wanted it for. Sorry if any of you were hurt, but I have a family to protect."

"We weren't hurt," Valkyrie said. "But Deacon Maybury... he was killed a few days ago."

Crasis looked at her for a moment, saying nothing. He swallowed, and nodded. "That's a shame," he said, his eyes drifting down. "He was... I'd like to say he was a good man, but he was... Deacon. I owed him, though. He's the one who actually introduced me to Sarah. He'd asked her out the previous week and she'd laughed so hard she fell over. It was love at first sight for Sarah and me. So I owed him, I did. It's a... it's a real pity I'll never get to repay him."

Ryan tried opening his Coke quietly. It fizzed and they all looked at him. He blushed.

"Maybe you can repay him," Skulduggery said, looking back at Crasis. "When you were working on Mercy, did any of them say anything? They have the Doomsday Machine hidden away somewhere and we need to find it."

"Foe has the Doomsday Machine?" Crasis said, his eyes widening. "And Deacon was working with those guys?"

"He planned to sell the key to whoever paid him enough," Valkyrie said.

Crasis stared at her, stared at Skulduggery, stared at Ryan, then stared at his hands. "It's a good thing he's dead," he said. "Because if I had the chance, I'd kill him myself. I did hear something, actually. I heard Obloquy complain that there were always people around whenever they'd check on 'it'. They never said what it was, but obviously it was the Machine. Mercy was supposed to stay still and quiet while I worked, but she kept moving and joining in with the conversation. She was joking that if their car broke down, they'd all have to get the Luas. She said they'd be riding the tram to the end of the world. I told her to shut up or I'd have to start again. I should have let her keep talking."

"You wouldn't happen to have a street map of Dublin, would you?" Skulduggery asked.

"Uh, yeah," Crasis said. "I think I have one somewhere around here."

He went off to search, and Skulduggery picked up a thick felt pen off a desk that was littered with paperwork. "They've hidden the Machine in a public place," he said, "and it's somewhere on or near a tram line."

Crasis came back with a tattered map and laid it out on a large, freshly carved table. Skulduggery started drawing lines down streets, drawing in the routes the Luas tram went down. Crasis and Valkyrie pored over the map and Ryan, not wanting to feel left out, did the same. He put his Coke on the table and did his best to appear as smart as the other people in the room.

When Skulduggery had marked all the routes they examined the map anew.

"Lot of public places," Valkyrie murmured.

"A very large amount," Ryan said, nodding like he was contributing.

"Ryan," Skulduggery said, and for a moment Ryan thought that he'd accidentally solved the mystery.

"Yes?" he said eagerly.

"Could you take your Coke off the map, please?"

"Oh," Ryan said. "Sorry." He lifted his bottle. There was now a wet circle around Dundrum. To hide his blush he took a long swig from his drink.

"The heaviest population centres would be here, here and here," Skulduggery said, marking the map with Xs. "If the Machine is hidden outdoors, we should be looking for areas that have had extensive construction work in the last few years. If it's indoors, then we're looking for new public buildings or shopping areas."

The Coke went down the wrong way and Ryan choked, gagged, and spat a mouthful all over the map.

Skulduggery, Crasis and Valkyrie looked at him.

"Sorry," he wheezed, before doubling over into a coughing fit.

"Maybe you should get some air," Skulduggery suggested.

Ryan nodded, coughing too much to respond, and staggered out of the door. His eyes were streaming and he knew his face was glowing an attractive shade of red. He went to the Bentley and leaned against it, finally getting the coughing under control. Not his finest moment.

"How're you doing, Ryan?"

He looked round as Valkyrie walked up.

"I'm OK," he said. "Just choking a bit. Sorry about that. I hope I didn't spit any on you."

"Don't worry about it."

He became aware of her looking at him and he looked away.

"Why do you do that?" she asked.

"Why do I do what?"

"Why do you look away whenever I look at you?"

"Um," Ryan said, "I don't know. I think, once I realise that I'm looking someone in the eye, I forget how long I'm supposed to do it. So I don't know, I suppose I look away before it gets weird."

She smiled. "You're an oddball."

"Yeah," he said, sagging.

Valkyrie didn't notice the sag. She was looking up the street, watching the people pass. "But that's OK. We're all oddballs here."

Now that she wasn't paying attention, he could look at her. He liked her face. She was very pretty, had a cute nose and a single dimple when she smiled. He'd always wanted a girlfriend like her – someone impressive, someone confident. He'd like to go back to school once the summer was over and have her beside him. Then everyone would stop and stare, and they'd think to themselves that there must be more to this Ryan guy after all.

But he'd never get a girlfriend like her. He knew that. Girls like Valkyrie saw him as a friend only. They went off with the good-looking guys or the cool guys or the guys who didn't make fools of themselves at regular intervals. A girl like Valkyrie would never be impressed with someone like Ryan.

He looked away before she looked back. He didn't want her to catch him watching.

"You're coping pretty well, you know," she said, facing him again. "When I first saw Skulduggery and all this stuff, I freaked. I actually blacked out."

"You fainted?"

"No," she said, her good humour fading. "I blacked out. There's a difference."

He grinned. "You fainted."

"Shut up. You're handling this well, that's all I'm saying. You haven't once asked to go home."

His grin went away. "Why would I? You're not that much older than me, you know."

She frowned. "What's that got to do with anything?"

"I'm fifteen. You're, I don't know, seventeen?"

"So?"

"That's only two years' difference," Ryan said hotly. "We're practically the same age and you're treating me like I'm a child. Fine, OK? You have no interest in me. I'm used to that. But don't stand there and talk down to me like you're so much better than I am."

Valkyrie looked at him and didn't say anything. He started to feel stupid.

Then she folded her arms and tilted her hips and it only got worse. "First of all," she said, "I'm not talking down to you *or* treating you like a child."

"But you expect me to want to go home."

"Of course I do. You were attacked. You're in danger. You're hanging around with people who can do magic. You've had what we call in the business a shock. Usually, when people get a shock they want to retreat to a safe place so that they can process what they've seen. Most people would want to go home right now. But not you. You haven't mentioned home, haven't mentioned your family, haven't tried to run off or call the cops. You are coping well, Ryan. That's all I said. That's all I meant. I have no idea what our ages have to do with anything or what you're talking about when you say I have no interest."

"Oh," he said.

"And the only time you have actually acted like a child," she said, "is right now. I don't like petulance, Ryan. I don't respond well to it."

"Right."

"When it comes to this kind of stuff, I'm the only one who is allowed to sulk. Skulduggery understands that. Do you?"

"Yes," he said, nodding quickly. "I'm sorry."

"You better be."

"I really am."

"I gave you a compliment and you jumped down my throat." She narrowed her eyes at him. "And what was all that about having no interest? Having no interest in what?"

"Uh, nothing."

"Don't make me hit you, Ryan."

He winced. "I don't know, I was just... I thought you saw me as a, you know, as a kid and... I was just saying that while, obviously, you'd never, like, go out with someone like me, that's still no reason to talk down to me. Which you weren't doing, and I apologise again for thinking you were."

"But what does me going out or not going out with someone like you have to do with anything?"

Ryan tried a smile. "I really don't know any more. It made sense when I said it."

She shook her head, looked about to say something else, then stopped. "Oh," she said. She was looking at him now like Andrea from school had looked at him when he'd asked her to the movies. She was looking at him with a kind of gentle pity.

"It's OK," he said. "You don't have to worry about it."

"Ryan, we only just met."

He nodded. "Absolutely."

"It's not that I never would," Valkyrie said, "but I generally go for guys... older than me, you know?"

Ryan tried a laugh. "Like vampires."

Her tone turned sharp. "We don't joke about vampires, Ryan."

"Right. Sorry."

"I think you're nice," Valkyrie said, softening again. "But let's concentrate on being friends for the time being, all right?"

"Sure. Yep. Don't worry."

The workshop door opened and Skulduggery emerged. "Ryan," he said, "stop leaning against my car."

"Sorry," Ryan mumbled, straightening up.

Skulduggery stopped in front of them. He was wearing a different face, and he put his hat on. "I have solved the mystery," he announced. "Before I take you to where the Doomsday Machine is located, I would like you both to acknowledge how brilliant I am."

"Uh," said Ryan, "you're brilliant."

"You're OK," said Valkyrie.

"That's good enough for me," Skulduggery nodded. "Get in the car. We've got a world to save."

7

They drove into Dundrum town centre and parked in the multistorey. Along the way, Skulduggery had pulled over three times to allow Ryan to pee. If Ryan had wanted Valkyrie to start thinking of him as older and more mature than he was, he knew he was not going about it the right way.

Once the Bentley found a place to park, they got out.

"How did you know it was here?" Valkyrie asked.

Skulduggery checked his façade in the wing mirror, then straightened up. "Simple detective work," he said. "We're going to need somewhere quiet to wait until everyone's gone. We'll search for the Machine tonight, dismantle it and then it'll all be over."

They started walking. "Shouldn't we call in the Cleavers?" Valkyrie asked. "We'll find it faster with a hundred people looking for it."

"I'd prefer to approach this with a little more delicacy," Skulduggery said. "The three of us should be fine." He looked at Ryan. "Nervous?"

"A little," Ryan admitted. "What if Foe and the others are waiting for us?"

"They might pay a visit to the Machine," Skulduggery conceded, "but they're not going to be lying in wait. They have no idea that we know it's here."

They passed from the car park into the mall. Valkyrie appeared to trust Skulduggery without hesitation, but Ryan was more cautious. Every time someone walked too close, he'd hop away, waiting for their image to flicker and drop, revealing Mercy or Obloquy or Foe. But the people in the mall seemed to be actual people, focused on their conversations or their shopping, and the only time they glanced at Ryan was when he stumbled awkwardly away from them.

Valkyrie raised an eyebrow at him. "You're not very good at acting casual."

"I forget how," Ryan confessed, skipping away from a suspicious-looking two-year-old holding a balloon.

Skulduggery and Valkyrie walked up the travelator and Ryan followed, flinching away from an elderly woman with a wrinkled prune-face. They approached a stocky security guard.

"Excuse me, good sir," Skulduggery began.

The security guard turned to them. "I'm a woman," she said.

"And a fetching one you are, too," Skulduggery continued, smiling. "Which way to the security control room?"

The security guard frowned. "Why? What business do you have there? Who are you?"

"All good questions," Skulduggery said, nodding, "and all questions I would love to answer. Unfortunately, we only have time for *one* answer, and since my question was the *first* and, let's be honest, the most *important* question, I feel that it is the question that deserves an answer. So, your security control room?"

The security guard folded her arms. "Do you have the authority to be there?"

Skulduggery's false face fixed her with a glare. "Do I have the authority?" he repeated. "Do *I* have the *authority*? Tell me, my dear, do I not *look* like I have the authority? Do I not *look* like the type of person who goes wherever he sees fit to go? Or do I look like the kind of person who needs *permission* to do the things that need to be done?"

"Uh," said the security guard, her arms no longer folded.

Skulduggery loomed over her. "There are things in this world that would turn your hair *white*. Threats and dangers to your very way of life that would send you shrieking into the corner to tremble and sob. Someone needs to protect the world from these dangers and threats. Is that someone going to be you? Is it? Because if it is, my companions and I will leave, right now, and entrust to you our continued survival. But if you have doubts, if you think you might falter right when you are needed to make the ultimate sacrifice, then tell us now and step back, for saving the world is what we do, and we're really very good at it."

The security guard's lip trembled, and she pointed to a door. "That way," she said. "Turn left."

Skulduggery clamped a hand on to her shoulder. "You are doing fine work," he told her, and led the way to the door. When they were through he walked past the left turn, to a room at the end of the concrete corridor. Inside was a table and two chairs. Ryan reckoned this must be where they kept shoplifters while they waited for the cops to arrive.

"We shouldn't be bothered in here," Skulduggery said, closing the door behind them. His false face melted away as he looked at his pocket watch. "Three hours until closing. Make yourselves comfortable."

He sat at the table and took off his hat. Ryan and Valkyrie remained standing.

"I still don't understand why they want to destroy the world," said Ryan. "Foe said he couldn't see the point of life but, I mean, that's a really *silly* reason..."

"They're bad guys," Valkyrie told him. "Villains. Some villains have proper plans. Others don't. They've just been around for a few hundred years. Given enough time, a stray thought can become an obsession, and then a purpose. They're nuts, Ryan. They're actually insane people who all agree with one another."

"Insanity fuels insanity," Skulduggery said, nodding, "just as stupidity fuels stupidity."

"Speaking of stupidity," Valkyrie said, "I'm just going to ask this one more time and you better give me an answer, because I haven't a clue how you worked it out. How do we know the Machine is here?"

A moment passed before Skulduggery spoke again. "Ryan told me," he said.

Ryan looked at him. "I told you what?"

Skulduggery raised his head, and he looked at Ryan with those hollow eye sockets. "You told me the Machine was hidden in Dundrum. Completely unconsciously, of course. You tried to hide Dundrum on the map with your bottle of Coke, then you tried to distract us with a coughing fit."

"Uh," Ryan said, "what?"

"The drive over confirmed it. Stopping three times to relieve yourself? You were only delaying the inevitable."

"No, I wasn't," Ryan said. "What are you talking about? How would I know where the Machine was hidden?"

"And why would Ryan be trying to stop us from finding it?" Valkyrie asked.

Skulduggery hesitated. "Ryan, why haven't you asked to go home?"

Ryan frowned, genuinely and completely puzzled. "What?"

"You haven't asked to go home," Skulduggery said. "You haven't tried to *call* home to tell them you're OK, even though they must be worried about you by now."

Ryan glowered, angry at having to admit this in front of Valkyrie. "I'm... I'm running away."

Valkyrie's eyes widened. "What? Why?"

"It's a long story."

"No, it isn't," said Skulduggery.

Valkyrie swatted the skeleton's arm. "Skulduggery, shut up. Ryan, what's wrong?"

"My... my dad died. My mum remarried. He's an OK guy but... I don't like being in that house. It reminds me—"

"No, it doesn't," Skulduggery said.

"Stop interrupting!" Ryan shouted. "You don't know what it's like! You don't know!"

"You don't know, either," Skulduggery said. "I'm really sorry to have to tell you this, Ryan, but the reason you don't want to go home is because there is no home to go to. Ryan, you're not real. You don't exist."

Ryan stared at him. "What?"

"You're Deacon Maybury," Skulduggery said. "You're a hiding place who thinks it's a boy."

8

Ryan backed away. "You're crazy."

"I am," Skulduggery said. "I'm also right. Deacon planned this whole thing – as much as he could, anyway. He hid the key, faked his own death and then went to Crasis – called in that old favour. He told Crasis to make him look inconspicuous – someone Foe would never suspect of having anything to do with any of this."

"Skulduggery," Valkyrie said softly. "Are you sure?"

"Crasis only looked at Ryan twice in the whole time we were there. He wanted to tell us, but I expect he'd made a promise to stay quiet. Once his new image was in place, Deacon went to work on his own mind. He couldn't take the chance that Obloquy would be able to read his thoughts. He had to disappear completely. He subdued his personality and replaced it with Ryan – a good boy. A decent person."

"You're wrong," Ryan said. "I don't know what you're talking about, but you're wrong."

"I wish I was," Skulduggery said, "but I rarely am. Deacon planned to hide away until Foe lost his trail. Ryan, can you remember what you did this morning?"

"I got up," Ryan said. "Had breakfast with my mum."

"Again, I'm sorry to tell you, but that's a false memory. The person you think is your mother doesn't exist."

Ryan had an ache, somewhere in his chest. "No. She's my mum. She's my mum and I love her."

"I know you do," Skulduggery said. "Deacon is very thorough. But there's only so much a Sensitive can do to suppress a personality, especially when he works on himself. Cracks start to show much earlier. That's why you were at the library today. Somewhere in your subconscious, you knew it was important. You knew exactly where to find that key."

Ryan realised he was crying. He wiped away tears.

"When we were looking at the map, you knew we wanted to dismantle the Machine. Your subconscious didn't want that. So it tried to block our way here."

"You're wrong," Ryan said.

"I'm right. You know I'm right."

"No. No, you're not. I know who I am."

"Which is why you're crying."

"No," Ryan said. "Shut up. Stop it. I know who I am. I'm me. What you're saying is stupid. It's ridiculous. I'd know if I wasn't me. I'd know it."

"No, you wouldn't. And I'm very sorry."

They hadn't spoken to him in three hours. They sat over there, at the table. Occasionally, he'd hear them talking softly. They were giving him space.

From somewhere outside, he could hear the announcements, alerting shoppers that the mall was closing. He imagined all the friends and families hurrying out, chatting and laughing and mothers dragging kids and kids wailing and crying...

Ryan remembered being a kid. He remembered his mum. And his dad. He remembered how much he loved his mum, and how much he missed his dad. He didn't want to run away any more. He wanted to go home. But the more he thought about going home, the less real it became.

It was dark in the room when Valkyrie came over. She sat on the ground beside him, her back against the wall.

"Hey, Ryan," she said, her voice quiet.

"That's not my name," he told her. His own voice shook like it always did when he was emotional. At least, that's what he remembered.

"I'm going to call you Ryan until I can't call you Ryan any more," Valkyrie said. "I don't care about Deacon. I've never met him. I don't know him. I know you, Ryan. And I like you."

He nodded. Didn't answer.

"We're going to go looking for the Machine now," she said. "We have a few hours before the cleaning crews get here. Skulduggery thinks dismantling the bomb won't be a problem. Do you still want to do it?"

Ryan tried to see her pretty face in the gloom. "What would you do if I didn't? Would you cut off my hand and dismantle it yourself? How do you know you can trust me? I'm Deacon, after all."

"You're still you."

"There *is* no me."

Her hand found his. Despite himself, Ryan's heartbeat quickened. "We all have a side to ourselves that we don't like," she said. "Skulduggery has one. I have one. Now you have one. But you don't have to be ruled by it. You can make your own choices, Ryan. Deacon wants to sell the Machine – to make some money and then leave the mess for someone else to deal with. You want to take it apart so that nobody can ever use it. You can choose to help us. You can choose to help *me*."

"And me," Skulduggery said from the other side of the room.

"Shut up," Valkyrie said, not turning away from Ryan.

"Right," said Skulduggery.

The ghost of a smile found its way on to Ryan's lips. "If I do help you," he said, "that would really annoy Deacon, wouldn't it?"

"Oh," said Valkyrie, "it would."

Ryan liked that idea. It was the only way he could think of to have his revenge on a man who had snatched away a family and a life that were never real in the first place. But Ryan's hurt was real. His pain was real. And for the next few hours, at least, Ryan himself was determined that he himself would be real.

"I have one condition," Ryan said.

He saw the outline of Valkyrie's head tilting to one side. "OK," she said cautiously.

"If I do this, and I dismantle the bomb, can I kiss you?"

He felt her slow, slow smile. "We'll have to see about that," she said, and got up. She pulled him to his feet.

Skulduggery led the way out into the mall. The shops themselves were dark and shuttered, but the main strip of the mall was still lit. It was odd, being in a space designed for crowds and seeing it empty. It didn't fit. It wasn't right. It was, all of a sudden, incredibly lonely.

They walked down the deactivated travelator, no one talking. They reached the ground floor and Ryan wandered around, his hand held open in front of him. Skulduggery had insisted that once he got close to the Machine, he'd start to feel something. A buzzing, maybe. A tingle. Ryan had asked if it would be sore. Skulduggery couldn't promise anything.

Valkyrie walked behind him. She pitied him. He knew she did. Of course she did. Who wouldn't? He was a pitiful person who wasn't even a person. He didn't even know what he looked like, not really. He knew he wasn't fifteen. He knew he was older. He wondered what colour hair he had. He wondered what his face was like. How his voice sounded. He wondered what his thoughts were like. The only thing he knew was that he wasn't a very nice person – not really. Not truly. A nice person wouldn't do something like this.

His hand tingled. Slight pins and needles. "I think we're close," he said. His words sounded weird in this place.

"It's below us," said Skulduggery, "built into the foundations. There's an activation panel somewhere around here. Follow the buzzing."

Ryan did as he was told, and led them to a section of the wall. Skulduggery tapped it with his knuckle. It sounded normal to Ryan, but Skulduggery obviously heard something that he didn't. It must have been great to be Skulduggery – to always know what to do, to always know what needed to be done. Even in the false life Deacon Maybury had given him, Ryan had never known that kind of certainty.

"Why didn't he make me better?" he asked as Skulduggery continued to tap.

Valkyrie looked at him. "What do you mean?"

Ryan's laugh came out of nowhere and didn't last long. "I mean, look at me. Why didn't he make me cooler, or smarter, or better-looking? He was creating a whole new person, right? So why did he make him as rubbish as me?"

"You're... you're not rubbish, Ryan."

"Yes, I am. I'm fat and ugly and useless."

"Skulduggery," Valkyrie said, "tell him."

Skulduggery stopped tapping the wall, and looked at Ryan. "Deacon made someone who would blend in with the background, someone too unexceptional to notice."

Valkyrie shook her head. "You're meant to make him feel better."

"I'm about to," Skulduggery said. "He made you unexceptional, Ryan. He made you normal. As normal as he could. And in doing so, he has single-handedly proven how exceptional normal people can be. When we were at Deacon's apartment, you could have run and left Valkyrie and myself to fight them off ourselves. But you turned back. You turned back to help. You stood up to terrifying people who want to kill the world, who would snap you in two and tear you apart and not lose one wink of sleep over it, and you did so without training or magic. You did so because you are a good person, and you have true courage. You have the kind of courage Deacon Maybury himself never had. He made you the most normal boy he could, and inadvertently he made you so much better than he could ever hope to be."

"Oh," Valkyrie said, "well... OK, that's better than I thought it was going to be. How are you feeling now, Ryan?"

Ryan looked at her. "I'm feeling pretty special, actually," he said, and she laughed.

Skulduggery pressed his thumbs into the wall, and a large section slid to one side. Instead of the mass of wires that Ryan expected, however, there was a carving of the key in the centre of what looked like a complicated metal maze.

"Oh, good," Skulduggery said.

Valkyrie peered closer. "Is it going to be easy to dismantle?"

"Not in the slightest."

"Do you think you can manage it?"

Skulduggery tapped his chin. "Only with an inordinate amount of luck."

"So we should probably wait for an expert."

"Good God, no," Skulduggery said, jerking his head round. "Where's the fun in that?"

"But... but if you get it wrong, we might all die."

"Yes, that is true, but I probably won't get it wrong."

Valkyrie's eyes flickered to Ryan, then back to Skulduggery. "You *probably* won't?"

"The odds are in my favour."

"Really?"

"Almost."

"I vote we wait for an expert."

"But that might take twenty minutes or *longer*, Valkyrie."

"So? It's not like it's counting down or anything. We have all the time in the world."

"And there's no time like the present. Ryan, I'm going to need you to press your hand against the carving. I'll guide you every step of the way from then on."

Valkyrie's tone was firm. "Skulduggery. We are calling this in and then we're waiting for a bomb-disposal expert."

"What will he know that I don't?"

"About the disposal of bombs? Lots."

Skulduggery waved a hand dismissively. "Bombs are simple things. They're designed to go off. What we have to do in order to thwart the bomb is to *stop* it from going off. What could be more straightforward?"

Valkyrie's fingers closed round Ryan's wrist and she pulled him away. "We are waiting for an expert."

"I think we should let him try," said a voice from behind them. They spun, saw Foe and his gang walking up. Foe was grinning. "It might save us the bother of destroying the world ourselves."

9

Valkyrie stepped in front of Ryan, and Skulduggery straightened his tie. "Excellent," he said. "You've fallen right into our trap."

Foe looked around at the otherwise empty mall, eyebrow raised. "This is a trap, is it? So this is the bit where all the Cleavers appear? This is the part where we surrender due to being completely outnumbered and you cart us off to our cells?"

"Roughly, yes."

Foe's grin grew wider. "Has the trap been sprung yet?"

"I'm simply not going to dignify that with an answer," said Skulduggery.

Standing behind Obloquy, Samuel was sweating badly. Ryan could see the lines of tension on his face. He looked to be in pain.

"Your pet doesn't look too good," Valkyrie said.

Foe glanced back, then shrugged. "When the sun goes down, all a vampire wants to do is rip off his skin and kill everything in sight. Right now, the only thing keeping all of us safe is the last drop of a serum he took. Your boyfriend took something similar, didn't he? What was his name? Caelan?"

Valkyrie's shoulders stiffened and her voice grew harder. "He was *not* my boyfriend."

"Bad break-up, was it? Actually, don't answer that. I heard it was. Bad for him more than you, though, wasn't it?"

"We don't talk about vampires," Ryan muttered.

Foe smiled and Mercy laughed. "See?" she said. "Told you he fancies her."

"So what if he does?" Valkyrie snapped back. "He's a nice guy. After we've smacked you lot around, we may as well give it a go. What's the matter, Mercy – jealous that two people can like each other when nobody in their right mind would ever like you?"

Mercy glared. "Plenty have liked me."

"Yeah," Valkyrie said, "I've heard."

The glare turned to a scowl. "Not like that."

"You don't have to justify yourself to me."

"Says the girl who dated a vampire."

"Says the psycho who dated everyone."

"Detective Pleasant," Foe said, interrupting the conversation just when it was getting interesting, "you've gone suspiciously quiet. It's not like you to miss an argument."

"Carry on," Skulduggery said, his head down. "Don't mind me..."

Foe frowned. "What are you doing?"

Skulduggery waited a moment, then looked up, and showed them his phone. "Just sending a message. Reinforcements should be here soon."

Obloquy sagged. "I told you we should have just attacked them," he rumbled. "But, no, you wanted to talk and trade witty banter."

"Shut up, Obloquy," Foe said. "Fine, Detective. You want to skip straight to business? Fine with me. Kill them."

Valkyrie pushed Ryan back slightly as Obloquy headed for her and Mercy zeroed in on Skulduggery.

"Oh, sure," Valkyrie said, "I'll take the big one, no problem."

Foe stayed where he was, his eyes on Ryan. Behind him, Samuel sweated.

Mercy opened her mouth and Skulduggery ducked the stream of energy that carved a furrow across the wall behind him. He dodged behind a pillar, but the stream intensified, melting right through the pillar and taking Skulduggery's hat off his head.

Obloquy pressed his hands to his temples and he squeezed, like he wanted to pop his own head open. Valkyrie staggered. She fell to one knee, bringing up her own hands like she was trying to shield herself. Ryan wanted to run and help, but now Foe was walking towards him.

"This doesn't have to hurt," Foe said.

Ryan turned, ran up the still travelator, swung round at the top and ran up the next one. He was halfway up when he started to seriously regret his choice. His legs were already screaming at him and his lungs were burning. He'd never been able to run for any length of time – not even in the school that he remembered but had never actually attended.

He glanced down, saw Skulduggery waving a hand and Mercy flying backwards. Valkyrie was on both knees now, with Obloquy standing directly over her. Darkness pulsed from the ring on her finger and Obloquy jerked back in shock. His psychic attack must have faltered, because Valkyrie immediately wrapped an arm round each leg. She pressed her shoulder against his belly and as she lifted she launched herself forward. Obloquy yelled as he hit the ground, Valkyrie on top, and Ryan saw her first headbutt go in before he reached the top floor and lost her to sight.

Staggering slightly, Ryan ran on, no idea where he was going or what he would do when he got there. The mall was terrifying at night. The few lights that were on cast the deepest shadows. Anyone could be hiding in those shadows.

Foe stepped out ahead of him and Ryan yelled and changed course and ran into a potted plant, tripped over it and sprawled on to the floor.

"I'd ask you to activate the Machine," Foe said, walking up, "but I don't have the time for an argument. So I'm going to be rude. I hope you don't mind, me being rude. It's nothing personal. I'm not going to kill you. Don't think I'm going to kill you. I'm just going to cut off your hand a little bit. You might die from blood loss or trauma or shock – let's not kid ourselves – but you will not die from me cutting off your hand. When you think about it like that, you have nothing to fear from me or my giant knife."

Foe took a machete from his jacket.

Ryan crawled away on his hands and knees, panting too hard to get up.

"I know some people say they like the thrill of the chase," Foe said, stepping on Ryan's ankle and pinning it there, "but I'm not one of those people. The only thing I care about is ending this world."

Ryan collapsed, and rolled over on to his back. "Why?" he gasped. "Why do you want to... want to kill everyone?"

Foe looked down at him, and shrugged. "Because it's Wednesday."

The machete swung and Ryan screamed and Skulduggery crashed into Foe from behind. They both went stumbling off. Ryan sat up, looking at his hand, making sure it was where it was supposed to be. He realised he was still screaming so he stopped that and looked around. Skulduggery kicked at Foe's knee, grabbed his head when he bent forward and cracked it against a narrow pillar. Foe staggered and swung a fist, but Skulduggery stepped inside the swing, latched on and started hitting him with elbows. It was all very violent. Ryan's mother, if she'd existed, would not have approved.

"Skulduggery!" Valkyrie shouted from below them.

"Ryan," Skulduggery muttered, as Foe grabbed him round the waist and slammed him back against the wall, "could you take a look and see what she's shouting about now?"

Ryan got up, hurried to the railing, looked over. Mercy and Obloquy were down and not moving, but Valkyrie was backing away from Samuel, who was lurching towards her, bent over like he had stomach cramps.

Ryan looked back. Foe had his arm wrapped around Skulduggery's neck from behind, and he was dragging him like he wanted to pull Skulduggery's head from his spinal column. Skulduggery twisted but Foe adapted, turning his hold into a headlock. Skulduggery reached up, his gloved fingers digging into Foe's eyes. Foe jerked away and lost his grip and Skulduggery pushed against him, tripping him with a sneaky sweep to the ankle. Foe went down and Skulduggery landed on top of him.

"Well?" Skulduggery asked as he pounded Foe with punches.

"Uh, I don't know," said Ryan. "Samuel looks like he's about to throw up."

Surprisingly, Skulduggery and Foe stopped fighting.

"He's doubled over?" Foe asked, panting for breath.

"Yeah," said Ryan.

Foe looked at Skulduggery, and they both stood up.

"You're on your own," Foe said, and ran.

Ryan frowned, looked down at Samuel again. Samuel's moan of pain drifted up, and then suddenly it turned to a growl. Samuel straightened, digging his fingers into his shirt and ripping it open. No, not just his shirt. His skin, too. Samuel ripped his flesh and his clothes from his body, from the bone-white body that lay beneath. His hands, and even from where he stood, Ryan could see the claws on those hands, tore Samuel's face off and threw it to one side, revealing the smooth head and big black eyes and jagged, jagged teeth.

Valkyrie turned and ran, and the vampire bounded after her. Something blurred out of the corner of Ryan's eye and suddenly Skulduggery was vaulting over the railing and dropping to the ground far below.

Ryan ran for the travelator, heading down, heading down to help Valkyrie. He heard her cry out and nearly tripped, nearly went head first. There was a crash of breaking glass and Ryan glimpsed Skulduggery disappearing through a shop window. He was almost at the ground floor when he saw her, saw Valkyrie, hurling fireballs and whipping shadows at the vampire that came at her like a wild animal. It twisted in mid-air, avoiding the slash of darkness Valkyrie sent its way. It landed on her, took her down, its claws raking across her body. She gasped and it raked again, and again, trying to get through her protective clothing, trying to rend flesh and puncture skin, trying to draw blood.

"Hey!" Ryan screamed, running into full view of the monster. "Hey, you! Hey! Come and get me! Come on!"

The vampire snapped its head up, snarling.

"I've got what you want!" Ryan shouted, holding up his imprinted palm. If Samuel the man was still in there somewhere, maybe he'd remember why all this was going on in the first place. Maybe he'd remember that Ryan was the real target. Or maybe the vampire would just see an easy kill and—

The vampire leaped off Valkyrie. Ryan howled in terror and started running again. He glanced back in time to see its claws and its teeth and feel the rush of air as it swooped up and over him.

Ryan's feet got mixed up and he tripped over himself. He sat on the ground, looking up. The vampire hung in the air, looking down. It writhed and snarled, slashed at him with its claws.

Skulduggery walked over, hands open, fingers flexing slightly as he held the creature in place. His suit was torn and his tie was crooked. Valkyrie limped over, holding his hat. She showed it to him, and he groaned. There was a large hole burned through the top.

The vampire snarled at them all.

Skulduggery raised his arms, and the vampire rose in the air. Higher and higher it went, up past every floor. Valkyrie took Ryan's arm, escorted him to the benches. When the vampire couldn't rise any higher, Skulduggery dropped his hands quickly, and the vampire plunged downwards.

"This won't kill it," Valkyrie told Ryan as the vampire fell. "But it'll break enough bones to stop it from bothering us."

The vampire hit the ground with a satisfying *thwack*, and didn't get up.

Skulduggery examined his poor hat, and laid it to one side. "Ryan," he said, "I know you've been through a lot, but there is the small matter of dismantling a bomb to get through, and then I'll let you rest. I promise."

IO

With Skulduggery's guidance, Ryan dismantled the Doomsday Machine. He rendered each and every part of it inert. When it was done, when the last piece was made useless, his hand started to burn. He hissed, looked at his palm, and the imprint faded to nothing.

"Well done, Ryan," Skulduggery said. "You saved the world."

"You knew exactly what to do," Ryan said. "You *did* know how to dismantle it after all."

"I'm glad you got that impression," Skulduggery said kindly. "But really I could have just as easily killed us all. Still, it's better than waiting around for the experts, isn't it?"

He took a set of handcuffs from his belt and went to shackle the unconscious prisoners, leaving Ryan and Valkyrie alone.

"How long do I have?" Ryan asked.

Valkyrie hesitated. "Skulduggery said... he said that as soon as this was over, one way or the other, Deacon's personality would start to reassert itself."

"So I don't have long," Ryan said quietly.

"I'm... I'm afraid not."

Ryan nodded. He didn't say anything. He didn't trust his voice not to break.

"You probably saved my life back there," Valkyrie said. "That was a very brave thing you did."

Ryan managed a smile. "Maybe it's something you'll remember me for."

"I definitely think so."

"I don't feel very brave right now. To be honest, I kind of feel like crying."

Valkyrie's hand rested on his shoulder.

"I really don't want to die," Ryan said. He was crying now. He didn't care. The only thing he cared about was that in a few moments he wouldn't be here any more. He wouldn't exist. They'd stopped Foe and the others from destroying the world, but Ryan's world was ending just the same. "It's not fair. How come Deacon gets to live and I don't?"

"I don't know," Valkyrie said softly.

"Isn't there anything you can do? Maybe Skulduggery can do something? Maybe he knows someone who can, who can block Deacon from coming back or…"

"I'm sorry, Ryan," Valkyrie said. She was crying, too. This pretty girl with the single dimple when she smiled, she was crying for him. This pretty girl who would never go out with a guy like Ryan, not in a million years, was sitting here with her arm round him, and they were crying together.

He fought to control his sobs. When he could speak, he spoke quietly. "Could I have that kiss now?"

She looked at him. "Definitely," she said, and leaned in. He turned his head slightly, didn't know if he should close his eyes or keep them open, but when their lips met his eyes closed. His first kiss in fifteen years of false memories. His only kiss in fifteen hours of real life.

They parted. His head was clouded. His thoughts were fuzzy.

"I really like you, Valkyrie," he managed to mumble.

"I really like you, Ryan," she said back to him.

Ryan smiled and tried to kiss her again, this pretty girl with the dimple, what was her name again, Valkyrie, that was it, seventeen years old and cute as a button, the kind of girl who had never even noticed Deacon when he was that age. He grinned and leaned in and felt her hand against his chest, keeping him back, and then her eyes were narrowing.

"Ryan?"

"I'll be whoever you want me to be," Deacon said, and she hit him so hard the whole world spun.

She stood over him. "Get rid of that face," she said. "Stop using Ryan's face right now or I swear to God I'll batter you."

"OK!" he cried. "Just don't hit me again!"

Deacon got to his feet, his jaw aching. "Ain't that something?" he muttered, and at those words, the image around him flickered and withdrew, and suddenly he was back to his old self again.

Valkyrie's eyes sparkled with tears. She was looking at him like she was going to hit him again anyway.

"I just want to thank you," he said before she did. "I was in a serious bind and you, you came in and you really helped me. I was in over my head, I don't mind admitting it. If it makes any difference, I never intended for the Machine to end up in enemy hands. The moment I sold the key, I was going to alert the Sanctuary and get an army of Cleavers in here to—"

"You risked the lives of everyone on the *planet*," Valkyrie said, her voice tight.

"I did," he said, nodding sadly, "and I truly regret that. It was stupid. It was short-sighted, and selfish. If I knew then what I know now, I would never have tried it. But we all make mistakes, isn't that right? And I made a mistake. A terrible, terrible mistake that could have had untold consequences for—"

He didn't even see the punch. He saw her shoulder shift and then he was toppling backwards. He hit the ground and his face felt three sizes too big. Good *God*, she hit hard.

"You better get up," she said, standing over him. "The Cleavers are coming, and if you're here when they arrive, you'll get arrested, too."

He blinked. "You're letting me go?"

"We're letting *Ryan* go," Skulduggery Pleasant said, walking up behind her. "Ryan was a friend of ours. He deserved better than to be you, Deacon."

"I know he did," Deacon said, rising slowly to his feet for the second time in the last sixty seconds. "I only hope I can make it up to him somehow, maybe by being a better person, by treating people with the same kind of—"

"If you want me to hit you again, you'll keep talking like that," Valkyrie said.

Deacon shut up. If looks could kill, he'd be skewered. "I know I did wrong," he said, hanging his head. "I know I did. And I've already paid for it. My brother. My poor brother Dafydd. Foe thought Dafydd was me. He chased him and Dafydd... Dafydd fell into that wood chipper. He was always the clumsy one, was Dafydd. So, so clumsy..."

Valkyrie shoved him to get his attention, and when he looked up she leaned in. "If we ever hear of you doing something like that again, creating an innocent person just so you can hide behind them..."

Deacon held up his hands. "I won't, I swear. I've learned my lesson. I was greedy, and selfish. But now I see that it was wrong to—"

"We don't care," Skulduggery said. "Run away before I shoot you."

Deacon nodded, and started walking.

"He said *run*," Valkyrie snarled, and Deacon did just that.

TRICK OR TREAT

Tanith wiped the blood off the carving knife and, ignoring the body of the man she had just stabbed to death, went back to carving her jack-o'-lantern.

Her skill with a blade always came in useful this time of year. While other people would be satisfied with triangular eyes and jagged teeth, Tanith transformed her Halloween pumpkins into works of slowly rotting art. Tonight she was carving a portrait of her dear friend and object of worship Valkyrie Cain. By all accounts, poor Valkyrie still refused to embrace her destiny as destroyer of the world, but Tanith could forgive her this little moment of self-doubt. After all, if Tanith herself hadn't been corrupted by a Remnant, then she would have been *helping* Val run from the inevitable.

It was the Remnant inside her, the thing of cruelty and nastiness, that had shared with Tanith this vision of the future, when Valkyrie would become Darquesse and burn all life to a cinder. It had been a glorious revelation, one that had spurred Tanith on to schemes and plans she had never before thought herself capable of. But the fact was there were no more Remnants out there. Her kith and kin were all trapped and locked away and hidden from her – so Tanith was on her own. More or less. She had a Texan psychopath who was besotted with her, and there were times when he certainly did come in useful.

But she didn't love him. Her love was reserved for Darquesse, and Darquesse alone.

She put down the carving knife and picked up a candle, placed it carefully inside the jack-o'-lantern. She lit it and stepped back. It was a good likeness. No, it was a *great* likeness. Valkyrie was such a pretty girl, and Tanith had to resist the urge to take a picture and send it to her. But she knew that Valkyrie would only tell Skulduggery, and Skulduggery would trace the picture back here to this small town in Ohio, and suddenly there'd be Cleavers, Cleavers everywhere. It was all so unfair. All Tanith wanted to do was protect Darquesse from the people who were planning on harming her, after all. She was on Valkyrie's side, in a way. Why couldn't Val see that?

Headlights looped in around the room, and Tanith went to the window, looked out. A battered old car lurched to a stop outside the house next door, and a shabby, middle-aged man climbed out. As she watched him hitch his trousers higher round his waist, Tanith made sure to keep her mind calm and free of violent thoughts. There were Sensitives who could pick up feelings of hostility and, while she didn't know if Jerry Ordain was one of them, she couldn't take the chance. There was too much riding on tonight to risk a stray thought at the wrong time. The fact that he came home at all meant that he hadn't foreseen tonight's events, and that was a promising start.

Of course, it was entirely possible that Jerry knew full well she was there, and he had a trap waiting for her the moment she made a move. That was the trouble with Sensitives – it was very hard to sneak up on them.

She took her sword from the table and left through the back door. She sprang lightly over the fence, landed without a sound in Jerry's yard as lights flicked on in the house. She crept to the window. No sign of an ambush. She saw Jerry ambling into the kitchenette. If he sensed her watching him, he gave no sign.

Taking a breath, Tanith moved to the door and rested her hand against the lock. It clicked open and she moved in silently. Jerry was a bachelor and lived like it. The house smelled of dust and old socks. She slid her sword from its scabbard and walked up the wall. Those floorboards were old and she didn't trust them not to creak. She crept upside down along the ceiling, careful not to disturb the bulb as she passed it or cast her shadow on to her target. Jerry had his back to her, and was making himself a massive sandwich. She reached the far wall and walked down until she was standing normally again. He still didn't turn round. She took out her phone, sent a text. A few moments later, Billy-Ray Sanguine rose up from the floor beside her.

They waited for Jerry to sense the hostility that only a psychopath of Sanguine's stature could radiate – the kind of hostility that he could never conceal, no matter how hard he tried. Instead, Jerry continued making his sandwich. Tanith was impressed at how cool and collected he was. It was almost as if he wasn't even aware of their presence. Jerry started humming to himself, and Sanguine looked at her. She frowned back. Now it *really* seemed like he wasn't aware of their presence.

Once he had piled every conceivable type of meat on to his sandwich, Jerry cut off the crusts and then sliced it down the middle. He picked up one half, raised it slowly to his mouth and bit into it as he turned. He saw them and shrieked, spitting it all out again as he stumbled back against the fridge. A bit of lettuce hung wetly off his chin.

"Hi," said Tanith. "Just checking – you *are* Jerry Ordain, right?"

The man stood there, eyes bulging. "Whuh," he said.

"Jerry Ordain? You *are* Jerry the psychic, aren't you?"

He shook his head. The piece of lettuce fell away. "No. Not me. No. Wrong person."

"Then who are you?" Sanguine asked.

The man gaped at him. "Me?"

It was Jerry. It was obviously Jerry, from the look on his face as his fear-frozen mind tried coming up with a false name. "I'm... I'm..."

Sanguine added an edge to his voice. "What's your damn name?"

"Jerry!" Jerry blurted. "But not the Jerry you're looking for! I'm a different Jerry!"

Jerry had to be the worst liar Tanith had ever met.

"I'll get him, though," Jerry said, stepping sideways. "If you stay right there, I'll get him. Just stay there. I'll be right back, with Jerry. The Jerry you're looking for."

Sanguine strolled over to intercept him, and Jerry reversed direction, started heading for the window.

"Make yourselves at home," he was saying. "Want a sandwich? I just made a sandwich. You can have my sandwich. I won't be long. Thirty seconds, tops."

"Jerry," Tanith said, "we've come a long way to talk to you."

He shook his head. "You've come a long way to talk to the *other* Jerry..."

Tanith showed him her sword. Jerry stared. And then he bolted for the window.

In his haste, however, he completely forgot about the coffee table and, when his shin smacked into it, he barely had time to howl before his face hit the floor. Tanith watched him contort in pain, one hand over his shin, the other covering his mouth. He'd bitten his tongue. She winced. She hated that.

Tears in his eyes, Jerry launched himself up and ran into the wall. He rebounded impressively, gave a little whirl and staggered to the window. Clumsy hands fumbled at the latch. He finally raised it, glanced behind him to make sure he still had time, and in that moment the window closed. Jerry turned back and dived into the glass, cracking it and careering backwards. He collapsed on to the rug and curled up into a sobbing, moaning ball.

"Pleathe," he lisped, "shtop hurting me."

Tanith sighed. "We haven't touched you, Jerry."

"I seen a lot of things in my time," Sanguine said, "but I ain't never seen a man beat himself up before. That was highly entertainin'."

Tanith walked over to Jerry as he continued to sob.

"Pleathe don't kill me."

"Don't worry," Tanith said, her voice soothing. "We weren't planning on it."

Sanguine looked at her, surprised. "We weren't? Why not? He's clearly an idiot."

She glared. "We're not here to hurt anyone. We're here to ask some questions and leave."

"But we'll be killin' him before we go, won't we?"

Jerry squealed softly.

"No, we won't," Tanith insisted. "Violence is not always the answer, Billy-Ray. This time, Jerry here gets to live out the rest of his life in peace – understand?"

"Barely."

She hunkered down and patted Jerry on the shoulder. "Don't mind him, Jerry. He's cranky. He's used to being the only American in my life, but now there's you. Jealousy is a terrible thing in a grown man, isn't it?"

"I ain't jealous."

"Of course not, dear. Jerry, what do you say you answer our questions and then we leave you alone? Does that sound good to you?"

Jerry nodded.

"Good man. How's your tongue?"

"I bith it."

"I can see that."

"Ith bleeding."

"I can see that, too."

He stuck his tongue out at her. "Ith it bad?"

His tongue was bloody and horrible. She took a small leaf from her coat and placed it delicately into his mouth. "Don't say anything for a few seconds. Let that heal."

Jerry blinked at her. His eyes were wet. He wasn't an impressive human being.

"Show me," she said, and he stuck his tongue out again. She nodded. "It's healing. It was only a small bite. Now you can answer our questions, can't you?"

He nodded, and she stood.

"You're involved with a group of people, aren't you? A group of sorcerers from different Sanctuaries around the world."

"How... how did you know that?"

"I've spent the last few months asking a lot of people a lot of questions. See, I figured there'd be someone out there who would be trying to do something about Darquesse before she even turned up. That's when I heard your name for the first time. You're a psychic, aren't you, Jerry?"

"I... I prefer the term clairvoyant."

Tanith did her best not to roll her eyes. "Clairvoyant, of course. And, as a clairvoyant, you would have seen visions of Darquesse."

"Of course," Jerry said, nodding. He was still on the floor, but he was sitting a little straighter now. His chest puffed out slightly. "Even low-level Sensitives picked up something. For a clairvoyant of my ability, it was a veritable tsunami of images and sensations and emotions. Very powerful."

"What did you see?"

"I saw death."

Sanguine gave a barely suppressed sigh.

"What do you mean?" Tanith asked, smiling at Jerry.

"I saw a city destroyed. Streets cracked and broken. Buildings burning. And I saw her. I saw Darquesse."

"Did you see her face?"

"Alas, no, I did not," said Jerry, and Tanith resisted smacking him for using the word *alas* in an irony-free context. "But there is no doubt in my mind that it was her. Ten foot tall, she was. A terrible sight to behold."

"Ten foot tall?" Sanguine asked.

Jerry nodded. "Oh, yes. Easily. And the way she moved... like a cat."

Sanguine frowned behind his sunglasses. "What, on all fours?"

"Pardon me?"

Sanguine continued. "I heard from another psychic – sorry, *clairvoyant* – that Darquesse had long black fingernails that she used to cut off people's heads. Did you see that?"

Jerry nodded. "It was awful."

"And she shot laser beams out of her eyes."

"Well," Jerry said with a shrug, "I don't know if they were laser beams, but yes. Devastating blasts, they were."

"This clairvoyant friend of ours," Sanguine continued, "he also caught a glimpse of red hair beneath her hood. Did you see that? Don't worry if you didn't. Our friend is probably the most powerful Sensitive in the world. I wouldn't be surprised if you didn't see as much as him."

"Red hair?" Jerry said. "Yes. Yes, I saw that too, now that you mention it. Long tousled red hair."

"He said it was straight."

"Long straight red hair, yes."

"He said it was short."

"Short straight red hair, that's what I meant to say."

Sanguine looked at Tanith, who glowered and poked Jerry. He screamed. She had poked him with her sword.

"You're lying to us," she said. He screamed again. "We don't have a psychic friend. Billy-Ray made all that stuff up. You didn't see a vision, did you?"

She twisted the sword and his screams reached a new pitch. "No! No, I didn't! I'm sorry! Please stop stabbing me!"

She withdrew the sword and wiped the tip of the blade on his shirt. "Are you even a Sensitive, Jerry?"

"I am," he whimpered, cradling his wound, "but I'm not a very good one. Sometimes... sometimes I can predict the weather, if it's a nice day."

"Is it going to rain tomorrow?" Sanguine asked.

"I don't know," Jerry confessed. "I can only predict a few minutes into the future. Most of the time I have to watch the forecast like everyone else."

"You," Sanguine said, "are the worst psychic I've ever met."

"Does anyone else know that you're a fraud?" asked Tanith.

"No," Jerry said, sobbing. "I've managed to keep them fooled. It hasn't been easy, but whenever they ask me to look into the future I always try to be as vague as possible. I talk about shadows and death and ominous feelings, and they generally infer their own meanings into that and then leave me alone."

"So when this group of sorcerers asked you to find out more about Darquesse," Tanith said, "you basically just copied what every other Sensitive was saying?"

"Essentially, yes," Jerry said. "Can I have a bandage? I'm bleeding quite badly here."

"First you tell us what they're planning, and then we'll see about bandages."

"I'm losing a lot of blood."

Tanith let the veins rise beneath her skin, and her black lips curled into a smile. "Tell us what they're planning."

Jerry paled, his face going slack. "Yes. Yes, of course. They're going after weapons. Four God-Killer weapons that they think could hurt Darquesse."

"Where are these weapons?"

"Scattered," said Jerry. "All over the world. They're going to go after them."

"And you know where they're goin'?" Sanguine asked.

"I have a list of the possible locations." Jerry took out his wallet, rifled through it, came out with a crumpled piece of paper.

Tanith took it from him, examined it and nodded. "Looks like we won't be needing you any more."

He brightened. "So that's it? I can go?"

She pulled him to his feet. "You can go," she smiled, and her sword flashed and she took off his head.

"You," Sanguine said, "are delicious when you're vicious."

She gave him a smirk, and led the way to the front door. She opened it and froze.

Six little children in Halloween outfits looked up at her.

"Trick or treat," said the little witch. Surrounding the witch was a pirate, a zombie, a vampire, a Mad Hatter and a rabbit. They rattled their buckets.

"Uh," said Tanith.

Sanguine appeared at her elbow and grinned at the kids. "Look," he said, "there's a little zombie. Smells a darn sight better than the real thing, doesn't he? And a vampire! Doesn't she look cute? And a rabbit!" He faltered. "A rabbit. That... that ain't exactly scary, though, is it?"

The rabbit looked up at him. "It is if you're scared of rabbits."

Tanith nodded. "You've got to admit he makes a good point."

"You talk funny," said the witch. "Where are you from?"

Tanith smiled. "I'm from London."

The pirate frowned. "Is that in France?"

The Mad Hatter scowled. "It's in England, dummy." He looked at Tanith. "You're English. Why do you have a sword?"

"Because I'm an English ninja," Tanith replied. "We're just like regular ninjas, except we wear leather and flirt more."

The kids nodded, satisfied with the definition, and then rattled their buckets again. "Trick or treat," they chorused.

"This isn't actually our house," Tanith told them, "but whatever you find in there is yours to keep."

The pirate perked up. "Even the TV?"

"Especially the TV."

The kids glanced at each other, then stormed the house. Tanith waited a moment, watching them approach Jerry's headless corpse warily. The rabbit hesitated, then nudged Jerry's head with his fluffy foot. The head rolled in its own blood, and the rabbit shrugged. "That's so fake," he said, and turned to help the pirate with the TV.

GET THEE BEHIND ME, BUBBA MOON

I

Every town has a haunted house, I guess, and Bredon, small as it was, was no different. My older brother and his friends used to go up there, dare each other to knock on the door. He told me once that when his time came, he accepted the dare like there was nothing else he'd rather be doing. He'd mocked others for being scared and he wasn't about to turn around and show anything like that kind of fear in his own eyes.

He said one Wednesday night, at the height of summer, they sneaked out and cycled over by the light of the full moon. Full moons were important for this kind of thing, he said. We were kids, and we knew this stuff. They reached the house a little before midnight and waited until Ryan Sanderson's brand-new digital watch beeped 11:59. My brother now had one minute to open that gate, walk up that weed-cracked path, and knock on that door. Midnight was important for this kind of thing. That was something else we knew.

So my brother pushed open the iron gate that creaked with rust and age, and he laughed at how creepy it was. Behind him, his friends laughed, too. He pretended the path was one big hopscotch game, and he jumped and hopped the whole way up to the sound of laughter and cheers. But my brother wasn't laughing any more. He told me he'd nailed that grin to his face when he felt it starting to slide off. He told me the closer he got to that door, the more real it all became. All the stories. All the rumours. All the scary, scary dreams.

He reached the three steps that led up to the front door. This close, he could see how old the wood was. He could see the broken doorbell with the wires hanging out. This part of town was all dark. No streetlights. Behind the house were the woods, and the trees there never seemed to grow any leaves. They stood against the dark sky and didn't move, like they were waiting for something bad to happen.

All these thoughts, my brother said, flickered through his mind. Them and more. The biggest and darkest thought, and the heaviest, the one that pressed down on all the others, was the feeling that he was being watched by someone with no goodness in them. He felt eyes on him that were mean and greedy and so full of hate, and he felt like the house would swallow him up if he got too close.

So he stood on the first step, leaned in as far as he could get, and knocked three times on the door.

Three loud knocks, so loud they could have woken the dead and, even though he was the one who made it, the noise broke something within him and he turned tail and bolted, back to the hooting and hollering of his friends, and they grabbed their bikes and cycled away from there like the devil himself was on their tails.

All this he told me one Saturday night years later, right before he went out with his college buddies. This was his version of a pep talk, because tonight it was my turn to knock on that door and my brother knew it, and he went away laughing at how white my face had gotten.

I told my parents I was going to bed early, and my dad grunted like he'd barely heard me and didn't lift his head from the book he was reading. My mom didn't drag her gaze away from the TV. She was watching some game show. Her favourite was *Wheel of Fortune.* Dad said he hated game shows, but I caught him enough times glued to *Jeopardy!* that we ended up watching it in secret, just us. That's one of my fondest memories of my dad, even now.

I went to my room and turned out the light and got into bed fully dressed. I don't know why I did that. My parents never checked on me, anyway.

At 11:20 pm, I got up. I could still hear the sounds of the TV from the living room. I put my flashlight in my pocket and climbed out the window, scuttled across the garage roof, and dropped down to where my bicycle lay. I cycled over to Pete Green's house, and together we cycled over to the school. Pete had been my friend since we were little kids. We liked the same things. We liked skateboards and comic books and *Star Wars* movies and arcade games. Haven't had a friend like him since, and I doubt I'll find one now.

When we got to the school, Benny and Tyler were already there, waiting for us, and so was Chrissy. I hadn't expected Chrissy to be there, and neither had Pete. She was something else we both liked.

Pete braked and brought the rear wheel of his bike around in an impressive skid. If I tried that, I'd have ended up on my face, so I slowed and stopped normally. I looked at the guys, pretending not to notice Chrissy or else I'd start blushing.

"Ready for this?" Benny asked, his grin in place.

I gave him a shrug, doing my best to act cool.

"He's peeing his pants," Pete said, laughing, and I laughed along with them just to show what a joke it was. As much as we were friends, I'd found it best to laugh along with Pete. He had a sharp tongue that'd turn on you if you weren't careful.

We rode up along Mulgarvey Street, got to the edge of town where the Streets started becoming Roads, and ended up on King Road. We turned off that before the junkyard, cycled on for another few minutes, and we came to the house at the very top of King Hill.

It stood on its own like a bad idea. It was dark and ramshackle, with some boarded-up windows and a boarded-up door. No graffiti, though. I didn't know of any kid brave enough to tag the yellowing sides of this house.

We left our bikes on their kickstands, and I went to the gate. Going to the gate was the easy part. Looking brave doing it wasn't much of an effort, either. It was the passing through the gate that was the problem. The house had a feeling about it. The closer you got, the more you felt it. It was a sick feeling, made you queasy and light-headed while your arms rippled with gooseflesh. It was a bad house. Everyone knew it.

But I guess I had a secret weapon. I had Chrissy Brennan watching me, and I knew there was no way, there was just no way, that I was going to chicken out in front of her. My hand went to the gate, pushed it open.

It creaked, just like in a horror movie.

I didn't look back. They'd see how white I was. How scared. I took my first step on to the garden path – though there'd never been much of a garden and there wasn't much left of a path. A few paving stones, islands in a sea of long grass. I stepped from island to island, focusing on that, letting my mind slip away from the house that suddenly seemed to loom over me. Island to island. Step to step. I was dimly aware of how much time I was taking, and when I looked up I was dismayed to find out I was only halfway there.

Something in me faltered.

"You OK, buddy?" Pete called.

I nodded, and looked back. Chrissy stood surrounded by the others, clasping her hands at her throat.

"He's too scared!" Benny cried.

"No, he isn't," said Pete, and to my horror he kicked the gate open and strode up the path after me, waving his hands in the air. "Ooooh, Bubba Moon! We're so scared of you! We're so scared of you, Bubba Moon!"

And then he was striding past me, and I stood there like the paving stones had latched on to my feet, and there was nothing I could do as he bounded up those steps and slammed his fist against the door.

"Yoo-hoo!" he called. "Anybody home?"

The cold feeling in my chest was gone, and in its place was a dreadful hollowness. He'd robbed me of my moment. I didn't have the words back then and I didn't have the frame of reference, but walking up that path and knocking on that door was a rite of passage for kids like me, and my friend Pete had denied me that one small foothold into adulthood and, I suppose, manliness. And he hadn't done it for me. He hadn't done it as a show of solidarity. He'd done it simply to show off to Chrissy, who hadn't come along the first time he'd knocked on that door, three months earlier.

"Come on, buddy," he said, grabbing my sleeve and pulling me forward. "Show Mr Moon we're not scared of him!"

I didn't want to, there was no point in it, but I knocked, anyway. It was a feeble effort. I couldn't believe Pete had done that to me. He wrapped an arm round my shoulders and turned me to face the others.

"See?" he said. "He did it! Happy now?"

"Yeah, big deal," said Benny. "Bet you wouldn't break in, though."

I was a good kid. I never shoplifted, I never spoke back to teachers, I never even carved my name into my desk at school. I obeyed the rules and I never got the feeling I was missing out on too much by doing so. Obeying the rules meant a smoother life, all things considered. But when I saw the look on Pete's face, when I saw how truly scared that idea made him, I saw a chance to prove myself.

"Sure I would," I said, and I started round the house, testing the windows, seeing if any would open. When I got round the corner, I lost the confident smile and started praying that I wouldn't be able to find a way in. It was dark round here, so I took out my flashlight, which glared back at me from the grimy window panes as I looked in.

Pete and the others came after me and I ignored them, adopting an air of casual indifference. They weren't speaking. Not even Pete. Chrissy was wide-eyed. Three windows in a row were boarded up, so I could skip them, but I made a big show of trying to force open the ones on either side. Sadly, my burglary skills were not up to the task, and I stood back and exhaled in exasperation.

"Hey, look," said Tyler. "You can get in here."

He stood by the wall, lightly nudging open the narrow window at his foot. The basement window.

Everyone knew the story of Bubba Moon. When he died, they found all kinds of black magic stuff in his house. There were books and scrolls and all sorts of daggers and things, and there were jars of preserved human remains. That's what my brother said, anyway. He said Bubba Moon used these human remains in his satanic rituals. I didn't know how much of that was true, but what I did know for sure, what everyone knew for sure, was that when Bubba Moon's dead body was found, it was found in the basement.

"Don't," said Chrissy.

"He said he'd do it," said Benny. "Let him do it."

"Will I be able to fit?" I asked, struggling to keep the tremor from my voice as I wandered over. It was pretty obvious I'd fit, but all I needed was for one of them to say something like I was too fat, or I'd get stuck, and that'd give me reason enough to back out.

"You'll fit no problem," said Pete. It had to be Pete.

I crouched, lifted the window, and shone my light in. There was a load of junk piled up, just like in any other basement.

"If there are rats in there, I'm not going," I said. "I hate rats. No way am I going in if there are rats."

The others crouched down beside me. More flashlights flicked on.

"Can't see any rats," said Benny.

"They'd hardly come out to see what the fuss was about," Tyler said. "They're probably scampering off into the corners or something. You'll be fine."

"This is stupid," Chrissy said. "You might cut yourself on a rusty nail and need a tetanus shot. And we don't know if there's anybody in there. There might be homeless people living here."

"Or the ghost of Bubba Moon," Pete said in a scary voice.

"Shut up," Chrissy said sharply, and Pete laughed, but I could tell the laugh was forced. He wanted her to like him as much as I wanted her to like me.

"Hold it open," I said, and I lay down on my belly. Tyler did the honours, and I slithered forward, my flashlight in my lead hand. There were a load of cobwebs that I had to brush aside, and I forced myself not to cry out when I saw the huge spider scurrying away from the destruction of its home and dinner plate. I got my head through, shone the light on the floor below, making sure it was clear. All I saw were small piles of dead, dried leaves. No one waiting to grab me.

I brought my legs up and turned, lifting my hips slightly to avoid the latch, and let my feet go first. I was looking back at my friends as I lowered myself down. There could be anyone sneaking towards me now, any number of gnarled hands reaching for my ankles.

When my legs were down as far as they could go and I was halfway in, I glanced up and for the first time looked Chrissy right in the eyes. She had such beautiful blue eyes. Her dark hair fell in slight waves to the middle of her back.

She was as tall as me and so pretty. She was the prettiest girl in school, but she refused to act like it, and here she was, out with a bunch of guys at a haunted house at a little past midnight on the weekend, and she was looking at me like she was scared she was going to lose me. I'd never felt braver.

I let myself go, and dropped into the basement.

I turned quickly, adding my beam to the shaking lights held by my friends. I wished they wouldn't shake like that – it threw moving shadows across the far wall. I took three small steps, making sure there was nothing waiting for me in my immediate vicinity, and then broadened the sweep of my flashlight. My fleeting moment of bravery was gone, replaced by a flesh-rippling fear that was creeping up behind me no matter which direction I faced.

"See anything?" Tyler asked.

"Junk," I managed to say. My voice sounded weird. Strangled.

"Any black magic stuff?"

I shook my head. My shadow, which was the biggest and starkest of them all, replicated the movement right in front of me. It occurred to me that someone could literally be hiding in my shadow and I'd never see him. "Just old lamps and furniture," I said. "A table. Sofa."

It was a big basement. My light couldn't even reach the side walls.

"If you see a Ouija board, grab it," said Benny.

"Don't you dare," said Chrissy. "My aunt did the Ouija board once and she doesn't believe in any of that stuff, but she said that Ouija boards are actually dangerous."

"Can't see any," I said, taking a single step to my left. Twenty more seconds and then I was done. Twenty more seconds.

"Can you see the circle?" Pete asked.

I knew what circle he meant. We all did. Bubba Moon had been found lying on a blanket in a circle he'd painted on the floor.

GET THEE BEHIND ME, BUBBA MOON

"Can't see it," I said.

"Go in further."

I took another step, sighed, and shifted my weight, did my best to look energised. "Nope," I said. "Just junk. It was years ago, anyway. It's probably faded away to—"

One of the lights jiggled fiercely, and before I even looked back I knew what was happening. Pete was crawling through the window. He was taking my moment away from me again, and I was too weak to stop him.

He dropped down. "Right," he said, walking past me like he didn't have a care in the world, "where is it?"

The others came after him. I don't know how. Didn't they feel the same cold, sickly dread that I did? Didn't they feel that something in this house, something down here in this basement with us, was just fundamentally wrong, and out of step with how the world was supposed to be?

I could feel the unnatural malevolence that hung heavy in the air, but I'd forced myself to come down here because I needed to do it. I needed to do it to prove to myself, and to Chrissy, that I could. That I wasn't about to let my fear beat me. Pete was probably the same, but Benny and Tyler and Chrissy herself? Why they came down I will never know. They regretted it, though. Later, they regretted it.

We spread out. The basement wasn't that big, not really, but there were moments when it looked big. There were moments, glimpses out of the corner of my eye, when the walls disappeared and the basement went on forever.

"Found it," said Chrissy.

Nobody rushed to her side. We all walked like condemned men, each step like wading through treacle. We joined our light to hers. On the floor before us was a circle that had maybe once been red. Time and dust and air and whatever had turned it dark, almost black. It was a wide circle, big enough for a tall man to lie down and die in. There were symbols on the outside. Black magic stuff. Satanic stuff. Not that any of us knew what satanic stuff looked like.

Not back then.

"I didn't think that part was true," said Benny. He sounded quiet. He sounded young.

We stood there and looked at this circle. Later, I asked the others if they felt what I felt, that electric tingle of panic beginning to crackle at the back of the neck. They all had. None of us let on, though. It was just an empty circle, after all. There was nothing in there that could hurt us.

"Big bad Bubba Moon," Pete said in a soft voice.

"Don't tease him," said Chrissy.

The softness left Pete's voice, and he laughed. "Tease him? He's dead, Chrissy! He's not around any more!"

"I didn't mean it like that," Chrissy said, defensive, her face flushing in the light.

"Don't tease him!" Pete cried, laughing again. "Don't make fun of the poor dead guy! We'll hurt his little dead feelings!"

"Pete," I said, "stop."

"Don't tease him, she says!" Pete continued, howling with laughter.

I knew what he was doing. I'd gone into the basement first, I'd gotten her attention, so this was his clumsy way of pulling her pigtails, of getting her to notice him again. That probably made him do what he did next. He was just showing off. He didn't deserve what happened. He was just showing off.

"Don't tease the big bad Bubba Moon!" he called, and jumped into the circle.

"Pete!" Tyler cried.

Benny tried to snatch him back, almost toppled, almost stepped over the painted line himself, but Chrissy grabbed him, pulled him to her side. She said later she didn't know why she did that – she'd had no way of knowing how important that had been – but her hands had moved and they'd probably saved Benny's life. He's still alive today because of her.

Pete spun and danced in the circle and he laughed and howled Bubba Moon's name like a wolf. We stared, horrified. It took me a few seconds to realise how cold it had gotten. At first I thought it was just me, but in the light I could see little puffs of vapour leaving Chrissy's mouth.

"We should go," Tyler said.

"Run away!" Pete shouted. "Run away all you like! You'll never get away from big bad Bubba Moon!"

He stopped singing and dancing and suddenly dropped to the ground, crossed his hands over his chest and said, "Hey, guys, who am I?" He laid his head back and closed his eyes and pretended to be dead.

And then all our flashlights went out.

Chrissy cursed and Tyler cried out and Benny stumbled back and someone stumbled into me and Chrissy was beside me and I grabbed her and she grabbed me and we hit a pile of junk behind us and it all came crashing down, and then we were running for the window. Tyler was first, trying to haul himself out of there. I shoved a chair into him and he got a foot up on that and boosted himself up. I wanted Chrissy to go next, but Benny was shrieking too loud to reason with, so when he was halfway out I pushed Chrissy forward and she didn't object. Tyler took hold of her left arm and helped her out, and her long legs vanished like spaghetti being sucked into a hungry mouth.

I got one foot on the chair, reached up, looked over my shoulder into the darkness and called Pete's name, and there was sudden silence.

The world beyond the window was dull. I could hear the others scrambling, their faint voices. There was light now, their flashlights active once again, flooding my little patch of basement. I existed in a cocoon of yellow and white that kept the darkness back.

"Pete!" I said again.

Pete was silent.

I couldn't go without him. I'd never be able to face him if I ran out on him. The panic was fading. I was starting to think rationally again.

In the shaking light of my cocoon, I saw the tips of Pete's shoes. Chrissy saw them, too, and shifted her flashlight. I could see Pete's legs now. He stood on the very edge of the darkness, his hands by his sides, his upper body in shadow. Not moving. Not speaking.

Every last bit of moisture left my mouth. I tried to say his name, but my heart was thudding so loudly that I couldn't even hear how it sounded. Pete's arms rose and he stood like that for a moment.

And then he ran at me, teeth bared, face frozen in a mask of hatred.

I screamed and Chrissy screamed and Benny and Tyler probably screamed as well, and Pete had almost reached me when he fell sideways, laughing so hard I thought he was crying.

"Your face!" he gasped. "Oh my God, your face!"

And he collapsed again with laughter.

"You're such a tool," I said, turning my back on him and climbing out. Chrissy helped me to my feet, but I shook off her hands and walked away, my whole body trembling. Tyler helped Pete out of the basement, which wasn't an easy task due to how much Pete was laughing.

"Your face!" was all he could say. I left him there, left all of them, and I got on my bike and cycled home.

2

I didn't see any of them the next day, but the day after that school started again and we were back together, all of us except Chrissy, who I passed a few times in the hall, but didn't say anything to. What happened at Bubba Moon's house was quickly forgotten about amid the hustle of a new school year. Pete didn't come in the next day, though, or the day after that, and on the third day in a row when he didn't come in Chrissy Brennan tracked me down at my locker.

"Have you heard from Pete?" she asked, without even saying hello first. Her hair, a rich brown that always shone so healthily, was tied back off her face. I may have only been a kid, but I knew enough to know that she probably wasn't as beautiful as I thought she was. My brother had once talked about a girl he'd liked, the prettiest girl he'd ever known, and then I met her and she was OK, but nothing special. She had a nice smile, but her eyes were too close together. My brother couldn't see it, though. He was blinded by his own infatuation, and I reckoned I was, too.

What I saw when I looked at Chrissy Brennan was pretty blue eyes and an amazing smile and a face I could gaze at for hours. She was lean and athletic and she wore ripped jeans and T-shirts, and even though her friends thought we were dorks she still hung out with us whenever she felt like it. I knew she liked *Moonlighting* and *Knight Rider* and I thought she was beautiful, but I was fully aware that I probably couldn't trust my own judgement.

It was only years later when I was looking back through old photographs that I realised that yeah, Chrissy Brennan really was as beautiful as I'd always thought, and that realisation made me smile a little.

"He hasn't been in for a few days," I said, but of course she already knew that. That's why she was asking.

"I was going to call by his place after school," she said, "to see if he's OK. Do you want to come?"

She probably didn't want to go there alone, that was all, and yet there was a small flicker of hope that lit inside me that maybe, perhaps, she wanted to spend some time with me without the other guys getting in the way.

"Sure," I said. "Straight after?"

"Yeah. Were you doing anything?"

I shook my head and kept my mouth shut so I wouldn't ask any more questions. Pressing for insignificant details was something I did when I was excited, and it was a dead giveaway. We arranged to meet at the school gates and then Chrissy walked off, her books under her arm, and I went to double history and served my time until the bell rang. I grabbed my bag, hurried to the gates, waited there for Chrissy. She walked up and we went off together in full view of everyone on the bus. It was a good moment for me.

"What do you know about Bubba Moon?" she asked, breaking the silence that followed immediately after.

I suddenly suspected that this time together was going to be all business. "When he was alive? He was a Satanist. He had a black magic cult that met at his house. My brother says you used to be able to hear chanting if you passed late at night and the wind was coming from the right direction, and sometimes screams. He says."

"Did you know the police were investigating him?"

I didn't know that. "What for?"

Chrissy looked at me. "Murder. Kids were going missing and they thought Bubba Moon and his cult were doing it."

"I didn't hear anything about any kids going missing."

"Not here, not in this town. Not even in this state. But in areas where his cult members lived, a kid would go missing before each one of his meetings. It started years ago, way back in the sixties. Why do you think they dug up his yard after he died?"

"I didn't know they had."

"Well, they did," said Chrissy. "Dug it all up, looking for the bodies. They never found any."

"Jeez," I said. "Where did you hear all this?"

"My housekeeper. She says everyone knows, but they don't like to talk about it."

"That's creepy," I said. "Someone like that, living in our town... Any one of us could have disappeared."

"My housekeeper says Bubba Moon was an evil man. Like real, actual evil. Not just bad. You know?"

I nodded.

"Did you feel it?" she asked. "You did, right? In the basement? You felt how evil he was, didn't you?"

That feeling, that dreadful feeling of malevolence that had made the hairs on my neck stand up. "I guess."

Chrissy's eyes flashed. "You *guess*? That's it? You *guess* you felt something?"

"No," I said quickly, "I mean I did. I felt it."

Satisfied by my answer, Chrissy nodded. "I think he was so evil he infected his house, that's what I think. That's why the place felt like that. The basement especially. It's probably strongest in the basement because that's where he died. And that circle, the circle Pete lay down in..."

She was scared. She was actually scared as we walked along on that beautiful warm afternoon.

"You think that's why he hasn't been in?" I asked, not sure I wanted an answer.

Chrissy blushed, and didn't look at me. "I don't know. Maybe. If Bubba Moon's evil can infect a house, why not a person?"

"Because he was living in that house for years," I said, as if it was a scientific principle. "It's like a bad smell that's been around for ages. It doesn't just go when you take the rotten thing out the room. It takes a while. You have to open windows and stuff. If it's been there for long enough, the smell lingers. Pete was only in that circle for a few seconds. He was lying down for less than that."

"Did you see how sick he looked on the first day back, though? He was all pale, and he had bags under his eyes."

I hadn't noticed that. But I did notice that Chrissy had led the way to Pete's neighbourhood without once having to ask me for directions.

Pete's house stood on a quiet street, and like all the other houses it had a sectioned-off front lawn and a back yard closed off by a wooden fence. We passed a man waiting for a bus and crossed to the other side of the road where a woman stood leaning against a lamp post, reading a paper. There were a few other people standing around, everyone doing their best to mind their own business. Chrissy glanced at me, frowning slightly.

We walked up the path and I knocked on Pete's front door.

"They're looking at us," Chrissy whispered.

I kept my eyes forward. Seeing a whole bunch of random people on the street all with their heads turned, staring at me and Chrissy, would have been more than I could have handled. It would have been like something out of *Invasion of the Bodysnatchers*, a film I'd caught on TV the previous year that had given me nightmares. I shivered. My mouth was dry. No one was coming to the door.

I tugged Chrissy's sleeve and she followed me round the side of the house. We paused at the living-room window. Pete's mom and dad sat sleeping on the couch. The TV was on and so were all the lights, even though there were still hours to go before the sun dipped. We moved on without saying anything, all the way round the house to the back, to Pete's window. We peered in.

Pete sat in the middle of the floor, legs splayed in front of him and shoulders hunched. His head was down. Eyes closed. There was something above him. Something that flickered, like heat rising off asphalt. It made my head hurt to look at it. Every few seconds, it became almost solid, and that solid form was a man, leaning down with his hands grasping Pete's head.

Chrissy made a sound, halfway between a gasp and a whimper, and the next time the form flickered into view the man was looking straight at us.

We both cried out, stumbled back from the window, and bolted for the street. We had just reached the path when Pete's front door opened and his mom stepped out.

"Well, hello there," she said brightly.

We faltered in our escape, came to an awkward, stilted stop.

"Pete's in his room," Pete's mom said, standing aside. "Come on in. I'll tell him you're here."

We should have run. I knew we should have run. Every instinct in my body was telling me to run, to get out of there. But instead we bowed our heads, the both of us, and walked dutifully into the house. The door shut behind us.

"Pete," Pete's mom called, "your friends are here!" She smiled at us. "You're so good to come by," she said. "He hasn't been feeling well lately."

Then she turned, went to the couch, and sat down beside her husband. Instantly, her chin dropped to her chest, and she was back asleep.

"Hey, guys," Pete said as he passed us on his way to the kitchen.

Chrissy and I looked at each other, then we followed him in. He stood with his back to us, looking at the fridge.

"Come to see how I'm doing, eh?" he asked.

"You haven't been in school," said Chrissy. Her voice sounded weirdly thick.

"No, I haven't," said Pete. After another moment, he opened the fridge door. "I've been feeling under the weather. I'm getting better now, though. Would either of you like a juice box?"

"No, thank you," said Chrissy.

"No, thanks," I said.

"I'm going to have one," said Pete, and he took out a juice box, closed the fridge, and turned. "Have you been getting much homework?"

Chrissy didn't answer. She probably figured it was my turn.

"Not really," I said. "What's been wrong with you?"

"I've been under the weather."

"The flu?"

"Just under the weather."

"Pete," said Chrissy, "does it have anything to do with what happened at Bubba Moon's house?"

Pete looked at her, looked at us both, and then down at his juice box. A moment passed. His right hand trembled. I was reminded of my grandpa, who'd had Parkinson's, which made his hands shake constantly. It got so bad he couldn't even take his own pills without spilling them all over the floor.

Then Pete's tremble passed, and he opened the juice box with ease and took a long, slow drink. When he was done, he wiped his mouth with his sleeve, burped, and grinned like a little kid. "Sorry, Chrissy, what did you say?"

"Nothing," I said before Chrissy could repeat her question. "We just called by, to make sure you're OK. So you're OK, you're doing fine, and that's good. We have to go now."

Pete's face fell, almost comically. "Already? But you just got here!"

"We have to go," I said again.

"Yeah," said Chrissy. "My mom's waiting in the car outside."

Pete frowned. "But you walked here."

Chrissy was moving back, but I froze. "How did you know?" I asked, and he looked at me. When he locked eyes with me, I could see that haze again, just over his head, and the flickering image of the man looming over his shoulder.

My thoughts slowed and a weight pressed down on my mind like a thick, heavy blanket, smothering the sharp edges, deadening the sharp voices, darkening everything and bringing it all to a slow and lethargic crawl. My eyelids lowered. My strength drained. My energy sank from my body, to my feet, and out across the floor. A yearning for rest filled me, like too much food at Thanksgiving, and I yawned, such a big yawn, and my head nodded forward with such a slow and gentle—

Chrissy yanked on my arm, pulling me out from under that blanket, and strength and fright surged through me, and before I knew it I was following her out of the house, up the path. The people on the street swung their heads towards us.

I pushed Chrissy and we ran.

There was a shout and I glanced back and they were chasing, all those people, running after us. They were bigger and stronger and faster, they were full-grown adults, and in a flat-out race they were going to catch us. I grabbed Chrissy's hand, pulled her off the street again, trampling the flowers in some nice old lady's front lawn. We ran into her back yard, jumped and scrambled over the fence, landed in a garden, and sprinted for the street beyond the house. There was a loud crack and we both looked back to see the wooden fence explode, a man running through the gap.

Still gripping Chrissy's hand, I took a short cut through the narrow alley that led to the rear of the parking lot at the Green Fields Mall. We hopped over the low wall, dropped the two metres to the ground on the other side, and ran on across the sparse lot. This time of day, most people would be parking out front. We needed to get to a populated area. They wouldn't do anything in a populated area. I hoped.

Chrissy looked back, gave a cry. I didn't need to look. I knew they were behind us. I knew they were gaining. I also knew we only needed a few more moments and then we'd be safe.

We ran up to the rear doors of the mall, which slid open much too slowly for my liking. I squeezed through the gap, dragging Chrissy after me, ran up the steps, and we burst through an invisible barrier into a bubble of safety. Suddenly we were surrounded by people – mothers and kids and teenagers and fathers and businessmen and working women and shops and stalls and muzak and people handing out pamphlets and people collecting for charities – and we slowed to a fast walk and got into the middle of them all.

Only then did I turn, only then did I look back at the ones chasing us. They stood at the edge of this imagined bubble of mine, their eyes on me and Chrissy, cheated out of their prey. Slowly, they drifted back, until we lost them in the crowd.

I was still trying to get my breathing under control, but Chrissy was fitter than me, and already looking around for help. She spotted a mall cop and squeezed my arm. We hurried over. He stood on the periphery of the Food Court, thumbs hooked into his belt. He looked bored and unimpressive, but he was a mall cop with a walkie-talkie, and a mall cop with a walkie-talkie could get real cops over here in two minutes flat.

Right before we left the forest of people, literally two steps before we emerged into the empty space in front of the mall cop, Chrissy pulled me to a sudden stop.

The mall cop said something into his walkie-talkie. He chuckled at the response. A thought, completely unconnected to the danger we'd found ourselves in, floated to the surface of my mind like a stray balloon that had lost its tether. I wondered if mall cops, or anyone who used a walkie-talkie for that matter, had to undergo specialised training in order to understand what anyone else was saying on those walkie-talkies. Every time I passed one and it gurgled to life, all I heard was a confusing mess of abrupt sounds and crackle.

The thought went away when I caught sight of the man standing behind the mall cop. He looked straight at us and smiled. To his left stood a woman, also with her eyes fixed on us. Another man walked by, nodded good-naturedly to the mall cop, who nodded back, and then he smiled at us and lifted his shirt slightly. We saw the knife in his waistband, and backed off.

At the very centre of the Green Fields Mall there was an area of recessed seating. Chrissy and I sat there for an hour, huddled together but not speaking. A neighbour of Chrissy's passed, saw us sitting there and made a teasing comment about me being Chrissy's new boyfriend. Despite everything, I blushed. Chrissy's neighbour asked her if she'd like a lift home. Chrissy looked at me, desperate to say yes, but reluctant to leave me. I told her to go on, I'd be fine.

And I was fine. I walked home quickly, leaving the mall amid a mass exodus of shoppers. I didn't see any of the people who'd been chasing us. Nobody followed me – at least that I was aware of. I got home and everything was normal, and my dad got back from work and we had dinner and I watched *Airwolf* and then *Knight Rider*, and I didn't say a single word about what had happened.

The threat was clear. *You talk to the mall cop, and he dies.* And it hadn't just been a threat to mall cops. Somehow I knew it was a threat to anyone I might go to for help.

I didn't sleep that night. Chrissy told me later that she didn't, either.

* * *

I spent the weekend in my house, refusing to leave my bedroom for the most part. I tried doing my homework, I tried reading. I dreaded Monday morning. What if Pete was back in school? What if I walked into class and he was there, sitting in his usual seat, with the flickering image of that man looming over him?

Monday came, though, and Pete's seat remained empty. It was empty for the rest of that week, and the week after. Then came the news that Pete's folks had pulled him out of school. Everyone came to me and asked what had happened, what was wrong with my friend, but I just shrugged and told them I hadn't been speaking to him. Eventually, they stopped asking.

Four months after that, I woke up one night to my name being called outside my window. I got out of bed, parted the curtains. There was a sliver of moon in the cloudy sky that barely lit anything in my backyard, but I could see Pete's face, pale and smiling up at me.

He called my name softly, and I heard him giggle. Then the clouds covered the moon, and when the moon came back Pete was gone.

I went back to bed and I didn't sleep that night, either.

3

I left home when I was eighteen, glad to see the back of the place, glad to leave all those bad memories behind. By then, of course, my selective memory had long since sorted through it all and thrown out the more outlandish elements of what had happened. The version of the truth it left me with was a lot more palatable to a reasonable mind such as mine.

In this new version, elegant in its simplicity and carefully censored to protect the innocent, me and my friends had broken into this creepy old house when we were kids and we'd scared each other witless. A few days later, I went for a walk with a pretty girl to see my sick buddy, then ended up getting chased over fences by irate neighbours after we trampled some flowers. This revised version of events didn't feature the flickering figure or the subtle threats and it made absolutely no mention of Bubba Moon, and that was OK by me.

I went to college in NYU and studied hard. I guess I knew that dropping out or failing would mean an inevitable return to my hometown, and I had no intention of going back there any time soon.

In my second year in New York, I met a girl in the library. She was surrounded by coursework and weighty tomes, and I glimpsed the lurid cover of a Gordon Edgley paperback peeking out from behind a textbook. I sat opposite, threatened to expose her for the fraud she was if she didn't agree to have a coffee with me. I'd never been that forward before, but there was something about her, something about the way her attention was completely and utterly focused on the horror story in her hands, that made her irresistible to a bookworm like me.

She gave me a smile that only hinted at her mischievous nature, and five years later we were married. Two years after that we had our first kid. Three years after that, our second. I got a good job in a bank and Felicity stayed at home and took care of the kids, and for a nice long while life was sweet.

Then the subprime crisis came along and the bank I was working for went under, and I lost my job and most of our savings in the same month. We'd invested heavily in rock-solid shares built on shaky foundations, and when the tremors began it all came crashing down. We were surviving, barely keeping our heads above water, holding on to our home with the tips of our fingers.

Felicity and I started arguing. A little at first, a cross word or a snapped comment, and those icy silences that grew into cold nights. We kept the edge from our voices when the kids were around, or at least we thought we did. I guess kids notice a lot more than we want them to.

Then, in February of the next year, my brother called, told me our dad had died. This odd kind of numbness crept over me as I talked to him, as I listened to his voice, leaden with grief, and when the call was done I put down the phone and sat in my study, surrounded by bills and notices and demands for payment, and cried.

We packed our bags and drove home. I did most of the driving. I thought about my dad a lot, of course, but also my childhood, my old friends. I thought about Tyler and Benny and the girl, the pretty one, what was her name? Chrissy, that was it. Chrissy Brennan. Man, I had such a crush on her. It was all coming back to me, like the miles were bricks in a wall that blocked me from my memories, and each mile we ticked off was one less brick.

I remembered Pete Green, too, my earliest childhood friend. I'd lost touch with him. Couldn't really remember why.

The town had grown since I was there last. Bits and pieces were the same, but mostly it looked like a large alien city had been superimposed over it. The old cinema was gone, but around the next corner there was a giant sprawling mall that had a multiscreen cinema of its very own. Chapters Second-hand Bookstore, a store that had once been like a church to me, was now a tanning salon. They did nails, too, announced the sign in the window. My eleven-year-old self would have been horrified. I mentioned this to my kids in the back seat. My son grunted. My daughter ignored me.

We arrived at my old house. Mom started fussing over us immediately. She didn't know about the problems Felicity and I were having, but I think she suspected. My brother was there. He said Mom had been trying to keep busy, like she was determined to work so hard that the sadness never had a chance to settle. We let her. Everyone grieves in their own way.

I was tired after the long drive, but that evening I went with my brother to a local bar, and we sat and talked. He told me about his life and I gave him an edited version of mine. I hadn't seen him in over seven years. He'd put on weight and he'd lost some more hair. He looked like a real grown-up now. I told him this and he laughed ruefully, and went to get us another drink.

When he was gone, a pretty girl at the table beside me gave me a smile. She couldn't have been much more than seventeen, but I smiled back, anyway, out of politeness more than anything. A woman approached my table. She was a few years older than me, pretty but strained, with grey in her hair, and a little too thin to be healthy.

"I was sorry to hear about your father," she said.

I looked at her and fished for a name, but it wouldn't come. Not at first. Someone laughed at the bar and she glanced over, and I caught an angle and the realisation hit me like a wrecking ball.

"Chrissy Brennan," I said, like I had no breath in my lungs.

She smiled, sat opposite me, setting her glass neatly on a coaster. I remembered the smile. It used to be such a beautiful smile. It still had echoes of that beauty, but now it threw up all those lines around her mouth. She looked old. She was my age, but she looked old. "Didn't think you'd recognise me," she said, brushing a strand of hair back over her ear, the way she used to.

"You're looking well," I said.

She smiled again. "How long are you here for?"

"Funeral's tomorrow. We'll stick around for a few days after that, to keep my mom busy. It's good to see you. I was just thinking about you, actually, on the drive over."

"I've been thinking about you, too," she said, in a way that nagged at me slightly.

My brother caught my eye, gestured over his shoulder to a few friends of his, and I nodded as he left me and Chrissy alone.

"So what have you been up to?" I asked. "How've you been?"

"I've been better," she said, and then laughed. "Sorry. Didn't mean to be a buzzkill quite so early on in the conversation. I saw you half an hour ago and I was sitting over there, debating whether or not to come and talk to you. Now I'm here and suddenly the mood goes way down."

She was blushing, and I leaned forward. "Hey, don't worry about it. Things have been better for me, too. My marriage, for one. I lost my job a few months ago. Before we see the summer, we'll probably lose the house as well." I hadn't even told my brother that part. "And that's not even mentioning my dad, OK?

So don't feel bad about bringing down the mood. The mood is pretty low to begin with."

I'd wanted to make her feel better, but it hadn't even raised a sympathetic smile.

"I got married," she said. "I have a son, Scott, who'll be fourteen in May. I'm not with my husband any more. He's not a very nice man. I have two jobs, neither of which pays me enough to give up the other. And I'm scared."

I nodded. "These are scary times."

She looked up at me, frowning. "No. I'm scared of *him*."

I answered her frown with one of my own. "Your husband?"

Now it was her turn to lean forward. "*Pete*," she said in a whisper.

"Pete Green?"

"Who else? What's wrong with you?"

"I'm sorry, Chrissy, I'm not really sure what you're talking about."

She stared at me.

She stared at me for so long I thought something brittle had snapped off in her mind.

"Don't do this," she said. "Don't you dare do this to me. You're the only other one who was there. You're the only other one who knows what happened."

"What happened when? I'm really not—"

"Bubba Moon," she said sharply, and the edge of a migraine stabbed at me behind my eyes.

"Bubba Moon," I repeated. "Yeah, OK. The town bogeyman. We broke into his house when we were kids. But we weren't the only ones there. Tyler McCormick and Benny Alverez were with us, and Pete."

Chrissy nodded. "And then a few days later we went to see if Pete was all right. We went to his house, you and me. Do you remember that?"

I smiled. "I remember us running from some particularly angry neighbours. I do remember that much."

"Angry neighbours? What are you talking about? They weren't angry neighbours. They were his followers."

"Whose followers? Pete's? Pete was an eleven-year-old boy."

"*Bubba Moon's* followers," Chrissy said, with a vehemence that made me sit back warily. "They were outside his house. Remember? You told me later it reminded you of a movie. That one with Donald Sutherland and Jeff Goldblum."

"*Invasion of the Bodysnatchers*," I said automatically, and something loosened in my mind. More bricks fell, enough to let an old feeling seep out. Fear.

I shifted in my seat. "Chrissy, it was a long time ago. Obviously I remember it differently than you do."

"You left," she said, like she was accusing me of treason. "Looks like you blocked it out. You didn't want to think of it any more. But I stayed. I remember everything, exactly the way it happened. You know those people who chased us into the Green Fields Mall? I see them practically every day. They haven't changed. They have not aged one little bit since that time we saw them. And there are more of them now. Over a dozen, I think, all living on the same street as Pete."

"I don't remember their faces, Chrissy, so I wouldn't be able to tell if they'd aged or not. But before we go any further, I want you to take a moment and think about the things you're saying."

She chewed her lip and nodded, then she looked down at the table, and I let out a breath. My hands were clenched, though I didn't know why. I drained the last dregs from my beer and was about to cut our encounter short by standing up, when she raised her eyes. She was calmer.

"I understand that it sounds insane," she said. "And I apologise for that. I also apologise for all this... anger. I suppose... I suppose I've been angry with you for leaving, and angry with you for the way our friendship ended, but neither of those things are your fault."

I didn't remember how our friendship ended, but I wanted this conversation to be over so I didn't ask.

"Here are the facts as I know them," Chrissy said. "Please bear with me. Some of them might jog some memories. A lot won't. Please don't walk out until I'm done."

I hesitated, but there was still enough of the beautiful girl I had once known in her face that I couldn't deny her this one request. "OK. Say what you have to."

"Thank you," she said. "Bubba Moon was a serial killer. Just because he was never called one by the police or the papers doesn't make this simple fact any less true. He was a serial killer, and he had his followers. As far as I know, they called themselves the People. They were a black magic cult. Maybe Satanists or devil worshippers."

"Satanists," I repeated, raising an eyebrow.

"It's not uncommon. Or it wasn't, anyway. People like Bubba Moon and Charles Manson, they attract people who live on the fringes of society – Satanists, fascists, convicted felons."

"OK," I said. "Go on."

"Moon's People would meet every month here in town, at his house. They'd take it in turns to bring an offering."

"What kind of offering?"

Chrissy looked me in the eye and said, in that same calm tone, "Kids. Fourteen-year-old kids. Girls or boys, it didn't matter, they just had to be fourteen years old. I don't know why. From what I've worked out, they were brought down to the basement and ritually murdered while the People chanted around them."

"Uh-huh. And what proof do you have of this?"

"No proof. Just stories."

"Right."

"Can I continue?"

I sighed. "Sure."

"Bubba Moon was also a psychic. He didn't read palms or tell fortunes, but he was clairvoyant. I've spoken to police officers who swear that he knew things about them during interrogations that he couldn't possibly have known."

"And the officers in question admitted this to you, did they?"

"Some of them did, yes. Though of course they'd never admit it in public."

"Oh, of course," I said.

"They'd been bringing him in for questioning for years, all related to various murders. They could get nothing to stick, until one of his People slipped up and got himself arrested. He told the cops everything. He told them more than everything. He told them about stuff so bizarre and insane that he had to be making it up, but within all that craziness he knew enough details about open murder cases that they were forced to take him seriously."

"So did they have enough to arrest Moon?"

Chrissy took a moment to sip her drink. "It didn't make any difference. Their key witness, who had agreed to testify and name Moon as the one who'd done all the killing, died in his cell the same night they went to search Moon's house. He hanged himself with a sheet."

"How inconvenient," I said, but Chrissy ignored me and continued.

"You should know this part," she said. "The cops have their warrant, knock on the door, don't get an answer, and they break the door down. They find Bubba Moon's body in the basement, lying in the middle of a circle, surrounded by occult symbols."

The circle. I remembered it now.

"They put him in a body bag, take him away, and search the house. They find a lot of old bloodstains, but tests are inconclusive. They dig up the back yard, looking for bodies. They don't find any. They find no evidence at all, actually. Bubba Moon is buried in some crappy little grave, his house is boarded up and never sold, and that's the end of the story."

"OK, then."

"Until a bunch of stupid kids break into that old house eighteen years later, and one of them, showing off to the others, jumps into that circle, and lies down where Bubba Moon had been lying down when they found him."

I needed another drink. My mouth was dry. "Pete," I said.

"That's right. Pete. He was perfectly fine for a couple of days, and then he didn't turn up at school. That Thursday afternoon, you and me paid him a visit. We wanted to see if he was OK. We walked there."

"There were people looking at us," I said softly.

Chrissy nodded. "We knocked on his door, then went round the back of the house. We saw Pete sitting on the floor and there was someone standing over him, only we couldn't see him properly because he kept flickering—"

"Like a heat haze," I said.

"Yes. Just like that. We tried to run, but Pete's mom called us in. Do you remember she went right back to the couch?"

"And fell asleep," I said. "Then Pete came out. There was something weird about the way he moved sometimes. He had a drink or something..."

"A juice box," said Chrissy.

"A juice box, yeah. It was like he wanted to open it, but it took a while for the message to reach his hands. Then... then something happened to me."

"He looked at you and all of a sudden you were falling asleep," said Chrissy. "He was doing the same thing to you as he'd done to his parents."

"But you saved me," I said. "We ran. They chased us. Into the mall. The security guard..."

"They were going to kill him," said Chrissy. "I'm certain of it. If we'd even tried to alert him, they'd have killed him there and then. They'd have killed anyone we told. Our parents. Teachers. Cops. Anyone."

"My God. I remember."

"Pete was taken out of school. We didn't really see him much after that. I'd come across him occasionally on the street, but I'd always hide until he was gone. His People were around him at all times. It should have been funny seeing all these grown-ups trailing after a kid, obeying his every command... but it wasn't funny. It wasn't funny one little bit."

Chrissy took another drink. "We stopped talking. You and me. We were too scared to talk, to be honest. We were too scared to remain friends. It was my fault as much as it was yours, but I blamed you for as long as I could. So you went away, all the way to New York City. And I met Toby, and I fell in what I thought was love, and I got a fantastic kid out of it, and then I realised Toby wasn't worth much as a human being, and I kicked him out. I took on another job, raised Scott myself."

"Must have been hard."

She shrugged. "People do it every day. But I did my best to live my life, to put the past behind me."

"Where it belongs," I said.

A thin smile. "If only we were that lucky. A few years ago, I started searching, just out of pure curiosity."

"Searching for what?"

"Disappearances," she said. "Fourteen-year-old kids going missing. I figured, if it was still happening, it'd be easy to spot. All of Moon's People are living in the same town now, after all. Their victims wouldn't be spread out halfway across America like last time."

"And... and did you find anything? Were they doing it again?"

Chrissy held her glass, but didn't raise it to her lips. She just smiled, a smile that was the furthest thing from peaceful I had ever seen. "They'd never stopped," she said. "Every month, a fourteen-year-old goes missing. People go missing all the time, of course they do, everyone knows that, but these kids get lost in the statistics. They're classed as *lost teenagers* instead of *lost fourteen-year-olds*. No one has made the connection. And they're local, but this town isn't as small as it used to be. Neither are the towns around us. Moon's People are choosing targets close to home."

"OK... OK, if that's true—"

"I've got the numbers, I can show you—"

"I don't want to see them," I said, a little more sharply than I'd intended. "Sorry. I mean I don't need to see them. I believe you that there does seem to be a... trend. But let's say you're right... I still don't know what this has to do with Pete Green."

"Yes, you do," said Chrissy.

"No, I don't."

"You saw the flickering man. That wasn't a hallucination. We both saw it."

"Yeah. I admit it. I saw it. It was real. But what *was* it?"

That strand of hair had come loose again. Chrissy tucked it behind her ear with her left hand. There was a band of lighter skin around her ring finger. "You know what it was," she said. "I told you, Moon was a psychic."

"I don't believe in psychics."

"You don't believe in the fakes and the frauds and the shysters who con grieving widows out of their life savings... But that's not what we're talking about here. Bubba Moon was a psychic. He died in that circle doing black magic. Pete lay down in the same circle, and when he got up we started seeing a figure hunched over him."

"You think... you think the figure was Bubba Moon?"

"Yes."

"And... what do you think Moon was doing with Pete?"

"Controlling him. That's what it looked like, right?"

I nodded. "You think he's still controlling him, even now?"

"More than that," said Chrissy. "I think Bubba Moon is possessing him."

"This is crazy."

"I know. And I've been living with it for most of my life, too afraid to talk about it, or tell anyone, or do anything... But now you're back. I'm not alone any more."

Her eyes were filled with such hope that it killed a little part of me. "Chrissy," I said slowly, "what do you think is going to happen now? If this is all true and Moon is that powerful and there are that many of them... what can the two of us do about it?"

She smiled, a sweet, trusting smile. "We can stop them."

"No, we can't," I said. "These are dangerous people. They're killers. What good would we be against a bunch of murderers?"

The smile faltered. "I... we'd come up with a plan."

"What kind of plan? Have you ever had to come up with any kind of plan like this before? Would you even know where to begin? I wouldn't. Here's our plan, Chrissy. We go to the police. They won't believe us, but we tell them everything we know. We have a responsibility to do that, but that's as far as it goes."

She shook her head. "The police can't stop them."

"We don't know that."

"They'll kill the police."

"Back when we were kids, sure," I said. "Back when they were a handful of small-town cops. But this isn't a small town any more. The cops are better trained and better equipped. We'll tell them Moon's People are planning a mass shooting. They'll get a SWAT team in, they'll get helicopters..."

"That won't work."

"We have to try."

"If we try and it doesn't work, it'll make things worse."

"What do you mean worse?"

Chrissy took a drink, drained her glass. "His People know me. When I see them in the street, they look at me. They smile. A few of them have tapped their watches."

"I don't get it."

Tears brimmed. "Scott is turning fourteen next month. They're going to take my son. I know they are."

I didn't have anything to say to that, so she continued. "I was going to move. A few weeks ago, I was all set to quit my jobs, take Scott out of school, and just run. I'd made some calls, managed to get an interview for a job in Utah, of all places. And then I get a postcard. A big bright 'Welcome to Utah' postcard, and on the back someone had written 'Can't wait for you to get here!' They knew. He knew. Moon knew I was planning to run. He was telling me there's nowhere I can go where Scott will be safe."

"Chrissy, I—"

"Please," she said, tears welling. "I can't lose my son. Please, help me."

4

The cemetery was on Bredon's southernmost hill. When I was a kid, we used to cycle up there on a summer's day and have picnics of peanut butter and jelly sandwiches and Dr Peppers. Back then, you could see practically the whole town from up here. Not any more. Now the town's sprawl was too wide and the buildings too high. Whole neighbourhoods were hidden from view and locked away, like old secrets.

Benny Alverez came to the funeral. When it was done, he walked up to me and we shook hands.

"I always liked your dad," Benny said. "He'd make those stupid jokes, then act surprised when we laughed *at* him rather than *with* him."

"That was no act," I said, feigning a lighter kind of sadness. "You're looking well. Middle age must agree with you."

He blanched. "Is that what we are now? Middle-aged? I thought being in your fifties was middle-aged. I read that somewhere. In a science magazine."

I nodded. "Oh, that's right, I read that, too. Middle age is always the decade ahead of the one you're in now."

"That's it," he said, grinning. "Yeah, I'm doing OK. Married a woman ten years younger than me, had our first kid last year."

"You dog."

He shrugged. "It is what it is." He nodded to my kids. "They yours?"

"They are," I said, my eyes on my wife for a moment. She looked tired. Even

Chrissy Brennan hadn't looked so tired. "Wait till your bouncing baby becomes a temperamental teen," I said. "That'll put some grey hairs on your chest."

"Looking forward to it," Benny said, smiling. "So how's life in the big city?"

I looked away, pretending to scan the crowd. "Chaotic. Uncertain. All the words you don't want to hear with a family to support." I looked back at him. "This place has changed a lot."

"Hasn't it?"

"I could barely recognise some of the streets," I said. "The Palladium is gone."

"Replaced with a twenty-screen behemoth on the next block over. Which, to be honest, is so much better than the Palladium ever was. Remember the sticky floors and the tattered seats and the dreadful sound system? Most of the movies we saw there started off as silent films before the projectionist heard the booing."

I laughed. "I'd forgotten that. Rose-tinted glasses, I suppose."

Benny's smile faded. "Yeah. Nostalgia's a killer. In town for long?"

"Don't know," I said. "After this, we'll be taking it day by day. All depends on what Mom needs."

"Tell her I was asking after her. I'd offer her my condolences, but she wouldn't know who the hell I was. Last time she saw me I was, what, twelve?"

"Eleven or twelve, yeah. You and Tyler, pulling wheelies on the street outside, showing off. Ever hear anything about him?"

Benny looked at me, his eyes narrow. "What do you mean?"

"After he ran away. Did he ever come back?"

"Man, Tyler didn't run away. He was snatched."

I frowned. "What?"

"He disappeared one afternoon on his way home from school. I can't believe you don't remember this."

"I remember him running away."

"Why do you keep saying that? They said he ran away for the first few days he was gone, then they found his bike and his bag and evidence of a struggle. It was all anyone talked about in school for months."

"So what happened to him?"

"He was murdered, most likely. His remains are probably still lying in some shallow grave in the woods even now. You seriously don't remember that?"

"It... it's coming back to me..."

"Last day of April, it was. I remember it vividly." Benny put his hands in his pockets and turned slightly, looking out over the town. "Poor kid. He was only fourteen."

"I can't believe I missed it," Chrissy said on the phone later. "I suppose... I suppose when it happened I didn't know what was going on, and when I started to look back a few years ago it was a cursory glance. Just enough to convince myself the murders were still taking place. I'd never even considered that Tyler's disappearance had anything to do with Bubba Moon."

"Well, don't feel too bad," I said, speaking softly as I stood in the back yard behind my old house. "All I'd remembered about it was those first few days when everyone said he'd run away because of his dad. I'd convinced myself that's what happened, even though I was here when the cops decided he'd been murdered. What the hell is wrong with me?"

"You wanted to leave it all behind, and I can't blame you," Chrissy said. "But do you believe me? If Moon went after Tyler, one of Pete's best friends, then he won't think twice about going after the kids of Pete's other friends now."

"But why Tyler?" I asked. "Why just him? We all turned fourteen the same year. If Moon kills one kid every month, why didn't he snatch all four of us?"

"That would have been way too suspicious," Chrissy said. "The cops would be investigating everyone we'd ever spoken to, and that would have led straight to Pete Green's door."

"So Moon just took one of us," I said, my voice dull. "Snatched him away like he was playing a game."

"I think that's exactly what this is," Chrissy said. "With all the People smiling at me, tapping their watches... it's a game. He wants to scare me. He has to be stopped."

"How? If Pete's possessed... what do we do? Call an exorcist? Hold a prayer meeting? I don't even know what the first step is. The best thing we can do, and I know you've already objected to this, is go to the police. At the very least they'll put Scott into protective custody or something."

"Are you sure about that? Are you absolutely, one hundred per cent sure about that? Because if we tell the police, and the police don't believe us, or they can't do anything, then Bubba Moon will make us pay. I know he will, and so do you. He'll make us pay for ruining this game of his, and that means Scott or someone or..."

"What? Chrissy, what?"

"How... how old is your son?"

I looked at the phone like it was an odd thing, like it was a foreign object that did not belong in my hand. On stiff legs, I walked back inside. I hadn't seen my son all evening. He'd been in my old bedroom. That's where he was now. Probably sitting in my old room, watching TV on his laptop or something. Not bothering to come up for air, or say hi, and definitely not feeling the urge to communicate. I knew this behaviour well. It had started last year. It had started when he turned thirteen.

I knocked on the bedroom door and opened it. My daughter passed me. "Where is he?" I asked.

She knew who I meant. She just shrugged, walked on.

On stiff legs, with a dry mouth, I went to the living room, where Felicity was sitting with Mom and my aunt. "Anyone seen Sammy?" I asked.

Shaking of heads all round. I nodded. My keys were in my pocket. I walked out the front door, closed it gently behind me, and bolted to my car. I jumped in, slid the key into the ignition. The engine came to life and I snapped it into gear and the passenger-side doors opened, two of them at the same time. A slender black man in a good suit got in beside me. On the back seat, a girl in black.

"I wouldn't do that if I were you," the man said.

"Where's my son?" I screamed, making a grab for him. My hands were pushed down with unsettling ease and the man reached over and smacked my head painfully against the steering wheel.

"We don't know," he said, "but I'm sure we'll figure it out easily enough. How's your nose? Sorry about that, but we can't afford to let you drive to Pete Green's house and get yourself killed."

"Where is my son?" I repeated, through gritted teeth.

"He could be in one of three places," the man said, "or he could be in a fourth that we don't yet know about. We didn't take him, if that's what you're thinking."

"That's what he's thinking," said the girl in the back seat.

"That's what I thought," said the man. "But we didn't. Take him, that is."

I looked at the man in the seat beside me. He was well-groomed. Clean-shaven. He wore gloves and had a hat sitting on his lap. He didn't strike me as a Satanist. I turned to peer at the girl. I'd seen her before. She smiled at me and I recognised her from the bar the previous night – she'd been sitting at the next table when Chrissy came over.

"You're Moon's People," I said.

"We're not," she told me.

"You've been spying on me."

"Only a little." She gave another smile. "And we've been listening to your phone calls slightly."

They both spoke with an accent. Irish, though his was a little less distinct than hers. Maybe he travelled a lot.

"What do you want?" I asked.

"We're here to help," the man said. "We're your exorcists."

"My name's Valkyrie," said the girl.

"And you can call me Mr Pleasant," said the man.

5

They made me drive to the bottom of King Hill, and left me in the car with the engine still running. I could have driven away right there and then. Instead, I turned the engine off, killed the lights, and got out.

Mr Pleasant stood looking up at Bubba Moon's old house on the top of the hill. He had his hat on now, which made him look like an old-time private eye, the kind I used to watch on TV when I was a kid. A black Humphrey Bogart. The girl sat on the bonnet of my car and swung her legs.

"Why did you bring me here?" I asked.

Pleasant looked round. "We didn't," he said. "You drove us."

"You made me drive you."

"We asked you to and you did. We didn't force you to do anything."

Valkyrie looked at me. "I heard what your friend said last night about Bubba Moon. She got it right. Well, most of it. Moon isn't a Satanist, though."

"That's right," Pleasant murmured. "He's just sick."

He started walking up the hill. Valkyrie hopped off the bonnet and followed. I didn't know what was expected of me, so I followed, too.

"Where's my son?" I asked, for what felt like the hundredth time.

"I should have thought it was obvious," said Pleasant. "The People have him."

"Then we call the police. We have to call the police."

"We don't know where he is," Valkyrie interjected, and it struck me that she was playing the good cop role in this partnership. He was allowed to be as rude as he liked, as long as she was there to smooth things over.

"If you call the police, they'll rush in and whoever's holding Sammy will kill him immediately and dump the body. He's not in any danger right now. They do their killings on the fourteenth of each month. That's tomorrow night. He's safe for now."

"Is he here?" I asked, my eyes flicking ahead of us. The house loomed, a dark thing in the darkness, its faded paint peeling like burst blisters, its windows blanked out by rotten wood, its roof patchy with old tiles.

"This is the most obvious place," Pleasant said, "so I doubt it. But before we go charging in to the rescue, first we eliminate all the places we shouldn't be charging."

I frowned. "Rescue? You're going to rescue Sammy? You're going to help me?"

"Of course," said Pleasant. "You're only just getting that? We announced ourselves as the exorcists. How much clearer can we make it?"

"Don't mind him," said Valkyrie, patting my arm. "He's just cranky. He didn't even want to come here in the first place."

Pleasant looked around sharply. "We are in the middle of a very important investigation. Very important. Things are happening."

"We were in Chicago," Valkyrie said, "doing a thing. About to go home. Then we're asked to come here, to do a little digging if we had the time."

"Which of course we don't," said Pleasant. "But your Sanctuary asked, and our Sanctuary said sure, let's put our investigation on hold, let's ignore the possibility of a disease that turns ordinary people into ticking time bombs and send our two best detectives to Bredon. Even though you have your own."

I frowned. "Sorry?"

"Detectives," he said. "America. America has its own detectives. Some good ones, too. None as good as me, of course."

"And that's the burden you bear with such humility," Valkyrie said, but her voice was softer now as we neared the house.

Pleasant led the way around the full circumference. The place looked even deader than it had when I was a kid. It also looked infinitely creepier. If I had thought that adulthood meant I wasn't going to find my flesh crawling, I was about as wrong as I could possibly be.

"You feel that?" Valkyrie said, pulling back the sleeve of her jacket and examining her arm. "Goosebumps. Skulduggery, I have goosebumps."

Pleasant looked round. "Interesting," he said.

"Your name is Skulduggery Pleasant?" I asked.

"Yes," he said. "Have you heard of me?"

"No. What kind of name is Skulduggery Pleasant? It sounds made up."

"It is made up. All names are made up. Why are we talking about this? The basement, wasn't it? That's where you broke in? Through this window, I take it?"

He pointed to the narrow window close to the ground, and I realised I was standing exactly where I had been all those years ago. I nodded.

Pleasant handed his hat to Valkyrie. "Do not wear it," he said, then crouched, prising the window open with his fingers. When it was open, he lay flat and slid through easily. It was like his body momentarily deflated, his clothes sinking to allow him access. A moment later, the window was lit from inside by a warm, flickering orange light.

Valkyrie put the hat on and looked at me. "Your friend was right. Bubba Moon is a psychic, or what we call a Sensitive. His followers have similar gifts. The same way Skulduggery and I have gifts. Some of his followers are Sensitives, some are... other things. You don't have to worry about any of that."

Her phone buzzed. She held it to her ear. She wore a big clunky black ring. She listened for a moment, then hung up. "They're not there," she said. "He'll be out in a sec. He's just looking around."

"Who *are* you?" I asked.

She hesitated. "We take care of things like this. Like Skulduggery said, we're exorcists. Of a sort. Except instead of praying and waving a crucifix we, y'know... punch. And shoot. There's a bit of stabbing, too. Lots of screaming. Some running."

A gust of wind snatched the hat from her head, took it up to one of the windows, and Skulduggery Pleasant reached through the wooden boards and grabbed it.

Valkyrie glared. "He never lets me wear it."

I wanted to drive right up to Pete's house and hammer on the door, but Pleasant made me park a block away, and we got out and walked.

"You said Sammy is at one of three places," I said. "Bubba Moon's house was the first, this is the second. What's the third?"

"A warehouse on the edge of town," said Pleasant. "We followed one of his People there yesterday. It's owned by a business that doesn't exist. Fudged paperwork, not done with any degree of style or finesse, but enough to pass routine inspection. High level of security, though, for a building that, as far as we can see, doesn't actually contain anything."

"That sounds like it's where they do their... killings," I said, then frowned. "Doesn't it?"

"It does," Pleasant agreed. "But it may not necessarily be where they keep their offerings."

"Shouldn't we get backup? Do you *have* backup? Chrissy said Pete has over a dozen followers."

"I wouldn't worry about that," said Pleasant. "Valkyrie and I have faced worse odds than this."

"You have?"

"We have," said Valkyrie, and then her reassuring smile slipped. "We've never actually *won* against those odds, but..."

"But we've come close," Pleasant said, "and trying is the main thing when it comes to life-and-death situations. Or one of the main things, anyway. It's in the top three. Well, top five. You need to stop thinking of him as Pete Green, by the way. He's Bubba Moon now. By this stage there'll be no trace of your old friend left in there at all, and any assumption otherwise could prove fatal."

"But can you get rid of him? Get rid of Moon?"

"Not if he doesn't want to go," said Pleasant, "and not without a powerful Sensitive of our own."

"So how are you going to exorcise him? Do you say prayers or...?"

Pleasant glanced at Valkyrie, then looked at me. "I'm going to have to kill him. Do you have a problem with that?"

I went cold, but my legs didn't stop moving. "Pete's innocent," I said. "But Bubba Moon is a serial killer and... I just want my son back."

"And even if they worked, prayers wouldn't do any good," said Valkyrie. "It wasn't Moon's spirit that possessed your friend – it was his disembodied consciousness. Apparently, there's a difference. Bubba Moon wasn't dead when the cops found him. He was doing some astral projection. You know what that is?"

"I think so," I said. "Didn't the CIA try that in the seventies? They'd have their agents go into a trance and send their minds out to spy on the Russians or something."

"Very much like that," said Valkyrie. "Although Moon could do a lot more than spy."

We got to the corner. A hundred yards down the block lay Pete Green's house. The lights were on.

"Moon knew the cops had one of his People," she continued, "and he knew this guy was talking. So he sent out his astral self and killed his follower in his jail cell. Made it look like a suicide. It all would have worked out fine if the cops hadn't burst in with that search warrant. When they found him, he wasn't dead, he was comatose. The circle was keeping his body alive."

"So when they moved him out of the circle," I said, "his body died."

Valkyrie nodded. "And his consciousness had nowhere to return to. It was drawn back to that circle where it stayed, trapped, until you kids came along."

"Eighteen years of Bubba Moon seething in that circle," Pleasant said. "He infected the whole house with his foul thoughts. That's why you felt uneasy. That's why the both of you had goosebumps."

"What about you?" I asked. "Did you have goosebumps?"

Pleasant looked at me, and Valkyrie grinned. Neither of them said anything, and then Pleasant moved off. Valkyrie stayed where she was, and I stayed beside her.

"Where's he going?"

"He's just checking out the house," she said.

I looked back, but Pleasant was gone. The suddenness of his disappearance alarmed me. I scanned the area. It was dark, but it wasn't that dark. There was nowhere for him to hide, and he couldn't possibly have jumped one of the fences in the three seconds I was looking away. I was going to ask Valkyrie where he'd gone, but I was struck by the quiet knowledge that she wasn't going to tell me. So I stayed beside her, and we both looked at Pete Green's house.

The street wasn't much different than I remembered. The houses were the same. Some of them, Pete's included, may have had an extension added on, but they were basically unchanged. There were a few tall walls where there had once been only fences. The lawns were neater.

I was suddenly struck by the insanity of the situation. Here I was, sneaking around the town I grew up in with two Irish exorcists who planned to kill my childhood friend because he was possessed by the consciousness of a serial killer.

But just as that wave of insanity hit me, another one followed, and this brought with it a cold determination to do whatever I had to do, to believe whatever I had to believe, in order to get my son back. Because behind all this madness was the reality, the only reality that mattered. I had carried my son in my arms and on my back, administered more Band-Aids than I could remember, held him when he cried, made up bedtime stories every night for ten years, and laughed with him at a thousand dumb things.

With him gone, it was like a piece of me had been sliced away – stolen. Once Sammy was back, once my family was safe, I could afford to allow plain, boring, run-of-the-mill reality to creep back into my world view. Until then, sneaking around with Irish exorcists was the place for me.

"Your son's not in there," Skulduggery Pleasant said from behind us. I turned sharply, stifling a curse, but he was already walking away. Valkyrie's reaction was much calmer, like she knew he was there. How he had snuck up on us, though, I had no idea.

"How do you know?" I asked, hurrying after him.

"Because I looked."

"You can't have looked. You were only gone a few minutes."

"A few minutes are all I need," Pleasant said. He touched his face, kneading the skin, and I saw him frown. "We'll have to hurry to the warehouse. We don't have much time."

The warehouse was empty. It was obviously empty. Somehow I just knew it. The others did, too, but Pleasant had to make sure. Like before, I stayed outside with Valkyrie while he vanished into the shadows. He came back a few minutes later, shaking his head.

"It's set up, ready for a ritual sacrifice, but there's no sign of your son," he said. He was touching his face again. "They could be keeping him anywhere. We're going to have to wait until tomorrow."

"What?" I said. "No. No, we can't leave Sammy with them overnight."

"Of course we can," Pleasant said, "and we'll catch them red-handed tomorrow. It'll all be very dramatic. You'll love it, believe me."

"No," I said. "We have to keep searching."

"It's pointless. Even if you knew this town, which you don't, not any more, it'd be a waste of time. Go home, get some sleep. We'll pick you up at three in the afternoon. I'll tell you the plan then."

"You're... you're sure? You're sure this is the best course of action?"

"This is the only course of action. Be ready at three."

I nodded, sagging against my car. I suddenly realised how tired I was. How utterly exhausted. "Can I give you a lift anywhere? To your hotel?"

"We're fine," Valkyrie said. "And try not to worry, OK? Saving people is what we do."

I gave another nod, then got in the car. I swung round, pointing the nose back the way I'd come. I glanced in the rear-view mirror, saw Pleasant and Valkyrie standing close to each other. His arm was round her waist. My eyes flickered to the road ahead, then back to the rear-view. The road behind me was empty.

6

I got no sleep. My son was in the hands of a madman. Every ten minutes, I grabbed the phone, ready to dial for the cops. But I didn't. I don't know why I was trusting these strangers, but trusting them I was, and so I didn't dial. I just thought about it a lot.

Three o'clock the following day I was sitting in my car outside my old home, waiting for Skulduggery Pleasant and Valkyrie to suddenly open the doors and get in.

At four o'clock, I was standing in the kitchen, a mug of cold coffee in my hand, my eyes on the street outside.

"You seen Sammy?" Felicity asked, passing behind me.

"He's checking out the places I used to go as a kid," I said. The words came out quickly, spilled out like a lie I'd been waiting to tell. "I drew him a map."

She came up, put her hand on my arm. "How're you doing?"

I stiffened, and she took her hand away. Then left.

At ten minutes to five, my phone rang.

"Hi," said Chrissy.

"Oh," I said, "hey."

"You sound disappointed."

"I'm just waiting for someone. They're late."

"Oh. OK. Listen, I'm sorry if I upset you last night."

"You didn't," I said, making sure no one was around before I continued in a softer voice. "They have him. They have Sammy. You were right, Chrissy. About all of it."

"They have Sammy? Oh, God."

"Chrissy, I met some people last night. A man called Pleasant and a girl called Valkyrie. They knew everything. They said they could help."

There was a pause. "Be careful," Chrissy said. "This sounds like something Pete would do."

"No, it's not him. They're genuine. I really think they're genuine. They knew everything. They knew stuff we don't know. They do this kind of thing for a living."

"I don't like it. I don't—"

"Dammit, Chrissy, yesterday we said we needed exorcists, didn't we? Well, now we have them. They took me to the warehouse where they think Moon kills the kids. They can help. Only... only they were supposed to meet me here two hours ago and they haven't shown."

"And you trust them?"

I hesitated. "Yeah. Yes, I do."

"Do you think they're in trouble?"

My heart became something heavy, weighing down on my lungs. "Yes."

I stood there in the kitchen, the phone pressed to my ear, as helpless and useless in the face of true evil as any child.

"Then do you want to go help them?" Chrissy asked.

"Yes," I said.

I picked Chrissy up outside her house, a small Cape Cod on what used to be called Dearson Street, but which now went by the rather more grander-sounding Eastview Drive. If they'd thought renaming the street would elevate the neighbourhood, they must surely have been disappointed. The houses stood forlorn, the spaces between them filled with coarse grasses and the rusted detritus of modern living – flat-wheeled bicycles, broken-down dishwashers, and old cars run on nothing but hope, spit and desperation.

Chrissy was waiting for me outside the neatest of these houses, and she got in quickly, her purse in her lap. Even now, with the lines on her face and the grey in her hair, I felt a little buzz in my stomach when I met those blue eyes of hers. A buzz that I hadn't felt with my wife for a long time.

I felt guilty about that.

We didn't meet much traffic as we drove to the warehouse, but it was already getting dark as I pulled over.

"Is this it?" Chrissy asked.

"No, it's further up," I said, having learned from the experts. "We'll walk the rest of the way."

She nodded. "OK, yeah. I brought something. For us. For protection."

Glancing at me nervously, she pulled a nickel-plated revolver from her purse.

"It was my husband's," she said. "I kept it when he left. It's loaded, I checked. This little lever here is the safety."

I looked at it. "I've never fired a gun in my life."

"Me, either. But I thought we might need it."

She held it out to me. I took it, felt how heavy it was. I kept my finger away from the trigger. "OK," I said. "OK, this is probably... probably a good idea."

She gave me a smile, a thin, brittle smile, and got out. I hesitated only a moment before joining her.

I tried sticking the gun into the waistband of my trousers, but it didn't feel secure, so I just put it in my jacket pocket as we walked. I kept an eye out for cameras. Pleasant had said something about the security being impressive, but I didn't see any, not even when we were peering through the chain-link fence.

There were lights on in the warehouse and a few cars parked outside that hadn't been there the day before. But I couldn't see any guards, and still no sign of cameras.

The gate was heavy and closed and the fence was twice my height. I realised that our first hurdle might also be our last.

"How the hell do we get in?" I murmured.

Chrissy hugged herself. It was cold out here. "Bruce Willis would just drive through the gate," she said. "Or if he wanted to be sneaky he'd drop down from a neighbouring roof." She craned her neck. "But how would he get up there?"

"This is ridiculous," I said. "We're intelligent people. We should be able to get past a fence."

"We could climb it."

We were going to have to. Even though I hadn't indulged in any strenuous physical activity for over six years, I was going to have to climb a fence in front of my childhood crush. I offered up a silent prayer that I wouldn't make too much of a fool of myself, then extended my arm, my fingers curling into the chain-link. Once I had a good grip, I rattled it a little, just to get an idea of what I had to work with, and then I jumped, grabbing a handhold further up. It wouldn't take much for my fingers to start burning, so I wasted no time. I dug my feet in against the fence, tried to get the toes of my shoes through the links. I hung there, scrabbling for purchase mere inches off the sidewalk.

"You have never stopped being sexy," Chrissy said in a quiet voice, and, despite the danger to ourselves and the threat to my son, I couldn't help it, I laughed, and I laughed so hard I had to let go and stagger away from my failed attempt at being impressive.

Chrissy covered her laugh with her hands, eyes glittering with mirth. We both knew what it was, of course. The laughter was a nervous reaction to a scary situation. It didn't make it any less funny.

"Boost me up," she said. "If I can reach the top, I'll try to pull you up after me."

I went back to the fence, interlaced my fingers and bent my knees, keeping my back straight. Chrissy put her right foot in the cradle my hands formed. Her hands rested lightly on my shoulders. She was taking deep breaths.

"One," I said, rocking slightly, "two... three."

On *three*, I straightened and lifted and she sprang. She got a hand round the bar on the top of the fence and hauled herself up quickly till she was resting on her belly. Steadying herself with her hands, she lifted her right leg and straddled the bar, looking down at me.

"I'm not going to be able to pull you up," she said. Her words were fast and clipped. She was up high and she was scared. She leaned forward, her knees tight and her right hand curled into the links. With her free left hand, she reached down to me. "That's as far as I can go."

"I can't reach that high, Chrissy."

"Then find something to step on. If I lean down any more, I'll fall."

I looked around for something to stand on, but the street was empty. "I'll be right back."

"Where're you going?"

"I'll have to get the car."

"Hurry."

I ran back to the car, not liking this one bit. I turned the key gently, like that would make the engine quieter, and drove very slowly to the warehouse with the lights off. I mounted the sidewalk, slowing down even more until the wing mirror scraped against the fence just below Chrissy. I turned off the ignition, got out, and clambered up on to the hood. Using the fence to steady me, I lunged up on to the roof. It clunked dully under my weight. I got into position, bent my knees, took a breath, and sprang. I hit the fence and clung on and Chrissy grabbed me with her free hand, then, after lots of grunting and exertion, I was straddling the fence, facing her. We held on to each other.

"We're going to have to jump down," I said.

She smiled without a whole lot of humour. "You first."

She let go of me and I gripped the bar with both hands, swinging my other leg over the side. I lowered myself down as far as I could go, then dropped. My heels slammed painfully to the ground and the fence rattled and I bit my tongue.

"You OK?" Chrissy whispered. "Are you all right?"

I nodded up to her, one hand over my mouth, blinking away tears of pain as I hobbled around in a small circle. She swung her other leg over, lowered herself down just like I had done.

"Catch me," she whispered and let go. She fell into my arms. She was heavier than I'd expected, but I didn't drop her. I set her back on her feet and she looked at me, frowning. "You sure you're OK?"

"Bit my tongue," I said, a little shamefacedly.

"Maybe I'll kiss it better for you later," she said, a grin on her face. "Providing we live through the—"

She grabbed me, pulled me down behind one of the parked cars. We stayed there for a few seconds, frozen. I peeked up. There was a sentry. He walked like he had walked this route a hundred times tonight already. He was watchful, but not wary – otherwise he'd have noticed my car on the other side of the fence. It was pure luck he missed us.

He glanced at his watch, then put his hands back in his coat. When he passed through the side door of the warehouse, a blue light in an obscure pattern glowed briefly on the doorframe. I was reminded of the security pads I'd seen in movies – where a green light would mean authorised, and red would mean intruder. I got the feeling that the light would glow red if we tried going in.

When he was gone, when we were sure we weren't going to be discovered, we jogged to the door, slowing as we approached.

I had expected an electronic pad fitted to the wall. Instead, the pattern, some kind of obscure symbol, was simply painted on. I ran my finger against the surface. No sign of any electronics at all. Maybe it wasn't an alarm. Maybe it had been a trick of the light. Even so, I was wary of passing it before testing its—

Chrissy took a giant step through the doorway and I sucked in a breath... but the symbol stayed dark. No alarms sounded. She shrugged at me while I got my heart back under control. I took the gun from my pocket and joined her.

We moved quietly by a small office, got to the corner that led to the main warehouse. There were two tables set up. One, in the centre of the cavernous space, was broad and heavy and covered in a white sheet. The other, over by the wall, held a coffee pot and two trays of sandwiches. Five of Bubba Moon's People stood here, chatting in soft voices.

Skulduggery Pleasant and Valkyrie sat with their backs to a steel pillar. Chains kept them in place. Pleasant was facing away from the door, but Valkyrie was looking right at us. Her left eye was swollen almost shut and she had dried blood on her chin. When she saw me, she turned slightly, whispered something. I could see Pleasant's shoulder move as he nodded. I showed her the gun and she immediately shook her head. I looked over at the People. None of them appeared to be armed.

The door rattled suddenly and opened. A blue van drove in, killing its lights once inside. The sentry pulled the door closed and the van trundled to the left side of the warehouse, leaving the centre clear but for the cloth-covered table. It stopped and the engine was cut off.

Bubba Moon got out. He looked like Pete Green all grown up, but he wasn't. There was something extra about him, something extra in the way he moved – like he still, even after all these years, hadn't fully figured out how to work his new body. Like he didn't quite fit into it. He was tall and lean and still had all his hair. He wore ripped jeans and cowboy boots, and as he sauntered forward he took off his shirt, let it drop to the ground.

Underneath he was scarred.

Someone, years ago, had gone to work on him with a blade. Bizarre symbols, like the one on the warehouse door, like the ones we'd found in the basement when we were kids, had been meticulously cut into his flesh like savage tattoos. The way he was showing off to his People made me realise he'd probably commissioned the work himself – and something about his grin made me think he'd been fully conscious the entire time.

"Brothers and sisters," he announced, his voice echoing in the great expanse, "I thank you for coming on what is truly a special day."

Bubba Moon spoke with a Southern accent, an accent that Pete Green had never had.

"We are blessed, we are truly blessed, to have two witnesses to this month's offering. Two valued guests, over from the Emerald Isle, here for one night only. Ladies and gentlemen, I give you Skulduggery Pleasant and Valkyrie Cain!"

The People applauded. Now that I was focusing on them, I could see the cuts and bruises they sported. One of them had his arm in a cast. They each looked like they'd gone twelve rounds with a prizefighter.

"Pleasant and Cain," Moon continued, wandering over to his captives, "we have heard tales of your exploits and adventures. I am truly honoured. Never in my life did I expect that our modest little operation here would warrant your attention. We are but simple folk."

He grinned. Some of his People laughed. The grin didn't stay on for long. "Of course, you did put six of my people in hospital this morning. We did what we could with our limited knowledge of medical procedures, but our friends, our very good friends, are now languishing in hospital wards being seen to by clumsy mortal doctors, and that's... that's just not cool."

He lashed a kick into Pleasant's side.

"But I'm not one to hold grudges," he said. "I have a simple philosophy in life. Do unto others as they do unto you. You have honoured me by coming to this nowhere little town. You have honoured me by taking an interest in me, in us, and in the work we do here. So allow me to repay you in kind. I will honour you, sir, you and your partner."

He smiled down at her. "Valkyrie, Valkyrie, Valkyrie... what age are you, Valkyrie? Seventeen, aren't you? A little old to be an offering, strictly speaking... but tonight is a night for exceptions, is it not?"

Two of his People hurried forward. They undid the chains holding Valkyrie to the pillar, and pulled her to her feet. She lunged at one of them, but her hands were cuffed behind her back and Moon stepped forward, slapped her so hard she almost fell.

"Play nice," said Moon, "or you don't get to play at all."

The two men dragged her to the table, and Moon's attention returned to Pleasant as Pleasant spoke.

"An offering?" Pleasant said as the two men dragged Valkyrie to the table. "A blood sacrifice? You people are still doing that?"

I wished I could catch a glimpse of his face, just to see if he looked as cool as he sounded.

Moon shrugged. "It's a little retro, sure, but we've been doing it for decades and we've received no complaints so far."

"What about the sacrifices?"

"Oh, well, yes, *they* complain, but they're always in a bad mood, anyway."

"And do you mind me asking who you're making the offerings to? Just for my own personal amusement, you understand."

Moon laughed. "That's just the thing, Detective Pleasant, I don't even know myself. All I know is that a being of wonderment and awe came to me in a particularly vivid dream, and he told me that I was an integral part of the anti-Sanctuary. He told me I was to gather around me like-minded individuals and every time we met we were to offer him the blood of a mortal."

"There is no anti-Sanctuary," Pleasant responded.

"Well, the only thing I can say to that is there *is*, and I am an integral part of it."

"Because you had a dream."

Moon smiled. "Doubt all you want, Detective Cynic, Detective Sceptic, but I know the truth and so do my People. We have seen what lurks on the other side. And within minutes you will see, too."

I was running through things to say in my head – *Freeze! Nobody move!* – when another of Moon's People went to the back of the van and pulled out Sammy. His mouth was gagged, his hands tied. He'd been crying. He looked terrified as he was pushed towards the table, which had become a sacrificial altar in my mind, and I stepped out and raised the gun.

"Stop!" I shrieked. "Just stop! Let my son go! Let them all go!"

Bubba Moon and his People looked at me with nothing more than surprise in their eyes. Chrissy hurried out beside me, sticking close.

Moon began to smile. "Look at this. Look at this situation we currently find ourselves in. Why, this is nothing less than a class reunion! My oldest friend and my oldest crush. And there was I thinking this night could not get any more special..."

"You're not Pete," I said. The gun was shaking badly in my hand, so I brought my left in to steady it. "You're Bubba Moon. I know all about you."

"I doubt it," said Moon, and gave another smile. "Chrissy. The years have not been good to you, now, have they? Probably down to that thug of a man you married. Yes, I know all about that. Your life has never quite taken flight, has it? You had your wings clipped young."

"Sammy," I said. "Come over here."

Sammy looked around, making sure no one was going to try and stop him, then he ran over. Moon chuckled.

I pointed the gun at the man holding Valkyrie down. "Release her. Take off the handcuffs."

The man looked over at Moon, who glanced at his watch. For some reason that made his smile grow wider. "Do what my friend says."

A few seconds later, Valkyrie was free. The moment the cuffs were off, she sighed, like freedom hadn't been the only thing that had been kept from her. She grabbed the key from the man and threw it to Chrissy.

"Help my friend," she said.

Chrissy immediately went to the pillar where Pleasant sat.

Moon didn't seem to care about any of this. He was looking straight at me. "How've you been, old buddy? Done any skateboarding lately? Sammy, you might not know this about your old man, but he was quite the skateboarder when we were kids, just a few years younger than you are now. He was cool back then. We used to skate in the park, even though we weren't allowed. We frightened the pigeons and the old people. Good times, were they not?"

Things were going according to plan. The gun trembled less as I pointed it at him. "You're not Pete."

"But I'm in here with Pete," said Moon. "I know everything he knows. I know you and me were both in love with Chrissy Brennan. I know she preferred me."

"I'm pretty sure she's changed her mind about that now," I said, and Moon laughed.

I looked over when the chain fell, and saw Pleasant getting to his feet. Before he came round the pillar, his hand went to his collar, like he was fixing his tie. He stepped into view and I frowned. It wasn't Pleasant. He was as tall and as slender, he was dressed in a similar suit, but this man was white, handsome but unshaven, his brown hair tousled.

It wasn't the man I'd met the previous night, but when he spoke, he spoke with Skulduggery Pleasant's voice. "I must admit, this is disconcerting. You could have disarmed my gun-toting friend here without a second thought, but you didn't."

"No, we didn't," said Moon, and then gestured to the man's face. "I like this, by the way. Inspires trust."

This man – Pleasant in disguise? – observed Moon through narrowed eyes. "All of which leads me to suspect you have something up your sleeve. Which is not a nice thought, to be honest."

Moon smiled. "I wouldn't say it is."

"You looked at your watch before you allowed Valkyrie to be released. Time is not on our side, is it? It's on yours, but not ours. Are we expecting company?"

"We are."

"Someone who will cancel out the threat posed by Valkyrie and myself?"

"Indeed."

Skulduggery Pleasant, for I had come to the conclusion now that it was definitely him, wearing a disguise of some kind, nodded. "I really don't like the way this is going. Still, at least I'm no longer in shackles. That's something, at least."

"I'm glad you think so."

Chrissy came over, standing beside me with Sammy behind us. Sammy was pale, frightened, still bound and gagged, but his eyes were fixed on Pleasant, not Moon.

Moon looked at his watch again, and a brand-new smile broke out.

"Here we—" was all he had time to say before a hole tore open in empty space and a light poured through and I glimpsed something, something within that light, which I somehow knew to be a portal to somewhere else, somewhere terrible, and I saw a monster's face in that light and the light grew and grew and burst and—

7

I uncovered my eyes, blinking rapidly, and found myself in a dark room that smelled of settled dust and mothballs.

I was alone. It was cold. There was a bed in the corner without a mattress. I crossed to the window, peered out through the grime-streaked glass at Bredon. The warehouse was on the east side, but I was on the west, looking down on to King Road and the junkyard. From here I could see the church and the lights of the gas station, and if there hadn't been that line of trees on Hyland Street I'd have been able to see my school.

I was in Bubba Moon's old house. Only... I'd passed Hyland Street a few times since I'd been home, and those trees weren't there any more. They hadn't been there since I was a kid.

There was a sound, somewhere below me.

I wiped the perspiration from my right hand, then gripped the gun tighter. I opened the door and immediately stepped away, expecting something to rush in at me. My back rippled with gooseflesh as I stood there, looking out into the gloom, waiting for horror. Finally, I started moving again, the floorboards creaking gently under my weight.

The landing was empty. There were no lights on in the house. The usual smells one would expect in an abandoned house – smells resulting from drunk teenagers breaking in or passing vagrants spending the night – were absent. No teenager had ever been drunk enough to break in here, and no vagrant had ever been cold enough to seek shelter under this roof. The only smell, apart from the dust, was a damp, unhealthy rot that seeped through the walls. It was like the house was sick, riddled with some wasting disease.

I reached the stairs and looked over the banisters. I had to go down there. I didn't know how I had got here, but I knew I had to go down there.

I started down the stairs.

Whether this was illusion or madness or magic, or if I had died in that warehouse and this was the hell I was to spend eternity in, mattered little to me at this point. For all I knew, I was still in the warehouse and this was all happening in my mind. Maybe it had affected everyone there. Maybe that bright flash of light had hypnotised me, hypnotised all of us.

Or maybe I was really here. And that thing I had glimpsed, that thing coming through the portal, maybe it was here, too.

I got to the bottom of the stairs without a clawed hand reaching through the banisters and grabbing my ankle. The front door was just ahead of me. I could have run straight to it, pulled it open, and fled. But what would I be fleeing into? Or when? Whatever had happened to bring me here had not only sent me across town, it had sent me across time. I knew, with no doubt in my mind, that this was the night we had snuck into Bubba Moon's house, all those years ago.

And that meant I had to go down, into the basement.

The basement door was under the stairs. The doorknob was black and loose and rattled when I turned it. I had to give it an extra turn it was fitted so badly. When it opened, the darkness from the basement spread upwards, passing me, darkening the hall, turning everything colder still, and then it settled, my eyes adjusted, and I started down the wooden steps.

There were more steps than there should have been. They descended into a gaping mouth of pitch-black. Twice on my way down I almost lost my nerve

– but if I was here, then Sammy might be down here, too, and I wasn't going to abandon my son.

Gradually, the gloom began to lift, ever so slightly, and I saw the concrete floor below. When I reached the bottom, I looked back, unsurprised to find that there were, at most, maybe ten steps in all leading up to the open door.

The house was playing tricks on me.

Navigating my way round the stacks of piled-up junk was like being caught in a maze. I didn't remember there being this many stacks, and I didn't remember them being this high. It was the house again, growing and widening, adding more twists and turns to the journey. Playing its games.

There were shouts in among the stacks, but shouts from far away. Something else, too. Like distant gunfire.

I entered a clearing of sorts, getting my first real impression of just how big the basement had grown. It was massive, as big as the warehouse. Maybe it *was* the warehouse. Maybe the bright light had hypnotised me into confusing the two. But the warehouse hadn't had all this junk, and along the walls it didn't have all those wooden steps leading upwards.

Someone emerged from the stacks on my right.

"Chrissy!" I hissed.

She jumped, covering her mouth with both hands, stifling a yell. Then she hurried over, clinging to my right arm.

"We're in his house," she whispered.

"I know," I said. "Stay close to me."

We moved onwards, through the clearing and back into the stacks. We approached a low table on which sat a dollhouse. As we passed, a light switched on in one of the small windows.

"That's mine," Chrissy said softly. "I used to have that. That exact one."

We stared at it for a few more moments. Another light turned on. Chrissy let go of my arm and stepped towards it.

"What are you doing? Chrissy, don't."

She looked back at me, her face strained. "I have to," she said, and reached out, fingers hooking into the exterior wall of the dollhouse. She pulled it open and all the lights came on and she stepped back with a cry of disgust. Cockroaches skittered over the toy furniture, burrowing under the thin blankets on the beds to get out of the sudden light and pushing over the plastic plates on the kitchen table. Some of them had got on to her hand and Chrissy cursed, swiping at them as they tried to scuttle up her sleeve.

I pulled her away and the lights in the dollhouse went out, though we could still hear the cockroaches spilling over the edge of the table and hitting the ground.

Chrissy pushed against me and we moved on quickly. My foot nudged something so solid I almost tripped. I looked down, cursed, stepped back right into Chrissy. Together, we looked down at the still form, half hidden by the stacks. When the figure didn't move, I inched forward, nudged it again. Then I got my foot under it and pushed the shoulder back far enough to reveal the face of the warehouse sentry. Blood leaked from a gash over his eye. He was either asleep or dead. I took my foot away, let the body slump back, and we stepped over it and carried on.

Ahead of us, around the next corner, another light flickered, and I heard the sound of a helicopter's rotor blades before it was replaced by synthesiser music. I recognised it immediately as the theme tune to *Airwolf*. Keeping the gun out in front, I led the way to an old TV with rabbit ears and terrible reception, the same TV that I had sat in front of, cross-legged in my living room, when I was a kid. We'd had that TV until the day my brother and I were throwing around the baseball indoors, and the ball bounced off the wall and hit the screen and cracked it. Our mom was not happy that day. Our dad was furious.

Even as this memory swam through my head, the crack appeared on the TV in front of us. The screen bulged slightly and retracted, like it was breathing. Every time it bulged, the crack would widen a little, and then it stopped retracting, it kept bulging, and black liquid (*blood*) started to drip from the screen, and then flow like an open wound. Then the screen burst open and the black liquid gushed out in a torrent that hit me square in the chest, forced me back, splashed into my mouth as I cried out.

Chrissy slipped and I fell over her and the black liquid covered us, drenched us, and then the torrent weakened, and went back to being a trickle, and then it stopped altogether and there was nothing except the busted TV.

I went to wipe my eyes clear, but I was dry. I was clean. I looked at Chrissy. There'd been no black liquid. No gushing blood.

"Playing games," I said.

We got up. Ahead, we heard voices. Children's voices.

We reached another clearing in time to watch myself, aged eleven, drop down from the narrow window into the basement.

"Oh my God," Chrissy whispered.

I was so small. So tiny. So young. I stared.

"See anything?" a voice asked from the window. Tyler's voice.

"Junk," my younger self said.

"Any black magic stuff?"

My younger self shone his flashlight right into my face and then moved it on without seeing me.

"Just old lamps and furniture. A table. Sofa."

We heard Benny telling me to grab a Ouija board if I saw one, and then Chrissy's voice came through loud and clear.

"Don't you dare. My aunt did the Ouija board once and she doesn't believe in any of that stuff, but she said that Ouija boards are actually dangerous."

Chrissy's fingers dug into my arm.

We watched history repeat itself until there were five eleven-year-olds down in the basement with us, the beams of their flashlights cutting through the murk.

Chrissy yanked on my shirt and I looked round. From behind a distant stack there came a fast-moving, flickering light, like someone going crazy with a flame-thrower. Then it cut off. No light, no flames, no smoke. The kids hadn't noticed it.

"Found it," Chrissy's younger self said. We walked after Tyler, joined the kids at the circle. Standing inside the circle was Bubba Moon.

Not the Pete Green Bubba Moon, but the original. A bald man, once heavily muscled, but with all that going to seed now. His gut was expanding, stretching the scars, distorting the symbols on his bare torso. He watched the kids crowd round him. They couldn't see him and he couldn't see us.

"Big bad Bubba Moon," Pete said in a soft voice.

Chrissy shrieked as the stacks beside us exploded, sending junk flying and old magazines fluttering like dying bats. A man hurtled through the air, bursting from one stack and disappearing into another. All this went unnoticed by the kids, unnoticed by Moon, but Chrissy and I ran over and I lunged into the stacks, gun at the ready, but of the man there was no sign.

We looked back at the circle. Pete was lying down in it while Bubba Moon stood over him. "Hey, guys, who am I?" he said, and laid his head back and pretended to be dead.

Grinning, Moon lay down with him, on top of him and over him, and all the flashlights went out.

The kids screamed, panicked, ran for the window, but Chrissy and I stayed and watched with mounting horror as Bubba Moon slowly got up, Pete moving within him, aping every movement. When they were both on their feet, Moon stepped back slightly, allowed Pete to stand on his own. Then Moon's hands went to Pete's shoulders, fingers digging into his shirt. When he lifted one shoulder, Pete lifted his foot, and together they lurched back towards the window.

I turned away from the unfolding scene, towards the sound of shouting. Gun in one hand, Chrissy's hand in another, I stepped cautiously towards a tall pile of shoeboxes. There was sudden movement, and one of Moon's People staggered out of the darkness. His shoulder hit the pile and he hit the ground and the shoeboxes toppled, spilling out hundreds of cassette tapes that clattered across the floor.

There was something else now, a sound like the snarl that thing had made as it passed through the portal. It was above us, and around us, moving through the stacks, and with it were more shouts and more gunshots. I heard Valkyrie Cain's voice.

When we looked back to the kids, they were gone. All but one.

Pete Green remained. He stood in the circle, looking at us, an eleven-year-old boy. At his feet, my son, unconscious.

I fought the urge to rush forward. "Why?" I asked.

Pete shrugged. "It likes the taste. The thing you saw. It likes the taste of mortal children. Fourteen years old, that's when they taste best, that's when it gets all the nutrients it needs. Who am I to disagree?"

"But why Sammy? Why our children?"

"Because I couldn't take *you*," said Pete. "I wanted all of you. You two and Benny. We all went down here, but I was the only one who stayed. How is that fair?"

"You killed Tyler," I said.

He grew up before our eyes. He grew taller and older and his clothes changed and his shirt disappeared and he was bare-chested and tattooed with scars again, just like he had been in the warehouse.

"Tyler was the only one I could take," he said. "But I made plans. Contingency plans. I was too late to stop you from leaving, my buddy, my pal, but I made sure Chrissy never got beyond the town limits, didn't I, sweetheart? I saddled her with a husband who was going to drain the fight right out of her. I left her with nowhere to turn. I left her with one option, and one option only."

Chrissy stiffened, and Bubba Moon looked at me and laughed. "All part of the game, you understand. I needed a way to get you to bring your family back to the old homestead for a few days, and really, what choice did she have? It was either your kid... or hers."

I frowned, raising the gun. "What?"

"I'm sorry," Chrissy said. She stepped away from me. She went to stand beside Moon.

I stared at them both. My hand started to tremble.

"You want to shoot me?" said Moon. "Or do you want to shoot the person who broke in and suffocated your dear old dad?"

He took one single step to the side, distancing himself from Chrissy.

"No..." I whispered. "Chrissy... what...?"

"He made me do it," she said, tears running down her face. "He said he'd take Scott next. He wouldn't let me leave—"

"Excuses, excuses," said Moon. "The point is, she killed your daddy, betrayed you to me, and now she wants me to kill your son instead of hers. You can't go home again, isn't that what they say?"

"I'll kill you," I said, pointing the gun at him.

"Go ahead."

The gun shook. He deserved it. For everything he'd done, he deserved it.

He wasn't my friend. He was a killer. He was a killer and he was going to kill my son.

I pulled the trigger. Nothing happened.

Moon laughed. "You really think she'd give you a loaded gun?"

A scream pierced the air, and Moon grinned. "That would be your friends, I imagine," he said. "What, you thought they were going to come save you? They've never gone up against anything like this before. You have no one to..."

He faltered. The scream twisted and undulated and screeched. No human being could ever make anything close to that kind of sound.

Then there was silence.

Darkness swarmed my vision and dissipated like smoke...

...and then we were back in the warehouse with Moon's People sprawled unconscious around us. Sammy stood beside me, his hands still tied and his mouth still gagged. Next to the cloth-covered table, Moon stood with Chrissy, shaking his head, trying to clear it. Skulduggery Pleasant and Valkyrie Cain stood behind them both.

Valkyrie pushed Chrissy aside and Moon spun, too startled to do anything more than curse, just before Pleasant stepped into him and flipped him over his hip. Moon crashed to the ground and Valkyrie moved in. The handcuffs that had been used to bind her snapped over his wrists.

Moon got to his knees, shaking his head. "You can't stand up to it, you'll never defeat it—"

"We already have," said Valkyrie.

Moon screamed in abject rage as I dropped the gun and turned, untied Sammy. His hands free, he pulled the gag from his mouth, too startled, too shocked to speak.

I looked at Chrissy as she ran from the warehouse, then at Moon, tears streaming down his face, and finally I turned to Pleasant. "Are you going to kill him?"

"I thought we'd have to," he said. "We didn't think we'd be able to capture him. But now that we have…"

Valkyrie held Moon as well as she could while Pleasant picked the knife up off the table and cut a new symbol into Moon's forehead. When it was done, Pleasant stood over him, his gloved hand splayed against his bloody wound. He looked at me.

"Before I begin," he said, "I need you to understand that the words I am about to recite in no way indicate the presence, or indeed the existence, of a Divine Being of any sort. Words are words, and they have power, and arranged in a particular way they can have a particular effect. Is that understood?"

I nodded.

Pleasant looked down at his prisoner. "I command you, unclean spirit, in the name of whichever god you believe in, I command you to depart. Depart, then, transgressor. Depart, seducer, full of lies and cunning, foe of virtue, persecutor of the innocent."

"Get away from me," said Moon. "Get away!"

Pleasant ignored him. "Give place, abominable creature, give way, you monster. Depart, then, depart, accursed one, depart with all your deceits."

Valkyrie grinned. "Say it."

"I'm not saying it," said Pleasant.

"Go on," said Valkyrie. "Say it for me. Please."

Pleasant sighed, and returned his attention to the exorcism, and then, in a loud voice, he commanded, "*Get thee behind me, Bubba Moon!*" and Valkyrie cheered.

We went home. Felicity had tried to stay up, but she'd fallen asleep on the couch. I helped Sammy to bed, and he hugged me before I turned out the light. For a moment he was a little kid again, a little kid who needed me.

I stayed with him until he was asleep, and then I sat on the couch and waited for Felicity to wake. When she did, we talked. I didn't tell her about Bubba Moon. We didn't talk about what I had just been through. Instead, we talked about us, and our great kids, and our life together. We talked for hours, until the sun bled into the night and turned the sky orange.

Bubba Moon's van pulled up and I went outside. Valkyrie Cain got out, and so did a tall man with dark hair. Skulduggery Pleasant in yet another astonishing disguise.

Valkyrie told us that the exorcism had lasted three hours. When Pete Green's body finally slumped into unconsciousness, she'd dragged him out of the circle, leaving only the flickering image of the original Bubba Moon trapped within. By that stage, she said, a team of Sensitives had arrived to drain him of his power. Pleasant told us that Moon would never again get the chance to infect anyone. He would stay there, in that warehouse, in that circle, too weak to possess even a passing pigeon, and that's where he would remain until the end of days.

I thanked them. Not only for saving my life, not only for saving the life of my son, but also for saving the lives of all the other children who would otherwise have been sacrificed to whatever creature had lived in that light. Valkyrie smiled, thanked *me* for rescuing *them*, and ignored Pleasant when he insisted that he'd had the situation under control. He made a joke about not telling anyone what had happened, or he'd have to send in his friends who'd wipe our memories.

I'm pretty sure it was a joke.

They left without saying much else. They didn't tell me who they were, who they worked for, or what all this meant. Pleasant didn't explain why he wore so many disguises, although Sammy told me later that he'd caught a glimpse of him when he was handcuffed to the pillar, and he could have sworn Pleasant had a skull for a head. At this point, nothing would have surprised me.

Bubba Moon's People were scooped up by whoever scoops people like that up, and Chrissy left town with her son. I asked Pleasant not to send anyone after her. She'd suffered enough, I reckoned.

Pete Green was introduced to a team of psychiatrists who were very curious to find out what trauma had led a grown man with all those unusual scars to revert to his eleven-year-old self overnight. They told me they didn't dare reunite him with any old friends for fear it would traumatise him further – but maybe at some stage in the future...

That suits me fine. Pete's my best friend, and I'm not going anywhere. This is my home, after all.

The original version of *Theatre of Shadows* was written in a single day and sent out to all participants of a massive live-action, role-playing event held in Dublin, on September 27th, 2014.

This new version is drastically rewritten in parts, and takes the original's place in canon.

The original story, flaws and all, is exclusive to the Theatre of Shadows participants, and will never be reissued.

THEATRE OF SHADOWS

B odies, stiff and frozen and covered in frost, hung from the ceiling on chains. Women, some long dead, some fresh, all swathed in ill-fitting grey, like hospital gowns. A draught sweeping through the giant makeshift freezer kept some of them swaying ever so slightly. The dead creaked when they swayed.

There were over a dozen of them, at Valkyrie's glance. Maybe fifteen or sixteen. She stepped between them, moving slowly. The black ring on her finger burned as cold as the freezer. She was only conscious of her breathing because of the long stream of crystallised vapour that escaped her lips. She was breathing slow and steady, forcing herself to remain calm.

There was a deckchair set up ahead. She had expected this. When they were reading through the killer's profile they'd come to the conclusion that, when choosing where to build his kill zone, he'd pick a place where he could sit for hours, gazing at the bodies of his victims, reliving the moments when he took their lives.

She emerged from the freezer, continuing on her path through the decrepit old theatre. There was light up ahead.

Silas Nadir sat on the stage in the candlelight, his back to the door. He was sewing. Another grey hospital gown. Music played. 'I Only Have Eyes For You'. On the floor before him was a bucket, the area around it stained with dried blood. Above the bucket, a thick chain dangled from the vaulted ceiling. On the end of that chain was a wrought-iron hook. Susie Pearse, her hands tied with rope that looped over the hook, hung there, quiet but alive.

Valkyrie looked around. They had a plan: find Nadir and then go in together. Skulduggery had come through the back entrance, Valkyrie through the front. He had made her swear not to take on Nadir without him.

An old-fashioned alarm clock went off on the table beside Nadir, nearly making Valkyrie jump out of her skin. Nadir tapped the clock, shutting off the alarm, and he put the hospital gown to one side and stood up.

Susie twisted on the hook; looked down at him. "Let me go. You hear me? Let me go right now."

Nadir ignored her. He opened a bag sitting on the table and pulled out a long coat. When he put it on, Valkyrie could see the bloodstains. That coat probably bore the lifeblood of everyone Nadir had ever killed. She looked around again. Where the hell was Skulduggery?

"They'll find you," Susie said. "The cops will find you. My family, they won't stop. They'll find you and kill you for this."

"I doubt that very much," Nadir said, only half listening. He opened a wooden box, and took out a small knife, its blade crusted with dried blood. He gazed at it lovingly, took a deep breath. "This is my favourite thing in the world," he told Susie. "It's a part of me, as much a part of me as a finger or a toe or an eye or an ear."

"Let me down," Susie said, her voice trembling. "Please."

Nadir ignored her and went back to the table. He took something from the bag, fixed it over his face, and turned. A plastic pig mask, the cheap kind with the elastic string to hold it on. It was cracked and battered and faded and, like everything else, it was splattered with blood.

The pig mask was just too much for Susie. She screamed and kicked and twisted, and Nadir watched her, enjoying her torment.

It was too much for Valkyrie, as well. She stepped from the wings and clicked her fingers. Nadir whirled and she threw the fireball. It hit him in the face and he screamed, stumbled back, his head ablaze, and she snapped her hands against the air and he shot backwards, off the stage.

Valkyrie ran up, wrapped her arms around Susie's legs and tried hoisting her off the hook. When that didn't work, she let go, stepped back, felt for the air and seized it. Susie cried out in shock as she rose higher, but she didn't fight against it. When she was high enough to free herself, she scooped her hands out of the hook, and Valkyrie brought her down. Susie collapsed against her.

Nadir had beaten out the flames, but the air was suddenly ripe with the smell of burnt flesh. Whimpering in pain, he pulled off the pig mask, taking a good deal of skin along with it. Howling, he jumped on to the stage and ran at them, knocking Susie out of the way and falling on top of Valkyrie.

He thrust the knife at her belly, but the blade couldn't get through her jacket. Nadir snarled, slashed at her face, but Valkyrie brought her arms up. She grabbed his wrist, got her right knee between them. He came forward and she scissored her legs, flipping him on to his back and now she was on top, pinning his knife hand to the floor and slamming palm shots into his head.

"Go!" she yelled to Susie. "Run!"

Out of the corner of her eye, she saw Susie hesitate, then turn and flee.

Nadir still had the knife, and Valkyrie had hurt him with those palm shots, but hadn't stunned him. This wasn't working out like she'd practised. He got his free hand to her chest and started pushing, tying to turn her, to throw her off, to get the knife back under his control. Valkyrie pressed against him, struggling to remain in the dominant position, but it was no use: they were turning. She was lying on her back again.

Nadir leaned over her, spittle flying from his burnt lips, eyes blazing beneath his scorched brow. His fist crunched against her cheek and the world rocked. She lost focus, only dimly aware of the knife coming down.

Something cracked against Nadir's head and he went sideways. The knife clattered away. When her vision cleared, the first thing Valkyrie saw was a rusted old pipe. The second thing she saw was Susie Pearse holding it, tears running down her face. Nadir tried to get up and Susie swung the pipe like a baseball bat, crunching it into his ribs. Nadir went tumbling and Susie followed, hitting him again.

Valkyrie tried to stand, but had to stay where she was, crouched down, waiting for her head to stop spinning.

She heard the pipe hit the ground and Susie cry out. She heard Nadir's curses, punctuated by the sound of his fists smacking into flesh.

Damn it.

Valkyrie forced herself up, turned to see Nadir standing over Susie, slamming kicks into her side. Poor Susie. She had no idea what was going on. She was just a normal, ordinary, average, everyday mortal. The only reason she was here at all was because she happened to fit the requirements Nadir looked for in a victim. Dark-haired. Young. Pretty.

Valkyrie reached up for the darkness, found a shadow, and stripped it back until it was as thin and pointed as a spear. Then she focused on Nadir, and flicked her hand. The shadow-spear hit him in the shoulder, taking him off his feet and pinning him against the wall. Nadir shrieked and hollered and Valkyrie pulled the shadow back. Nadir dropped, sniffling in pain.

"Hey there," Valkyrie said, helping Susie get to her feet. "You OK, Susie?"

"He was... he was going to kill me," Susie said. Her eyes danced on the edge of hysteria.

"But he didn't," said Valkyrie, keeping her voice calm. "You fought back. You saved my life, do you know that? You're going to be OK."

She heard Skulduggery shout her name and she shouted back. A few seconds passed and he ran in, leaped on to the stage and activated his façade before Susie saw him.

"You were to wait for me," he said.

"You were taking too long," Valkyrie said. "This place has half a dozen different stages – how was I supposed to know which ones I was meant to search? Besides, look at us. We're good. Susie's alive and we've got Nadir. Job done."

"Valkyrie—"

"He was going to kill her. I didn't have a choice."

There was no arguing with that, so Skulduggery turned back to the wounded serial killer. "Silas Nadir, you're under arrest."

"Look what she did to me," Nadir whined. "Look what she did to my face!"

"He had a pig mask on," Valkyrie said.

"That's disconcerting," Skulduggery responded.

"Look what she did!" Nadir screamed, jumping to his feet. "She burned me! Burned my face! I can smell my own skin burning!"

"Well," Skulduggery said, "that's what you get when you decide to be a serial killer. You'll have plenty of time to regret your life choices from the comfort of your brand-new cell."

The hatred on Nadir's ravaged face twisted into an angry smile. "You think you've won? You think you've beaten me? You don't think I had a contingency plan?"

"To be honest," said Skulduggery, "I didn't think you knew what contingency *meant*."

"The first lesson I was ever taught about how to murder people was to have a contingency plan. And you're standing right in the middle of it."

Nadir moved suddenly, pressing his hand to a sigil on the wall, a sigil connected to another sigil, and another, in a trail that led down to the floor and across the stage to where they were standing. The ground pulsed beneath Valkyrie's feet.

"Oh, hell," Valkyrie muttered.

"Run!" Skulduggery shouted.

Valkyrie shoved Susie Pearse towards the door and tried to follow as the world started flickering around her. She knew she was too late because she'd been through this before.

They were being shunted.

The flickering grew faster, and faster, and Valkyrie lost her balance and fell against someone – Skulduggery – and then with a jolt the theatre solidified around them.

Valkyrie looked up. "It didn't work. We didn't shunt." She looked back, but Nadir was gone. "Damn it! Come on." She went to run after him, but Skulduggery gripped her arm.

"Wait a moment," he said.

"What? What's wrong? Skulduggery, he's getting away!"

Skulduggery deactivated his façade, the face flowing off his skull, and looked around. "Nadir is no longer our main problem."

"Then what is?" Valkyrie asked. He let go of her arm and she stepped back. "Well? What's... what's so..." She frowned. "It's really quiet, isn't it?"

"It is."

Valkyrie jumped down from the stage and hurried for the door. The theatre was a labyrinth of corridors and dead ends, but she found her way to the exit and emerged on to a street devoid of life. Nothing moved in the city but the breeze. No cars on the road, people on the footpaths, birds in the air. Not even any litter.

"What happened to all the people?"

"We've been shunted," Skulduggery said, joining her.

"So we're in another dimension."

"No, not quite. This is still quite obviously our world, but we don't seem to fit any more. Shunting works by locating and changing the frequency of existence – I think Nadir nudged us slightly out of synch with the rest of the world. Where we are there are no people, no animals."

They started walking.

"So how do we fix it?" Valkyrie asked.

"I have no idea."

"Is it permanent?"

"Unless we can find a way to phase back into this reality, I doubt it will happen by itself."

She blinked. "So... so what do we do?"

"I don't really know. We just have to hope that Ghastly realises we're missing and does something about it."

Valkyrie looked around. "This is creepy."

"I suppose."

"You don't find it creepy?"

"I find it peaceful. Relaxing. Almost soothing, in a way. No traffic, no mobile phones, no people..."

"I'm here."

"I didn't say it was perfect."

"I'm just creeped out. This is way too eerie for me. It's just... it's empty. Doesn't that scare you? It scares me. It's unnatural. I don't like how quiet it is. It's very quiet. You feel like you have to keep talking just to make up for it, you know? Like you have to compensate for how quiet it is. You just have to talk. Say stuff. Utter words. Sounds. Anything, really. Barnyard animal noises would be better than this kind of silence. What's your favourite barnyard animal noise? Mine would be a cow, mooing. Do you have a favourite? Is it a sheep? There's something about sheep baaing that'd be quite reassuring right now. Like, you know... *baaaaaa*. There. That's kind of nice, isn't it? *Baaaaaaaaa*. Very relaxing. *Baaaaaaaaaa*. What? Why are you looking at me like that?"

They stopped walking.

"I'm just surprised by the speed at which you've gone insane," said Skulduggery. "I think it happened mid-sentence, too. That's impressive."

"Well, I wouldn't have to talk so much if you'd contribute a little to the conversation."

"About favourite barnyard noises?"

"About anything. Instead, you're standing there with a serene look on your face."

"I'm not wearing a face."

"A serene look on your skull, then."

"I just like the silence. Is that so wrong?"

"Yes it is. It's very wrong. You should be helping me make some noise. Don't you have anything to say? Anything at all? Anything in the slightest—"

"I do, actually."

"Good. Good! What?"

"Don't look behind you."

Valkyrie froze. "What?"

"Don't move," said Skulduggery quietly, "and don't look behind you."

Her eyes widened. "What's behind me? You said we were alone."

"No, I said there did not appear to be any people or animals."

"So what's behind me? A fish?"

He shook his head.

"I'm going to turn round," she whispered.

"I wouldn't do that."

"It's a monster, isn't it?"

"It may have some monster-like qualities, yes."

"I'm turning round."

"Just don't scream."

"I reserve the right to scream."

"It might be attracted to loud noises."

"I won't scream, then."

Valkyrie turned.

A creature the size of a football crawled up the side of a lamp post, a giant bug with many terrible eyes. Its pale skin pulsated with a sickly throb, and its wings were folded over its back.

So far, it hadn't noticed them. Valkyrie crouched immediately.

"What are you doing?" Skulduggery asked.

"Hiding," she whispered.

"Behind what?"

"Shush." Keeping low, she moved back round a corner. Skulduggery strolled after her.

"I don't like this place," said Valkyrie. "It has giant bugs. What do we do now?"

"There's not really much we can do, so I suppose we wait until Ghastly figures out a way to bring us back."

They returned to the theatre, closing the doors behind them. Keeping away from the doors to the various stages, where anything could be lurking in the darkness, they stayed in the foyer with the large windows. Valkyrie was not looking forward to the sun going down.

"How many of those bugs do you think there are?" she asked, keeping watch.

"We have no way of knowing."

"Do you think there are any that are nocturnal?"

"Possibly."

She let a few moments go by. "I'm hungry."

"We could try to catch the bug, if you want. Cook it."

She made a face. "God, no. Are you crazy? It looks disgusting."

"Might taste nice."

"I'd rather eat my own foot."

"You said you were hungry."

"Not *that* hungry." She went back to peering out of the window. "Wonder where Nadir learned to use sigils like that."

"It's pretty basic stuff, actually. You should read a book every now and then. Maybe you'll learn something."

"I read plenty."

"What was the last book you read?"

Valkyrie looked round. "The last one?"

"The last book, yes."

"The last book I read?"

"You can't remember, can you?"

"Of course I can. It was... *Moby Dick*."

"You read *Moby Dick*? Really?"

"No," she confessed, her shoulders sagging. "I was going to, but then I realised it was about a whale, and I don't like stories about whales. Not since *Free Willy*."

"Ah, yes," said Skulduggery. "That other great whale story."

"I don't get a lot of time to read these days," Valkyrie said. "I'm always doing this or that. Look at me now. I'm stuck in limbo world, hoping our friend comes looking for us. This is how I spend my time now. I'd love to be able to sit down on a porch somewhere and just read a book and have no one bother me or try to kill me, but hey, this is the life I chose, so I have to make the best of it."

"You talk a lot when you're hungry."

"I'm bored."

"You're incorrigible."

"If I read more books, I'd probably know what that means, but for now I'll just take it as a compliment and smile."

Skulduggery stood up. "Did you hear that?"

"Hear what?"

"That voice," Skulduggery said. "You didn't hear it?"

"No. What did it say?"

"I couldn't make it out."

Valkyrie got to her feet. "How come you heard it and I didn't? You don't even have ears. Which direction did it come from?"

"I'm not sure."

"Maybe you imagined it."

"There!" he said. "Did you hear it that time?"

She frowned. "That was me."

"Not the voice I'm talking about."

"I didn't hear anything."

Then she heard it, loud but distant, like a bad broadcast.

"Skulduggery? Valkyrie?"

It came from all around them. Valkyrie's frown deepened. "God?" she whispered.

"Ghastly," Skulduggery said.

"There you are," the voice responded. It *was* Ghastly, but distorted. Suddenly Valkyrie felt a little stupid about the whole God thing. "You're OK?"

"We are," Skulduggery said. "Where are you?"

"In the theatre foyer. Finbar's here. He sensed your presence and he's boosting my words so we can communicate. It's a psychic thing. I haven't a clue how it works."

"Hi, guys," said Finbar.

"Nadir shunted us out of phase," Skulduggery said. "We're stuck, and we're not alone. There are creatures here, and they might not be friendly. The sooner we can get back, the better."

"Any idea how to do that?" Ghastly asked.

"We're hoping you'd know, to be honest."

There was a moment of silence. "Oh, right. Sure."

Valkyrie sagged. "That did not sound optimistic."

"It'll be fine," Ghastly said. "We'll figure it out. We'll get a Shunter over here and he'll bring you right back."

"I take it Nadir got away?" Skulduggery asked.

"No sign of him," said Ghastly. "But don't worry about that for the moment. Let's focus on getting you home."

"What about Susie?" Valkyrie asked.

There was a pause. "What about her?"

"She's OK, isn't she?"

"There's been no sign of her. I thought she was shunted along with you."

Valkyrie looked at Skulduggery, her eyes widening.

"She may well have been," Skulduggery said. "Ghastly, we have to go. If she's out there, we have to find her."

"We'll be here when you get back," Ghastly promised.

Skulduggery took out his gun, nodded to Valkyrie, and she led the way out.

They searched for an hour. The silence was quickly becoming claustrophobic, like a mist had descended to dampen the sounds of the natural world. They moved through this unnatural world, this unnatural city, and the longer they searched, the less confident they became of ever finding the missing girl.

They only spoke when they absolutely had to. The solitude made words seem too loud. Instead of reassuring Valkyrie, they put her on edge. Even the sounds of her own footsteps were too loud on these streets.

Skulduggery held up a hand and she stopped. He pointed ahead. Three bugs flew towards the open door of a café. Resisting the urge to run in the opposite direction, Valkyrie followed Skulduggery to the back entrance. She heard buzzing, coming from above.

Skulduggery turned to her, motioned her to stay put. She nodded gratefully. He moved into the backroom, towards the stairs. The Necromancer ring on Valkyrie's finger wasn't getting cold, which meant no one in the immediate vicinity was dead. Yet.

Minutes passed.

The buzzing grew louder in the next room and she backed out, into the narrow alleyway. It grew louder still and she ducked down as a bug came flying out. It twisted lazily into the sky, disappeared.

Valkyrie leaned against the wall, doing her best not to shiver, and felt something touch her neck.

She threw herself forward, but it was too late: the bug had already crawled from the wall on to her shoulder. She tried to swat it off, but it was heavy, way too heavy. It was cold to the touch, its skin both tough and thin at the same time, as if the tiniest scratch would open it up and all its blood and bits would come bursting out. Her touch seemed to annoy it, however, because it hissed and its wings buzzed and it unfurled a tail with a stinger.

It had a stinger in its tail.

It jabbed at her, the stinger failing to penetrate her jacket, and she cried out and swung her arm against the wall. The impact dislodged the bug and it fell heavily to the ground. Valkyrie kicked it, sent it spinning, but it regained its senses and those wings started buzzing again. It lifted off, came at her, and she clicked her fingers, filled her hand with flame, and thrust it straight out. The bug became a ball of fire and weird insect screeching. It flew up, hit the wall multiple times, like a fly on a window, and then the flames overwhelmed it and it dropped.

Valkyrie stared, in fascination and revulsion, as it moved weakly along the ground towards her. Then it stopped, and didn't move again. It smelled of burning fat.

Suddenly the air was filled with more screeching, and she looked up in time to see flames belch from breaking windows above. She jumped back, avoiding the falling glass, and watched as dozens of fiery bugs swarmed into the open air to die.

Moments later, Skulduggery rejoined her. "Found a nest," he said. "And a body. Not Susie. Male, badly decomposed. You OK?"

"One of those things attacked me," she said. "Can we get away from here?"

"That's probably a good idea."

Making sure the skies were clear of buzzing enemies, they headed back to the theatre via an alternate route.

"What would happen if it had stung me?" Valkyrie asked, her reluctance to speak now a thing of the past. "Do you think it'd be bad?"

"Maybe," Skulduggery said. "Or maybe it would just have been like a wasp sting."

"Yeah. Yeah, I mean... why not? Why would it have to kill me? It might be just like a wasp sting. I've never been stung by a wasp. Have you? I've gone through my entire life without being stung by a wasp. For all I know, I'm allergic. If a wasp stung me, I might swell up and die within minutes. My throat would constrict and I wouldn't be able to breathe and—"

"You're in luck," Skulduggery interrupted. "There are no wasps here. Just those big, horrible, stinging bugs."

"I'm panicking a bit."

"Understandable."

"Allergies aren't going to kill me. Not when there are so many monsters around to do the job."

"That's the spirit. Come on. Susie's this way."

Valkyrie frowned. "How do you know?"

"I can hear her."

And there it was, floating like the scent of pollen on the breeze. Singing.

Skulduggery wrapped his arm round Valkyrie's waist and they flew upwards, landing on the roof of a multistorey car park that had no cars.

Susie Pearce stood with her back to them, her arms outstretched in the sunlight, singing a sweet lullaby as the air around her filled with those buzzing, bloated bugs.

"Susie?" Skulduggery said quietly, his façade flowing over his face.

Susie stopped singing and turned, and Valkyrie stifled a gasp. She was thin, much thinner than she had been only a few hours earlier. She looked almost skeletal, and her eyes were dull, but the expression on her face was peaceful. Happy.

"Hello?" she said.

"Susie, we're here to help you," Skulduggery said.

Susie smiled. "Help me? Why would I need any help? You are kind, but no, no, thank you. I'm perfectly happy where I am."

"Are you in pain?" Valkyrie asked.

"Not at all," said Susie.

"What happened to you?"

Susie's smile faltered for a moment. "I don't remember," she said, and then the smile came back. "And I don't care. I don't have a care in the world. If you don't believe me, come over here. Do you see these beautiful birds? Aren't they extraordinary?"

Valkyrie looked at the ugly, bloated, buzzing bugs. "Birds?"

"Magnificent, aren't they? We don't have birds like these back home."

"Susie," Skulduggery said, "where are we? Do you know?"

"We're in Dublin, of course."

"But where is everyone else?"

"Oh," Susie said, laughing lightly. "Is that what's worrying you? We're in Dublin, but it's not the Dublin we're used to. This is where the special people come, the people he chooses. Only good people are allowed here. None of the bad ones. No one like that man who..."

She shuddered. The insects grew agitated around her.

"His name is Silas Nadir," Skulduggery said. "Don't worry, he's long gone. He's the one who sent us here."

She shook her head. "No. He sent us away, but we didn't go where he wanted to send us. We were pulled here instead."

"Who pulled us?"

"He doesn't have a name," Susie said happily.

"Did you meet him?" Valkyrie asked.

"Sort of." Some of the insects settled on Susie's outstretched arms. Their weight didn't seem to bother her. "I heard him. He led me here, and he told me what had happened, explained it all. I'm OK now. I was scared. Now I'm fine."

"Could we talk to him?" Skulduggery asked.

"Maybe," said Susie. "If you're lucky. If he decides to let you hear him."

"How do we make contact?"

Susie laughed. "He's already listening, you silly man."

Skulduggery looked around. "Hello?"

A voice. Soft, but everywhere at once. "Hello."

"Who are you?"

Silence.

Skulduggery waited a moment, then tried again. "You brought us here. Why?"

"To help me," said the voice.

"Help you do what?"

"Get home."

"OK," Skulduggery said. "How do we do that? What do you need?"

No answer.

"If we help you," Valkyrie said, "will you send us back to *our* home?"

A beat. "Yes."

Valkyrie frowned. That had sounded like an amazingly big lie.

"What do you need us to do?" Skulduggery asked.

"Your companion," said the voice. "She is to wait."

"For what?" Skulduggery asked.

"I hate waiting," Valkyrie said.

"She really does."

"I'm very impatient."

"Extraordinarily impatient."

"Wait," said the voice.

Skulduggery tilted his head. "Wait like Susie is waiting?"

"Yes," said the voice.

Valkyrie's gooseflesh rippled at the thought of those bugs landing on her.

"What good does waiting do?" Skulduggery asked. "And why only Valkyrie? Why not me?"

"Is it because I'm a girl?" Valkyrie asked.

"Or because she's alive?" Skulduggery pressed.

Silence.

"Susie Pearse is going to die here," Skulduggery said. "If we don't help her, if we don't bring her home, she's going to die. You do know that, right? Something is happening to her."

"She's thinner," Valkyrie said.

"She's wasting away," Skulduggery said. "Will you let us help her?"

Silence. Then, "No."

Valkyrie looked back at Susie. All of the bugs had landed on her now. They crawled over her stick-thin body, each one vying for space.

"Susie," Skulduggery said, "what are the birds doing now?"

Susie's smile was briefly obscured by a rising stinger. "What birds?" she asked.

The bugs struck at once. Valkyrie cried out in horror and Skulduggery leaped forward, but it was too late. Susie's entire body stiffened. Skulduggery fired his gun and three bugs exploded and the rest panicked, lifted off, filling the air with that awful buzzing as they fled.

Susie took a step to balance herself. Red welts were appearing all over her body. Skulduggery caught her as she fell. The welts grew to hives, massive hives or boils. He lowered her into a sitting position. Her breathing was laboured.

"What did you do?" Valkyrie shouted. "What did you do to her?"

The voice didn't answer.

Skulduggery scooped Susie into his arms. "We'll take her back to the theatre," he said, then walked to the edge of the rooftop and stepped off.

Valkyrie ran after him, leaped, and used the air to control her descent. She landed heavily, but without injury, and covered Skulduggery's back as he carried Susie through the streets.

When they got back to the theatre, she shut the doors as Skulduggery let Susie stand on her own.

"I can't see," Susie murmured.

The hives were enormous. She had three on her face alone. The one on her cheek was mangling her words and the one on her forehead had swollen her eyes. The rest of her body bulged with them. The stingers had even managed to get through her hospital gown.

"You're going to be OK," Skulduggery said. "We're going to get you to a hospital."

"Ghastly," Valkyrie said loudly. "Can you hear us?"

"We're still here," Ghastly said, his voice coming through clearly. "Finbar has found something. A presence, he calls it, in the theatre with you. It's strongest on the main stage. Any idea what it might be?"

"I think we've been talking to it," Skulduggery said. "Nadir shunted us, but this thing, whatever it is, latched on, redirected us here. I don't know how, but it seems to be draining the life out of Susie Pearse. All we've been talking to is a disembodied voice, though."

"Then maybe its physical form is in hiding."

Skulduggery nodded. "It'd be nice to have something solid to hit."

"I don't feel well," Susie murmured.

Valkyrie looked back to reassure her, but gasped and stepped away instead. The hives were pulsating. There was something inside them.

The boil on Susie's neck ruptured wetly and a bug, a small version of the stinger bugs, came crawling out. It spread its wings, covered with pus and slime, and they began to beat. In moments, the beat was a buzz, and it lifted off Susie's shoulder, rising drunkenly through the air.

Valkyrie was too horrified to say anything.

Susie whimpered a little as a boil on her hand burst. The insect fell to the floor and started to crawl.

Skulduggery pulled Valkyrie back.

More boils burst. The boil on the side of Susie's face ruptured, then the one on her forehead. Newly hatched bugs crawled all over her. Susie had stopped whimpering. What remained of her features went slack. She swayed, and toppled backwards. When she hit the ground, she burst the hives on her back with a sickly wet sound.

Valkyrie was running before she knew what was going on. Skulduggery was behind her, pushing her ahead of him, away from the buzzing. They crashed through a door and ran down into darkness. Skulduggery held fire in his right hand, illuminating the stage.

The being who stood there was tall. Human but also not. Yellowing white skin, like unbrushed teeth. He was maybe nine feet tall, naked but perfectly smooth. Large eyes blinked at them as they came to a stop.

Valkyrie's Necromancer ring went cold.

Skulduggery allowed his façade to recede, and tossed the ball of flames at the curtain behind the stage. It caught fire quickly, throwing more light across the floorboards. Then Skulduggery took out his gun, thumbed back the hammer, and pointed. "You know what this is?"

The figure observed him. "A weapon," he said. His voice came both from his own mouth and from all around them.

"Yes, it is," Skulduggery replied. "And it can splatter your brains all over the wall if you don't take us home right now."

"Your weapons cannot hurt me."

"I disagree. You have a body. Bodies are made to be damaged."

"I will not do as you ask."

Skulduggery jumped on to the stage. Valkyrie followed.

"You drained the life out of the girl," Skulduggery said. "You killed her. Why?"

"I need to be strong," said the figure.

"How many people have you managed to drag here and use up?"

A moment of silence. "Not enough. One more. I will be strong with one more."

"You're not getting Valkyrie," said Skulduggery. "If you try, we'll stop you. That's what we do. We stop things like you from getting what they want. So do yourself a favour. Admit defeat. Give up. Let us go. It won't end happily for you if you don't."

Skulduggery hadn't noticed them yet, but there were bugs in the rafters above them. As if they knew Valkyrie was watching, they detached themselves and started flying. Their buzzing filled the air. Such a pretty sound. She didn't know why she hadn't noticed before. In fact, the bugs themselves were kind of pretty, now she got a good look at them. They reminded her of hummingbirds.

Something was shaking her arm. A gloved hand. Skulduggery's gloved hand.

"Valkyrie," he said. He sounded so far away. Even his grip on her arm seemed dull. Numbed.

"Release her!" Skulduggery demanded.

That tall man with the white skin had a small smile on his face. A peaceful smile. Valkyrie realised her own lips were curling upwards. She wondered if her smile was as peaceful as his. She didn't mind if it wasn't. She didn't mind anything any more. Her whole body was warm and numb. Except for her finger. That Necromancer ring was making her finger cold. She wanted to take it off, let it fall, and just be warm all over.

If you do that, you die. He's controlling you. He's dampening your thoughts.

She smiled at the voice in her head. It was her own voice, but different. This was another thing she didn't mind. Not even Darquesse could ruin her good mood.

The ring is cold. It senses death.

Silly Darquesse. Darquesse didn't matter. The only things that mattered were those pretty, pretty hummingbirds flying down towards her. She raised her arms so that they could land, but shadows curled round her right hand. Was she doing that? Some part of her was. Some part of her was listening to Darquesse.

Fight it. Fight or die.

The shadows lashed at the ground, tearing through the floorboards, like they knew exactly where to go. Valkyrie watched the wood splinter, giggling at the way it came apart. The shadows convulsed, lashed again, and now Skulduggery was hurrying over. The tall white-skinned man frowned.

There was another tall white-skinned man lying beneath the floorboards. His eyes were closed. He was resting. No. The ring was cold. He was dead. It was the same white-skinned man. How was that possible?

Valkyrie frowned.

The hummingbirds came to settle on her arms and she blinked at them. Those hummingbirds looked a lot like bugs...

"Get off me!" Valkyrie shouted, stumbling back. Her shadows slashed at the bloated bodies and the bugs went into a frenzy. She pushed at the air to give herself some space, then clicked the fingers of both hands. The fire kept them away, but they buzzed round her angrily, their stingers flexed.

"Are you back with me?" Skulduggery shouted, pulling at floorboards.

"I am," she called. "Is that him?"

"Let's find out," Skulduggery said, pressing his gun against the corpse's head. "Hey, big guy. This is your physical body, am I right?"

The white-skinned man didn't answer.

"That's what I thought," Skulduggery continued. "So you hide your body here while you collect enough energy to kick-start it again. That's perfectly normal. Nothing strange about that. But if I pull this trigger, all that work is for nothing. And, while you might be able to siphon off enough life force from your victims to bring yourself back from the dead, scooping up your own brains wouldn't be quite so easy, would it?"

"Step away from there," said the white-skinned man.

"Call off your insect friends."

One of the bugs got too close. Valkyrie prepared to thrust a fistful of fire into its underside – and then all at once they withdrew. The buzzing died until she couldn't hear it any more.

She let the flames go out, but kept a watchful eye on their flame-lapped surroundings. Smoke was quickly filling the theatre.

"Send us home," Skulduggery said.

"I cannot," the white-skinned man responded. "I only have the power to bring you to me when you travel. If I could initiate travel myself, I would not be trapped here."

Skulduggery didn't move the gun from the corpse's head. "Ghastly," he said loudly. "Can you hear me?"

Valkyrie moved a little closer to him in case the bugs came back.

"I'm here," Ghastly said. "Any progress?"

"We've reached an understanding. All we need is a Shunter."

"Bear with me," said Ghastly. "I should have one here in under an hour."

Skulduggery waved his hand and the fire was instantly under his control. He looked at the white-skinned man.

"Get comfortable," he said.

Less than forty minutes later, Skulduggery was sitting at the edge of the floorboard grave site, his feet resting on the corpse's chest. Valkyrie sat with her back against his, keeping watch. A perimeter of fire encircled them. The white-skinned man, or the ghost of the white-skinned man, stood in the middle of the stage. Nobody had said anything in all that time.

Then Ghastly broke the silence. "We have our Shunter. He's trying to lock on to you, but there's something blocking him."

Valkyrie got up while Skulduggery leaned over, tapping his gun against the corpse's nose. "Whatever you used to redirect us here, turn it off."

"You must help me," said the ghost. "I have been trapped here for centuries. All I want to do is return home."

"Where is home?"

"Far from here. A dimension of peace and wonder."

"You didn't show Susie Pearse much peace and wonder," Valkyrie said. "And we don't even *know* how many other people you've killed."

"I did what I had to do, and I was saddened by it," said the ghost. "But if you stop me from returning home, their deaths will have been in vain."

"Their deaths are already in vain," Skulduggery said. "Stopping you from benefiting from those deaths doesn't make that any less true."

The ghost shook his head slowly, and looked away.

"We have a lock," Ghastly said. "Get ready."

Valkyrie started to flicker. After a moment, Skulduggery did, too.

"I'll be waiting for you," the ghost said.

"No, you won't," Skulduggery replied, and pulled the trigger.

Dublin City was packed full of people and cars crammed the streets. Valkyrie stood on the pavement and watched the world move around her.

Skulduggery appeared at her elbow, his façade in place. "No sign of Nadir," he said.

"The hunt continues," Valkyrie murmured. She looked at him. "Don't suppose Susie's body came back with us?"

"I'm afraid not. We'll do what we can for her family, though. Ghastly is seeing to it."

Valkyrie nodded. "She saved my life."

"She deserved better."

A driver blasted his horn at another driver. Curses followed. Valkyrie welcomed the distraction.

"I missed," Skulduggery said.

"Sorry?"

"When I fired," he said. "I missed. I pulled the trigger when I was leaning over the body, but I flickered out. I found the bullet in the floor when I was talking to Ghastly just now."

"So that... *thing*, whatever it is, is still there? Still waiting to pluck someone out of their shunt?"

"I'm afraid so."

"Damn it."

"Indeed."

The city darkened and the lights came on.

EYES OF THE BEHOLDER

It was a subjective thing, beauty.

Billy-Ray Sanguine had known this since he was a kid, since before he'd had to scoop out his own eyes to make room for the magic. Back then, though, it was a pretty face that would catch his attention or, if he was feeling in a particularly soulful mood, a sunset that held the sky just right. Beautiful things, yes, but nothing extraordinary about them. Nothing life-changing.

Then he'd taken those instruments to his eyes. He remembered the feel of them vividly. Cold and sharp. He remembered the pain, and the way his hands trembled. His body had resisted, had fought against his intention. A curious sensation, that, to have your own body try to sabotage your ambition. His will proved stronger than his natural instincts, of course, and he emerged triumphant, traumatised, and blind.

In the year that followed, he feared he would never see again. But gradually a new kind of sight came to him. A different kind. He saw what was in front of him – he saw the physical, he saw what everyone saw – but he also saw deeper. He saw colours both as they appeared and as they were. Darkness became light. Light became more. The most ordinary thing became a beauty powerful enough to stop his heart.

But nothing, in all his years and his travels, had prepared him for the transfixing beauty that was Tanith Low.

She was a pretty girl – he knew that when he first saw her. Fun, too, although that sword of hers caused him some problems. But over the years he noticed something. She was growing more beautiful every time he saw her.

A subjective thing, beauty, but his eyeless gaze allowed him to appreciate her in a way no one else could. She shone. She shone with a light so brilliant it scared him. Her face, her smile... These were things that stayed in his mind. Took root there. Grew. Flourished.

He was in love.

The idea thrilled him. He'd never expected to fall in love. Sociopaths often found it difficult. But he'd managed it because he'd met the right person. He'd found *her*.

He'd asked Tanith Low to marry him, and she'd said yes.

He would have danced if he'd been a dancer. He would have sung if he'd been a singer. But Billy-Ray was a killer, and so he celebrated his love by killing.

It felt good, to have purpose again. He didn't mind admitting that he'd been through some dark times recently. He had wandered aimlessly, made bad decisions, battled injury and doubt and wrestled with existential demons. But he had emerged the other side, stronger and more positive than ever before. With the world in turmoil around him, with the Sanctuaries about to go to war, it made a nice change for him to be the one to have found his centre. And it was all because of a crazy little thing called love.

The song played in his head as he burrowed through the earth.

They had their problems, of course they did. What couple didn't? She was possessed by a Remnant and he had four God-Killer weapons stashed away that he'd told her he'd destroyed. Big deal. Every couple keeps secrets. It was the way of things. It was all part of being in a grown-up relationship.

He didn't mind that she called the shots, either. He was happy to do whatever she asked and kill whoever she told him to. He'd just killed a sorcerer in Nantucket after the idiot had announced that he'd figured out where to find Darquesse. What a dumb move. The guy hadn't even been telling the truth. It didn't matter. He had to die. Tanith had asked Billy-Ray to do it, and Billy-Ray was going to do whatever made his fiancée happy.

Fiancée. He smiled.

He adjusted his heading, turning north, trusting in his unerring sense of direction to guide him back into her arms. He was enjoying the sensation of tunnelling. For too long, it looked like he might never be able to use his magic properly again – not since the girl had cut him, and then that 'doctor' had made such a mess of stitching him back together.

But he was whole again, and healthy, and he sped through the ground like a fish through water. It was just like old times. Just like...

He frowned. Wait. What the hell was this?

Something moving up behind him. Something big and fast. He glanced back, glimpsing it through the shifting rock. A worm, bigger than a man, with teeth bigger than his head.

Adrenaline shot through his body and he piled on the speed. So concerned was he about what was on his tail that he almost missed the vibrations coming towards him. At the last moment he veered left, and now they were both after him. More vibrations on either side. Three of them. He was being herded.

He broke for the surface, the rock opening and spitting him out into an old house, big and dark and cold. The worms didn't follow him up here. They didn't have to.

Two men and a woman stood waiting. He knew them. Gepard Voke, narrow and tall and blue-eyed. Persephone Grief was to his left, willowy and dark-haired with eyes the colour of blood. To Voke's right stood Barnaby, black-eyed and black-hearted.

None of those eyes were real, of course. They were cryolite glass, sitting easily in empty sockets.

"Billy-Ray," said Voke. "What *are* you doing? The Sanctuaries are almost at war, friend will soon be fighting friend, brother fighting brother... This is the perfect time for people like you to work both sides against the other and make some serious money. Or whatever it is you're actually paid in these days. Instead, here you are, killing for free."

"All for the love of a good woman," said Persephone. "You've changed, William."

"Don't call me that," Sanguine said. "You, of all people, are not allowed to call me that."

Voke laughed. "Hear that? Hear the way he talks now? What happened to the accent? Where's all the *y'awls* and the *yee-hars*? Billy-Ray, you have done sold out, boy."

"He's been away from us too long," said Persephone. "He's let his accent fade. Probably wants to fit in with his English lady friend. Is that it? Is that why you're softening?"

"I think you're right," Voke said, nodding. "When he's working on his own for long periods of time, as he likes to do, he sounds as though he just came in off the ranch. But when he's around people, our boy here has a tendency to forget who he is. Ain't that right, Billy-Ray?"

Sanguine ignored them, switched his gaze to the silent member of the trio. "Been a while, Barnaby."

"It has at that," Barnaby replied in his quiet voice.

"What're you doing running with these two? Thought you had more discriminating taste."

Barnaby shrugged.

Sanguine turned his attention back to Voke. "What are those things in the ground?"

"Aren't they special?" Persephone asked, smiling. "Aren't they just too cute? The big one's called Rex. The slightly bigger one is Spot. And the runt of the litter? That's William. He's my favourite."

"Yeah," Sanguine said. "Adorable. Now what the hell are they?"

"They don't have an actual name," Voke said. "A Shunter took an expedition team to an alternate world where these critters are at the top of the food chain. They caught these ones, brought them back, and we've been training them ever since. We call them groundsharks."

Sanguine shook his head immediately. "That's a stupid name. Makes them sound like little shark fins slicing through the living-room carpet."

"I wanted to call them razorworms," said Persephone.

"That's a damn sight better than groundsharks."

Voke frowned. "They've been named. You can't rename them. We wrote the name down."

"Scribble it out and write razorworms," Sanguine said.

"No, we will not be doing that. We decided on a name and we're going to stick to it. We took a vote."

"I've changed my mind," Barnaby said. "I prefer razorworms."

Sanguine ignored Voke's glower. "And congratulations, by the way, on introducing a new species into the food chain on this world. Absolutely nothing could possibly go wrong there."

"You think we didn't consider the implications?" Voke asked. "They're all male, so they can't breed and they won't spread."

"How do you know they're all male?" Sanguine asked. "How can you tell? They're big worms. Worms are hermaphrodites. What's their life cycle? How do they reproduce? For all we know, all three of them are pregnant and they're laying thousands of eggs right now. But then that's just like you, Gepard. You don't think things through. You never have."

"And you're the mastermind, are you?" Voke laughed. "You're a hitman, Billy-Ray. That's all you are. You take orders and you do what you're told. Where's the great strategy there?"

Sanguine shrugged. "I have my own plans, ticking away in the background. And I may take orders, but it's always on my terms. I'm my own man, Gepard. You three, however? You've hired yourselves out to the Supreme Council, haven't you? It was your little razorworms I encountered protecting the London Sanctuary a few months ago, right? You're not guns for hire. You're lackeys. Lapdogs."

Persephone chuckled. "Oh, Billy-Ray. You are not doing yourself any favours right now by insulting us."

"Grand Mage Bisahalani sent us to track you down and bring you to him in shackles," Barnaby said.

"Something about the murder of Quintin Strom," said Voke, smiling. "We told him shackles won't hold you, no more than they'd hold any of us. But Sanctuary people... well. Some things they just don't understand."

"So you're here to kill me, that it?" Sanguine asked.

"That's it," Persephone said.

Sanguine held his arms open wide. "Then you're welcome to try."

They went for their guns and Sanguine ran at them and dived into the ground, the darkness enveloping him. He felt the instant tremor as a razorworm closed in from below, and two more tremors from in front as he swam through the cold earth.

A razorworm burst up and Sanguine spun sideways, rocks parting for him as he dodged those teeth. The razorworm's body was too long to turn on the spot. It kept going, arcing as it went, and Sanguine burrowed through the loop.

Voke was suddenly beside him, gun in hand, and Sanguine batted it to one side. The sound of the gunshot was lost amid the rumbling thunder of shifting rock, but the flash was as bright as a bolt of lightning. With one hand holding the gun at bay, Sanguine's other hand closed round Voke's throat. They spun through the cold rock, twisting and turning as tremors moved in from all sides.

Voke lost his grip on the gun and the earth swallowed it as they twirled. Sanguine's forehead crunched into Voke's nose and he left Voke where he was and rose quickly to the surface, bursting into the still air of the old house, Persephone and Barnaby emerging right behind him.

He ran as they fired, passing through a wall. He jumped on to the old table ahead and leaped for the ceiling. He got his fingertips to it and was sucked upwards just as Persephone appeared beneath him. He felt a bullet snap at his trouser leg.

The first floor of the old house was just as dark and cold and empty as the rest. He ran to the landing, found the stairs leading up. The staircase leading down had collapsed years ago.

The wall cracked beside him and he swung a punch as Barnaby emerged. His timing was off, though, and it merely clipped him. They fell against each other, struggling for the gun in Barnaby's hand. Sanguine tripped him, but lost his grip and was forced to reel backwards as Barnaby fired. He fell through the wall, the wood and the plaster resealing behind him. From the landing, Barnaby kept firing, the wall failing to even slow the bullets down. Sanguine rolled to his right, cursing, then sprang up and passed into the next room in time for Persephone to crack her elbow into his jaw.

Persephone jammed her gun into the side of her head as he fell to his knees. She was saying something, probably something cool as she was about to pull the trigger, but that had always been her problem. She talked too much.

His hand flashed up, fingers closing around the barrel, pushing it away as

Persephone fired. It was an automatic. Meant it needed the slide to rack back in order for the next bullet to enter the chamber. He kept his hand tight around the barrel, jamming the slide as he stood, his free hand flicking open his straight razor. Barnaby crashed into him as he slashed at Persephone. He missed her throat by a fraction.

Barnaby kept coming, shoving Sanguine back. Sanguine grabbed his wrist, keeping the gun away. Barnaby fired. Fired again. Sanguine hit a wall and it crumbled and he passed through into it. Barnaby fired again as his wrist emerged from the other side. Sanguine dropped his razor and bent Barnaby's arm back on itself and his finger closed over Barnaby's own, and as Barnaby's face followed his hand through the wall Sanguine squeezed the trigger and the gunshot was the loudest so far.

Sanguine stepped back in the sudden silence. Barnaby's body hung limply, half in, half out of the wall.

Sanguine stooped, picked up the straight razor and the fallen gun. Persephone ran in, eyes wide with alarm. She saw Barnaby and screamed, raised her gun to Sanguine and pulled the trigger three times before she realised nothing was happening.

"Still jammed," Sanguine told her, and shot her in the heart.

He passed through the floor, through the ceiling of the room below, and then dropped to the ground.

Gepard Voke stood there, blood running from his nose and dripping from his chin on to his shirt. He spat. "You kill them?"

Sanguine gave a little shrug. "They're dead."

"They were my friends. They were your friends, too, once upon a time."

"Naw," said Sanguine, walking towards him. "I never had friends. I just had people I hadn't killed yet. Hey, Gepard, what do you think of my accent now? Still think I've sold out?"

Voke held his ground, but his right leg was shaking so hard Sanguine thought it'd fall off.

With a trembling voice, Voke said, "We always knew there was something wrong with you."

"Damn right something's wrong with me," Sanguine said. "I'm in love."

He punched Voke so hard one of his glass eyes popped out. Voke reeled, stumbled, and Sanguine killed him before he straightened.

He watched the blood drip from his straight razor. It was a startling, mesmerising red. A beautiful red. Even the corpse was beautiful. The way it lay there, crumpled, devoid of life, but in its own way complete. It didn't need life to make it beautiful. Few corpses did. Sanguine struggled to think of one person he'd killed that death hadn't made more beautiful. There was only one person he knew whose perfection would be marred by death's veil. But he was never going to let that happen.

Beneath his feet, he felt the vibrations as the razorworms circled. Their activity brought a smile to his face. He'd been wondering about this, wondering what he could possibly get that would be as special as she was.

Three razorworms from another dimension, he reckoned, was as good a wedding gift as any.

THE BUTTON

S omewhere in the distance, a train rattled on its tracks.

Conor sat in his kitchen with the curtains drawn, the lamp on the table casting its searing eye over his handiwork. It was the size of a shoebox, and wooden. Heavy. Inside were things he did not, could not, understand. There were gears and levers and finely balanced cogs and symbols painstakingly etched into it all. He didn't know what they meant, didn't know what they were for, but he had seen them in his head for as long as he could remember. Transferring those symbols to metal and wood, after all these years, was... well, it was wonderful. It was a relief. It was like he'd been tense his whole life, every muscle knotted and his teeth gritted and his eyes screwed shut, and now suddenly he was relaxing, and a strange sort of euphoric calm spread through him.

He took a screwdriver from the junkyard of tools on the table and fixed the lid in place. His hands were covered in nicks and cuts. He had run out of plasters days ago. Some of the cuts still stung. There were particular gears and symbols that required blood. He didn't know why – he just knew that they did. He saw it in his head. He always had. This device, this box, these designs, these gears and levers and symbols – they had always been a part of who he was. This was all he thought about. It was why he didn't finish school. It was why he couldn't hold a job. It was why Cathy had left him. This device had ruined any chance he'd ever had at happiness – but here it was, finished. A wooden box with a big red button on its lid.

Conor straightened his back. Vertebrae cracked. How long had he been sitting hunched over like that? How long had he been sitting here? He became suddenly aware of how full his bladder was, and how empty his stomach. He needed to go for a walk. He needed fresh air. Was it even daytime? The curtains were closed and everywhere but the table was in darkness. It was night. But what night? Was it still the weekend?

There was something over by the door, a shape in the gloom. Like a man, standing very still. Conor squinted at it, then turned his head, looked at it out of the corner of his eye. No matter how he viewed the thing, this coat or this shadow or whatever it was, it still looked like a man. A tall man. In a hat.

Conor frowned at it.

"Hello, Conor," said the man.

A bolt of fear and fright shot from Conor's belly to his chest, but his body remained still. Would his legs even work if he tried to jump up? He'd been sitting here for so long he doubted it.

Conor's mouth was dry. How long had it been since he'd taken a drink of water? His voice cracked. The question he asked was not *Who are you?* or *What do you want?*, two questions he felt needed answers, but rather, "How long have you been standing there?"

"Just a few minutes," said the man. He had a reassuring voice. It was smooth. "You didn't hear me come in. You were otherwise occupied. What is that you've got there?"

"You can't have it," said Conor. "If you want to rob me, rob me. I have a little money somewhere. But you can't have this."

"I'm not here to rob you," said the man. "What happens if you press that button, Conor?"

The pressure on his bladder, the dryness of his mouth, the emptiness of his belly, and now a headache, rising slowly from the heat that was stinging his skin and making him sweat. He felt sick. He *was* sick. He needed to lie down.

"I don't know," said Conor.

The tall man in the hat moved his head ever so slightly. "You don't know what it does? But you made it, didn't you?"

Conor nodded.

"How did you know what to do?"

"I've always known," said Conor. "My whole life I've known. I had these images in my head. But I couldn't see them clear enough until... sorry, what date is it?"

"The twenty-first," said the tall man. "Four days before Christmas."

Conor frowned. "That can't be right. It was the eighth just... just a few days ago."

"Time got away from you," said another voice in the gloom, somewhere over by the window. It was a girl's voice.

"Who are you?" Conor asked at last.

"No one in particular," said the man. "We have a job to do, that's all. We help people."

"I don't need your help."

"You may not," said the girl, "but everyone else does." She walked forward a bit, until the peripheral glow from the lamp could pick out her features. She was pretty, with dark hair. Wearing black. Seventeen or eighteen, no older. "What does the button do?" she asked.

"I told you," said Conor. "I don't know."

"Then why is your finger on it?"

He looked down. There it was, his finger, resting on the big red button like it had no intention of ever moving. He frowned. He couldn't remember putting it there and yet... yet it seemed there was no other possible place he could put it. His finger belonged on that button.

"I'm sorry," Conor said. "I'm not feeling well."

"Conor Delaney," said the man, "take your finger off the button."

And Conor almost did it. Without thinking, his finger rose a fraction before the weight of his obligation forced it back down again.

Obligation? What obligation? What the hell was going on?

"How did you do that?" he asked the man. "How did you make me do that?"

The man made a sound, like a dissatisfied grunt, and it was the girl who spoke. "How did you disobey? Did you take a name?"

"What?" said Conor. "What do you mean?"

"How did you disobey?"

"I don't know what you're talking about, do you understand? I don't know who you are or what you're doing here."

"They're saying the world will end," said the girl.

This stopped Conor for a moment. "What?"

"They're saying the world will end," the girl repeated. "Did you hear that?"

"Are you... are you talking about that Mayan thing? What about it? The Mayan calendar ends on the twenty-first of December. So what? It's a calendar. They ran out of room, or they stopped calculating, or a new cycle begins again or something... I'm sorry, what does that have to do with anything? It's nonsense."

"Do you know what a Sensitive is, Conor?" the girl asked. "It's a psychic. You believe in psychics?"

"No," said Conor. "I don't believe in astrology, either, or tarot cards, or palm reading."

The girl nodded. "Palm reading is silly. So is astrology. Most tarot-card readers haven't a clue what they're doing. I met one once who assured me I had a happy life ahead of me – so she's pretty obviously an idiot. But psychics have been predicting the end of the world, Conor, to coincide with the end of the Mayan calendar."

"So?"

"So we think the end of the world starts here," said the man.

Conor frowned. "In Ireland? You think the end of the world starts here in this country?"

"Actually, I think it starts here in this kitchen."

Conor blinked. "You can't be serious."

"I can be, but rarely am."

"And what? You think this button kicks it all off?" Conor said, almost laughing. "You think that's what I've been making? This is a box of gears and junk and things that don't make sense! There's not a single computer chip or piece of technology in it. It's not connected to anything. I don't know what will happen when I push the button, but whatever it is will happen in this box and this box alone. It's not going to set off a chain reaction, or explode, or detonate nuclear warheads, or... It's just a silly box."

"A silly box that has been in your head for your entire life," said the man.

"But now it's out," said Conor. "It's not in my head any more. It's gone. I don't have to... I don't have to think about it any more."

"How's your mother, Conor?"

The smile faded from Conor's face.

"She's doing well, from what I gather," the man continued. "Responding to the treatment. She still draws on the wall, of course. Strange symbols. Strange designs. Gears and levers and a big red button."

"My mother is ill."

The man nodded his head in the shadows. "Like her father before her. And his father before him. Stretching back through the generations. And all of you with this design in your minds. This box. That button. But you, Conor, you're the only one who saw it clearly enough to construct it."

"I've broken the cycle," said Conor. "I'm not going to end up in an asylum like the rest of them. I've done it. I've made it. Now I get to have a normal life. Now that my duty is almost done, I get to be free of it."

"What duty?" asked the girl.

The headache was getting worse. He was getting hotter. He probably had a fever. "Did I say duty? I don't know. That's not the word I meant to use."

"But it's the one you did use," said the man. "Do you have a duty, Conor? Is that what it feels like?"

"I'm not sure I... I..."

"That box has cursed your bloodline for hundreds of years," the man said. "Maybe more. You were compelled to construct it, weren't you? You didn't have a choice. You may not even have been fully aware of what you were doing. You have a duty to that box, don't you, Conor?"

Conor nodded. "An obligation," he whispered.

"An obligation to that box. Why is your finger on the button, Conor? Is that part of your obligation? Once you build it, you set it off?"

Something broke in Conor's heart, and tears came to his eyes. "I have to press it," he said, his face crumpling. "I just have to press it once and it'll all be over. I'll be able to walk away and never think about it again."

"Pressing that button will hurt a lot of people."

"It's just a box," Conor sobbed.

"It's more than a box."

"It's just a box, I'm telling you. It doesn't do anything. I'm not a scientist or an engineer. I'm just a man. I'm just ordinary. I wouldn't know how to build anything that would hurt people. I don't want to hurt anyone. I just want to be able to walk away."

There was a sound outside. A car pulling up. A line of light swept in through the crack in the curtains and brushed by the man's jaw. It looked like his skin was white as chalk, or he was wearing a mask or something.

"Be right back," said the man, and slipped through the door.

"Who's out there?" Conor asked.

"Some people," said the girl. "There's been a race to find you. We got here first."

"What do they want?"

There was a cry from outside, and a sudden light like a bursting flame, and then it was gone again.

"They want the box," said the girl. "They want to sell it, or use it, or worship it. I don't know. Some of these people just don't make any sense to me. You look tired."

"I feel sick."

Outside there was another sound. Loud. Abrupt.

"Was that a gunshot?" asked Conor.

"It was," said the girl.

"Aren't you scared?"

"You've got your finger on a button that will end the world," the girl said. "Why should I be scared of guns that aren't even aimed at me?"

"I'm not going to end the world."

"You've got your finger on the button."

"I can barely work out how to make calls on my own phone – why do you think I know how to destroy the planet? This is ridiculous. Please leave me alone."

"I wish we could. But if we do, you'll press that button, and you'll kill us all. You'll kill my friends and my parents and my little sister. I can't let you do that, Conor."

"I won't be hurting anyone. The box doesn't do anything. It's just a stupid box with a stupid button, but it's been in my head for my entire life, like a constant whine in my ear. All I have to do to be rid of it is just press the thing. That's all. Easy as that. I'll press it, no one will get hurt, the world won't end, and I won't have to listen to that whine any more. I won't have to dream about gears and symbols. I'll be able to close my eyes and not see how one cog fits into the other. I'll be able to live in the kind of peace that my mother never could.

"You don't... you don't know. You don't know what it was like, seeing her... seeing what happened to her. Seeing how bad it got. When I was ten years old, she sat me down and told me these dreams I had would only get worse. She told me they'd consume my life, like they were consuming hers. This is my chance to escape that madness. Please, just leave me alone. This is the only chance I'll ever have."

"It isn't madness you're suffering from," said the girl. "My friend, the one that's out there right now fighting on your front lawn, told me what you are. You're a conduit for an idea, an idea that was planted centuries ago. It's grown inside the minds of your ancestors, been added to, been improved... and here, tonight, it's finally ready. You're not mad, Conor. Your mother isn't mad. You're just open to a stream of information that the rest of us aren't."

"So who planted it?" Conor asked. "This idea you're talking about. Whose idea was it? The Mayans?"

"The Mayan people just foresaw the end," said the man from beside the door. Conor hadn't even heard him come back in. "They had nothing to do with this. We don't know who started it. We don't even know if ending the world was what was originally intended. All we know is that our Sensitives had visions of a man in a dark room, building a box, and when he pressed the button everything just... ended."

"Then how did you know it was me?"

"They heard a train in the distance."

"That's it? That's all?"

"That narrowed it down," said the man. "A few other hints. A few other clues. Why haven't you pushed the button?"

"Why haven't I...? But you don't want me to."

"That's not why you haven't pushed it. Your finger's on it. There's nothing stopping you. Why haven't you?"

"I don't... I'm not sure."

"It's because you know that it isn't just a silly box and that isn't just a silly button. You believe us, don't you?"

"No, I... Oh, God. I don't know."

"Will you give us the box, Conor?"

"What will happen then?"

"We'll take it somewhere safe," said the girl. "We can't dismantle it and we can't destroy it – something might go wrong. But we'll take care of it. We'll hide it away where no one will ever find it."

"It won't be used to hurt anyone," the man said. "I promise."

"And me?" said Conor. "What will happen to me?"

The man hesitated. "I won't lie to you. You'll probably always feel that urge to push the button. That won't go away. You'll have to live with it for the rest of your life."

"But I'm so close. I'm so close to leaving it behind."

"We're asking you to make a sacrifice," the girl said. "We're asking you to continue living with this so that the rest of the world can continue living. Please, Conor."

More tears now, but they came silently. Conor lifted his finger from the button, and with his other hand he pushed the box slowly across the table. The girl came forward to take it. She wore a black ring, Conor noticed. For a moment it seemed to play with the shadows, and then the girl was lifting the box and stepping back, taking great care.

The last remaining dregs of strength drained from Conor's body. He was exhausted, confused, scared, and all he wanted to do was lunge across the table and push that big red button before the girl took it away.

"Thank you," said the man, and Conor just nodded.

The man looked down at something – a pocket watch? – and opened the door. "Two hours until midnight," he said. "Should be loads of time."

"Loads of time for what?" Conor asked, even though he knew the man hadn't been speaking to him.

The girl walked slowly out, taking the box with her. Conor forced himself to remain where he was.

"There's a woman who believes the souls of all her dead lovers are trapped in the centre of the earth," said the man. "She wants to crack the world open to free them."

Conor frowned. "Can she do it?"

"Yes. So we have to stop her before she kills us all."

"But... but didn't your psychics say that I'd be responsible for the end of the world?"

"Some of them did, yes. And some others said that she would. We've averted eight potential apocalypses already today, and she'll be our last. Once midnight comes, we can relax. Then we just have to hope the Americans don't mess up."

"The Americans?"

"A day can last forty-nine hours around the world," said the man, walking out and leaving Conor sitting there at his kitchen table. "A lot can happen in a day."

OUTSIDE THE MURDER-COTTAGE, BY THE SEA

A VALKYRIE CAIN ADVENTURE

S he didn't look especially weird.

That's what Valkyrie had been expecting: a weird-looking weirdo, maybe dressed in ragged, blood-splattered clothes, hissing abominable secrets to herself as she emerged from her murder-cottage.

But, now that she *had* emerged, she seemed pretty normal, all things considered. Not as tall as Valkyrie, but around the same age, with a good haircut, dressed in decidedly non-ragged jeans and a non-blood-splattered and actually-quite-nice crop top. It was off-white and lace-up. A cute outfit.

Valkyrie hopped down off the low wall and walked over, smiling. The murder-cottage was small and out of the way, nestling contentedly by the side of a narrow, rarely used road. Beyond the sand dunes and the grasses, the Atlantic threw itself against the shore with a pleasingly determined rhythm.

This girl didn't seem like the type to have a murder-cottage. They were normally reserved for the weirdos and the lunatics and the seriously evil. This girl didn't come across as seriously evil, despite her name.

"Can I help you?" Wretched Darling asked, frowning as Valkyrie neared.

"I like your top," Valkyrie told her. "Where'd you get it?"

"I don't remember," said Wretched, her frown deepening. "I know you. I recognise you. You're that girl who almost destroyed the world."

Valkyrie grinned. "That was my reflection, actually. Well, my reflection inhabited by a version of me that – you know what? It's way too complicated. Yeah, I'm the girl who almost destroyed the world. But that was ages ago. It was, what? Seven years ago? Eight? I've moved on. So has the world. Name's Valkyrie. And you're Wretched, right? I've heard about you, too."

There was a small wooden gate between them, old but freshly painted. Wretched's eyes flickered to the latch, probably wondering if it would be enough to delay Valkyrie if Wretched decided to dart back into the cottage. Valkyrie allowed her smile to broaden, letting her know that it most certainly would not. Not in the slightest.

Wretched folded her arms and cocked her hip and raised an eyebrow – all very casual, all very innocent. "So," she said, "what can I help you with?"

"I'm here to see your parents, actually."

"I'm afraid you got your details wrong. My parents live in Kildare."

Valkyrie shrugged. "I know. I still came to see them."

"Well, they're not here."

"Are you sure?"

"I'm very sure."

"I heard they were here."

"They're not, though."

"That's puzzling. That is puzzling. See, I heard you brought them with you when you left Kildare last night."

Wretched didn't say anything.

"That's where my partner is," Valkyrie continued. "Skulduggery Pleasant – you heard of him? I know you're not one to pay much attention to the goings-on of Sanctuaries and stuff like that... but if you recognise me then you *must* know who Skulduggery is."

She nodded. "I know who he is."

Valkyrie placed her hands on top of the gate and leaned in. "He's in Kildare – at your parents' house, actually. Looking around. Investigating."

It seemed as if Wretched wasn't going to respond to that, but then she said, "Why?", like she'd just remembered to act alarmed.

"Your mum called him," Valkyrie answered. "She said she and your dad were worried about you. They were worried you were headed to a dark place. Her words, not mine. You headed to a dark place, Wretched?"

Wretched shook her head.

"I drove here, and Skulduggery went to Kildare to talk to them. I don't want you to get mad or anything, but when he knocked no one answered – and so he broke the door down." Valkyrie winced. "Are you mad? It's OK to be mad. In fact, I wish you would be mad. He's always breaking doors down and he won't stop until more people get mad about it. Are you mad?"

"Yes."

"You don't look mad."

"I am."

"You don't look worried, either. I swear, if someone broke down the door of my parents' place, I'd be freaking the hell out, Wretched. I really would. I'd be all, like, *what did you do that for?* And *where are my folks? Are my folks OK? Are they in danger?* But you're pretty chill, standing there in that gorgeous top. Have you remembered where you got it yet, by the way?"

Wretched shook her head again.

"You sure?"

"Somewhere online," said Wretched.

"So, yeah, we can't find your parents. Just to remind you, in case you've forgotten or in case you didn't hear me right, because none of this appears to be bothering you too much, they were worried that you were heading down a dark path. Something to do with the Faceless Ones. Are you a worshipper, then? A follower? Your parents, they told Skulduggery *they* weren't, but they said you met someone...? Is that right? You met someone and you were basically recruited into the whole religion? I'm not big on religion myself. I don't like worshipping anything that isn't my girlfriend, know what I mean? But the way it sounds, and I might be wrong, but the way it sounds is that you were indoctrinated into a cult."

"The Church of the Faceless isn't a cult," Wretched said, her eyes narrowing slightly, her nostrils flaring.

"Huh," said Valkyrie. "That's the most emotion you've shown in all the time I've known you. Which, admittedly, is, like, four minutes. But still... interesting."

Wretched stood up straighter, and put her hands on her hips. "What do you want?"

"Like I said, I'm looking for your parents."

"And, like I said, they're not here."

"You did say that," said Valkyrie. "Yes, you did. And you're absolutely, positively, *resolutely* sure that they're not? I mean, I don't know your folks. They might be really quiet people. They might be in the back room of your lovely little murder-cottage and you might not even know it."

"My what?"

"Sorry?"

"My murder-cottage?"

"Your...? Who called it that?"

"You did."

"Seriously? I called it a murder-cottage?"

"You did."

"Oh wow," said Valkyrie, "that is embarrassing. I thought I was only *thinking* that. But, y'know, since you brought it up, *have* you murdered anyone in there?"

"No," Wretched said through gritted teeth.

"No, you haven't murdered anyone in there *recently*, or no, you haven't murdered anyone in there *at all*?"

"I haven't murdered *anyone*."

"That you can think of."

"Anyone!"

"In the last three hours."

"I'm not a murderer!"

"OK, OK," Valkyrie said, standing back now, holding up her hands. "Calm down. Let's not go crazy. Let's not kill me." She laughed. "You wouldn't kill me, would you? I know we've just met and everything, and I know I suspect you of murdering your parents, but I feel like we could be friends. I feel like we could hang out, maybe do each other's hair, maybe tell each other what websites we buy clothes from."

"You... you think I killed my parents?"

"I would have assumed that was obvious by now."

"How dare you."

Valkyrie laughed. "I know, right? You think *that's* rude, you should try being me for a day! I suspect *everyone* of *everything*! I meet someone and *bam!* I immediately think they're a bad guy, like a serial killer, or someone who started worshipping the Faceless Ones a few years ago and whose parents tried to convince her to stop worshipping them and in return she killed them to prove her loyalty to her new family in the Church... It is *exhausting* being me. You literally have no idea."

"Search the place," said Wretched.

"What's that?"

"Search the place," Wretched repeated, standing to one side and sweeping her arm back towards the cottage. "Go on. If you think I killed them and hid their bodies, go ahead and search the place."

"You're giving me permission?"

"I am," Wretched snarled. "Because this is ridiculous and I want it over with and I want you to go away."

Valkyrie bit her lip. "Hmm," she said.

"What? What's wrong now? I'm giving you permission!"

"Well, see, that's the problem," said Valkyrie. "If you're inviting me in to take a look, there's probably nothing to find. Unless, of course, you *want* me to think that, so I won't bother searching. That would be sneaky of you. But then you look at me and you think to yourself, *This girl's crazy-smart as well as being crazy-hot, so she'll probably know that I'm bluffing.* So then why would you give me permission if you know that I'll be inclined to *actually* search the place...? Unless you're planning to follow me in there so that you can whack me over the head with a shovel and just keep on whacking until I've joined your growing list of victims. On a completely unrelated note, do you *have* a shovel?"

Wretched frowned. "I think there's one in the shed out the back."

"Aha!" Valkyrie cried, and then frowned again. "Wait, what were we talking about?"

"I was giving you permission to search my home."

"Ah, but I don't think your parents are *in* your home."

"Then where are they?"

"I'm not sure," said Valkyrie, peering at Wretched's mouth. "Open wide?"

Wretched stared. "You think I ate my parents?"

"No. Yes. Kind of. Maybe not *all* of them. Maybe just the juicy bits."

"You think I'm a *cannibal*?"

"We try not to use that word," Valkyrie said, wincing again. "We prefer to call them people-eaters. It's a valid lifestyle choice and I'd thank you not to act so horrified."

"This is ridiculous. You're ridiculous."

"You should really meet Skulduggery."

"You think I ate my parents because they disapproved of the Church of the Faceless?"

"No!" Valkyrie said quickly. "Good God, no! I'm so sorry if I gave you that impression! Please, let me clarify. I think you ate your parents because you're an evil psychopath who has been convinced by even *eviller* psychopaths that eating your enemies is a good way of proving yourself. Whether or not your parents disapproved of your religion had nothing to do with why you ate them."

Wretched glowered. "Do you have any proof?"

"Not yet," Valkyrie admitted. "But I'm expecting some soon."

"How soon?"

"I'm not sure. When was the last time you had a bowel movement?"

Valkyrie's phone rang. She held up one finger to tell Wretched to wait, and put the phone to her ear.

"Has she come out of the cottage yet?" Skulduggery asked.

"Yes, she has, and I'm talking to her," said Valkyrie. "She's right in front of me."

"Oh. What's she like?"

"Kind of annoyed. Very impatient. She's not a great liar, which is a drawback if you've just eaten your folks and you want to get away with it. Speaking of which, she's asking about proof – have you found any?"

"I found a toe," said Skulduggery.

"Any idea who it belongs to?"

"I imagine it's her father's. It's quite hairy."

Valkyrie pressed the phone to her chest, and smiled at Wretched. "Could you describe your dad's toes?"

Wretched frowned. "What?"

"His toes. Would you describe them as hairy? Skulduggery found one at the crime scene, and yes, we'll be getting them analysed later, but if you could give us a hint as to what they looked like, maybe we could get through this a little faster."

Skulduggery's voice, muffled. Valkyrie put the phone back to her ear.

"What was that?" she asked.

"I could send a picture," Skulduggery repeated.

"He can send a picture," Valkyrie told Wretched. "Do you think you'd be able to identify your father from a picture of his toe?"

Wretched didn't say anything.

"What's she saying?" Skulduggery asked.

"Nothing," Valkyrie told him.

"What's she doing?"

"Staring."

"Is she doing it in a guilty way?"

"Pretty guilty, yeah. I'd say she's either going to try to run off or she's going to attack me."

"I'm assuming you can take her."

"Oh, God, yeah."

"Right. Well, I'll leave you to it. Oh – did you ever find out what was making that strange rattling noise in your car?"

"It was a stone caught in the... you know the inside wheel bit? The whatever-it's-called. Anyway, I found it and I took it out, and it's all fine now."

"OK then, just so long as it wasn't anything serious. Let me know how it goes with the people-eater."

"I will," said Valkyrie. "Bye."

She hung up, put the phone away, and turned her attention back to Wretched.

"Fine," Wretched said. "I killed them."

"I knew that."

"I ate them."

"I knew that, too."

"They were heathens. Just like you're a heathen. All heathens are going to die. You can either die now, or you can die later."

"Yeah," said Valkyrie. "That sounds like a threat until you realise it applies to just about everyone, doesn't it?"

Wretched shook her head. "Those who worship the Faceless Ones will live forever once the Dark Gods remake this world. First, they'll destroy it. They'll tear down the mortal civilisations, burn billions, and enslave the survivors. Then they'll build a new world, a better world, for people like me. You won't be in it."

"I wouldn't want to be."

"You'll be burned with the others."

"Good," said Valkyrie. "I'm glad."

"Or you'll die before that," Wretched said. "Maybe the Faceless Ones will tear you apart when they return because of all the harm you've done. Or maybe you're not even worth the effort. Maybe someone like me will kill you."

"Finally, we're getting to the good part of the conversation."

"The Faceless Ones would reward me greatly if I were to kill you," Wretched said, clearly warming to the idea. She raised the latch, nudged open the gate with her knee and came forward until she was standing within punching distance. "They'd make me a queen, I imagine. They'd give me my very own country to rule."

"I don't know about a whole country," Valkyrie said doubtfully. "But you might get a reality TV show out of it."

Wretched's face twisted. "They won't have *television* in the new world! That's a mortal invention!"

"So's the wheel. You're telling me they won't have the wheel, either? How's anyone going to cycle anywhere? And what about wheelbarrows? Will you not need wheelbarrows in the new world? How are you going to do any gardening?"

Wretched opened her mouth to snarl an answer and Valkyrie slapped her, the heel of her hand crashing into the hinge of Wretched's jaw so hard it pitched her backwards, unconscious before she even hit the ground.

"You've got to think about these things," Valkyrie said, rubbing her stinging hand. "You've got to take them into account, otherwise you're just going to look stupid when the time comes." She took a pair of cuffs from her pocket, turned Wretched on to her belly, and secured her hands behind her back. When she turned her over again, Wretched was moaning, and her eyes fluttered open.

"What did you do?" she asked, her voice frail.

"I knocked you the hell out," said Valkyrie, pulling Wretched to her unsteady feet. "You know what else mortals invented? Toasters. Are you telling me this new world of yours won't have any toasters? Are you crazy? Why would you want to live in a world without toast?"

"You have no idea," Wretched muttered.

"How to live in a world without toast?"

"No idea about what's coming. About what he's going to do." A bitter smile cracked through. "You're all dead. All of you. Everyone who works in the Sanctuaries. Anyone who could possibly stand against us. You're all going to die."

Valkyrie blinked at her. "You are a cheery lady."

"I'm going to watch you scream," said Wretched. "I want you to remember my words, OK? You can put me in prison, but I will be freed, and then I'm going to watch you scream."

"You're really not going to tell me where you got that top, are you?"

"No."

"Thought not," Valkyrie grumbled, one hand gripping Wretched's elbow as she led her to the car.

HAUNTED

Valkyrie knocked, and the woman who answered the door was cautious, wondering who could be calling at this time of night.

"Hello. You don't know us, but my name's Valkyrie."

"Valerie?"

"Sure. This is my associate, Mister Pleasant."

"I'm the approachable one," Skulduggery said, the moustache drooping on his façade as he nodded.

The woman, Lilly Ayers, didn't open the door any wider. Her eyes were tired. Her fingernails were polished but chewed. Recent stress had awoken a dormant nail-biting habit.

"I'm sorry, what do you want?"

"We were told you were having some problems," Valkyrie said, putting on her most quietly sympathetic smile. "With your son."

Lilly stiffened. "I don't know what you mean."

"It's quite all right," said Skulduggery. "You went to the authorities, and they either dismissed you immediately or simply didn't know how to help. Fortunately, somebody knew enough to alert a different kind of authority, and that's why we're here."

"You're... you're this different kind of authority?"

"No, we're not."

"But you work for them?"

"We work alongside them," Skulduggery said. "We're independent contractors, you might say, if you were going to say anything at all. It's complicated. Essentially, we operate as a—"

"Don't worry about him," Valkyrie said, still smiling. "We're the people who deal with this sort of thing all the time. Miss Ayers, could we come in?"

Lilly hesitated, then opened the door wider and stood aside. Valkyrie went in first, and Skulduggery removed his hat as he followed.

The house was a three-bedroom semi-detached at the end of a cul-de-sac. There was a single black-and-white photograph on the wall of a younger Lilly Ayers holding a baby, and below that a small table with a wireless router and a bowl with car keys in it. There was a pad beside the bowl and a pencil. Skulduggery picked up the pencil as Lilly closed the door, then led them into the living room, where a boy of ten was playing a game on his tablet. He put the tablet down when he saw they had guests.

"Zane," said Lilly, "this is Valerie and Mister Pleasant. They say they can help."

Skulduggery threw the pencil at the boy. It hit his forehead and bounced off.

The boy, Zane, frowned slightly. "Why did you do that?"

"Do what?" Skulduggery asked, walking over to him. With two gloved fingers, he gripped Zane's chin and tilted his head up and to the side.

"You threw a pencil at me," said Zane.

"Ah," Skulduggery responded. "Noticed that, did you? Would you say you're an especially observant child, Zane? Open your mouth, please, and say Wurzel."

Zane opened his mouth. "Wurzel."

Skulduggery peered at him. "Observation, Zane. Are you especially good at it?"

"I don't know. I don't think so."

"Please stand up, with your feet together, and lock your knees out straight."

Zane did as he was told, and Skulduggery pushed him over. Zane fell back on to the sofa before struggling to his feet again.

"I'm sorry," said Lilly, coming forward, "but what exactly are you doing?"

"Standard procedure," Skulduggery told her. "Just a few simple tests to establish that Zane is who he appears to be."

Valkyrie took Lilly's arm and led her to a chair. "Now that these completely unnecessary tests are out of the way, why don't you tell us what's been happening?"

Reluctantly, Lilly sat. "It started a few months ago. It was noises at first. Strange noises around the house. Then things began to move. Doors would open and shut. Taps would turn on. Books would fly off the shelves and hit me. I... I thought it was a ghost." She looked embarrassed by the admission.

Valkyrie gave a nod. "Logical assumption."

"But I don't believe in ghosts."

"That's rarely the most important factor in hauntings," Skulduggery told her. "Go on."

"Then it started happening in Zane's school. The principal thought Zane was pulling pranks. He got suspended twice, and then I just— I stopped sending him. It was too dangerous. Not to Zane, Zane was never targeted, but I was covered in bruises by this stage, and I didn't want any of the kids around him to be hurt like I was, so..."

Valkyrie sat beside Zane. "And how did you feel about all this?" she asked him.

"Scared," he said.

"I don't blame you. I'd be scared, too."

Zane swallowed. "I'm being haunted."

"No," said Valkyrie. "I mean, you might be – that's always a possibility – but hauntings are rarer than you'd imagine. What is probably happening, though, and this is very easy to find out, is that you're actually magic."

"What do you mean by magic?" Lilly asked.

"Precisely what you think we mean," said Skulduggery. "We believe your son has magic powers. Without instruction, without guidance, this magic can manifest in all sorts of ways. If left to his own devices, it may very well fade away as Zane gets older, but it could also become stronger. If this happens, and he doesn't receive any training, he will be what we call a Neoteric. This is not a route we would encourage."

"Magic powers?" said Lilly. "Like... like what?"

"There are many disciplines of magic, and new ones being discovered all the time."

Lilly stood. "No. No, you just wait. Just stop talking and wait a second. When you say magic, what do you actually mean?"

Skulduggery deactivated his façade, and the false face flowed away, revealing the skull beneath. "I mean magic."

Lilly shrieked and held Zane behind her. "Don't hurt him! Don't you dare hurt my son!"

"Why would I hurt your son?" Skulduggery asked, head tilting.

"Because you're a skeleton!"

"And do you have a history of skeletons hurting your family members?"

"Mum," said Zane. "Mum, it's OK. Look. He's not going to hurt us."

"He's really not," said Valkyrie. "I know this is a lot to take in, but just because he's a skeleton doesn't mean he's a bad guy."

Lilly stared at her. "Are you a skeleton, too? Is everyone a skeleton?"

"No," Valkyrie. "I mean, we all *have* skeletons, obviously, on the inside, but Skulduggery is the only *living* skeleton. You get used to it surprisingly quickly."

Lilly collapsed into her chair. "But this is impossible. Magic isn't real."

"I very much hope you're wrong, Miss Ayers," Skulduggery said, "or else people like us have been deluding ourselves for a long time."

"And... and you think Zane is magic, too?"

"Yes, but there's no reason to panic," Valkyrie said. "There's a school right here in Ireland that will take him without a problem. He'll be taught all the usual subjects, plus a load of magical ones. He'll be able to make new friends without worrying about hurting anyone because they'll all be just like him."

Lilly didn't have a response to this, so Valkyrie turned her smile on Zane. "What do you think of all this?"

"I'm magic? Are you sure?"

Valkyrie took a pouch from her pocket, drew out a pinch of dust, and let it sprinkle into Zane's hand. The dust sparkled with every colour imaginable.

"You're magic," she said.

For a moment, he went as quiet as his mother, and then he looked up again. "I'm not being haunted?"

"You're not being haunted."

"There's no ghost?"

"There's no ghost."

He frowned. "So what about the man in my room?"

Valkyrie hesitated, and Lilly sat forward.

"What man in your room?" his mother asked. "Zane? What man?"

Zane looked at her, and then at Valkyrie. "There's a man who comes to my room some days. He looks like a ghost. I can see through him sometimes. He stands there, but I can't hear him. He's shouting at me, though. He's always shouting."

"Do you recognise him?" Skulduggery asked.

"No," said Zane. "Not really. I think maybe I've seen him before, but I can't remember where."

"What does he look like? Is he as tall as me, or Valkyrie, or your mother?"

"Um," said Zane, screwing his face up in concentration. "Probably her," he said, pointing at Valkyrie. "And he's got black or brown hair. It's hard to tell because I see through him."

"Is he thin? Is he big? Does he look strong or weak?"

"He looks normal, I guess."

"And what's he wearing?" Valkyrie asked.

"I don't really know," Zane said. "Ordinary stuff."

"When was the last time you saw him?"

"This morning, when I woke up."

"Sweetheart," said Lilly, diving beside Zane and wrapping her arms round him, "why didn't you tell me?"

He shrugged. "I thought it was the ghost. I didn't want to tell you because I know ghost stuff upsets you."

She kissed the top of his head. "Don't you be worrying about me. Don't you be worrying about what upsets me. Things that upset me, they don't matter. What matters is you."

"What did the man do this morning?" Skulduggery asked.

Another shrug. "I just woke up, and he was standing in the corner, and he was shouting at me. He looked angry. He always looks angry."

"Can you show us your room, Zane? Would that be OK?"

Zane and Lilly led them upstairs, and sat on Zane's bed while Skulduggery and Valkyrie looked around. There were toys on the floor and posters on the wall, but no ghosts screaming silently or otherwise.

Valkyrie sprinkled some of the rainbow dust. It turned pretty colours as it drifted down, but that didn't prove much beyond the simple fact that something magical had occurred here.

"Maybe you could reach out," Skulduggery said to Valkyrie.

She glowered at him. "I wouldn't know what I was doing."

"Since when has that stopped you?"

"I'm sorry," said Lilly, "what are you talking about?"

Valkyrie tried smiling. "I'm a bit of a psychic. Just one of my many dubious talents. I'm really not very good at it, though, and generally don't know what I'm doing half the time, so..."

"But it could help? It could help us stop this ghost, or whatever it is?"

Valkyrie hesitated, then gave a reluctant nod. "I suppose it wouldn't hurt to try. Zane, do you mind if I put my hand on your head? Because the ghost is appearing to you, and he hasn't harmed you, there might be a connection between you."

His mother's arm wrapped round him again, and Zane nodded. "Sure. I don't mind."

Valkyrie stepped over, placed her hand on his head and closed her eyes.

"Anything?" Skulduggery asked.

"Literally just closed my eyes, dude."

"Sorry," he said. "Please continue."

As gently as she could, Valkyrie allowed her thoughts to hover around Zane's. She didn't enter his mind – she didn't like doing that and didn't want to do it now – but instead she probed the energy that surrounded him, ever so quietly, searching for the correct frequency.

"Oh my God," Lilly said, all in a rush, and Valkyrie took her hand away and opened her eyes.

The ghost stood in the corner of the room and through him Valkyrie could see the wall and the edge of the window. His shirt was scorched and there was blood on his face and matted in his hair. He shouted at Zane, then seemed to realise there were other people here. He glared at Skulduggery, glared at Valkyrie, then his gaze fell upon Lilly, and he roared like a maniac.

"He's angry," Valkyrie said. She was still attuned to whatever frequency had brought the ghost out, and it was driving a sharp pain into the space behind her eyes.

"We can see that," Skulduggery told her.

"He's blaming Zane for something. It's Zane's fault."

Tears glistened in Zane's eyes. "But I haven't done anything. What did I do? Why does he hate me?"

Valkyrie hesitated, then stepped forward, her hand outstretched.

"Careful," Skulduggery said.

"I'll be fine," she answered, and when her fingertips touched the ghost her mind exploded.

Her world was a rush of memories that weren't her own, her vision blocked by a blurring flickershow of people and places and noise – so much noise, voices talking over each other, crying and shouting and laughing and begging and screaming.

Valkyrie concentrated on the screaming, narrowing her focus to cut through the sensations around her, and suddenly she saw this man, but he was solid and he was real, and she knew him. She knew who he was.

She cursed, and withdrew, and Skulduggery caught her before she fell. The ghost stopped shouting and raging and just stood there, looking at her. Hating her.

"I'm OK," she said softly, and stood on her own. "I know who he is." She glanced at Skulduggery, then at Lilly, and then at Zane. "He's you, Zane."

A look came over the boy's face, a quiet realisation, even as Lilly gasped.

"That's Zane? How is that possible? How can he be haunted by the ghost of someone he hasn't even grown up to *be* yet?"

"Because it's not a ghost from the past," said Valkyrie. "It's a ghost from the future."

"Why is he here?" asked Zane, his voice soft.

Lilly gripped Zane tighter. "Is he here to warn us of something? Something that's going to happen? Is Zane in danger?"

Valkyrie's head was pounding. She could have found a gentler way to say this, she knew she could, but the pain was erasing any diplomacy she had left. "Zane *is* the danger," she said.

Lilly frowned. "What?"

"In two years, Zane joins Corrival Academy, and he learns magic. He chooses his discipline and makes friends. He's a natural. He gets very good very quickly. He grows up and falls in love and has his heart broken and carries on, meets new people, new friends and new loves, but something curdles inside him, and... I'm sorry, but innocent people die."

Zane swallowed. "Do I kill them?"

Valkyrie nodded.

"That's ridiculous," Lilly said, anger in her voice. "Zane would never hurt anyone! This is stupid! You can't know that! You can't say that!"

"Mum," said Zane, and Lilly bit back her next words. Zane blinked at Valkyrie. "What happens then?"

"Other sorcerers try to arrest you," she said, "but you're too powerful. You kill them. You have a plan – a big, ambitious, terrifying plan – and you have your followers, and you're a threat, Zane. You're a threat to the world. Skulduggery and I go to stop you."

Lilly hugged her son even tighter to her side.

"You kill friends of ours," said Valkyrie in barely more than a whisper. "You kill people we love. It all falls apart. Your plan collapses. We're closing in on you. That man, the ghost... Your adult self is in a room, right now, in the future, and we're about to burst in. You think the world has turned against you, and you don't think it's fair, and you're blaming all of this on your own weakness. You're tracing your misfortune back here, to your childhood. To your mother."

"To Mum?" said Zane. "Why? Why to my mum?"

"It's your love for your mother, and her love for you, that you blame for your weakness as an adult."

"Is that why he's here?" Zane asked. "Does he want to do something bad to Mum?"

"You want to kill her," said Valkyrie. "You think that by cutting out the source of your weakness, it'll make you stronger."

Zane looked at Lilly, tears running down his face. "I'm so sorry, Mum."

"Hey, no," Lilly responded, refusing to cry. "You don't have anything to be sorry about. If this is real, if what she's saying is true, then you still don't have anything to be sorry about. You, right here, the person you are right now, Zane, is a good person. You are a good, kind, decent boy."

"I don't want to hurt you, Mum."

"I know you don't," she said, hugging him. "I know."

Zane sobbed in his mother's arms, and then disentangled himself and walked up to the ghost. Valkyrie could still feel the rage emanating from his future self.

"I'm not going to let you hurt her," Zane said. "I'm not going to do the things you did. I'm not going to kill those people. I'm not going to learn magic, either. I won't do any of it. I won't let you do any of it. Go away now. Go away!"

Zane's ghost snarled, and started talking, snapping out silent words until Zane turned his back on him, and he vanished, like a picture deleted on a phone with a single tap.

Lilly hurried to her son, dropping to her knees and hugging him.

"I'm very sorry we couldn't do more to help," said Valkyrie, and Skulduggery followed her out of the house.

They walked in silence to the car, then stood by the doors and didn't get in.

"We can leave them alone," Valkyrie said.

"We can't," said Skulduggery.

"But he's not even going to attend Corrival."

"Then he'll grow up to be a Neoteric," Skulduggery said. "From what you describe, his power will be too great to ignore."

"That future has been averted, though."

"That *version* of the future, maybe."

"He's a good kid, Skulduggery."

"You saw what he does. If you're confident that he no longer poses a threat to those people he killed, then I'll accept your judgement, and we'll leave him be."

Valkyrie's headache was getting worse. "Otherwise, what? We operate on him? We send in our Sensitives to rearrange his thoughts? We can't change him. We don't have the right to change him."

"Those are two out of the three options available to us," Skulduggery said. "You know what the third one is."

She narrowed her eyes. "We sure as hell aren't doing that."

Skulduggery took his hat off, adjusted the brim. "We do the bad things so other people don't have to."

"We're not doing *that*."

"Then we call in the Sensitives," Skulduggery said. "We distract his mother, and we perform the procedure. He won't remember it. She won't even notice the difference. Their lives will return to normal."

"She'll notice."

"No, she won't."

"She'll notice, Skulduggery. I'm just… I'm not used to this. I'm used to us swooping in and saving the day. I'm used to us finding the impossible solution to an impossible problem."

He put his hat back on. "We can't save everyone."

Valkyrie pinched the bridge of her nose. "Call in the Sensitives."

"It's for the best. You know it is."

"Yeah." She opened the car door, and hesitated. "And what if it doesn't work? What if we change his thoughts, and he still travels down that same road?"

"Then we'll be waiting for him at the end of it," said Skulduggery, and got in.

THOSE WHO WATCH

The corpse hung by its neck from the tree like an oversized Christmas ornament, each gentle sway teasing a groan from the branch. There were bodies dangling from the trees on either side of it, and more beside them, forming lines that curved slightly to become an expansive circle – a border within the woods.

Valkyrie Cain observed this boundary of dead bodies. "That," she said, "is ever so slightly ominous."

Skulduggery Pleasant stepped up beside her, adjusting his hat. The suit was dark blue today, a three-piece with a white shirt and a blue tie. The face he'd been wearing as they'd talked with the sheriff flowed away now, revealing the skull beneath. His shoes, polished to a shine, sank into the soil. He didn't seem to care.

"This display does more than offer a warning," he said. "The moment we step through, we're in her territory."

"The monster's female?"

"We're dealing with a witch," Skulduggery said, nodding. "One of the old-fashioned, non-human variety. The kind that would pluck little children from their beds and nice old ladies from their gardens and gobble them all up."

"She hasn't eaten these people."

"No," he murmured. "She hasn't. I wonder why not."

"We should probably go and ask her," Valkyrie said. "You know, before she eats anyone else in the town. I doubt they'd be able to handle many more unexplained disappearances."

He dipped his head at her. "After you."

Valkyrie raised an eyebrow, and stepped across the boundary.

Twigs crunching beneath their feet, they moved through the woods. Valkyrie had never been to this part of America before. The sky was the colour of a bad mood, and the air couldn't quite summon up the energy to become warm. The further they walked, the fainter the birdsong became behind them, until it faded altogether.

The wood was holding its breath – the way a child might as it hid beneath the bed while the monster searched the house.

They stepped into a clearing. In the middle of that clearing was a cabin. Its roof dipped. Its windows sagged. Its stone chimney slumped.

Skulduggery nodded to Valkyrie. "Go ahead and knock."

"You think that'll be OK?" she asked, frowning. "A witch won't try to eat me or anything?"

"If she does, I've got my old friend here to talk her out of it." He tapped his jacket, right where his gun was holstered.

Sighing, Valkyrie approached the cabin, stepped up on the rotting porch and knocked. "Hello?" she called. "Anyone home?"

She heard movement inside. Footsteps. Shuffling. The door rattled, a heavy key turning in an old lock, the dragging back of the latch. The door opened.

A little old lady, wrapped in a shawl with a bonnet on her head, peered out. "Hello?" she said, her voice weak and hesitant. Nervous. Scared, even.

Valkyrie put on her best and most reassuring smile. "Hello there," she said.

"I was passing through, and was just wondering if you're the one eating people?"

The little old lady blinked in confusion. "I'm sorry? Eating who? What? I'm afraid I don't know quite what you mean."

"Oh," Valkyrie said, "sorry." She leaned down until she was level with the elderly woman. "Eating people," she said loudly and slowly. "Are you doing it, you decrepit old bag?"

The witch grew so fast Valkyrie barely had time to register it. One moment she was a stooped old woman in a shawl, the next she was twice the size and lunging from the cabin, an oversized fist knocking Valkyrie off her feet.

Valkyrie slammed to the ground and rolled in the twigs and the dirt and the dead leaves, and the witch thundered after her. Her skinny arms were too long for her body and her hands were way too big for her wrists. Her grey hair burst from the bonnet like she'd been electrocuted. Her jaw jutted at an angle, her gaping mouth overstuffed with yellowed, broken teeth.

Skulduggery pressed the muzzle of his gun into the side of her head, and said, "I'd stop moving if I were you."

The witch froze.

Valkyrie picked herself up, rubbing her cheek. "Ow," she said.

The witch's eyes – hazel eyes, they were – bulged in their sockets. "Don't kill me," she said. "I don't deserve to die."

"And the townspeople you've strung up around your home?" Skulduggery said, moving so that he was standing beside Valkyrie. "Did they deserve what you did to them?"

The witch licked her lips. She had a very, very long tongue. It was cracked, like old shoe leather. "I do what I do for a good reason," she said. "A very good reason. I'm protecting that town."

"By killing everyone in it?"

The witch didn't answer.

"What's your name?" Valkyrie asked.

"Esmerelda Montague," said the witch. "I have lived in these woods since I was a little girl, and that was a long time ago. I watched the town grow from an empty field to a single lodging to a home for hundreds. I have watched the people from a distance because they don't like me. They never have. But I protect them, nonetheless."

"Protect them from what?" Skulduggery asked.

"From the monster," said the witch.

A sound reached them, bleeding through the trees. A long and guttural roar. It faded, and silence reclaimed the clearing.

"That," Skulduggery said, "would be the monster, yes?"

"Please understand," said Esmerelda. "If it breaks free of its prison, you will see a slaughter the like of which you could scarcely imagine. The town I'm protecting. The next town over. The state. The country. It will attack, devour and disappear. There is no way to track it, and no way to kill it."

Valkyrie brushed a leaf from her hair. "And you're the only one who can keep it trapped?"

"Yes."

"And you do that by killing a bunch of people and hanging them from trees?"

"I have formed a magical boundary," Esmerelda said. "A border between life and death, a shield against—"

"And you do that by killing a bunch of people," Valkyrie repeated, "and hanging them from trees?"

The witch faltered. "Yes."

"See, that's where you lose me."

"Take us to the monster," said Skulduggery.

Esmerelda sagged. "That is not wise, skeleton."

"Probably not, but I'm the one with the gun."

The witch looked at them both, and shook her head regretfully. "Very well," she said, and started walking. They followed close behind.

"What kind of monster is it?" Valkyrie asked.

"I don't know," said the witch.

"Does it have a name?"

"I don't know that, either."

"How long has it been here?"

"As long as I have."

"How long is that?"

"I don't know."

"You don't know how long you've been here? What age are you?"

"What age is this tree?" asked Esmerelda. "Or that rock? What age is the air? I am old, I know that, and I remember when I was young, and I know that the time between the two has been long, and lonesome."

"Who named you?"

"I did. I took my name from a young woman I hung from a tree. She wasn't using it any more, and names were suddenly all the rage, so I tried it on and it's mine now."

"Cute story," Valkyrie murmured.

Esmerelda stopped walking, and turned to them. "We are close to the monster," she said, "and so I must beseech you to leave. It's not too late to walk away and leave this to me. The balance I have struck is delicate. Your very presence may be enough to tip the scales. My way is working."

"Your way kills innocent people," Skulduggery said. "It's time to try something new."

"You think new ways are better ways?" the witch asked. "Of course you do. You're centuries old, are you not? I can sense that about you. And yet your clothes, your weapon... You put all your faith in the new. But battling the old monsters requires the old ways. This is something you've forgotten, skeleton."

Her hazel eyes flickered to Valkyrie. "Your mind is more open. Walk away, girl. Convince your friend to walk away beside you, and I will give you a reward."

Valkyrie folded her arms. "I'm not interested in—"

"You have lost people."

"I'm sorry?"

"Loved ones. Yes? You've lost them."

"Everyone's lost people they love."

The witch nodded, leaned closer. "But I can bring them back."

"*Right*," said Valkyrie, drawing out the word. "So if we turn round, and leave this whole mess to you, you'll... what? Actually bring someone I've lost back to life?"

"Yes."

"And you can do that? You have that kind of power?"

Esmerelda hesitated.

"That's what I thought," Valkyrie said.

"I'm just a witch," said Esmerelda, "and my abilities are limited. But I possess the knowledge, and that knowledge is a key that can unlock the secrets of life and death."

"You're stalling."

"I swear to you, girl – I do not lie."

"Keep walking, witchy."

With great reluctance, the witch resumed her march through the woods. Skulduggery followed, just out of range of a sudden swipe, and Valkyrie walked parallel, ready to throw lightning if Esmerelda tried anything sneaky.

"You'll regret this," Esmerelda said. "I could have reunited you with a loved one, but you have spurned my offer."

"Yeah, yeah."

Esmerelda glanced behind her. "And what of you, skeleton? What would you give to have your wife and child at your side once more?"

Skulduggery's head tilted slowly. "How do you know about them?"

The witch shrugged as she walked. "These are the things I know."

"So you've heard of me?"

"I have not."

"Well, you certainly didn't read my mind."

"True, I don't have that ability. But I know loss, and I know sorrow. The people I hang from trees, they have all lost loved ones – either to me or to the monster. I reunite them with these spirits in death. I see your wife and child, and I see so many others. I see a scarred man, and a quiet man."

A glance at Valkyrie. "And you, girl. I see an uncle, and a... twin? No, another version of you, one without magic. How curious."

Valkyrie narrowed her eyes. "Just because you can see the people we've lost doesn't mean you can bring them back to us."

"You are correct," Esmerelda said. "It is not as simple as that. Not as simple as a click of the fingers or an incantation intoned. But I could have made it a possibility. I could have unlocked the door and allowed you to reach through, to pull your loved one from death. And now, alas, I fear it is too late for we have arrived."

They stepped through into another clearing, this one dotted with tree stumps. In the centre of the clearing was a small circle of trees carved with sigils. Valkyrie had been around enough of the various languages of magic to at least recognise the patterns of the most popular ones – but these weren't even the slightest bit familiar.

Something moved within the circle of trees, something dark. Valkyrie stepped closer, trying to get a good look.

Its skin was mottled green and black, and it was so big it could barely turn round in its wooden cell. Its arms were as long as Valkyrie was tall, and there was a claw on the end of each crooked finger. She spied a mouth, and teeth, and it growled as she neared.

"Hello, brother," said the witch.

The monster roared at her, a sound so violent it made Valkyrie step back.

Then the roar died away, and the monster glared. It had yellow eyes.

"Your brother," said Skulduggery.

Esmerelda gave another of her sighs. "I've always thought of it as such, but perhaps that's due to the fact that my life has been so sorely lacking in the love of family that I have latched on to it as my only companion. You must think me pathetic."

"Don't be so hard on yourself," said Skulduggery, trying to get a better look at the monster. "I just think of you as a murderer. Valkyrie, might we have a spare cell big enough for this charming creature?"

"I reckon," Valkyrie said. "Though we'll have to call in a squad or two of Cleavers to secure it for teleportation."

"I can help you with that," said Esmerelda, turning to them. "I can render the monster—"

She moved without warning, her fist crunching into Skulduggery. Valkyrie raised her arm and poured magic into her fingertips, and lightning leaped, but she was far too slow, as the witch was already upon her. Esmerelda picked her up and then brought her down, slamming her into the dirt.

The air rippled and struck Esmerelda from behind, making her stumble over Valkyrie, and Skulduggery hurled a fireball that caught in the witch's hair. Esmerelda screamed and batted at herself furiously, and Skulduggery's gun flew into his hand.

Then Esmerelda spoke three words that sliced into Valkyrie's head, and

Skulduggery grunted, and stiffened, and fell backwards. Gritting her teeth against the pain, Valkyrie released her lightning and this time it found its target. Esmerelda hollered and jerked back, fell, scrambled up. Valkyrie fired again but the witch moved, and the lightning tore a chunk from one of the trees holding the monster.

The sigil burned.

The monster burst from the trees, and Esmerelda spun, lunged, trying to grab it, but her legs gave out and she fell, even as the monster loped out of the clearing and vanished into the woods.

"No, no, no," Esmerelda mumbled, forcing herself to her feet. "What have you done? What have you done?"

"We can catch it," Valkyrie said, panicking. "We can catch it before it hurts anyone."

"We won't be able to contain it!" Esmerelda snapped. "This is your fault, girl! Now I have to take more innocent lives!"

Valkyrie stared at her. "What? No. No, we just have to—"

"You are responsible for what I am about to do," the witch snarled, and ran back the way they'd come.

Valkyrie got up, rushed over to Skulduggery, pulled him to his feet. "Did you hear that? Did you hear what she said? What do we do? Skulduggery, what do we do?"

"Split up," he said, snatching his hat off the ground.

"Seriously?"

"I'll go after the monster. You go after the witch."

"Splitting up is a terrible idea!"

"Then *you* go after the monster, and *I'll* go after the witch."

"That's still splitting up!"

"The monster has to be stopped, and we can't let Esmerelda sacrifice anyone else."

"Fine," Valkyrie growled, backing away from him, "I'll go after the witch. But I'm only doing this because it's my fault if she kills anyone."

She turned, ran a few steps and then leaped, energy crackling around her as she shot into the sky. She skimmed the treetops, the air rushing into her face, making it hard to breathe. She twisted, flew like she was doing the backstroke, her hair whipping over her eyes.

Valkyrie glimpsed the town approaching fast, and she twisted again, swooping low. She landed in a run that she slowed to a jog, hopping a wall behind a second-hand car lot. She made her way through the rows of vehicles. A salesman brightened when he saw her, but she just waved and kept walking.

The town was small, and it was nice, and it was quiet, and there was no one shouting or yelling or raising the alarm, so Valkyrie was pretty certain she'd beaten Esmerelda here. If she knew which part of the woods the witch would be emerging from, she could have hidden there and smacked her over the head with something heavy – but, as it was, all she could do was keep an eye on the treeline.

"Sheriff told me about you."

Valkyrie turned. A woman stood there, looking at her with red-rimmed eyes. She was in her forties, and her roots were showing. Her clothes were high-end but lived in. Someone who'd recently taken a substantial knock, then. Someone who'd lost someone, maybe, and hadn't had the time to deal with it.

"I'm here to help," Valkyrie said.

The woman nodded like she didn't believe her. "And your friend? You came with a friend, didn't you? Man in a suit?"

"I did. He's in the woods."

"I see," said the woman. "In the woods. And why is he in the woods? Is he here to kill the monster, maybe? The monster who's been snatching away the people of this town?"

"I don't know anything about any monsters," Valkyrie said carefully. "We're just here to—"

"Help," the woman said. "Yes, I heard you the first time. People are talking about the two of you, talking about seeing you both walk into those woods... Did you know we don't go in there? Did you know we never have? I was born here, raised here, and since I was a child I've known that you never go into the West Woods. Because of the monster, you understand. The *monster.*"

Her lip curled. "Grown men and women talking about monsters like they're real. Placing all the blame on some creature when our husbands and wives and children go missing and are never seen again. And now look. Here you are, feeding into that... that *hysteria.*"

"I'm not trying to make things any more difficult than they already are, Miss...?"

"Oh! You want to know my name, do you? My name is Joanne. Joanne Freely. My husband was Jacob Freely. I say *was* because he's gone. Snatched away. By the monster, apparently. But, instead of looking for clues and finding whoever is doing this, the sheriff of this godforsaken town is happy to blame it all on some supernatural being that lives in the trees. So who are you, I wonder, and what brings you to our town? You're not from here, obviously. You're not even from this country, are you?"

"I'm Irish."

"Good for you. Heard it's lovely over there."

"My name's Valerie. I'm here to—"

"You're lying."

Valkyrie blinked. "I'm sorry?"

"My husband lied to me," said Joanne. "He lied to me about a lot of things, that man. He wasn't... he wasn't strong, in the way you have to be strong. So he lied to me, and I got very good at spotting lies. And you lied to me when you told me your name. Why'd you do that? What are you hiding?"

Valkyrie took a moment to scan the treeline, then looked back. "OK," she said. "My name's Valkyrie. I know you don't believe that the monster exists, that it's some sort of town legend, but I know it's real, and so does my partner, and we're here to stop it."

Joanne shook her head. "You people... You come in here, charging grieving families to speak with their lost loved ones, and you take their money and—"

"We're not mediums," Valkyrie told her. "We're not charging money for this, and we don't want anything in return. When we've done our job, we'll leave and you'll never have to see us again."

"Your job. This is your job, is it?"

"Yes."

"You're monster fighters, are you?"

"Among other things."

Tears came trembling down Joanne's cheeks. "Do you know what I think? I think you and your friend are behind it all. I think you're taking those people. I think you're taking them and killing them. I think you killed my Jacob."

"Joanne, I'm so sorry for your loss, but I swear to you—"

Joanne had a gun in her hand now, and the tears were coming fast. "Why?" she asked. "Why'd you do it?"

Valkyrie raised her hands slowly and spoke very, very calmly. "Joanne, I haven't hurt anyone in this town. Anyone at all. You need to put the gun down."

"Why'd you kill him?"

"You're upset, and you're in pain, but I promise you I didn't kill your husband."

Joanne clicked back the hammer. "Then you're just here to profit from his death," she said, her hand shaking. "I'm sick of it. Sick of it all. It stops here. This town needs to wake up and stop dreaming of monsters and creatures and face reality."

"If you kill me, it's murder."

"Maybe that's what they need," Joanne responded. "A bit of everyday murder to snap them out of whatever delusion they're under."

Something blurred behind her, a mass of grey hair and broken teeth, and Valkyrie tried to shove Joanne out of the way. Joanne jerked back and fired. The suit absorbed the impact as best it could, but Valkyrie still went stumbling away, one hand at her belly. She watched the bullet fall from between her fingers, squashed-up like a crushed soft-drink can. She would have heard it hit the ground if her ears weren't ringing from the gunshot.

Joanne's gun bounced on the pavement near Valkyrie's foot. She looked up, saw Joanne's terrified face as Esmerelda grabbed her. Before Valkyrie could react, one of the witch's massive fists came swinging for her, and then the world juddered and went away.

Valkyrie blinked.

She was blinking. When had this started? When had her eyes opened? She had no idea, and yet here she was, blinking at the blue sky and the trees that slid by.

She went over a root. Hit her head. She didn't like that. She didn't like any of this. Her jaw was sore, her thoughts clouded. Her hand hurt, and there was a tightness round her ankle.

She was being dragged. Rustling filled her ears. She was being dragged across the ground in the woods, her hands trailing after her. Dragged by the ankle. Yep, that made sense.

Valkyrie raised her head. Oooooh, that made her feel sick. That made her want to puke. She put her head back down and closed her eyes and focused on her breathing.

When she was confident she wasn't going to throw up over herself, she raised her head again.

Yep, definitely being dragged through the woods.

Esmerelda gripped Valkyrie's left ankle in one hand and pulled her along behind her as she walked. With the other hand, she dragged Joanne. Joanne was unconscious, just like the man that was slung over Esmerelda's shoulder. Three of them, then. Three people to be killed and hung from branches.

Not if Valkyrie had anything to say about it.

She went to blast the witch with lightning and nothing happened. She examined her hand. A sigil had been scratched into the back of it. A little blood had trickled and dried against her skin.

Dammit.

"You're awake," said Esmerelda without looking round.

"Don't try to kill us," Valkyrie said. "It won't end well for you."

"I have to," the witch responded. "It's the only way to save the town."

"How can you be sure? Have you tried other ways?"

"I have tried all the ways."

"I think we both know that's an exaggeration."

Esmerelda glanced back. "At least your death will mean something, which is more than most can say."

Valkyrie was dragged over another tree root. "I hate to break it to you," she said, "but, if you do manage to kill me, it won't be the first time I've died. I've been around the block with this sort of thing."

"Sorcerers," said Esmerelda, and Valkyrie saw the edge of a smile.

"Also," Valkyrie said, "if you kill me, the skeleton in the suit is going to be super mad at you. Trust me, you do not want that hassle."

"I will kill the skeleton when I see him again," Esmerelda said. "It is a surprisingly easy thing, to kill the dead."

"Many people have tried."

"They should have tried harder."

"You want to know what I think?" Valkyrie said, and suddenly lashed her free foot into Esmerelda's wrist as she torqued her body violently to one side – but Esmerelda didn't let go, she just kept walking, and Valkyrie sighed and allowed herself to be dragged onwards.

"Lame," she said.

"Don't worry," said the witch, "we're almost there."

"Lame," Valkyrie said again, but louder this time.

They entered the clearing, and the cabin came into view.

"Are we going in there?" Valkyrie asked.

"We are."

"Is that where you're going to kill us?"

"It is."

"I see," said Valkyrie, and started shouting for Skulduggery.

"Do you really think that will do you any good?" Esmerelda asked. "He is in pursuit of my brother, and my brother is very fast indeed. They are both a long way off by now."

Valkyrie glowered. "Well, I'm going to keep shouting if it's all the same to you. Shouting and... fighting!"

She grabbed a branch, sat up and swung as hard as she could at Esmerelda's arm. But the branch was old, and dry, and the very act of swinging caused it to break in two, and so all she swung was a handful of crumbling wood.

"Ah, bloody hell," she muttered.

The door to the cabin swung open.

"Can I walk?" Valkyrie asked. "Can I at least walk to my doom, instead of being dragged? My magic is bound, I've got no weapons, and you're stronger and faster than me. There's no way I can escape. Just... come on. I feel stupid being pulled everywhere."

The witch stopped walking, considered it, and let go of her ankle. Valkyrie stood, brushed herself off. "Thank you," she said, and stepped through the door.

The cabin was wide and cold and smelled of something musty and unpleasant. There was a small bed in one corner, and a large table with a single chair. The table was stained with something dark. Blood, presumably.

Esmerelda came in, closing the door. She put Joanne and the man on the table, and reached for a long, thin knife.

"Whoa," said Valkyrie. "Just whoa. Hold on. Slow down. Skulduggery's going after the monster. You don't know him, but I do, and generally, when Skulduggery goes after a monster, the monster loses. Now, I don't want to tell you how to witch properly, I'm sure you do your job very well, but shouldn't you wait a little before you start killing these people?"

"I am going to wait," said Esmerelda.

"Oh. OK, cool."

"First I'm going to kill you, and, once that's done, only then will I kill them."

Valkyrie shook her head. "What I'm saying is, you might not have to. Skulduggery will bring your brother in, I'm sure of it. The monster will either be dead, or it'll be in shackles, or it'll be... I don't know what it'll be, but it'll be something. I wouldn't be surprised if Skulduggery rode it back like a horse."

"Your skeleton friend will not defeat it."

"You don't know him like I know him."

Esmerelda put the knife into a pocket somewhere in the folds of her ragged clothing. She closed her eyes and breathed out, and it was like she was breathing out her mass, because when that breath was done she was a little old lady again. Valkyrie watched her hobble over to the chair and sit in it with a heavy sigh.

"You poor girl," Esmerelda said. "You have no idea."

"No idea about what?"

"These woods. The town. What's happening here, between us. The people on this table. Your skeleton friend. My brother. You can't feel it?"

"I'm not entirely sure what you're on about, to be honest."

"I suppose I shouldn't be surprised," Esmerelda said. "It took me a long, long time before I started to sense what was going on. What was really going on."

"Maybe you could tell me."

"I doubt you'd believe it."

"You're a witch. My friend's a skeleton. My own reflection turned into a god. I think my mind's pretty open to new possibilities."

The old lady did her best to smooth down her hair. "I trapped my brother," she said. "I made a cell for him, a boundary he could not cross."

Valkyrie waited for her to continue.

"And there's another boundary," Esmerelda said at last, giving up on her hair and returning her hands to her lap. "A boundary made from the dead bodies of the townspeople that I have hung from trees. This boundary serves multiple purposes. It keeps unwanted visitors away – mostly – and it gives me the strength I need to do what I have to do. So there's a boundary outside a boundary."

"OK."

"But there's another boundary, outside even that. It encompasses my brother's cell, this cabin, the town and this county, small as it is. You passed through it when you arrived."

"I didn't see any boundary."

"It's not something you can see, but it is there, nonetheless."

Valkyrie nodded, like she was beginning to understand, even though she had no idea what the witch was talking about. As she nodded, she scanned the cabin for a weapon. Couldn't find one.

"And what does it do?" she asked. "What's it for, this boundary?"

"It changes things," said Esmerelda. "It changed you. It changed your friend."

"I don't feel any different."

"Of course not. If you felt the change, that would defeat the purpose."

"And what's the purpose?"

Esmerelda smiled thinly. "There's very little point in telling you. You'll be dead soon."

"I wish you wouldn't say things like that. But hey, satisfy my curiosity before I go."

"Ah, but I'm afraid to, you see. I'm sorry, what is your name?"

"Valkyrie. Valkyrie Cain. My friend's Skulduggery Pleasant."

"Valkyrie and Skulduggery," Esmerelda said, and her smile broadened. "I like those names. I'm afraid to tell you, Valkyrie, because I have never told anyone. I have never spoken the words aloud. I'm afraid that when I speak them, they'll know that I know. If they don't already know. Which they probably do."

"And what are you talking about?"

Esmerelda looked around, as if she was expecting the walls to come crashing down. "There are... beings. Watching us."

"Beings?"

"I don't know who they are or what they are. All I know is that they are watching. And controlling."

"Controlling what?"

"Me," said Esmerelda. "You. These people here on the table. Your friend Skulduggery."

Valkyrie frowned. "Um... No. Nobody's controlling me, thank you very much."

"These beings are powerful. You think they've endured for so long by being careless? Over time, I've developed a sense for their interference. When they make a change, the air is different somehow. It becomes charged."

"And what kind of changes do they make?"

"It happened just a few minutes ago, before you started shouting for

Skulduggery. It happened earlier in the town, when you tried to push this lady away from me," Esmerelda said, nodding at Joanne. "It happened right before you ran after me, and before that, when I offered you the choice between having a loved one returned to you and turning back before we reached my brother."

"I'm sorry?"

"These beings," said Esmerelda, whispering now. "They control this little pocket of reality. Do you understand? This is where they play their games. They watch us, and every so often they... they decide which direction we take. What we say. What we do."

"Are they watching us now?"

"Oh, Valkyrie, my dear. They're always watching."

"And they decide my actions? So they'd decide if I scratch my nose with my right hand or my left hand?"

Esmerelda's tongue flickered out, like she was tasting the air. "I can feel the charge," she said. "Yes. They will decide this."

"Uh-huh," said Valkyrie. "OK then, I've already made my mind up about which hand I'm going to scratch my nose with. You're saying they'll decide, is that right? Then let's see it." She looked up. "OK, you sick weirdos, let's see it in action. Decide for me."

She scratched her nose with her right hand, and immediately frowned.

"Well," said Esmerelda, "was that the one you were going to use?"

"I wasn't going to use either," Valkyrie said. "My nose wasn't itchy." She looked up. "You're saying someone made me do that? Who?"

The witch shrugged. "As I said, I don't know – but I've sensed them for years."

"Why don't you leave? What's keeping you here?"

"My brother. Making sure he doesn't hurt anyone."

"See, now just wait. OK, there might be a group of oddball beings out there watching us, dictating our movements – and don't get me wrong, that is creeping me the hell out – but let's not stray too far from the fact that you kill people to stop the monster from killing people. Doesn't that strike you as the slightest bit hypocritical?"

"My brother will kill a lot more than I ever would." The old woman clapped her hands. "But enough of such thoughts! The beings have watched, do watch and will watch, and I've grown accustomed to it! It's the way the world works. But today you die so that I can imprison my brother once more."

That knife again, in her hand, and she stood.

"Wait," said Valkyrie. "Just stop. Before you enter into your full witchy glory, just hear me out. I have a plan. I know how we can get the monster back in his cell and figure out what these mysterious beings are after. I mean, you're curious, right? After all this time?"

"I... yes," said Esmerelda. "My curiosity is piqued."

"Then help me conduct a little experiment. Will you do that?"

"You think you can make these beings reveal themselves?"

"And their intentions, yes."

"How?"

Valkyrie tapped her head. "I'm a little bit psychic. I don't have it all figured out yet, I'm not the most talented Sensitive the world has ever seen, but I reckon I'm good enough to sense them, like you've done. And I think I can go further."

Esmerelda frowned. "How much further?"

"They want something, right? They're watching us for a reason. From what you've told me, it could be something as simple as entertainment. These mysterious beings of yours just might be warped enough to derive some degree of satisfaction from watching others go through hell for their own amusement. If that's the case, I think I have a way to turn that against them."

"How?"

Valkyrie bit her lip. "I don't know if I can tell you without them overhearing."

"Whisper it."

"Will that work? Can't they hear whispers?"

"Yes," Esmerelda said miserably. "They can hear everything."

"Then maybe... maybe I can speak directly to your mind. Can we do that?"

"We could try," said the old woman, and came forward, and Valkyrie punched her across the jaw. Esmerelda fell in an unconscious heap.

Valkyrie hurried out of the cabin. Boots crunching over dead leaves, she ran to the clearing where the monster had been trapped and took off in the direction Skulduggery had gone.

She found his gun, and scooped it up and ran on.

She found his hat, and scooped it up and ran on.

Then she found Skulduggery.

He was standing just before the edge of the woods with his back to her, his arms folded, one finger tapping his chin.

"Ah," he said when she reached him, "you're here. Good." He held his hands out. She passed him his belongings. "Thank you," he said.

"I almost died," she told him. "The witch almost killed me."

"There's an old saying, Valkyrie: 'almost' only counts in horseshoes and hand grenades."

"What? What does that mean?"

"Old sayings don't have to make sense. They just have to be old."

"Where's the monster?"

"Nowhere."

"Sorry?"

"I chased it. We fought. It ran here... and vanished."

"It went invisible? It teleported?"

"I don't think so. It just... stopped. Very strange indeed."

"Huh."

Skulduggery looked at her. "What?"

"I've got something even stranger. Esmerelda seems to think there are beings watching us right now that control what we say and do."

"And you believe her?"

"I don't know. A few minutes ago, I scratched my nose and my nose wasn't even itchy."

"That does sound suspicious," Skulduggery muttered.

"My point is, she might be right. If she is, then that means they're watching us at this very moment. They're listening to everything we say."

Skulduggery's head tilted. "Even the boring bits?"

"What boring bits?"

"Good point. Come, tell me exactly what happened since we split up."

She filled him in as they walked back to the cabin.

"I might have a theory," he said as they approached the door.

"Already? OK then, what's going on?"

The door burst open and Esmerelda came sprinting out in all her witchy glory, the knife in her hand, and she leaped at Valkyrie but Skulduggery's gun was in his grip, and he fired a bullet into her leg. The leg crumpled beneath her and she stumbled but kept moving, the knife raking across Valkyrie's suit, barely missing her throat. They went down, scrambling, Valkyrie gripping Esmerelda's wrist in both hands, keeping that blade away from her.

Skulduggery hunkered down beside them, just out of reach, the gun pointed at Esmerelda's head. "I'm going to have to object to you killing Valkyrie," he said, and the struggling stopped immediately. "I've spent so much time training her up, and I really don't want to start again with someone new. I know you're tough, and you've been around a long time, but I assume that a shot to the head will kill you just as dead as it'd kill most people."

"I assume so also," said the witch.

"Then what do you say you drop the knife, before Valkyrie takes it from you and rams it into your eye?"

Esmerelda smiled. "I think you overestimate your friend's abilities."

Valkyrie twisted Esmerelda's wrist, plucked the weapon from her hand as it sprang open, and tapped the tip of the blade against the witch's cheek, just under the left eye.

"Oh," said Esmerelda, and leaned back, coming up to her knees. Valkyrie wriggled out from under her and stood.

"That was risky," Valkyrie said. "Shooting her leg like that."

"It was," Skulduggery murmured. "I should have shot her in the chest. Hitting a leg when the target's attacking is not something I would generally advise anyone to attempt." He cocked his head. "You're lucky I'm such an amazing shot."

"You didn't have a choice," said Esmerelda. "I felt it. The charge in the air. The beings took the option away from you."

"Ah, yes," Skulduggery said, "these mysterious beings. Do you have a name for them?"

"As I told Valkyrie, I don't know who they are."

"But you must have named them. You must think of them as a collective group."

"Not really. I just call them beings."

"Well," Valkyrie said, "that's not gonna work for us. We like things to have names. You get that, don't you? Why names are important? You took a name for yourself, after all."

Esmerelda frowned. "I suppose so..."

Skulduggery lowered his gun, but didn't put it away. "From what Valkyrie told me about you, you may have missed out on some of the new rules of magic.

And by new I mean anything that's cropped up in the last few eons. If we could figure out what these beings are called, or even if we just go ahead and name them right here and now, that gives us a certain amount of power over them. Not a whole lot, but it's something."

"I'm afraid I don't know anything that could help," said Esmerelda. Then she frowned. "Where is my brother?"

"Gone," Skulduggery said. "It left the woods and it disappeared. You say it's been around for as long as you have?"

"Yes," Esmerelda replied. "But what do you mean by 'gone'? Is it... is it dead?"

"Maybe. Or maybe it never lived. Maybe it never existed."

"But... but you saw it."

He shrugged. "I've seen plenty of things in my life, and even I'm not arrogant enough to assume that every one of them was real."

"You think the beings who are watching us made the monster?" Valkyrie asked.

"It's possible," he responded. "They made it, put it in these woods to act as a threat, and observed what happened next."

"But who'd have that kind of power? Are we talking about, like, a Darquesse situation? Someone learned their true name, and they've been acting as a god here in this little county ever since?"

"Perhaps," Skulduggery said, "but I don't think so. Someone of Darquesse's power would be able to control things a lot more tightly. These beings, whoever they are, are limited in the directions they can give."

"So it's not a bunch of gods we're talking about here?"

"I don't think so."

"Have you ever heard about this kind of situation before?"

Skulduggery nodded. "There have been instances over the years of people feeling like they had no input in their own decisions. There were occasions when mages would act out of character, particularly during the 1980s. I've personally known sorcerers who have died in bizarre circumstances, undertaking ridiculous tasks when they really should have known better. An old colleague of mine conducted one of the only investigations into the phenomena. He referred to the ones controlling it all as Horts."

"Ah," said Valkyrie. "So he wasn't into the idea of giving something a cool name. Good to know."

"He had a theory that there were both individual Horts and entire Councils of Horts," Skulduggery continued, "all casting votes to decide the fates of a select, unlucky few."

"And that's what you think is happening here?" Esmerelda asked. "Can I get up, by the way?"

"Yes, I do think that's what's happening here, and no, you cannot get up."

"But you shot me in the leg."

"Well, you tried to kill my friend."

"And who are these Horts?" Valkyrie asked.

"I think we can safely assume that they're not gods," Skulduggery answered, "but they do have a certain amount of power to wield over us."

Valkyrie resisted a shiver. "They probably don't like the fact that we're discussing them, do they?"

"For all we know, they're finding this highly amusing. Or they might be deciding that it's time we do something exciting, like fight, or kill each other."

"So what should we do?"

Skulduggery pondered this, and then he sat on the ground and indicated that Valkyrie should do the same.

"We should do absolutely nothing," he said. "If we commit to inaction, we may force their hand. If something spurs us into motion, then we'll know that not only are they watching, but they're also listening, and comprehending the discussion we're having."

"And what purpose does this serve?" Esmerelda asked.

Skulduggery dipped his head. "By forcing them to engage with us, we'll start to take away their power."

"By merely sitting here?"

"Sitting here peacefully, yes. They might decide to throw a pack of goblins at us; they might send the townspeople after us with pitchforks and burning torches; they might try something else entirely... But once they do any of this we'll gain the upper hand."

"But, if they're listening, then they know that's exactly what we're expecting," said Valkyrie. "So, like... they won't do anything, and they'll just wait us out instead."

"If we're dealing with a single Hort, then yes. That is entirely possible. But if, as we suspect, we're dealing with an entire Council of Horts, it will be much harder for them to control the outcome. All we need is for one of them to cast a vote, just one single Hort to cast that first vote, and then it will all come tumbling down."

They sat there and waited.

"My leg hurts," said Esmerelda.

"We don't care," said Valkyrie.

They waited some more, but no goblins attacked, and no townspeople swarmed them with pitchforks and burning torches.

"Nothing's happening," Valkyrie whispered. "Maybe we've got it wrong. Maybe there's no one watching us."

And then a rabbit hopped up.

They watched it sniff the air.

"Is that something?" Valkyrie asked Skulduggery. "Like, is that the something else you mentioned? Seems a little odd that they'd send a bunny. Or is that just a regular old bunny with nothing to do with any of this, that would have come by, anyway?"

"Shoot it," said Esmerelda.

Valkyrie glared. "Do not shoot it."

"I think you should shoot it," the witch said, nodding.

"He's not going to shoot it," Valkyrie told her. "It's a rabbit, for God's sake. He's not going to shoot a rabbit."

The rabbit twisted and contorted and expanded, its teeth turning sharp, its eyes glowing red, growing until it was the size of a man and growling like a wolf.

"Shoot it," said Valkyrie. "Shoot the bunny. Shoot the bunny in the face."

It hopped towards them, and they got up quickly. The rabbit snarled, and Skulduggery thumbed back the hammer on his gun. The animal lunged, and he fired three times, and the rabbit whirled and collapsed.

Skulduggery walked over, nudged the dead rabbit with his foot. It immediately dissolved into a red goo that was absorbed into the ground.

"Well," Valkyrie said, "this day just keeps getting weirder. Skulduggery? Do you have anything to add?"

"Not just yet," he said slowly. "But this is very interesting."

"Is that the word you meant to say? You sure you didn't mean to say baffling?"

His head tilted. "There's nothing baffling about this in the slightest. With every decision the Horts make, they're giving us vital information that we can use to beat them at their little game."

"So shooting the giant rabbit-monster was a learning experience?"

"Everything is a learning experience, Valkyrie. Except maybe this conversation."

She grinned. She couldn't help it.

"OK," said Skulduggery, "we have an opportunity to fight back. Esmerelda, can you walk?"

"I can limp if I must."

"That will suffice."

"I can hobble if I have to."

"Yes, I get it, I shot you and it hurts, but we really need to focus on other things right now."

"Sorry," said Esmerelda.

"Quite all right," Skulduggery said. "If you want this to stop, if you want to be released from whatever hold they have over you, you'll walk south through the woods. Valkyrie will walk east. I'll walk west."

"And why are we doing this?" Valkyrie asked.

"When I was chasing the monster, I did nothing that I would regard as unusual or out of character," he said. "This is purely a guess, you understand, but if I'm right, which I usually am, it means that the Council of Horts is only able to concentrate on one of us at a time. If they focus on Valkyrie, like they have done, that means they're not paying attention to Esmerelda or me. When they take their eyes off us, therefore, we can begin to strike back."

"Wait," Valkyrie said. "So what if they do focus on me again? Then I'll be the one in danger while you two are off somewhere." She held up her hand. "And my magic is bound, remember?"

"I can fix that," Esmerelda said, and reached out and scratched the back of Valkyrie's hand.

"Ow!"

"Sorry."

"That hurt! Ow!"

Valkyrie rubbed her hand vigorously, but the sigil had been successfully corrupted, and she could feel her magic again.

"Thank you," she muttered.

Esmerelda beamed.

"Are we all set?" Skulduggery asked. "Everyone clear on the plan?"

"Not in the slightest," Valkyrie responded. "What if the Horts focus on you? Then it'll be me and Esmerelda coming up with a plan and, I'll be honest with you, my plans usually involve people being punched. But I can't punch the Horts because I don't know where they are."

"I also like to punch people," said Esmerelda.

Skulduggery shrugged. "If they follow me, then we'll have another piece of information that we can use against them. Ready?"

"Not in the slightest," Valkyrie said again. "Which way's east?"

Skulduggery pointed.

"Right. And we just walk – is that it?"

"Walk until they send something after you," Skulduggery said. "Then run. Or fight. Whatever you're in the mood for."

"I'm in the mood for fighting," Valkyrie said, scowling, and they all set off in their different directions.

Valkyrie stomped through the undergrowth, kicking leaves and snapping twigs. She looked up at the sky, glimpsed between branches.

"Well?" she said. "You going to do something? Here I am, walking along. That's not very interesting, is it? If you're getting bored, you should probably throw something my way. Nothing big. Nothing sharp. An idiot, maybe. Someone I can punch, and I won't feel too bad about it."

She frowned. "But why would I feel bad? The bunny wasn't real – not really real. And it looks like the monster wasn't real, either. So whatever pops out at me won't actually exist – not in any meaningful way."

Her phone beeped, and she took it out, read the screen, scrolled a bit, then put it away again. She walked on, not bothering to even look up now.

"I read this book a few years ago. Massive book. Anyway, it was about a town that had a horrible thing happen to it, and all the people were forced to do terrible things, and it turns out that it was all because some, like, alien kids got bored one day and decided to persecute a bunch of humans. They didn't look at these humans as much more than ants, I suppose. Or maybe less than ants. But is that what this is? You're playing these games with us because you require entertainment?"

The ground started to slope downwards. Valkyrie leaned back as she went down. She slipped and fell, landing in a sitting position. Her frown deepened.

"Was that you?" she asked. "Or was that me? Did you make me slip, or did I just slip? God, this is nuts. This is doing my head in, it really is. It's giving me a headache. Is this a stress headache? It is. See what you've done?"

She closed her eyes and gently rubbed her temples for a few minutes.

When she was finished, she stood. "Was that fun for you?" she asked. "I hope it was. I hope you were thrilled, watching me get a headache."

She started down the little hill again, weaving between the trees, placing her hands on the trunks to slow her momentum until the ground levelled out.

"A word of warning, though," she said. "I don't know how long you've been at this, but things are different now. The moment you involved Skulduggery and me, it all changed. You're not gonna win this one. I don't know if you've done your research, but we're quite well known for stopping bad guys. Which is what you are, by the way. You're putting people through hell. You're responsible for so many of those townspeople being killed, for your own selfish amusement. You're the villains of this piece. I hope you realise that."

Valkyrie shrugged. "I mean, I get it. If you view us as something less than ants, then why would you care? If we mean absolutely nothing in the grand scheme of things, then why shouldn't you use us for entertainment? Entertainment's important, especially in times as messed-up as these, am I right? I'm right. I know I am. But I'm afraid we're going to have to put a stop to it."

The ground started to rise, and Valkyrie kept going, using the trees to pull herself up. When she got to the top, she took out her phone again, used the compass to set her in the right direction.

"You know what I can do, don't you?" she asked. "I don't mean the lightning or the flying. I mean the other stuff." She tapped her head. "In here, like. You know I'm a Sensitive, too, yeah? I'm not the best at it, by any means, but I've had some training. What's the point in having a talent if you don't develop it into a skill, you know? So I've got a little skill in the psychic department — enough to scan my surroundings for eager little minds... like yours."

She grinned. "Oh, I know you're there. I can sense you. I know you're watching me. I know you're listening, and I know this is piquing your interest — some of you more than others. That's OK. I'm not going to take offence. Some of you may not like to be addressed so directly. To you, I say don't worry. This'll be over soon enough."

Valkyrie entered the clearing where the witch's cabin stood. Skulduggery and Esmerelda were waiting for her.

"Any trouble?" Skulduggery asked as she walked over.

"Nope. Don't think they even noticed I was walking in a circle. But they're there. I can sense them. They're paying attention."

"I still don't understand," said Esmerelda.

"This is a device we use for communications," Skulduggery said, showing her his phone. "I used it to send Valkyrie a message in which I laid out my plan. If the Horts could read the message, they would have immediately done something to stop us returning to your delightful home. But, because we are all here, they weren't given the opportunity to read it — which proves my theory."

"What theory?"

"The Horts aren't all-powerful," Valkyrie said. "There's something else, maybe someone else, deciding what choices to offer them."

"How far did you get with the scan?" asked Skulduggery.

"I did as much as I could without making them suspicious, but I think it was enough. There's a... I suppose you'd call it a presence, beyond even the Horts. It knows this is coming to a close. I think you're right – I think it wants it all to stop. It feels it's time to end."

Skulduggery nodded. "That makes sense. We wouldn't have been allowed in, otherwise."

Esmerelda stiffened. "Something's about to change."

"I can sense it, too," said Valkyrie.

"I doubt there's any need to worry," Skulduggery responded. "The Horts are demanding a choice, but I don't think they'll get what they're after."

"We're gonna find out," Valkyrie said, feeling the charge in the air, feeling the fine hairs stand up on the back of her neck. "It's happening..."

The feeling passed, and she looked around. "Nothing," she said. "No changes, no nothing."

"That's never happened before," Esmerelda said. "As in nothing has never happened. Something has always happened. It's the way of things. I don't think I know what to do."

"I rarely suffer from that affliction," Skulduggery said. "Valkyrie, can you sense a mood?"

Valkyrie's thoughts became songbirds and flew away from her for a moment, and when they returned they sang to her.

"Finality," she said. "It's coming to an end, and they know it."

"Can you tell us anything about them?"

"They're... I don't know. They're like us in a lot of ways, I think, but also different."

Skulduggery nodded. "My colleague who opened the investigation, he had his theories about who the Horts were. At various times, he believed them to be a group of high-powered Sensitives, a group of Warlocks, or simply sorcerers grown bored of long life. But he had one theory that struck me as closer to the probable truth. He believed that the Horts exist outside our reality – close enough to take a peek every now and then, close enough to interfere in limited ways, but too far to actually live beside us."

"That would fit with what I'm sensing," Valkyrie said slowly. "But the presence behind them... I have no idea what that is. I don't know, maybe it's their god." She closed her eyes, and raised an eyebrow. "Someone's definitely amused at that idea."

"I'm glad we can still entertain," said Skulduggery. "But this is over. The game, the experiment, the trial, the show – whatever this is, it's done."

There was a deep, deep rumble from somewhere below them.

Valkyrie frowned. "Please don't tell me that's what I think it is. Please don't tell me that's someone packing up their toys and going home."

"Actually," Skulduggery said, "I'd say it's more like someone wiping the page clean. Either way, we should probably get the hell out of here."

"But my leg!" Esmerelda said as the ground began to shake. "You shot me in the leg, and I can't run!"

"Are you still complaining about that?" Skulduggery said, and gripped her round the waist. "Hold on to me."

"Oooh," the witch said, grinning.

As they rose into the air, Valkyrie ran to the cabin. "You go on!" she shouted. "There are two of the townspeople in here! I'll get—"

She barged in. Joanne and the man stood there, looking at her.

"Fun's over," Joanne said. "That's a shame. I was enjoying that."

The man began to dissolve into nothingness, starting at his feet and quickly rising until his head vanished and he was gone.

"Huh," said Valkyrie. "So... what? None of the townspeople are real? All those folks that Esmerelda killed?"

"She didn't kill anyone. She thought she did... but she didn't."

"And the town itself?"

"Disappearing even now," said Joanne. "Along with the woods. There were just fields here before I started. Just empty fields."

"How long have you been doing this?"

Joanne smiled. "A little while – but time moves differently for me. Not faster, not slower, just... differently."

"And I take it you're not Joanne."

"There is no Joanne. This is merely a mouthpiece I'm using. I just wanted to say hello. Just wanted to say 'well played'."

"What's your name?"

"You and your lot... always after the names, aren't you?"

"Are you a Hort, or are you the thing I sensed behind it all?"

"I'm a bit of both, actually. I'm the one behind it all, but I'm also curious to see what happens. Or at least I was. Ah, I suppose it was time it ended. I have no regrets."

The cabin shook, and Skulduggery called Valkyrie's name.

"I'll be out in a second!" she yelled back.

Joanne didn't have any legs. They'd dissolved, just like the man had. "The beings you call Horts... Once I involved them, I had no way of knowing what would happen next. They might have killed you. I'm glad they didn't."

"Yeah, me too."

"I'll miss this, I'll miss Esmerelda. She was fascinating to watch. The things she did to the few in order to save the many... Your world will be a less interesting place without her in it."

Valkyrie frowned. "What do you mean by that?"

"Her kind," Joanne said, "they live for a long time. But not this long. She became, however, a vital part of this entire experience, and I couldn't have done it without her. Will you tell her that I said thank you? Will you tell her that?"

"I don't think I will, to be honest. You've ruined her life, and now you're ending it. You get that, don't you?"

Joanne shrugged, and then her torso dissolved.

"Ah," said Valkyrie. "To you, she's not really real, is she?"

"Not really."

"And I'm not really real, either, am I?"

"No. I mean, you're more real than Joanne, or the town, but... not by much. You're mostly make-believe."

"Says the floating head."

Joanne laughed. "You have a point, Valkyrie. Yes, you do."

Gaps appeared in the cabin walls. Through them, Valkyrie could see the woods. The trees also had gaps in them.

"Right," Valkyrie said, "we're off. You want my advice? Never come back here."

"A threat?" Joanne asked, amused.

"Very much so, yeah. There's a reason you haven't told me your name, isn't there? Because you know that we'll be watching for you, and we'll be ready, and if you do come back we'll get a fix on your position, we'll find your dimension, and a load of us will shunt over and kick your ass. You got me?"

Joanne laughed, and then her head vanished.

Valkyrie spun, energy crackling, and she burst through the gaps in the roof and joined Skulduggery and Esmerelda, and they flew the hell away from that place.

Esmerelda sat on the stump of a tree and looked out at where her woods used to be. "So my whole life," she said, "has meant nothing. And now even that is going to cease to be."

Valkyrie glanced at Skulduggery, and they both stood there and didn't say anything.

"I've been alive for all this time, and I thought I was... I thought I was helping people and saving lives, and none of it mattered. Not one little bit. All those people I killed..."

"Well, that's the good news, isn't it?" Valkyrie said. "I mean... you haven't killed anyone. Not really."

"But I thought I did. For all this time, I thought I did." Tears ran down her cheeks. "I spent my youth here. I grew old here. My life has been a waste. My power..." She looked up. "I could have helped people. I could have healed people. I could have brought people back from the dead."

Valkyrie frowned. "You were serious about that?"

"I've been serious about everything," the witch said. "My whole life. But I don't have that power any more. I did have it when I offered you the choice. But it wasn't really you I was offering the choice to, was it? It was them. Maybe they knew what they were doing when they cast their votes, or maybe they didn't quite realise the opportunity that lay before them. Maybe they didn't believe that it would have been so easy."

"You said it was knowledge, right? You had the knowledge that was the key to life and death. Tell us. Tell us, and we'll take it from there."

"I don't think I have the time, girl."

"You could try," said Valkyrie.

Esmerelda smiled, started to speak, and grew so old so fast that she turned to dust.

The breeze picked up, tossed the dust into the air and swirled it around.

"I could have done it," Valkyrie said. "I could have brought someone back – someone we've lost."

"It wouldn't have been as easy as that," said Skulduggery. "There would have been complications. Loopholes."

"I could have tried, at least."

"No," he said. "You couldn't." He put his hand on her shoulder. "You didn't have a choice."